A
Cottage Affair

by

Sharon Sobel

This is a work of fiction. Names, characters, places, and incidents are either the product of the author's imagination or are used fictitiously, and any resemblance to actual persons living or dead, business establishments, events, or locales, is entirely coincidental.

A Cottage Affair

Cover Art by *Tina Lynn Stout*

The Wild Rose Press
PO Box 708
Adams Basin, NY 14410-0708
Visit us at www.thewildrosepress.com

Publishing History
First *Last Rose of Summer* Edition, 2012
Print ISBN 978-1-61217-026-8

Published in the United States of America

The last words were said into the hole as Alex pulled on the slab with his good hand.

Arden didn't think it was a good time to ask why he was so interested in studying the deed to her property. When she said nothing, he looked up at her and said, "Help me get rid of this thing, will you?"

He shrugged his sling over his head, but he seemed stuck there, tied in a knot of his own making.

"Haven't yet got the hang of it, I guess?" she murmured, leaning toward him and reaching over his head. Without waiting for his arms to be freed, he dropped them over her shoulders, capturing her in his web.

His lips closed over hers as he tentatively tasted her with his tongue, and she pressed against him, wanting more. She felt a sharp ache in her belly, neither of hunger nor indigestion.

He drew away, and without his support, Arden thought she'd lose her balance. The sensation seemed apt; she most certainly lost her balance a moment ago, unable to conjure the memory to support her.

They shared a moment thawed from time, warming them in the sunshine of another day. The kiss brought it back.

"Do you want to do it again?" he asked, hopefully. She realized she stared at him, mesmerized by the experience.

"Not yet," she said softly, hesitating to stir up more ghosts. Eastfield was working a spell on her.

Dedication

For Lillie Madeleine Alayne Freidel-Sobel

With the hope
that the love of books that begins with Little Bear
lasts for a long and wonderful lifetime.

Chapter 1

"Beware of volunteer recruiters bearing gifts."
~Eleanor Gilmartin Zane
(a Thrifty Means volunteer since 1990)

If Arden Alexander had known Eastfield would send over an official welcoming committee on her first morning in town, she would have changed out of the silk harem costume she wore to bed. But forgetting where she was, forgetting who she was, she staggered to the front door and opened it.

"Good morning! We hope we didn't wake..." One of the women, dressed in a blinding shade of light green, held out a loaf of bread, wrapped in plastic wrap and ribbon. When Arden didn't answer, the woman's arms dropped, leaving the lingering scent of yeast and flour in the space between them.

"It looks like we did, Miriam," said the youngest of the three. "We apologize, Miss Alexander. We forgot you wouldn't be used to Eastfield hours. We'll come back later."

The woman held a bottle of apple cider, and Arden knew if she turned the welcoming committee away, she might be foraging for breakfast in her sister's cobwebbed pantry.

"No, please come in," she said politely. Or it would have sounded polite if her voice didn't have a gravelly edge to it. Arden hadn't spoken to anyone in at least two days, and her throat felt rusty. She put her hand to her lips, coughed, then realized she ought to brush her teeth if she intended to sit down with her new neighbors. She knew enough about

1

small towns to imagine that whatever happened here in the next few minutes would be all over Eastfield in an hour. "Come in. I think I have a sofa here somewhere. Why don't you ladies look around, and I'll be with you in a second?"

She left them standing in the tiny mudroom, and ran off in the direction of the bathroom. Her bare feet felt every knot and peg in the wide hardwood floor and she slipped on a braided rug. She found her cosmetic bag where she left it the night before, and picked up a hairbrush with one hand while she brushed her teeth with the other. She managed to make herself presentable, unless one happened to notice the flimsy pink and red swaths of fabric stitched to a piece of ribbon over her breasts. But there was no time to do much about it now. Arden grabbed a musty flannel shirt hanging on a peg in the bathroom, and threw it on over her ridiculous costume. She had guests to entertain.

However, it seemed the three women knew how to entertain themselves. When she rounded the corner in to the den, she saw they were examining the cottage's dusty treasures.

"Ladies?" Arden asked.

The women did not look surprised to see her back so soon, and they certainly didn't look the least bit uneasy about making themselves comfortable in her—her sister's—house. Perhaps this is what they did, inspect Eastfield homes to ensure there were the requisite number of antiques, or that the furnishings were sufficiently "country."

They were well rehearsed. They smiled, came together in front of the old Eastlake sofa, placed their offerings on the Hitchcock coffee table, bent their knees in unison, and sat. Arden pulled up a chair that looked twentieth century, though she had no idea who manufactured it, and sat down to face them.

"We really do apologize," said the one who had not yet spoken. She was probably about forty, a few years older than Arden, but looked like she would be perfectly comfortable back in the college classroom. Her jeans were snug, flattering her curves, and she wore a fleece jacket over a turtleneck. Fall came early to New England. "And we haven't introduced ourselves. I'm Eleanor Zane, and I live up at Garland."

Arden remembered her sister talking about the old estate, with its large farmhouse and acres of land, home to two eccentric old ladies. The townspeople must have protested like mad when the property finally changed hands. She guessed Eastfield was like that.

"Let me introduce Miriam Pell, and Liza Silver."

"Are the three of you the official Eastfield Welcoming Committee?" Arden asked, as her guests put their offerings on the Hitchcock table.

Liza laughed. "No. That would be Dora Higgins. She may come by in a few weeks or so."

Arden settled down into her seat. "I may not be around that long. I'm not actually moving in, you know." To be perfectly honest, Arden had no idea what her future held, but vagueness had a practical advantage.

Miriam Pell started to speak, but Eleanor put her hand on her sleeve. Though she was younger, she clearly was the one in charge. "Oh, that would be disappointing. We were hoping you'd be able to help us."

As Arden wondered what they imagined a stranger in a silk harem costume could do to help, Eleanor unwrapped her offering, something flat and wide. She pulled a redware plate from layers of tissue paper, and held it under her chin, like a cue card. Across the shallow bowl of the plate a scrawling hand had written "Eastfield" in light

3

yellow glaze.

It was a lovely house gift, but before Arden could thank them, Eleanor asked a curious question.

"What is it?"

Arden looked at her, knowing there was more beyond the question than the obvious. This woman, arriving at her door on Old Tory Lane unannounced, probably knew everything about her.

Arden reached for the plate and studied it, giving herself time to consider her answer. She came to Eastfield to mourn the loss of the museum that had been her passion, to try to forgive a cash-strapped university that saw the Early American art collection as expendable, and to figure out what to do with the rest of her life. She had not yet unpacked her car, nor ventured into town, and she was already being lured into revealing her professional expertise. This was her sister's doing, to be sure. Why Anne couldn't allow her one blessed morning to sleep late was something they would discuss later.

"It's an excellent copy of Eastfield redware," Arden began, confidently. "Of the type made in this area in the early nineteenth century. The artisan is very skilled, and has replicated the glazes to perfection. But though we have seen antique redware with the names of other nearby towns written across the plate—like Norwell or Millwood— no one has yet discovered a true Eastfield. That's the first hint that this piece is a replica. The other has been left by the artist, who displays his honesty by etching his trademark in the back of the plate. Warren Effly, isn't it? He does beautiful work." Arden replaced the plate on the table and crossed her arms over her breast as she sat back.

Miriam Pell actually applauded.

"Okay, who are you ladies?" Arden asked again.

"We're some of the volunteers from The Thrifty Means, a treasure shop that benefits local charities.

This came in yesterday afternoon."

"Consigned?" Arden asked.

"Donated," Liza said. "As are most things we sell."

"I see," Arden said, though really didn't. Not yet. "A piece like this, by Effly, is worth about $2500, I'd say. He announced last winter that he was going to stop making pottery, and spend his time building birdhouses."

Eleanor nodded. "We already have one of those. It looks like Warren is going to need a little more practice. The opening he made is just large enough to admit a flea."

Arden raised her brows. "I didn't realize the birdhouses were on the market yet."

"I'm not sure they are. But we have some connections, and we never know what's going to come in."

"You said it was a 'treasure' shop? Is that another word for junk?" Arden was being unfair, because even a rough prototype of anything made by Effly was worth a fair amount of money. And if a redware repro just happened to show up one afternoon, theirs was surely a shop with a reputation.

"Sometimes," Eleanor said. "We get old clothing, toys, and the stuff that's been hidden in the attic. We get books that were on the bestseller list last month. But we also get antiques from people who just want to get rid of them. That's why we need your help."

Arden rubbed her forehead, trying to make sense of what they were saying. It really was too early in the morning for anything to be coherent.

"I don't understand."

Miriam leaned forward, with a conspiratorial air. "We would like you to volunteer at The Thrifty Means. Your time would be helpful, but your expertise would be a gift. None of us are really professionals, you see, and someone with your background would make a very big difference to us."

Arden looked down at her draped body, wondering what these earnest, cheerful women thought about their supposed professional in this harem get-up. She was an idiot to have put it on in the first place, but she arrived at the cottage late last night and she was tired, and fished around in her sister's closet for something in which to sleep. A T-shirt would have been just fine. A high-necked cotton nightgown would have been better suited to the autumn chill and the indifferent heating system. Instead, she found this silky thing, thought it was a negligee, and threw it on over her head. Now it seemed it was something Anne might have worn on the stage, in *Kismet*.

In the light of day, under the unbuttoned flannel shirt, it looked absurd, with tiny bells hemming the dropped waist, and sequins strategically placed on the sheer fabric over her nipples. If she even vaguely resembled a professional, the profession itself was slightly dubious, and probably illegal.

"Since you seem to know everything about me, you also know my error in judgment probably hastened the closing of the Bradford University art museum. I may never work in the antique and art auction business again."

"Of course we know. The business of the museum's closing made all the newspapers, even the *Eastfield Edition*. But, of course, there's the local connection." Liza Silver unwrapped the loaf of bread as she spoke, broke off the thickly crusted end, and passed it across the table.

The smell was as seductive as a Chippendale desk at a yard sale. Arden pulled off a substantial chunk of bread and sank her teeth into the soft, warm dough.

She paused, thinking about the local connection. Was it simply enough she owned this house with her sister? She had never been here, not even for a visit. Why would it matter to the people of Eastfield if a young curator made a very expensive mistake that precipitated the loss of a museum to a community several hours away?

"And the other thing," Arden said, "is that I have to find work, somewhere, in whatever field. I really can't volunteer for your shop or for anything else. To be honest, I need money."

Eleanor stood, walked into the kitchen as if she lived here herself, and opened a cabinet. Through the doorway, Arden watched her pull out some mismatched glasses and rinse them in the sink. Eleanor returned to the den, with a dishtowel over her arm and set down the glasses on the table. Liza opened the bottle of cider, and poured out the libations.

"But you don't have a job yet, do you?" Eleanor asked, and Arden realized this was the first thing in her personal life about which the ladies of The Thrifty Means seemed to be in doubt. Perhaps Eleanor was merely being rhetorical, because she went on. "Until you get back on your feet, we thought you might like to join us. We could use you, but you might be able to use us, as well. The Thrifty Means is Eastfield's clearinghouse, not just for antiques, but for gossip and networking. You never know whom you might meet."

"Eleanor met her husband there." Miriam said.

"Actually, I met Evan years ago when we were in high school," Eleanor corrected her, but smiled. "You never know who's going to know someone who knows someone who may know of a position. Plus, you'll get to meet everyone, and make some friends."

Arden paused, her hand hovering over the glass of cider on the table. These three knew everything.

7

Surely, they could not know about her utter lack of friends, of confidantes, of someone with whom to spend an afternoon at the movies. It never seemed to matter before, because Arden raced her way through college, on a fast track to a dream job at Bradford University. It was only in recent weeks that she came to realize how very much alone she was. Even her sister, who urged her to take possession of the unused cottage they jointly inherited on Old Tory Lane, hadn't been able to welcome her here herself.

Now, the prospect of friendship was more seductive than the fresh bread, the sweet cider, even a Chippendale at a yard sale.

"Friends are hard to make," Arden pointed out.

"Not at The Thrifty Means. We're all so different, and yet somehow we come together for this, and for other things. Some women have volunteered there for forty years," Miriam Pell said.

"I started when my kids went off to school. I had some time on my hands then, and somehow can't stay away now." Liza passed a look from one friend to another, and laughed.

"And I joined when I returned to town, after my divorce. I'm a writer, and need to get out and away from the computer for a while each day. There's always someone to talk to at the shop," Eleanor said. Arden wasn't surprised to hear Eleanor was a writer; there were darker currents beneath her calm exterior, some energy that needed an outlet.

"Most of us think Eleanor is writing a book about us. So be careful what you say in her hearing." Miriam took another pinch of the bread and stuffed it into her mouth, so she would say no more. Eleanor elbowed her and Liza groaned.

They were friends. Arden saw it and appreciated it for what it was. And here they were with their bread, their cider and their Warren Effly redware, trying to convince her to join their little not-so-exclusive club. She thought about the day she had planned, in which her goal was to unload the car, clean up the dusty cottage, and pick up some food in town. There really wasn't much of a decision to be made after all.

"Of course I'll give you a hand, for as long as I'm in town. Should I come over this afternoon when I settle in, after I shower and change?"

Something crashed very close to the cottage, and Arden, who had slipped to the edge of her chair to be closer to the loaf of bread, nearly fell off.

"Is that a tree? Did a tree just fall?" Arden asked, as the three women jumped up and ran to the large picture window. The drapes were open, as they had been last night when Arden arrived. But then all was dark, and Arden assumed she would look out on a view of deep Eastern woodlands.

Arden wrapped the flannel shirt around her, realizing it was far too large to have belonged to Anne. Well, her sister always seemed to have a man around, though most were more the black leather and chains type, rather than flannel and jeans. On the other hand, Anne sometimes sought refuge in this cottage in Eastfield, out in the woods, accessed by an unpaved road. Perhaps there was a flannel and jeans guy who followed her here.

As she stood at the window, shoulder to shoulder with Miriam, Liza, and Eleanor, Arden appreciated she was not quite as deep into the primal woodlands as she imagined. A large farmhouse stood on the slope of the hillside, its six-over-six windows staring down at her. Beyond it was a large red barn, into which four of her cottages might have neatly fit, and still have room to spare. A large truck moved slowly between the new buildings, where there must be a driveway.

"Am I about to get a new neighbor?" Arden asked the reflections of the four faces in the window.

9

"I doubt it," Eleanor said softly. "We tend to know who's coming and going in this town. When people are moving, a trip down to The Thrifty Means is usually their last errand in town."

"I would have thought they'd go to the post office. Or return an overdue book at the library."

"You would think," was all Liza said, her voice dropping off.

A man appeared at the back of the truck and it looked like he was trying to stop it with his outstretched hands.

"Alex Wingate isn't going anywhere," Eleanor murmured.

Arden knew who he was and knew he wasn't going anywhere. His interest in her cottage made her choice of retreating to Eastfield particularly desirable at this time. She understood a confrontation was inevitable, but hadn't quite realized he lived in her back yard. Or she lived in his.

"He's probably starting a new project," said Miriam.

"I think I read an article about it in the paper," added Liza.

"He must be getting a delivery of lumber," Eleanor said.

Arden looked at their faces in the window and wondered why this should be such a subject of fascination. In her tiny apartment in Boston's Beacon Hill, it was both rude and improper to speculate too loudly about one's neighbors, the noises that came out of their apartments, the smells wafting about in the dinner hour. Here in Eastfield, such considerations could very well be the town's pastime. She ran her fingers through her hair, untangling knots and snags.

"Is he building a new house?" Arden asked innocently. *And where?* she wondered. *On the slate patio?*

"He's a sculptor, and an art professor," Miriam said. "I'm surprised you haven't heard of him. He did the fireman's memorial up in Hartford, very controversial. Either you like his style or you don't."

Through the plate glass, they heard him yell and saw him point to a spot closer to the barn.

"Oh, I like his style," Eleanor said, and Arden knew it had nothing to do with the guy's artistic talent.

"Better not let Evan hear you say that," Miriam laughed.

"I think Evan knows he has nothing to worry about," Eleanor said, still smiling. "But that reminds me. I promised him I'd pick up some bagels and cream cheese at the market. I'd like to think I'm his muse, but his inspiration for writing more likely comes from the bakery."

"We ought to go," Liza said, and Arden heard the regret in her voice. Was Alex Wingate's style that good?

"I heard a carton of Wedgwood dishes came into the shop yesterday afternoon. Should we go check it out?" Miriam asked.

They turned away from the window, surrounding Arden. "Will you join us later?"

"Yes," Arden promised. "I have a few calls to make on some job leads. And I've got to shower and change."

They started to walk to the door, where a large collie sat gazing in on them. No one seemed in a hurry, as they paused to look first at a painting and then at the fireplace screen. When they opened the door, the dog threw herself at Eleanor's legs, but she held her ground.

"Yes, you definitely want to change," she said, looking over her shoulder.

"Oh, you may want to know that Alex Wingate

told us he thoroughly approves of that costume on you. I wouldn't put it away, just yet." Miriam pulled knitted gloves from her jacket pocket, though the day was already warmer than it was when they arrived.

Arden watched the women of The Thrifty Means and the beautiful dog climb into a dark blue van. When she could no longer see the dust kicked up by the van on Old Tory Lane, she dashed back into the house and pulled the drapes across the large window, through which her neighbor had apparently enjoyed a show the night before.

****

Alex shrugged off his denim jacket and brushed his hair off his damp brow. He didn't know where the usual delivery guys for Eastfield Mills were this morning, and didn't appreciate showing this new team where and how to pile the raw wood in his barn. He had been sketching some new designs, hard at work and thinking about his new neighbor, when the great lumbering delivery truck showed up in his drive and knocked over a totem pole he was restoring.

Now that some semblance of order had been restored, Alex saw these guys were just kids, probably taking courses at the local community college, and picking up a few extra dollars on the side. He didn't recognize them from town, but had to admit there might be some people he didn't know. That alone was so unusual, he wondered if the Eastfield police—who seemed to have little else to do—would track him down and arrest him for Insufficient Neighborliness.

However, after what he saw last night, he might have every good reason to hang around his property, and even get out on it a bit more. Take a walk in the woods, perhaps, to check on the drainage in front of the cottage on Old Tory Lane. He looked down the hill just as the draperies were swept closed in the large window. He smiled, thinking he might have to go down to be certain all was well.

He hadn't even realized Anne Alexander had a sister until she called to ask him to check if everything was in good working order in the cottage. It seemed an odd question at the time, since he had long ago agreed to keep an eye on the property. And he did, more for his own benefit than for hers, since he hoped to buy it from her one day. But now that he had his first glimpse of Arden Alexander, he wondered if Anne wanted him to check up on more than the heating system, and if Arden was anything like her sister.

Anne was an actress. Perhaps he shouldn't be surprised she never mentioned a sister, since she loved to talk about nothing so much as herself; even when she came up to the farmhouse to keep him company while he worked, he barely got a word in. That suited him just fine, for she rarely demanded proof that he listened, and the company of a beautiful woman was always pleasant enough. But if she had ever showed up in his barn wearing something like that flimsy silk thing, he might have been persuaded to take a break from his work. One needed inspiration for creative genius, after all.

Now there was another beautiful woman on his property and he was in the mood to be distracted. He emailed Anne this morning, to let her know of her sister's arrival, and had been thinking of little else since He heard Eleanor Zane's blue van crunch through the leaves and gravel to the driveway at the bottom of the hill and regretted he hadn't been first in line to welcome the new Ms. Alexander to town.

He wondered if she was still wearing that gauzy thing.

Whistling to himself, Alex started to walk down the hill on a path worn into the soil centuries ago, when he was called back to the barn. He thought about ignoring it, but when he heard a crash and tumble of wood decided he ought to check it out.

****

Arden was only in her new home for a few hours before she realized her sister, for once, was quite right. There was something calming, even redemptive, about this cottage in the woods, with its old dusty furniture and rugged lines. She tried to remember when it passed into their hands from their Great Aunt Portia, a very strange old lady who visited them in Boston once a year. Arden had been a little frightened of her. But Anne, more than ten years older, always seemed fascinated by Portia Trumbull, as she was by all odd characters. They provided inspiration for her. Anne was always looking for drama, and if Eastfield, Connecticut had a playshop, it was not likely to be compelling enough to bring Anne to town. She'd have to provide it herself.

By contrast, Arden never looked for drama or the spotlight, and yet it somehow found her in Boston. She came to Eastfield to hide from its glare.

She looked at her surroundings appraisingly. She was part owner of a rustic, slightly damp cottage, overgrown on the outside and indifferently decorated on the inside, where Anne didn't seem to have made her mark. Oh, there was the evidence of the harem costume and a few other things Anne would have considered appropriate dress for a quiet evening at home. And there was that old flannel shirt, smelling of mildew and man, which someone must have left behind. However, the rough furnishings and scattered plates and glasses in the cabinets revealed nothing of the two sisters who owned this place, other than the possibility that they didn't care much about it.

But one of the reasons Arden came to town was

to prove otherwise and she was now surprised to find she somehow came to care for the cottage almost at once. She fingered the Portuguese tiles in the bathroom, wondering where she might buy scatter rugs in just the right shade of blue. She found an old vacuum cleaner in a closet and hoped there were stores still selling bags to fit. Outside, she walked about in the overripe garden where the slightest breeze brought down a shower of gold leaves, and decided she would read up on maple sugaring. She doubted she would still be in Eastfield in late winter, but then, you never knew.

While she waited for the rusty water in the shower to run clear, she opened her suitcases on the bed in a spare room. What seemed sensible enough for a country retreat while she was packing in Boston was now almost comical. Where would she wear silk slacks and patent leather slides? She would probably kill herself just walking down the rough stone steps. And a sundress? Though there were still warm days in the city, the wooded landscapes of Eastfield demanded wool sweaters, fleece jackets and knitted caps. A sturdy pair of hiking boots would also be useful.

By the time she stepped out of the shower, Arden had a mental list of what she needed to buy in town. A few minutes later, she sat down at the kitchen table to write it all down. Her long hair started to dry and she decided to let it go natural today; it suited both her mood and her new style. And besides, until she joined the three Thrifty ladies at their shop, she wouldn't see anyone she knew.

After she dressed in jeans and a sweater she found in the closet, and slipped her feet into a basic pair of flats, she wasn't sure she knew herself, either. The person in the mirror looked more girl than woman, more collegial than professional. On the other hand, without a job, and bumming out in a cottage in the woods, she now was closer to the girl she had been in college than she had been in many years.

She left the cottage, cleared the leaves off her car in the driveway, and got into her car. She looked back, realizing she forgot to lock the door. It probably didn't matter since it would be easy enough to climb through the window or break down the darn door if anyone thought there was something worthwhile to steal.

Suddenly, it just didn't matter at all. She wasn't going anywhere. She turned the key and nothing happened. Thinking she was distracted and just missed the sound of the engine turning over, she tried again. The car was dead.

She was out in the middle of nowhere, and her car was dead. She had her cell phone, and there must be a phone book somewhere in the house, but what if her car couldn't be fixed today? What if it couldn't be fixed at all? Could one live in this town without a car? Arden crossed her arms over the steering wheel, and dropped her forehead onto her arms, her light mood gone as she considered the very worst-case scenarios. Nothing was as it ought to be, and she was utterly, miserably alone.

Arden wasn't sure how long her little spell of self-pity lasted, but the sound of crunching leaves was enough to pull her up and out of her black hole. She looked up, expecting to see something large, like a dog or even a deer. But it was even larger.

A man stood at the front of her car, looking as surprised to see her as she to see him. She had the advantage, for she realized at once who he must be. And understood precisely what Eleanor Zane meant when they spied on him a few hours ago.

He wasn't the tallest or broadest or best-looking man she ever seen but there was something immediately compelling and attractive about him.

His dark hair looked too short, as if his barber had a go at him without caring what the customer wanted, but was wavy and thick enough to suggest how it would curl once it grew in. He was either tanned or olive skinned; if the latter, his pale eyes were all the more extraordinary. Even at the distance of several feet, Arden could see how thick his lashes were, and how they shaded his eyes.

He put his hands on the hood of the car, as if he could prevent her from leaving, and she thought them the most extraordinary feature of all. His hands were overly large, very strong looking, yet graceful. They reminded her of the hands of Michelangelo's David.

Arden unsnapped her seat belt and got out of the car. After she closed the door, she leaned against it, keeping a safe distance from someone who was, after all, a perfect stranger.

Perfect. Well, she could hardly know that yet, could she?

"Was I in your way?" she asked tartly.

"Why? Were you going somewhere?" he asked and surprised her with a voice much deeper than she expected. But then, before today she's only heard his voice raised in anger. Looking at him now, she did not think he would be quick to anger. Or to judgment, for that matter. "It looks to me like you're stuck here. And considering your reaction, it looks like it goes beyond car troubles."

Okay, so the man was quick to judge.

"You know nothing about it," Arden said indifferently. "Except that the damned car won't start."

"Do you want me to take a look at it?"

"Are you a mechanic?"

"No, I'm your neighbor," he said, and pulled up the hood.

Well, that certainly made everything clear,

Arden thought ungraciously. She recalled all the warnings her mother ever gave her about men who sabotaged the cars of single women, then offered to help, and then attacked them. She backed away, stumbling on a tree root. He didn't seem to notice. From this new vantage point, she was able to notice him very well.

She recognized the look on his face, as she recognized it on the face of every boy who ever showed her a snake, or man who showed off his sound system in his apartment. He was fascinated by this filthy, greasy engine, examining each part as if it was the eighth wonder of the world. When he pulled a Swiss Army knife from his pocket, Arden backed even further away, but he was busy scraping away at something

"Well, look what we have here," he said, and pulled a loose wire out of something.

"Did you just do that?"

He finally spared her a glance, and his pale eyes settled on her for a few moments. Arden was suddenly too conscious of her wild, wet hair and her sister's scruffy jeans.

"Did I cut the wire?" he asked, and then smiled at her. *Dear God. Let him rip out the whole engine. I'll take my chances just on the chance of seeing that smile again.* "Why do you think that?"

"Maybe it's the knife in your hand. Or maybe it's because I drove here from Boston without any problem at all. I don't think I could have done that with my wires hanging out."

He looked at her as if he was checking to see if anything else was hanging out, but said, "But then you parked here all night."

"So? Do the police come around and disable foreign cars?"

"They might, but as you're from Red Sox Nation you probably get some dispensation. But it wasn't

18

the police. It probably was a mouse."

"A mouse?"

"You know, those gray squeaky things. Your car was warm and dry, and offered protection. Look, here's where the little guy built his nest." He motioned her to come forward. "He's gone. He's not going to bite you. Neither am I."

That was an interesting prospect, and very tempting.

"I believe you. So what should we...I...do?"

"I could probably tape it together, and it would hold you for a while. But we could just call Jeff at the gas station on Norwell Road and he'll come over."

Arden pulled her cell phone from her bag and punched in the numbers as her neighbor recited them from memory.

"I'm a good customer, unfortunately," he said, as the phone rang. He watched her as she spoke to Jeff, as she glanced at her watch, as she sighed in frustration.

"He can't get here for a few hours," she said as she clicked off. "What am I going to do?"

Again, he smiled. And again, her heart started to race. "What do you want to do?"

When she replaced her phone in its pocket, she pulled out her shopping list and waved it. "I wanted to go shopping. I have a million things to buy."

He backed away from her list, as if she were a teacher holding a test paper with a bad grade. "Well, if it's a million things, I'm not sure they can fit into my truck. But if you can shave a few things off that list, you're welcome to come with me into town. I've got a few errands to run also."

"What about my car? What if they come while we're gone?"

"Just leave the keys on the front seat," And then, when she looked at him in disbelief. "This is

Eastfield, Miss Alexander. We'll come back in a few hours, and your car will be all set to go and there'll be a handwritten bill along with your keys on the seat. Trust me."

"I don't even know your name."

"Alex Wingate. Alexander, like yours." he said, and seemed to hesitate. "If you've got everything you need, let's go up to my place and get my truck. There's a path here, but the leaves make it slippery."

Arden followed him up the hill, and the path got easier when they came through the trees and onto a hilly plateau, for the sun was strong and dried the dead leaves. Daisies and mums grew in soil basins between outcroppings and sated bees and other insects gave up their buzzing and lay in the center of the flowers. Though the effect was a little wild, someone spent hours gardening this place, and Arden knew it wasn't her sister. Anne wouldn't know a daisy from a cauliflower.

"Isn't it odd we have the same name?" she asked.

He stopped and she came up close behind him just as he turned. Too close, then. Arden took a step back.

"Not odd when you think about it. We're distantly related, though not on the Shakespearean side."

"You know about that?" Arden asked in disbelief. She didn't know many people who knew her famous sister was Anne Hathaway Alexander. Their mother claimed they were descended from William Shakespeare through fifteen generations or so, and named her older daughter for his wife, and Arden Shakespeare Alexander for his mother. Anne took her mother's passion as her own, and took to the stage, truncating her name to better fit a theatre marquee.

Arden Alexander also respected their mother's

passion, and came to appreciate…old things.

"Consider yourself lucky, for you might have been named Prospero or Donalbain. The Alexander side of the family always seemed more sensible. They'd never believe the coincidence that we're living next door to each other."

"But it's not a coincidence," he said, looking a little uncomfortable. "This is an old family property, and that's an old family name."

"Then we truly are cousins?" Arden asked in some wonderment. Why had Anne never mentioned it?

Alex Wingate turned and continued up the steep path.

"I hope not," she thought she heard him say.

****

His dog was waiting for them in an old red pickup truck, drooling on the rolled down window.

"It's not fancy, but it'll get us to town," Alex Winthrop said. He sounded a little apologetic, though why someone who lived in a house such as his should be apologetic about anything was a mystery. Arden stood in the autumn sunshine taking in the broad prospect of his antique farmhouse, its white clapboard siding freshly painted, the stone chimneys dotted with moss. It stood in the shelter of old shade trees; maple, oak, and catalpa, which showered gold and red leaves on the large gabled roof. A wide porch wrapped around much of the building, furnished with white wicker furniture and plaid pillows. Surely, this man had a wife.

"Her name is Miranda," he said.

"Well, she's done a beautiful job around here. I love the potted bamboo," Arden said, thinking there might be a Shakespearean connection after all. She also thought she might do something like this in her own garden.

"She loves it too. I think she's buried bones in

each pot."

Arden looked at him in surprise, as he opened the door of the pickup and helped the elderly lab down the step.

"Are we talking about your dog?"

He grinned, and Arden blushed, because he knew just what she had been thinking.

"We are, I hope. She used to belong to your sister, who finally realized Miranda loved it here too much to travel around the world with her. That was years ago. I sometimes call her Mrs. Miranda, out of respect, because she's such an old girl now. The dampness is a little rough on her arthritis, but she seems to have enough energy to torment squirrels, and dig up my bamboo." The elderly dog sauntered over to Arden, and pushed her nose into her open handbag. Arden rubbed her between her ears, and the dog, contented, sat on her shoe.

"That's how we get people to stay here. Miranda and I are pretty boring company, so we use every strategy to keep our audience captive."

He knew what she was thinking, about her assumptions about someone named Miranda, and now gave her the information she would have otherwise spent hours trying to get him to divulge. He lived with his dog, they lived a sedate life, they loved company. And here she was, practically in his back yard, and without a thing to do with her time.

"I don't intend to be around long," Arden said, too quickly. She realized her mistake at once, for it was her plan to dispel any notions that she and Anne didn't care about the property. Alex Wingate had already made an offer on the house, one Anne instantly rejected. She vaguely hinted to Arden that the man had some bargaining tool that he would use if pressed, and the sisters concluded that it must be abandonment of the land. It seemed a good time, by all reckonings, for Arden to make her presence felt.

"We'll see what we can do about that," Alex said casually and then gestured to the back of the truck. "If you can extricate yourself from under that paw, give me a hand with this, will you?"

Arden eased her foot out, and left Miranda in charge of her handbag as she went to help. Alex handed her a few metal poles and gestured toward the barn, where he had piled up a mound of what appeared to be scrap metals.

"Do you collect garbage?" she asked.

He hefted a two by four onto his shoulder and his shirt rode up on his stomach. He looked pretty solid.

"Do you mean, as a career? Yes, I suppose I do. I'm very keen on recycling." As if to punctuate his point, he pulled a water bottle out of the truck, aimed, and threw it into the open blue bin by a shed. "Nothing goes to waste around here."

He was right; there was not a spare ounce of fat on him.

"That must be the reason the ladies from The Mean Thrift like you so much," Arden said to his back, as she followed him to the barn.

"Do they?" he asked, over his shoulder. "Well, that's good to know. I thought that might have been Eleanor in the blue van. Are you already a full-fledged volunteer? Or did they just give you some advance buzz on our Eastfield personalities? We have more than a few characters here." He carefully set down the plank on a pile of similar wood. Some had nails and hinges still embedded.

"I'm related to a few. I should have guessed anywhere my sister felt comfortable would welcome the unconventional." She hoped her comment was not obviously tinged with bitterness and regret.

Alex rearranged his wood and other pieces of junk as if he didn't hear her.

"She doesn't spend all that much time here, you

know. Just look around the house and you'll see it hasn't been loved in a long time." Even if he didn't hear the undertones in her words, she heard them in his. He didn't waste any time on his campaign to buy the cottage.

"I hope to clean up the gardens," Arden said pointedly.

"The house needs work as well. Did you see the plastering over the fireplace in the kitchen? There was a leak, probably for months, before I happened to notice it and patch it up."

"How did you get in the house?" Arden asked. *Stupid, stupid question.*

He looked down at her, and for the first time she saw a splattering of paint on his forehead and cheeks, and some in his dark hair. She knew many men who studied painting, but none who actually picked up a brush.

"I have a key," he said, and waited, perhaps for her to hold out her hand and ask for it back.

She didn't. Everything in her experience screamed for her to demand its return or change the locks, or both. But strangely, it seemed comforting to know someone was close and available and able to help.

"Not that it really matters," he added. "Anyone could just climb in the pantry window. The one next to the freezer."

"Well, that's good to know," she said tartly, though she'd already thought the same thing.

"I wouldn't worry," he said and patted her on the shoulder, like one of his buddies. "Most of us never lock the doors at all. I don't know why your sister bothers."

"Is Eastfield so safe?"

"Funny you should ask." He reached for her shoulder again, turned her around, and they walked side-by-side back to the truck. "Just a few years ago there was a series of gentle murders here in town."

"How can murder be gentle? Is Eastfield a fantasy town, like Brigadoon or something?"

He laughed. "Well, let's just say those who died were pretty close to the end anyway."

"Euthanasia?"

"Except they weren't murdered to put them out of their misery. They were hastened to their end so that The Thrifty Means would have the advantage of their posthumous generosity."

"Those nice ladies? You can't be serious!"

"Oh, I'm dead serious; no pun intended. But it had nothing to do with the ladies you met, so you can relax. They didn't put arsenic in your tea or anything."

"Cider. And I got the name wrong."

"So you did, but I didn't bother to correct you. There seems something appropriate about Mean Thrift, when you think about it."

They arrived back at the truck, and Alex tentatively lifted a carton. "This is too heavy for you, I think. Try that metal box."

"What do you have in these boxes, anyway?"

"This one has old doorknobs. Yours has blueprints." He frowned. "I think."

Arden lifted the box, which was practically weightless. "Or feathers. What do you do with all this stuff?"

"Someday, if you're good, I'll show you."

"Is that a promise or a threat?"

"It depends on what you think about my work. James Meechan, in *Contemporary Sculpture,* thinks it sucks." He shrugged, tilting the box of doorknobs, but Arden saw he was not indifferent to the criticism. "Like you, he has a better eye for the classical, pure lines and predictable objects."

"If you know anything about me, Mr. Wingate, you know there's lots of room for unpredictability in classical art. It has been to my detriment."

He put the box on a chair and took hers from her hands.

"No, I know nothing about you, except what your sister told me. But now you have me interested. Never mind being good. I'll let you see what I have even if you're bad. Especially if you're bad."

Chapter 2

"A cracked vase may have been made by Wedgwood,
but it's still a cracked vase."
~Miriam Pell (volunteer since 1941)

As they turned off Norwell Road into the town center, he heard her give a little sound of pleasure. Even after all these years, Alex often had something of the same response himself. Eastfield was a beautiful place, quaint and very self aware of its charm. Street lights had been installed only in the last year, and now bore large baskets of autumn mums where there had been pinks and purples only a month before. No building stood higher than two stories, and most had been standing for over a hundred years. Those that did not tried to conform to the historical architecture and design of their neighbors.

Cars were a modern necessity, even in a town where farmers still drove tractors down the state highway, but Eastfield did its best to relegate the boxy reminders of modernity to parking lots behind the shops and homes. Ethnic restaurants were permitted, of course, though there had been a great deal of resistance to granting liquor permits or allowing any stores to sell any drink more serious than iced tea. Now it was possible. But still, most people who decided to eat out headed over to Ludlum's, where greasy hamburgers and indifferent service made it no less popular.

"Where do you want to go first? The Thrifty Means?" Alex asked. It was the first thing he said since his crack about her being bad.

Arden turned and looked at him as if she quite forgot he was there. Perhaps she had.

"I'm afraid that the minute I show up at The Thrifty Means, I'll be put to work. And there's a few things I need to do to get my life in order, before I get anyone else's life in order. Is that the hardware store? And is there a garden shop? I also need to pick up some food, but that should be the last thing, I think."

"The garden shop is next to the Market. And we'll go to the hardware store first. It's a few blocks away."

"Why not park here and we'll walk? I can meet you back here in a couple of hours or so? Would that work?"

"That works," he said, nodding. Either she already forgave him, or decided she needed him until her car was fixed. In any case, he was building a relationship of trust. He wanted the cottage, and things would be so much more congenial if he could convince the sisters that his was the only offer worth considering.

"Then take it," Arden said.

It was a moment before Alex realized she was referring to a parking spot. He pulled in a little too quickly, and missed a shopping cart by about three inches.

"Do you have an extra car key?" she asked, breathing out slowly.

"What is this? Don't you trust my driving? Or is it retaliation for having the key to your cottage?"

She frowned and he guessed he used up his meager portion of forgiveness. "No. But if I want to leave things in the car while I go into the next store, shouldn't I have the key?"

"If I'm not worried about people breaking into my house, I'm certainly not worried about someone stealing the floor mats out of my truck. Besides, everyone recognizes it. If a sixteen year old kid drives off with it, someone will call the police."

"You're very trusting," she murmured, and it didn't sound like a compliment.

"Well, aren't you?" he asked, gently, hoping it was true. He didn't know all that much about her, other than what Anne mentioned in a brief phone conversation, but already sensed the deep hurt she carried from the Bradford affair. About that, he knew a good deal. Anne told him she sent Arden to Eastfield to heal, but he guessed the closing of the university art museum provided an excellent reason for its curator to dig in her heels on the Eastfield property. There was no other reason for her to move here; most people in the business knew she had been set up for a bad deal at the museum, and there would be other doors opened for her.

Yet the hurt she carried like a weighty backpack seemed to bear heavily upon her, making her cautious about everything, when she really only had to be cautious of him.

"No, not any more," she said.

Arden looked out the window, apparently interested in shoppers unloading green fabric bags into their cars. Alex realized he made her uncomfortable; he should have kept his mouth shut. She didn't know him at all, and yet she already came up to his house, rode in his truck, and knew he had a key to her house. Why should she trust him? Because they were cousins a dozen times removed?

"Not any more," she repeated, and took a deep breath. "I don't make friends easily, but always got along with the people I worked with. I always assumed that meant that I could trust them, and count on them when needed. They somehow gave me the impression I could. And I believed it; they took me out to console me when I broke off my wedding plans, and cooked meals for me when I broke my arm. But recently…"

"Yes?" Alex asked. He already knew all about the business at Bradford. Right now, he really wanted to hear more about those nixed wedding plans.

She looked up at him and he liked everything he saw. Her eyes were large and brown, punctuated by dark eyebrows that turned up slightly at the corners. Her lips were parted to reveal small, even teeth, and faint creases—not quite dimples—framed them. Her hair, curled and shiny, was carelessly pinned up with a big tortoiseshell clip. He guessed she wore it neat and prim when she went to work. But he could imagine how it would look loose and cascading down her back and over her shoulders. He wasn't sure what he revealed as he looked at her, but she edged closer to the door.

"Recently, I changed my outlook. I trust myself, and that's about it."

"So, did you come to Eastfield to live as a hermit? I think you've already blown that chance."

She smiled, so unexpectedly, he wondered what he said. "That was the general idea. But here it is, my first day in town, and you're right. I think it's going to be impossible."

He nodded and they got out of the pickup. Alex looked over the hood, over Arden's shoulder, and saw a few guys he knew. They gave him a small victory sign, as if he made a conquest. Behind them, Miriam Pell waved while one of the kids from the market loaded groceries in her car. Arden Alexander was absolutely right. It was going to be impossible.

"You could refuse the women from The Thrifty Means, you know. They're persistent, but usually know when to give it up."

"I suppose I could," she said thoughtfully. "But what about you?"

"Me? What do I have to do about it?" Was she already shutting down any bargaining for her cottage?

"Well, you practically live in my back yard," she pointed out, and he could see she found this somewhat humorous. Perhaps they weren't talking business at all. In fact, if she weren't such a prickly little thing, he would think she was actually flirting with him.

"I think, more accurately, you live in my back yard." Alex flirted right back. He wasn't sure he could handle this. He was woefully out of practice.

She put her hands on her hips. "Well, I suppose it all depends on what window you're looking through."

"What's that supposed to mean?" he asked. But he had an uncomfortable feeling he already knew.

"Nothing. Nothing at all," she said. "But I think I'll stop into the linen shop and find some new curtains for the windows. So you might as well put your binoculars away, Mr. Wingate."

"I never...I don't know where..."

She came around the front of the pickup and put a finger on his lips to shut him up. He was tempted to take a bite; she smelled like cinnamon toast. "It's all about trust, isn't it? Or lack thereof?"

"Well, you can trust I'll be back here in two hours, if you can get everything done by then," he said. Stupid thing to say.

Arden nodded before she turned away. She looked down the row of small stores and seemed to have decided on the linen shop. Damn the place. They probably sold thermal lined, opaque, quilted drapes.

But really, the little show in the window last night was too good to last very long, anyway.

Alex looked up the street in the opposite direction. He thought about grabbing a bite at the luncheonette. But then he saw Miriam Pell enter The Thrifty Means, and realized he ought to have a word with those busybodies. If he wanted Arden Alexander to know how much he liked that harem get-up, he just would have shown up at her door in a caftan and holding a sword. Of course, he might be able to buy both at the shop.

****

The man was as transparent as the ridiculous nightgown she wore last night. Really, after dealing with months of subterfuge, rumor, and innuendo, she recognized the signs of kindly betrayal as clearly as if he had "Caution" written on a sticky note, stuck on his forehead. She scarcely knew Alex Wingate, and yet she already knew he was not what he appeared; a single guy who was kind to animals and helpless neighbors, collected scrap metal and made controversial statues in his barn. He knew what he wanted, and how to get it. Arden frowned, finally recalling some of the controversy up in Hartford. The story about his sculpture even made the pages of the *Bradford Beacon*, though she scarcely paid attention to it at the time. For all she knew, he made instruments of torture, or weapons of mass destruction.

But then, her sister liked him, even as she warned Arden about the man's motives. So Alex couldn't be a complete lunatic. On the other hand, her sister liked anyone who was well muscled and good-looking, so Captain Murderer would probably qualify.

"If you don't like that color, we also have it in cream and pink," someone said behind her.

Arden turned, holding pale green fabric, and realized she was still frowning. But the saleswoman was smiling, hopeful, eager to please. It was infectious.

"I like the green, actually. I was just wondering

how opaque it is. I'm replacing drapes that are old and faded, and as long as I'm going to the trouble, I might as well have some privacy."

"And warmth," the woman added and nodded. "It's easy to forget how cold our winters can be. And with the price of oil going up, you could use some extra insulation."

"Exactly," Arden agreed. At the moment insulation sounded like a good thing. In fact, if they had anything like a cocoon in this shop, she might buy it and wrap herself up in it, and not come out until spring. "I think I'll take them."

The woman smiled broadly. Arden glanced at the price tag, and was glad she could make someone so happy. All it took was buying something at retail.

"You'll like them," the woman said, sounding like she really meant it. "What size do you need?"

"I have no idea," Arden said truthfully, and felt like an idiot.

"You could always come back tomorrow with the measurements."

"I'm not sure I'll have a ride into town. Do you deliver?" She didn't know anyone who delivered anything except for pizza, but it was worth a shot.

"We can," the woman said, drawling out the two syllables. Arden wondered if she was considering doing her a favor, just to make the sale. "Where do you live?"

"On Old Tory Lane. Number 12. The little..."

"The Alexander place," the woman finished for her. "Are you thinking of these for the den? The picture windows or the French doors? If you want them for the windows, you'll need the largest size. I'm not sure I have them in green. Oh, here they are. You'll also need a double rod and some hardware. We include them in the price." She rummaged around in a few drawers and when she seemed satisfied, carried the whole thing to the front desk.

33

Arden remained where she was, speechless.

At the counter, her saleswoman spoke to two other women, who looked up to greet Arden as if she was the mayor. Did Eastfield have a mayor? Did Eastfield need a mayor when all decisions could probably be made at The Thrifty Means?

"And how is Anne?" one of the women asked, when Arden finally gathered up the courage to come closer.

"She's well." Arden did not want to admit she hadn't seen her sister in five years. But these women probably knew it anyway. "She's in London right now."

"Of course. We read the reviews of her show."

Of course.

"Well, you must be Arden. She talks about you all the time."

For the second time that day, Arden stood facing a tribunal, three women who knew more about her than she did herself.

"And now you must be planning to stay in town for a while, since you're redecorating." One of the women glanced around and then leaned over conspiratorially. "Anne is lovely, but she really never cared much about the cottage. She bought most of the furnishings at The Thrifty Means."

"I thought The Thrifty Means was the place to go for treasures."

"Junk," the three women said in unison.

"Other people's garbage," said one.

"The styles are so last century," said the youngest.

"There's no accounting for other people's taste," said the third, and shrugged.

Arden thought about some of the weirder things she'd seen her sister wear, and the costume she herself slept in last night. Perhaps they had a point.

"Alex Wingate gets things there."

The women laughed.

"Well, he's always collecting things! When you consider what he already has, the antiques he picks up at The Thrifty Means are just for fun. But the man definitely has a good eye."

Two of them as Arden recalled. Pale blue and heavily lashed, and likely not to miss a single thing that happened. She didn't know anything about his collection, but she nodded in agreement. There was probably a danger in that, but she didn't want these women to pick away at even more of her insecurities.

"I thought I might go over there, myself," Arden said. "Some of the women already introduced themselves to me this morning."

"Well, they certainly don't waste any time," one of the women murmured. "They must be desperate for new volunteers."

Arden shrugged. "They didn't seem desperate. I thought they were just being neighborly."

As if "neighborly" was a magic word, the tone of the conversation changed at once. Arden decided to file that piece of information for the future.

"Of course they were," the youngest saleswoman said. "Eastfield is a very friendly town"

"Then I'm sure I'm going to love living here," Arden said and smiled broadly. Perhaps she had some of her sister's talent, after all. "When do you think the curtains could be delivered?"

"Is this afternoon too soon? We'll send Mary Beth over and she'll hang them for you."

Arden thought about Alex Wingate, and their neighborly proximity.

"No, it's not too soon at all. I'll be home, probably working in the garden."

The three women nodded and one of them jotted some notes on the brown bag into which the draperies had been carefully folded.

"Mary Beth belongs to the Garden Club," said

the jotter. "She could probably give you some pointers on how to get the garden ready for winter. She lives on Norwell Road, just a few streets away. She's practically your neighbor."

Of course she was.

****

Since Mary Beth would probably arrive at Old Tory Lane with the draperies in one hand and a trowel in the other, Arden thought she should actually purchase a few mums or something to stick into the earth. She guessed she owned the smallest plot of earth in town, but that should make her job easier. She assumed the ancient stone walls surrounding the house bound her property, but perhaps it wouldn't be a bad idea to check that out in Town Hall when she had her car back. If she decided to plant a row of poplars between her windows and Alex Wingate's front lawn, she ought to be certain they were on her land.

Rosy Outlook, the nursery next to the market, also existed on an odd piece of land. From the road, it looked very modest, a small frontage of pots and flowers and an aging greenhouse. As Arden came up the brick path, pausing at a farm wagon laden with ripe pumpkins, she realized the nursery land stretched in a long strip right to the river. Rows and rows of mums were staged on rough wooden steps and a few customers were filling red wagons with pots of yellow, orange, and purple blossoms.

Arden hesitated, not yet ready to be welcomed by more Eastfielders, so she remained in front of the greenhouse, her hand hovering over the last coneflowers of the season.

"You won't be wanting those, Miss Alexander," said a voice behind her.

Arden closed her eyes, counted to ten, and turned around. She opened her eyes and saw a pleasant looking man a little older than herself. He wore a collared knit shirt with the Rosy Outlook logo and "Mike" embroidered on the chest.

"That's not very good salesmanship, Mike," she said as if she knew him her whole life. "Why wouldn't I want them? They're gorgeous."

"I bet you're thinking of putting them in those stone pots of yours, aren't you? The ones on the east wall? They'll be gone in a few weeks. It'll be too cold for them. You should put in mums. And pick up some bulbs for the spring."

Arden supposed if Mike thought that her pots were on the east wall, they were on the east wall. She had no idea.

"Why are you selling them, then?" she asked, more curious than annoyed.

"Well, that's just the thing, Miss Alexander. We're not." He opened his palm to the few shelves of flowers surrounding them, where a small hand-written sign encouraged people to help themselves to what they needed.

"That's very generous of you. I'll take a pot and hope for a heat wave." Arden blushed, thinking she already felt a little too close to the sun on Old Tory Lane. She smiled sweetly and asked, "But where are your bulbs?"

This seemed to be a more difficult question than she supposed, because Mike thrust his hands into his pockets and rocked on the balls of his feet. Did he notice her embarrassment?

"Do you have bulbs?" Arden reworded her question. The man looked a little confused. "Mike?"

"It's not that, Miss Alexander. It's just that now I've said it, I don't know where you'll put them. I'm thinking about your spring garden."

Already knowing she would regret the question, Arden asked, "Do you happen to know what it looks like?"

Mike took a deep breath. "Those bushes in the

front are lilacs, and your Aunt Portia had bunches of tulips up near the road. Unless the deer got 'em. There's a lot more of them than there used to be in the old days. Deer, I mean. Not the tulips. Let's see; there's crocus near the garage, mostly yellow, and some daffodils. No narcissus. Your sister had me pull it all out for her the first year she came to Eastfield. Said it was unlucky for an actress to have narcissus in her garden. Something about a poor boy drowning in a pond. Must have been a kid she knew. Anyway, we planted Siberian iris instead, but you'll see that later in the season. Seems strange, since they weather the cold days, but you won't see them until late May. Then, along by the well—don't draw water from it, it hasn't been tested—there's a bed of portulaca. The chipmunks like it, but it's been in there for a hundred years, I figure. And you'll see..."

"Mike?"

"You'll see a couple of yews by the brook. Alex put them in last year. Needed some help with them, so I went over one afternoon to give him a hand."

"My neighbor, Mr. Wingate?"

"Yeah. He needed my help."

"I see," Arden said thoughtfully. "Are you telling me my property is all used up? That there's no room for anything else there?"

Mike seemed to think this a very good joke. "Ha! Alex has acres! He's been buying up any adjoining lots when they come on the market. He has room to plant a forest to rival the cedars of Lebanon!"

Arden did not want to be reminded of her neighbor's empire building. "Whereas I would just be happy to have a few shady maples and some yellow daffodils in the spring. Look, I'm very glad Mr. Wingate can afford to buy half the town, but I'm only concerned about my own little garden."

Mike returned to his contemplative mode, looking down at the dirt. It looked like whatever he was thinking didn't make him happy. When he lifted his face, Arden expected to hear he only had white daffodils or something equally tragic.

"But he owns your garden," Mike said.

Arden shook her head. "No, he doesn't. I appreciate he may care for it while my sister is away, but the property belongs to us. We inherited it some years ago."

"The house, yes. But not the property. Everyone in town knows that."

Arden felt her face burn, and she struggled to catch her breath. What was she doing in this town, where there was no such thing as a private life? How could she have imagined she could bury herself in the little house in the woods, where no one would notice her? And why did a perfect stranger know more about her business affairs than she did herself?

Because she never bothered about the cottage on Old Tory Lane. She didn't pay the taxes, never saw the deed, never bothered to visit until now, when she needed a refuge. And now she was hearing something so absurd, it must be...

"Impossible," she said, feeling certain of it. Anne would have told her about it before she urged her to stake their claim by living in the cottage. "How can someone own the property beneath someone else's house?"

Mike scratched his head, sprinkling yellow pollen on his dark hair. "I don't really understand it myself. I think it's been like that for years. No one ever bothered to clean up the deed, I guess."

"Well, you can tell anyone who asks that that's one of the reasons I came to Eastfield. To settle it once and for all," Arden said with some certainty. It sounded good, even to her.

"I don't blame you," Mike said. "You never know what will happen in the future."

"Do you think Mr. Wingate wants my cottage?"

Arden asked, though she already knew that he did.

"I couldn't say but I wouldn't be surprised if he did. I heard he wants the zoning board to consider letting him set up an artists' retreat or something like that. I may have that wrong."

Arden doubted it. It was probably on the front page of the Eastfield newspaper.

"Then maybe he'll make me an offer." She hoped so, so she could have the pleasure of refusing it. "He'll need dorm space for those artists."

"Mebbe," Mike said, sounding very country. Arden began to suspect it was a bit of an act. "But I don't hear tell of that. So you can just go ahead and do what you like. He won't mind. Just steer clear of his lumber and paints."

"I've already seen his lumber and paints close at hand, but thanks for the advice. I haven't seen any of his work, though. What do you think of it, Mike?"

On this, the gardener was decisive. "It's not my style. I guess you just got to like it. I'd rather see a nice statue of a lady in a garden, not some contraption that looks like a couple of kids put it together. It's this modern stuff."

"I see," murmured Arden sympathetically. "Not exactly what you expect to see in a place like Eastfield."

"Oh, we don't have much of it around here. It's for much fancier places. Alex gets a lot for his work and he's pretty famous. He teaches at a few colleges, you know."

Arden nodded, wondering why their paths never crossed before. But then, her field was early American folk art, and Alex's work was anything but. "Do you know which colleges?" she asked, genuinely curious. Boston wasn't Eastfield, but people knew others in the business.

"Can't recall them," Mike admitted. "You can ask over at The Thrifty Means, though. Those gals seem to know everything."

"So I've heard," Arden said.

****

Arden delivered her daffodil bulbs and fading coneflowers to Alex's truck before she set off to find the shop along the Norwalk River. A small handwritten sign directed her, but even without it, she might have guessed that a couple of minivans with furniture tied to their roof racks would have provided the clues she needed to find the way. The outside of the shop looked modest enough, with a peeling painted sign over the front door with the name and a date of incorporation of over sixty years before. The two windows were laden with merchandise, set out somewhat haphazardly, but interesting enough to make you overlook the artlessness of the whole thing. There were several very fine pieces of pewter, a worthless fireplace screen, a very dark painting that might clean up very nicely and pass for a work of the Hudson River School. There also were several paperback best sellers and a few EZ Guides to History.

But the window display was a work of cunning next to the delightful chaos that reigned within.

Arden stood in the doorway, jostled by a few customers competing to lay claim to one treasure or another. She scarcely noticed as she struggled to take it all in.

Merchandise of every sort hung from the ceiling, filled the shelves, stood upright on top of other pieces in the shop. Genuine antiques vied for attention with junk from chain stores, vintage silk gowns hung shoulder to shoulder with T-shirts and fake fur coats. There were showcases of jewelry, racks of books and videos, chandeliers large enough for a castle, and plastic Halloween decorations.

Arden thought it was heaven.

"Miss Alexander! We knew you'd come!"

Arden turned to see Miriam Pell approaching, walking sideways as she angled down the crowded center aisle. Behind her, Liza Silver looked up from an open rusted box, and waved.

"Did you hear it from Alex Wingate or the women at the linen store?" Arden asked with just a touch of cynicism.

Miriam stopped, effectively blocking the aisle. She looked surprised. "Neither. We knew you'd come because we asked you to. "

"And how could I resist?" Arden laughed.

Miriam seemed to relax as well. "That's just the problem. None of us can resist. At home, we have dishes in the sink that need washing, floors that need vacuuming, gardens that need weeding. But we all show up here, instead, to volunteer and to be with each other. We have a very good time."

Arden looked around again, this time homing in on a delicate netsuke in an ivory case. It was priced, absurdly, at ten dollars. "I can see how, and why."

"Well, come with me, and I'll show you more," Miriam said, and reached for her hand.

****

Alex looked up from the *Eastfield Edition* to see Arden walking toward the truck. The bags in the back seat already told him she had a productive morning, and the smile on her face told him she was either glad to see him, or she had accomplished a few more errands. While he preferred to believe the former, it was most likely the latter that made her happy.

She was on time, which made him happy. As much as he wanted to spend time with his new neighbor, he had work to do in the barn.

"How was your morning?" he asked as she came close. He folded the paper, and opened the door for her.

As she raised herself up into the high seat, she

used his forearm for support and leaned into him ever so slightly. Her hair smelled like...something. He wasn't sure what. He had the feeling it was the flavor of something he drank, but it wasn't cola or orange juice and it certainly wasn't chardonnay.

"A little frustrating," she said. "There was something I wanted to buy, but someone beat me to it."

He walked around the front of the truck and got in. As he backed out, the paper bags shifted and one fell off the seat. "It doesn't look that way to me. It looks like you were first in line at each store, and did very well for yourself."

She looked out the window and waved to a guy who stood beneath an apple tree, plucking off the ripe fruit. Mike Riley, damn him. Alex realized he didn't want the gardener coming by Old Tory Lane, plucking other ripe things.

"It also looks like you made some friends," Alex said, under his breath.

"Oh, I did. In fact, that's why I missed out on that buy. I was so busy meeting everyone at The Thrifty Means, I was too late to buy a little netsuke I saw on the way in."

Alex pulled out onto Norwell Road, planning to take the scenic route home. "Do you collect them?" he asked.

"I don't know much about Japanese artifacts, but I do enjoy them. Who wouldn't? This one was of a cat curled around a tiny ball of twine." She paused as they came to an intersection, but said nothing when he went right instead of left. "I guess you could say that I collect anything that strikes my fancy, whether I know anything about it or not."

"But you...in your job...know about a lot of things," he said, realizing too late how lame it sounded.

"Not as much as I thought," she murmured. "Is

that the old quarry?"

He was surprised. "I thought you were never here before. How do you know about the quarry? Does its reputation precede it all the way to Boston?"

"Oh, it does. It's where the statue of King George III was dumped during the Revolution, isn't it? It was taken from its pedestal in lower Manhattan and brought by horse and wagon through southwestern Connecticut on its way to Hartford, where it was going to be melted down for ammunition. The driver spent the night in Eastfield, and when he returned to his wagon, the statue was gone. Most people thought it was taken by some angry colonists who threw it into the quarry. They were still finding pieces of it in the seventies. The nineteen-seventies."

"That's not entirely true, you know," Alex said.

She seemed excited. "Do you mean they found pieces more recently than that?"

"I don't know about that. But there are some people here who think it was taken by the Loyalists, to prevent it being made into musket balls. The Loyalists were..."

"I know. The Tories." She sat back into the seat, clearly deep in thought. "Is that where..."

"Yes," was all he said.

She laughed, and leaned closer to him. "How did you know what I was going to say?"

"What else could you be asking? You didn't think Old Tory Lane was named for your ancestor, Victoria Trumbull, did you?"

"Well, that's the family story. I rather thought it was," she said, clearly disappointed.

"I'm sorry. Our side of town was notorious as a safe refuge. Everyone knew the politics of everyone else, but neighbors protected neighbors before, during, and after the Revolution. The brook that runs past your cottage is called George Brook, and it wasn't named for Washington."

She leaned back again, and stared out the window. The hills and fields of Eastfield were already dressed for autumn, celebrating the last party before the long and cold New England winter. He let her enjoy the scenery, feeling no words could enhance the brilliant palette before them. He slowed behind a hay wagon pulled by a tractor, and hoped she noticed the single-lane stone bridge that took them over the Norwell River. She sucked in her breath, and he thought she admired the red-tailed hawks circling over a pumpkin field.

But then, he realized she saw none of this, for she was stuck on one point.

"And yet I understand it's not my property at all," she said, still looking out the window.

Alex turned sharply to the left, ready to get home.

"I was wondering when we'd get to that," he said.

Chapter 3

"Stone walls make for good neighbors."
~Lucille Armitage
(volunteer since 1980, and a devotee of Robert Frost)

Back on Old Tory Lane, the spirit of revolution still sparked and threatened to ignite. Arden vowed to spend a few hours each day working the soil, after deciding her first line of assault was going to be fought by taking control of the land. If she farmed it, she claimed it, like some old homesteader. She knew almost nothing about it, and even less about farming, but surely it wasn't too hard to dig some holes and stick the daffodil bulbs in.

Her first surprise was finding a small set of very shiny garden tools in the garage. Her sister must have been inspired to stake her own claim at one time, and bought what someone told her she needed. There was, however, not a fleck of soil on them, and their price tags hung limply off their handles, so perhaps things had not gone as planned. Arden put down one of the bags of bulbs so she could rip off the tags, which seemed to be a very positive step. She felt better already.

She wore the flannel shirt she found in the closet and a wool cardigan, and wisely pulled her thick hair back with a ribbon she had found in one of the old trunks. There was always a temptation to trim the whole curly weight to her shoulders, but vanity always warned her to deal less drastically with one of her best features. And although her reason for coming to Eastfield had very much to do with getting out of the public eye, she was beginning to feel that there might be someone whose eye she would like to catch.

Arden walked out of the garage and looked up toward his large barn. She hadn't seen Alex Wingate for a couple of days. She saw several large panels propped against the wall of the barn, and the sound of a power saw mingled with the buzzing of bees in the late summer flowers. She could admit, but only to herself, some curiosity about what he did there, how he crafted odd pieces into noteworthy sculpture for public spaces, what he planned for the property. His property.

Her property too, if she had something to say about it.

Arden attacked the window boxes first, cleaning out the decaying leaves and finding a cache of buried walnuts and hickories. Feeling a little guilty, she dug a hole beneath the window, and dropped the food store into it, hoping its hoarder would find it in the dead of winter and not come seeking it in her ancient basement. Arden lined the bottom of the wooden containers with gravel from the driveway and dug up some herbs growing wild by the kitchen door. She thought she might prolong their season if they were pressed against the warmth of the house.

Though she didn't know much about gardening, she did know how to cook. Access to fresh parsley, mint, and dill was worth a little of her bother.

When the boxes were full, Arden scouted the plot with a critical eye, understanding a lot more about artistic placement than practical considerations. She put a clump of yellow flowers near the weathered mailbox, and bedded a few pots in the marshy soil near George Brook. She planted the coneflowers around the well—from which she wasn't even tempted to draw the greenish water— and hoped the dead flowers would drop their seeds and regenerate in the spring.

When she was done with the coneflowers, she was pretty well exhausted. Arden wiped a dirty hand across her brow, and fought off the impulse to leave the remaining flowers for the following day. Her sweater and shirt were a mess, and the knees of her jeans were soiled and damp. Tempting as it was, it would be too impractical to abandon the project just yet.

She rounded the house toward the garage, and to the little niche it created by the back door. It was an odd space, but designed for convenience, and calculated to keep a modern addition discreetly hidden behind the colonial facade. In that, it was successful, for Arden hadn't even noticed it when she first pulled into the driveway. Now that she— literally—better understood the lay of the land, she wondered if there had been another purpose in mind when the garage was built; although designed to preserve the integrity of the antique cottage, it was in plain view of the owners of the large house on the hill. It seemed almost a deliberate snub.

Arden glanced up toward it now, wondering what the present owner was doing and when he intended to come down the hill and resume their discussion about his property and her rights. Would he notice her efforts to clean up the garden? Would it even matter to him?

As if in response, the harsh grind of the power saw from within the barn revved up in sharp acceleration just as Arden knelt at the cornerstone of the garage. She was now sensitive to the sound and was able to distinguish the shifting sounds of the blade, as it turned a corner, or hit a knot in the wood. In the clear, sharp air, it nearly obliterated the sounds of the woodlands, the rushing of George Brook, the passing of an occasional car down Old Tory Lane. It polluted the tranquility of the sunny autumn day as the industry of men and women tainted the world since the first tools were fashioned, and recreated the natural environment.

Arden was suddenly so incensed by it all and so absorbed in the rough music, she didn't notice when her spade struck rock. Not hearing the familiar clinking sound, she continued to hack at its resistant surface, thinking it was just hard soil. Finally, making no progress at all in getting through, she banged hard in frustration and bent the spade double.

The power saw droned on.

Arden lifted the now useless spade out of the sizable hole and wondered if her sister's original intent for the tool had been ornamental, for it hadn't served her all that well. Then Arden looked down into the hole and swore softly when she saw the impermeable obstacle of flat, gray slate that she had been doing no more than chiseling away. She shifted her position, and the sun illuminated the stone to reveal something other than the scratch marks her own spade produced. Arden got down on her hands and knees and leaned very close into the earthy pit.

The power saw whirred to a sudden crescendo, as if lifting into flight, and then was just as abruptly subdued. A man's voice rose abruptly above it, and was cut off.

Arden was already on her feet and had turned toward the barn when she heard the sound of a crash.

She ran quickly over the brushy ground stretching beyond the garage. Pausing a moment to catch her breath, she scrambled over a very low stone wall that might have been put up as a boundary marker at one time, and scared off a couple of chipmunks. A hard-packed footpath suggested steady traffic through the woods, by either humans or animals.

The path diverged into two narrow trails, both seeming to lead to the same place. Arden hesitated only a second, hearing nothing but the dull whirring of the blade and bare branches bending in the breeze, and opted for the lower trail that looped down to George Brook and brought her up to the back door of the barn.

The distance wasn't all that far and yet she was breathless and her brow was damp as she pulled on the heavy steel handle that would slide the door open. It had been an uphill run, and a rugged one, and stark fear proved as exhausting as any emotion could be. And now Arden was absolutely certain something was wrong.

She pulled on the handle, and after a moment the great door moved out of its stops and onto the linear track. A series of tiny bulbs positioned over the frame suggested an alarm system at work, and Arden wondered if she would set something off.

But hearing nothing, she entered the barn.

Like the great medieval cathedrals, the huge structure filtered what natural light there was to suit its own purposes. White shafts of sun beamed through the open skylights and through the large windows, and invoked the sense of some primeval dawn. The original loft had been opened so that as one stood in the center of the building, one could see clear up to the arched ceiling, but the enormous space was broken by balconies lining the upper walls.

The building was extraordinary, but might well have looked naked if it hadn't been for the even more extraordinary display arranged somewhat haphazardly within. Great monuments were poised everywhere, rich in color, daring in style, evocative in meaning. Worlds away from the early American colonial style of Eastfield, these works mingled...

"Are you going to just stand there gawking at

the damn things or are you going to give me a hand?"

Arden turned, remembering why she had just dashed up here in the first place, and wondered where Alex Wingate was to be found in the mess of wood and paint strewn about the floor.

"I'm over here," he said nastily, and as Arden turned in his direction, he kicked a broken board off his lower legs. Nearby, just beyond him, the enormous saw continued to buzz like a wounded housefly caught under a swatter.

Arden approached it first, realizing she didn't know what to do about it. When had she ever touched such a thing? Couldn't it sever a finger poking around where it didn't belong? She leaned in as close as she dared and tried hard not to look at the whirring blade.

"Those who can read usually notice there's an off switch," said Alex, settling back against a support beam and closing his eyes.

"I thought they're supposed to have automatic shut-offs or something like that," Arden said, straightening up and crossing her arms. Maybe the damned thing would shut itself down in a few moments, exhausted.

"I disabled it."

"Well, that's very clever. What if it came after you one day, chopping up everything in its path?"

Alex laughed, but the tremor of his underlying pain was evident. "It's not alive, you know. It's a machine, a tool. The switch is red. You won't amputate anything by putting your finger on it. Just do it." His strained voice trailed off. "Please."

"What if Miranda came in and sniffed too close to it?"

"Please," he repeated. "She's afraid of the sound. Of power saws and vacuum cleaners."

Arden could put if off no longer. Her eyes

wandered down the length of the powerful tool, over the splattering of paint and plaster to where there was a handhold.

"Just do it!"

"Shut up!" Arden cried out over the noise of the saw, and wished she had never come near the place. But she did the deed. She leaned down quickly, pressed a red switch, and put the hateful thing out of its mechanical misery. Lifting her hand, she confirmed that all her fingers were in place.

"Remind me never to hire you to do repairs around here," Alex said into the deafening silence. "If that's what..."

"And remind me never to come running over when it sounds like you've killed yourself in here! Next time, you can take care of your own problems."

"Well, Wonder Woman, if it was just dealing with the tools of my trade, I think I could handle it. But as it is..."

"How badly are you hurt?" Arden interrupted. The power tool was a diversion, for she should have tried to help him first.

Alex sat on the floor amidst wood shavings and chips, his left foot still hooked into the rung of a large metal ladder. His hair, dusty and damp, stood up in little spikes around his head. He braced himself with one hand as he started to rise, but the other hand remained at an odd angle against his side.

"It's nothing," he said. His attempt at bravado was somewhat endearing, all the more because there was no conviction in it. In fact, it wasn't simply the obvious underlying sense of pain, but the truer, stronger, emotion of anger that came through. It couldn't, and shouldn't, have been directed at her. But another glance at the monumental works of art he created, and at his wretchedly crooked wrist, told Arden a great deal.

"Is it broken, do you think?" she asked gently and made her way over the lumber toward him. She was no Wonder Woman, and certainly no Florence Nightingale, but she could manage to get him to a hospital, if necessary. "Does it hurt?"

Alex bit his lower lip and glared at her.

"Okay, I suppose it hurts like hell," she said quickly. "And it looks broken to me. And we've got to get it set, I think. Are you going to drop the stoic act and just tell me how it happened? Never mind. I can see for myself. Didn't anyone ever tell you that climbing ladders can be dangerous? Especially while holding a power saw?"

She stood directly over him, and tried to extricate his foot from the ladder.

"It's what I do. I'm an artist. Maybe soon-to-be late artist."

"You sound as dramatic as my sister. This fall isn't going to kill you."

"Maybe not, but if you keep twisting that ladder like that, you will."

Arden turned to meet his eyes, and saw all the signs of pain had replaced the anger. A muscle was twitching in the corner of his mouth and his lower lip was white where his teeth bit into it.

"I'm sorry. I really am." She positioned herself differently, with her knees practically at his waist, and lifted the heavy ladder off to the left. "There's blood on the floor. Can you wiggle your toes?"

The rung of the ladder had knocked off his shoe, and a red stain was seeping across the white cotton of his sock. But the movement within was plainly reassuring as he experimented with one toe after another.

"Okay, that's good. Your dancing days aren't over yet," she said lightly.

"Well, yeah, as long as my two left feet are fine." He leaned back against a box Arden pulled up behind him and shut his eyes. "I think the real question is, will I still be able to work?"

Arden looked down at his twisted hand, which hadn't moved an inch in spite of his other exertions. "You're right-handed, aren't you? Look, I'm sure it'll just be a momentary set back. But now you've made me very nervous, as if I'm guarding a national treasure. We'd better get you to a hospital." Arden reached over for a narrow plank of wood that looked like it served as a paint palette. But the paint had dried now, and the size was about right for a splint.

"What are you doing with that?"

"Just relax, will you? I used to be a Girl Scout," she said, though she could not disguise the tremor in her voice. The twisted wrist with a bone jutting out beneath its skin was at once more terrifying and more threatening than a runaway power saw, and there was something unsettling about touching the painfully vulnerable place.

Arden eased the palette under Alex's wrist and carefully lifted it a few inches off the ground. She felt him wince as she did so, and saw him start to pull out, but she caught him just above the elbow and eased him back to where he could do himself no further harm. She felt the muscle of his arm, tight with pain and anxiety.

"Let's call an ambulance," she said. "There must be a hospital nearby."

"There is, about ten minutes away in Norwell. But if you're willing to drive me, I'd rather not wait."

"Okay, if you're sure," Arden said, knowing she was not. "But I need something to tie this up." She cleared her throat.

"There's a shirt over by the desk," he answered after a moment. "Just shred it."

Arden stood a little awkwardly, feeling sore from her gardening binge. She saw he had a small office set up in a corner of the barn, dominated by a large oak rolltop desk. She made for it at once, specifically for the flannel shirt tossed over the back of the desk chair. As she fingered it, wondering if she could avoid ripping it up, she glanced down at the desk where some pencil sketches were pulled from a pad. There, she recognized herself. The gray lines were light and airy, but the artist's touch was assured. Arden blushed, almost feeling the caress of his fingers. Why had he been sketching her? Were her lips really that full?

"Let's get on with it," Alex called out, and when she turned, she saw that he had been watching her. He shifted his position and brought his broken wrist to rest in his lap.

"Stay right there!" she said and, with reluctance, turned away from his desk. "Did anyone ever tell you that you're a lousy patient?"

She walked over with his shirt and kneeled at his side.

"I don't think I've ever been a patient before," Alex said thoughtfully, and she sensed that his eyes were on her rather than on what she was doing. "But this isn't the first time I've been tied up."

It wasn't so much what he said, as the way that he said it, that made her look up. His face was just inches from her own and somehow the good humor was back in his light eyes. Whatever it was he remembered managed to drive away some of the pain; Arden wasn't confident enough to imagine it had anything to do with her own amateur ministrations.

"Is that a fact?" Arden asked sweetly, and then, "I hope whoever did the deed also had the good sense to gag you as well."

She watched the grin begin in the corners of his mouth and stretch the thin lines of his lips. Then they parted to reveal his teeth, even and white, and to allow the sudden escape of his laugh.

"Oh, I don't think..." she began, but then was silenced as his lips caught hers in a kiss that gave no indication whatsoever of his newly vulnerable state. It was the gentlest of touches, but he was absolutely sure of himself, and Arden wasn't prepared to put up any defenses against this sweet possession. He smelled of turpentine and of pine wood, but his mouth was minty and warm.

"You don't think what?" he asked, moving only slightly away.

Arden opened her eyes and his questioning expression appeared in duplicate. His eyes looked even lighter in the sunlit room and at this unbearably close distance, she could see flecks of amber in them.

"I don't think—" What? The problem was, she was thinking too much. Thinking that she wanted this since the moment she met him, most of all. "I don't think you would have done that to the ambulance driver."

"That would depend, I suppose. If they gave me enough pain killers, I'd kiss a coyote."

"Now, there's a thought. I guess I should be flattered you're not yet floating on codeine?" She helped him to his feet, and he swayed over her like a sapling in a hurricane. "Or was that the bribe to get me to drive you to the hospital?"

"Bribe?" Alex leaned back against the wall. His shirt was unbuttoned, and Arden saw a smear of red paint on the blue T-shirt he wore beneath it. Caught up in the peculiar intimacy of the moment, she reached out and straightened his collar.

"Bribe?" he repeated. "You have it the wrong way around. I was taking my reward for helping you out the other day."

"I didn't realize doing a favor for a neighbor came with conditions. But all the same, you could have asked."

"And spoil the surprise? It was only a kiss."

He's wrong about that, Arden thought. Perhaps it was only a kiss for him, but it moved her in ways she thought she had outgrown. It aroused the sweetest dreams of longing and fulfillment. He could not be immune to it, she knew he couldn't. "Well, no more surprises, okay?" Arden asked in a voice that didn't sound like her own.

"No more surprises," he echoed, and swayed away from the wall.

Arden pulled up his good arm and slipped under his shoulder. He leaned heavily against her. "There's something else wrong, isn't there?" And then, with growing suspicion, "Did you hit your head or something?"

Arden slipped one arm behind him and allowed her hand to wander up his spine to the back of his neck, and through the thick dark hair smelling slightly of sawdust. The bump on his head was as large as a golf ball.

"Great," she sighed, speaking against his chest. "You probably have a concussion, as well. Is there anything else you haven't told me?"

He didn't answer, and she guessed all his energy was channeled into the business of staying upright. That took a great deal of her energy as well. He was heavier than he looked. He was at least six inches taller than she, lean and tightly muscular. The other day she had admired his legs in their close fitting jeans, and felt the strength of his arms. But neither were doing very much to help her now.

"Just lean on me," she said. "We'll walk out to your drive and I'll bring my car around to you."

"We're as far away from your driveway as we are from mine. I can make it to the car."

Arden looked up at him a little doubtfully, but from her peculiar angle as his crutch, she could only see the determined line of his jaw.

"The ground is a little rough here. I think..."

"I know it a lot better than you. Let's just get going."

Though he was undoubtedly concussed, he managed to keep up a fairly vivid monologue of curses as they made their way down the wooded path. Miranda followed them until Alex gently told her to go back to the house. He was kinder to the elderly dog than he was to Arden.

"I'll feed her when I get back," Arden murmured. "You'll tell me what to do."

"I'll feed her myself. I'm not staying in the hospital."

"How do you know that, Dr. Wingate?"

"Because I'm not."

They continued in determined silence for several moments, until they came to the stone wall. Arden had already stepped over it a few times but had forgotten it was there.

"Let me go over first," Arden said.

Alex answered her by raising his foot right over the wall, and coming down hard on something that clanged like a can.

"Damn squirrels," he muttered. "What'll they think of next?"

"Oh!" Arden said guiltily. "Did you hurt yourself? I must have dropped that when I scrambled my way up to the barn. I heard the crash." It was the broken spade, lying where she dropped it a half-hour before.

"Didn't Robert Frost write something about good fences making good neighbors? I guess he wasn't thinking about sounds of destruction and rescue operations."

Arden looked up at him again, thinking how only a true blooded New Englander could quote Frost while suffering a concussion.

"I think he was writing metaphorically," she

said. "Like espousing the virtues of heavy draperies when one's neighbor lives in the back yard."

"I guess there's drawbacks to everything," Alex said, and winced again. "And just when I thought I was through with my suffering today."

"Obviously you haven't spent much time around hospitals. Unfortunately, the fun is just beginning."

Chapter 4

"A little tansy can cure anything that ails you.
Of course, if you take a little too much,
it'll just kill you."
~*Deb Mallowan (volunteer since 1975)*

Actually, it started just a few moments later, when they reached Arden's garage.

She left Alex seated on a concrete planter as she ran into the cottage to get her keys and purse. Catching a glance of herself in the crazed mirror, she could only wonder what possessed him to kiss her; her forehead and cheeks were smeared with soil and her hair fell loosely around her face in a tangle of curls. The lack of makeup and sunshine had left her skin pale and her eyes were unusually large and dark. And yet, he managed to find something flattering in those rough sketches she found on his desk.

Arden put those thoughts aside, as she pulled an afghan off the couch. Her quick movement released a faint odor of lavender, which presumably prevented the release of a colony of moths. Sometimes old-fashioned remedies continued to work just fine.

Alex stood next to the planter when Arden returned to the garage, jingling the keys.

They already agreed the building was too narrow for him to navigate his way into a seat and he waited until she pulled the car out. Once inside the garage, she felt grateful she had the presence of mind to bring the afghan, because the car was as chilled and damp as a tomb.

Alex's hand was already on the door handle before Arden stopped the car. She braked and opened her door to help him, but when she looked over the roof of the car, he was gone. She ran around the hood, to find him sprawled on the upturned earth.

"Alex! Oh, dear God!"

"I take back what I said about pain," he said wearily as she helped him to his feet. "It can get worse. Did you booby-trap the place or something? What the hell is this?"

"Well, I wasn't trying to snare a rabbit for dinner."

Alex looked down at the gaping hole in the ground, which had apparently thrown him off balance. "What were you burying?"

"I was only planting daffodils. I assume the lord of the manor has no objections? Good. But I have a feeling that someone else was doing the..."

"What?" he asked as her voice drifted off.

"Nothing." This was not the time to tell him about the engraved slab she uncovered. Nor was it the time to discuss poetry or anything else. "Can you manage this?" she asked instead.

With her help, Alex slid down heavily into the front seat of the car, and closed his eyes. For all his bravado, he looked awful.

Once again, Arden rounded the hood of the car, pulled down the garage door to lock it at its base, and jumped in beside him.

They arrived at Norwell Hospital without incident, though the ten minutes of driving time seemed an eternity. Alex wasn't sure what he expected, but it wasn't a scene of desperate humanity tempered by mechanical efficiency. It soon became evident the hospital was the central clearinghouse for all sorts of incidents, from gunshot wounds to stomach cramps. Wheelchairs lined up at the emergency entrance like taxis at an airport, and a steady stream of ambulances and private vehicles delivered accidents and illnesses with alarming regularity.

Efficient but indifferent hands helped Alex from the seat while Arden idled the car at the curb, and a nurse's aide in scrubs gave every indication he was simply going to whisk him away into the bowels of the enormous building. Alex summoned up the strength to stop him with an authoritative gesture.

"Wait for her. She comes with me."

"Of course, sir," said a nurse, standing guard with a clipboard in hand. "What is her relationship to you?"

"She's my wife." Alex was not in the mood to decipher the nature of their relationship and he doubted Arden even heard what he said. She looked worried enough to be his wife, but he had seen that expression on her face before. Perhaps she was worried about squirrels getting into her bags of bulbs back on Old Tory Lane, or perhaps she was thinking about what she'd have for dinner. But no matter; the nurse looked from one to the other, and checked off something on the pad on her clipboard. A valet appeared from behind her, caught Arden's car keys as she tossed them to him, and when the aide started to push Alex through the door of the hospital, Arden went right in with him.

The place was a teeming mass of pain, and so incongruous was it with the beauty of the day, the effect was even more jarring. Alex felt humbled in this place, angry about his own carelessness that made coming here necessary, but grateful for the woman who came to his rescue and remained by his side.

Arden took several steps ahead of him, and opened the door to the small room in which he was apparently going to pay the price of this day's work.

A man waited for them within, concerned about another price.

"Stay here until a doctor can see you," he barked. "And we'll need to see your insurance card."

Alex lifted himself out of the wheelchair, and the aide helped him up onto the examining table. He then drew an absurdly cheerful curtain around as a makeshift enclosure, and left Alex with Arden in a space that made the inside proportions of her car look generous.

He couldn't read her expression, but he guessed she wasn't happy.

"Now I see why they want to be sure that people who actually have some relationship with each other are together in here. You wouldn't want to be stuck in this tent with the stranger who happened to find you," he said cheerfully, trying to get his mind off the incessant pain. "Well, you're hardly a stranger, are you?"

"I'm not exactly an old friend, on the basis of a few days' acquaintance," she said. "And neither am I a wife."

Even so, she hoisted herself beside him, so they sat shoulder to shoulder. He resisted the impulse to lean against her, and was surprised and oddly comforted when she leaned against him.

"Well, now you've explained their reasoning, what about yours? You needed me in here like the garden needed more daffodils. This isn't going to be pleasant, you know," she said.

To her credit, there was nothing but concern in her tone.

"I need someone to protect my interests," he said at last, and felt her body shift against his. He turned his head to meet her eyes and the gesture was painful enough so he closed his. "I need someone here to tell the doc that I need my fingers, that I work with my hands, that I have to have the use of them. I can't have them do a quick bandaging and send me home. I want to see a specialist, someone who will know what he—or she—is doing."

"You're pretty demanding, aren't you? I thought you wanted to be home today. You didn't want an ambulance to get you here. And you didn't ask to see a specialist." She leaned forward, and he almost fell over. "What kind of reputation does this hospital have? They seem to be pretty popular."

"I have no idea, and I'm sure they are. Your sister once cut her cheek and was able to get a plastic surgeon here to sew it up for her. Of course, everyone recognized her, and took pictures with her, and treated her like royalty."

"Maybe they'll do the same to you when they see your insurance card. Do you have one, by the way? I may be your wife, but I'm sure my policy doesn't cover you."

"It's in my wallet." Alex twisted on the table, trying to leverage his good hand into the tight rear pocket of his jeans. "Arden, do you mind?"

She gave him an odd look, and continued looking at him as her hand went into his pocket against his backside, and fished out the overstuffed wallet.

He held his breath, and was sorely tempted to kiss her again, but just then the brightly striped curtains were cast aside by a white-coated doctor who burst into their little sanctuary.

"What do we have here?" he asked gruffly. One glance was apparently all he needed to make an assessment, for he called for a nurse before either of them said a word. As Alex was wheeled out for x-rays, the doctor thrust a clipboard into Arden's hands.

"Fill this out while you're waiting," he said, and left her.

****

Arden glanced at the empty examining table, with its creased sheet and smudges of Eastfield soil. She was exhausted, drained of the energy that had prompted her to do her gardening only hours before, and wondered if Alex would be gone long enough for her to take a quick nap. But if she stretched out on the table, no doubt someone would spot her, bark out a few orders, and the next thing she'd know, she would have her appendix out or something. That's why a patient needed an advocate, someone to look after his or her interests. That's why she was spending this lovely day in the hospital, staring at an insurance form and holding the wallet of a man who was, despite his protestations to the contrary, a stranger.

Well, if she was his wife, she had every right to rifle through his wallet.

Alexander John Wingate was forty—younger than she thought, and older than he looked—and had blue eyes. She thought the description hardly adequate for their strange pale shade, but the plastic card didn't have much room for a detailed description. The State of Connecticut was right about his dark brown hair, however, and probably about his height. The house on Old Tory Lane was his principal address. He was an organ donor.

Mr. Wingate carried pictures of children in his wallet. Arden studied the small faces of several boys and girls and wondered about their mother. But then she flipped the plastic sheath to the next picture, and guessed he was a doting uncle, rather than father. Two men who looked the very image of him appeared in a posed print probably taken at someone's wedding. Alex was not the one with the lily-of-the-valley stuck in his lapel.

Alex also carried a little file of papers in his wallet—clearly avoiding the transition to a sophisticated cell phone—and Arden's eyes passed over a series of addresses and phone numbers. Anne's was there as was her own in Boston. There were business cards of municipal title-holders, and various people in the arts community. A well-worn slip of paper bore the name and number of the president of Bradford University, her boss until very, very recently.

The curtain was pulled aside, this time by a nurse. Arden stuffed Alex's papers back into the wallet, and moved out of the way of the bulky equipment being delivered to her small space.

"You doing okay, honey?" The nurse asked kindly. In contrast to the doctor, she seemed to have nothing else on her mind, nothing else to do.

Arden was not so delusional to think it was so, so she didn't waste time on her own state of mind.

"How is Mr. Wingate?" she asked.

The nurse blinked and studied her for a moment. "He looks a lot worse than he is. He has a mild concussion. And he has a broken wrist and hand. They're going to bring him back in here and set it right now. I don't know if you want to stay around for that; your husband may not want an audience. But don't go far. He'll be out in no time."

Arden barely had time to consider this, when Alex was wheeled back in. Judging by the expression on his face, "no time" was not soon enough. Arden could only guess what had been manipulated and prodded in the name of diagnosis, but she knew at once that it hadn't gone well. He looked grim and uncomfortable and refused to meet her eyes. He was wearing a hospital gown and the bare skin on his arm reflected the harsh overhead light on its thin layer of sweat.

"How are you?" Arden asked, genuinely concerned. She certainly wasn't play-acting, and she had a feeling Alex knew it too. He looked up at her with narrowed eyes and raised his brow in the quirky way she was coming to know well. But he didn't answer her.

"It's not just the wrist," the doctor said tersely, over his shoulder as he assembled a massive array of materials, including the plaster permeated bandages that would harden into a close-fitting cast. "He's also broken three fingers and bruised one of his knuckle bones."

"He needs that hand to work with," Arden began, as if that would make a difference. But she'd promised she would help Alex and didn't know what else to say. "Could he have a separate cast on his fingers so he could move them?"

The doctor laughed, making Arden feel like a fool.

"Look, Mrs. Wingate, I've already explained to your husband. He's not going to be doing anything with this hand for a while."

"But he's an artist..." Arden broke off, feeling helpless, when she promised to be his advocate.

"I don't care if he's Norman Rockwell. He isn't going to be doing anything for a while, except catching up on his reading."

Alex moved with what looked like a little spurt of frustration, but channeled it into getting up on the table again. He acknowledged Arden with a shrug of his shoulders, already resigned to the inevitability of being punished for a moment of carelessness.

She understood it all too well. Hadn't she just gone through it herself? How does one cope with the sudden loss of doing what one loves best? She had been one of the most respected young curators in her field, rising to prominence as she bought and borrowed historical paintings and artifacts for the neglected art museum of Bradford University; she had determined it her life's mission. When the fall came, following an ill-advised purchase and the subsequent decision of the Board of Trustees to sell the collection and close the museum, she felt the walls of her identity collapsing around her, and scarcely had the heart to dig herself out of the rubble. The loss of her livelihood was secondary; the loss of purpose was, and remained, even greater.

They would console each other, two neighbors out of work. Or kill each other, as they bargained for ownership of the cottage. But now she would not be alone in the special society of the unemployed, though he was as unlikely and as desirable a companion as she could have wished.

She watched him grit his teeth as the doctor got down to business, and told herself Alex's setback was only momentary, for it surely would only be a matter of months before his hand would be able to pick up that damned power saw again. If he behaved himself, it might even be sooner.

Arden, on the other hand, might never again find a museum's trustees to entrust her with their treasures. It was too bad Alex Wingate wanted the cottage, for she might decide to remain there for the rest of her life.

****

"Are you cold?" Arden asked the invalid as Alex hunched over in the passenger seat, holding the unbuttoned tails of his torn shirt around him. He had sacrificed the garment to this great effort, and it looked like he was unable to part with the tatters. Beneath the old afghan, it hung loosely from his shoulders. The sleeve had been too narrow to slip over the bulky cast, so half of the shirt was now draped over his rigidly bent arm. He stared out the window into the growing darkness and said nothing.

"Did you ever read *The Red Badge of Courage*?" Arden asked.

She came to a stop at a traffic light and watched him turn away from whatever it was that fascinated him at the window, and look directly at her. Lines of weariness etched across his angular features, and he still looked pale, but his eyes were bright in sudden amusement.

"Are you thinking I should take the doctor's advice and form a book group? What made you think of that old onion?"

The car behind them honked its horn, and Arden started up with a jerk that must have hurt Alex's arm.

"You did," she said tartly. "Don't get me wrong. There was nothing heroic about your behavior this afternoon. You were rude to me the whole time, and then left me to fill out the damned forms. But it was something in the way you looked just now. All you need is a blood-soaked bandage around your forehead."

"I'm sorry to disappoint you." He tapped gently on his new fashion accessory. "I'm also sorry I was rude to you. Thank you for everything you did."

Arden glanced at him and thought he looked sincere. She ought to leave it at that. Her conscience told her most emphatically to leave it at that. But she was also tired, and frustrated, and the words slipped out anyway.

"You're not going to find me so agreeable about other things," she said. "You may have bullied me this afternoon, but you ought to know that Anne and I have no intention of giving up the cottage."

The tapping stopped.

"Why are you bringing that up now? Did you and your sister have a conference call while I was being wrapped up like a mummy?"

"Oh, please," Arden said, abandoning her vow of sympathy for a fellow wanderer. "It's just your wrist and fingers. People break their limbs all the time."

"Those people, as you say, are usually ten years old. Their bones set easily. I'm an old man."

Arden made a sound deep in your throat. "I

know just how old you are. I saw your license."

He looked at her in amusement.

"You looked through my wallet?"

"You gave it to me, remember? I had to find your insurance card before they threw us out on the curb. I also found the phone number of my boss—my former boss—at Bradford."

"Make a left turn here. It's a shortcut," he said curtly.

She turned. "Why do I feel like I've been set up?"

"Why do I feel like you're going to accuse me of something I didn't do? Look, it's a small community, even smaller than Eastfield. There are a few dozen art museums in New England. I'm an artist. You're a curator. Everyone knows each other."

"I didn't know you until a few days ago."

"Aren't you glad you now do?" he asked, unable to hide the sarcasm in his voice.

"I'm not sure. I thought I was moving to Eastfield to escape from my past. Now, it seems I've never left it."

"I thought you might have come to Eastfield to find your past."

"I might ask what any of this has to do with you," Arden said tartly. "Unless you tried to get me fired from my job so I would come down here and realize how rustic the place is so I would be happy to unload the cottage. Was that your plan?"

"My plan? That would be quite a plan. Don't forget the part about breaking my wrist so I could lure you to the hospital so we could have this conversation."

"Very funny."

"Yeah, I thought so. I just didn't plan on everything hurting like hell." He caught his breath and Arden realized her anger probably was misplaced for now. It didn't seem fair to pin an injured man against the wall.

Alex wasn't ready to let it go, despite his pain.

"I have a plan, and would have told you about it myself. It's more of a dream, really, I would like to start an artist's retreat on the property and bring students to work in the studio and on the land, I will need to have a place for them to stay, and wondered if you and your sister would sell me the cottage before I built something else." In the reflection of the windshield, she saw him looking at her. "It's not as if the two of you actually use the place."

"Well, that's changed now."

He didn't answer her, but she saw him smile. "I had James Warren's number because I've been calling colleges to see if an internship for art students might work with their programs and accreditation. It had nothing to do with you, or the Bradford Museum."

"That's quite a coincidence," she said.

He didn't answer for several moments. "Yeah, so we've already said. But why are you berating me about this now? Is it so you can kick me while I'm down?"

Arden glanced at him and finally relented. She was being stupid, after all. But her frustration was real.

"No. It's just that I didn't think my whole life was going to be so transparent, or that coming to Eastfield was going to push me back into the game."

"What did you expect?" he asked.

She certainly wasn't expecting him. Why did Anne never mention that a good-looking and talented guy—who was clearly available—would be willing to claim her as his wife on a few days' acquaintance?

"Anne only told me that there was someone who looked after the property, who lived nearby, and who was interested in buying the cottage if we weren't interested in it anymore. She thought it might be a good idea, since I was at a loose end anyway, to live in the place and see how I liked it. I didn't know if I would ever meet you. To be honest, she led me to believe you were some elderly curmudgeon."

"I'll oblige the two of you in forty years. Although after today, crankiness may come on sooner than I thought." He made a face, as if trying out the feel of a perpetual grimace. "Anyway, I come from a long line of curmudgeons."

"And I suppose your ancestors have been behaving very curmudgeonly to your poor cousins in the cottage all these years?"

He seemed to find this amusing, for the grimace easily became a smile. "We do our best. I believe my Uncle Edward once asked for your Aunt Portia's hand. If she married him then, we wouldn't be having this conversation now."

"The cottage would have already been yours," she said, thoughtfully.

"More likely, the property would have gone to their children. You and Anne and I have benefited from the fact there were none from a marriage between them, or from anyone else."

"It's surprising, isn't it? Either of them would have been considered a catch in their day."

"Have you seen pictures of them? Unborn generations of children ought to be grateful those two didn't reproduce."

Arden stole a glance at him and considered how there must have been some dipping into a very favorable gene pool in more recent years. He smiled without looking at her, and she had a feeling he knew what she was thinking.

"Well, looks aside, there were other assets. A woman who owned even a small cottage had some equity. After all, Shakespeare may have married Anne Hathaway for that reason."

"I thought she was pregnant," Alex said.

"That, too," Arden mused. "Between property and pregnancy, she must have held the cards. Not for long, though, as he more or less abandoned her and the kids."

Alex held his breath as she went through an intersection on a red light. "But they still had the house in Stratford-on-Avon."

"And Aunt Portia somehow managed because she still had the cottage in Eastfield. But she must have needed some income to keep the property going."

"She was a beekeeper and sold honey to all the local markets. That's how my uncle died, you know."

"I don't know. What are you talking about?"

"Uncle Edward was stung by a bee and collapsed on the path between our houses. Portia found him hours later, when it was far too late to save him. She had the hives removed the next day." He turned his head. "You missed the turn."

Arden wanted to hear more of this tragedy, but she realized her patient was probably just anxious to get home.

"Maybe she loved him, after all," she said.

"Well, she could have had him," Alex said and shrugged.

"Perhaps she did," Arden said, making the next turn. She felt a light touch on her cheek, as soft as the stroke of a paintbrush. But Alex's good hand was firmly planted on his stiff, ungainly cast.

"I didn't realize you were a romantic, Ms. Alexander," Alex said lightly.

"Oh, I'm not, Mr. Wingate. I'm not only a realist, but I can get really grouchy. And let me warn you: if I stay in my little cottage on Old Tory Lane, I'm going to become a curmudgeon long before you do."

"I doubt it," he said. "You're just feeling down because you've had a long day."

But the day wasn't over yet.

****

"Just drop me off in the driveway," Alex said casually. He didn't want to give her any reason to believe he wasn't entirely grateful for her help, or that her driving gave him a bigger headache than the bump on his head.

"I'm coming with you," she said.

"I thought you couldn't wait to get rid of me."

"I do want to get rid of you. But the doctor told me to watch over your concussed head. And besides, I ought to feed Miranda." She frowned. "Are you hungry?"

"Don't worry about me. I lost my appetite at the hospital after I saw that guy with the gunshot wound. But I think I could manage on my own."

"Who's going to look after you?"

The thought of having Arden in the house, hovering over his prone body, and helping him into his bed was appealing. But he much preferred those things when he wasn't dizzy and sick, and didn't want to use up all his chips now.

"Miranda will take care of me. She'll bark for help if I fall off the couch or something."

"She sounds very well trained. Does this sort of this happen to you often?"

"If it did, I'd have a good stock of food in the house. But I don't and you're probably hungry yourself."

"So, if you can bear it, let's stop at my house first and I'll grab a few things, and then we'll drive up the hill to your house."

It was easier to agree than to argue. If Arden wanted to continue to play the part of his wife, he would let her. In fact, the more he thought about it, it sounded better and better.

They turned the corner of Old Tory Lane, and her small cottage came into sight. For months it had been buried behind the canopy of ancient trees, but now, with leaves already on the ground, its fine old lines were plainly visible. The trim needed a paint job, he noticed, but it would have to wait until the spring. If his neighbor became bored with Eastfield or him, he could do the paint job after renovations were completed.

"Oh, no!" Arden cried.

Alex blinked, thinking he was not so far gone as to have said his thoughts aloud.

"Oh no, no, no," she repeated. "Look at my door!"

Lots of people left their doors ajar in Eastfield, but Alex suspected Arden was not one of them. Of course, they had left in a hurry, and she might have forgotten to close it. But then, Alex noticed that one of the windows reflected the fading light oddly, as if it was broken. Something that looked like a bean pot was lying on the front lawn.

Arden pulled up into her drive, jammed on her brakes, put the car into park, and leapt out of her seat.

"Where the hell are you going?' Alex yelled after her, and struggled with his damaged hand to unbuckle his seat belt.

"I've been robbed! Who would have done this?" Arden cried over her shoulder and reached the landing in front of the open door.

"Stay where you are!" Alex commanded, and finally extricated himself from the running vehicle. His words echoed in his wounded skull, bouncing around like a stone. Clutching his forehead, he added, "Don't even think of going in there by yourself!"

Arden waited, but only just. As soon as Alex made his clumsy way to the bottom step, she went through the door, but then stopped where she was.

He couldn't see what she saw, but her reaction was all he needed to know. She gave a little cry, and staggered backward, until she came up against his chest. Any thoughts of protest were short-lived. Her body molded against his, stirring up entirely inappropriate responses, and he put his good arm around her shoulder.

"Who could have done such a thing?" she whispered, already in tears. "What could they have been looking for?"

Perfectly content with his nose buried in the soft waves of her hair, Alex forced himself to look over her head.

If the intruder sought something, the malicious damage done to the cottage seemed merely gratuitous.

The home of the Alexander sisters, usually so ordered and neat, lay in veritable shambles. The contents of every drawer lay strewn about the place. Cushions and bedding had been thrown off the couches and mattresses. Furniture was toppled in careless abandon, and a chair lay broken under a window. The small china figurines that had been on the mantel since the beginning of time had been swept clean away and lay in a small pile on the thick hearthrug. And it looked like a crow bar had been taken to the painting over the mantel—one that always reminded Alex of Gainsborough's *The Harvest Wagon*.

A pity; he liked that piece.

Alex pushed Arden gently aside. They were losing the light, and he wanted nothing more than to take to his bed, possibly with a companion other than Miranda.

"Is anything missing?" he asked, walking around her. Unsteadily, he dropped to his knees and poked through the rubble of a china vase. It must have been filled with marbles, because the floor was treacherously scattered with them.

"How would I know?" Arden cried, wiping tears from her eyes. "It'll take me days to sort through this. And I don't know what Anne had here anyway. There's an inventory somewhere; an old document that comes with the deed to the house. But that just manages to tell us what was around in old Victoria Trumbull's day, before the Revolution. And where she wanted them to be placed for all eternity. The old biddy is probably twirling in her grave over this!"

"Don't be too sure." Alex said, without conviction. "The place weathered storms for a few hundred years and it'll survive this as well." With the help of an upturned table, he stood up and turned back to her. She hadn't moved.

"What will I do?" Her voice had something he hadn't heard before, some note of desperation having more to do with other things than a room of broken antiques.

She came forward and wrapped her arms around his body.

"You'll spend the night up at my place, that's for sure," he said, savoring the unexpected moment. He would have liked to stay like this for hours. "But, for now, I think we have to call the police."

"Oh, no. Everyone in town will know," she sighed against his chest

"Get used to it," he said gruffly, but with some sympathy.

He led her through the labyrinth of broken pottery and furniture, over spilled flowerpots and scattered magazines. She followed along at his side, murmuring over one thing and another.

When they stepped into the kitchen, he expected her loudest protest, but she seemed resigned, stoic. The vandals had helped themselves to the contents of her refrigerator, and washed it down with the water that dripped insistently in the sink. Salad was strewn all over the table.

"There goes dinner," she sighed.

"We'll get something delivered," Alex said,

feeling in charge of his life once again. "My cell phone is in my left back pocket. Ludlum's is in my address book, and the police are at 911. Call them first, and then we'll know how many to order for."

Chapter 5

"Nothing reveals dirt like
the bright and honest light of day."
~*Lauralee Crawford (volunteer since 1998)*

Arden woke up to a mid-day sun streaming through the slats of a shuttered window, the groggy uncertainty of where she was, and how she came to be there. She was dressed in an unfamiliar pair of boxer shorts, and an oversized white T-shirt, and her pillow was damp where her head had made an impression.

She heard movement from somewhere below her in the house, and sat up in alarm. Voices, men's voices. One louder and more insistent than the others, and then the banging of a door.

With a rush, the events of the day before came back to her, and she settled back onto the pillows and contemplated what had occurred, while she studied the glimmerings of light on the white painted ceiling.

The Eastfield police officer arrived before she and Alex made their way out of the kitchen the night before. Arden had the sense there hadn't been much to do in town since The Thrifty Means murders of a few years before, and combined with the news about Alex's broken wrist, this made for a rollicking good time. During it all, Arden managed to extricate herself from under Alex's shoulder and clear a space for herself on her sister's ancient sofa. She picked up a three year old copy of *Fairfield County Living* and was happy to learn that ceramic geese centerpieces were once all the rage.

In time, the police remembered who was the victim in this crime scene and dutifully questioned Arden about what she believed was missing (she didn't know), who had done the deed (she couldn't imagine), and what their motives might have been (she had no idea). The consensus was, in her rush to get Alex to the hospital, she probably left the door open herself, but she managed to persuade them such a circumstance was unlikely to spontaneously generate criminal activity in her living room. And it didn't seem to be the work of squirrels.

They took a good many notes, and poked and prodded around the ruins. And, with a promise to do all they could, and probably sensing the party had gone on long enough, the officers left.

Alex was somewhat more efficient. He walked around the cottage with a flashlight, checking windows and closets, and shut off the dripping faucet. Back inside, he scooped some clothing off the floor, coaxed Arden off her nest on the sofa, and made good on his promise to shelter her for the night.

Poor Miranda barely paused to greet them at the farmhouse door before dashing off into the woods to take care of her business, while Alex and Arden entered the dark house. Alex wasted no time in getting her upstairs to a bedroom that was plain and clean, and pointed her in the general direction of the shower. Arden found some clothes in one of the chests and just managed to get into them before she tumbled into bed and blissful oblivion.

It had been quite a day. What started in peaceful contemplation of her projected spring garden now seemed like the placid lake behind the rapids; the hours had rushed through like a rain-swollen torrent, washing over a series of crises and emotional upheavals, and finally leaving the travelers broken and exhausted at its end. Like fellow survivors, she and Alex had naturally been drawn to each other in very real and immediate need. It had been gratifying and necessary while it lasted, but there were no guarantees that would hold up in the light of a new day.

Arden sat up again and listened for the sounds of the house. All was still. She looked around the room, appreciating it more in the light of day; one that from the looks of it, was fast approaching noon.

Arden gingerly stepped out onto the small rag rug and wondered if Alex was still around. Belatedly, she remembered she was supposed to look in on him last night, to make sure he wasn't comatose.

She walked carefully to the door, and opened it into the hallway.

His house was splendid, the veritable definition of a New England farmhouse. What had been only vaguely noted in her sleepy-eyed glances the night before had seemed dreamlike in its loveliness.

And what she saw this morning told her it hadn't been imagined.

Alex's house was of a similar vintage to the cottage, but graced with higher ceilings and better living space. Alcoves at either end of the hall were crowned with semicircular windows and fine wooden frames. The wide floorboards were authentically irregular, highly polished, and protected by a long braided runner. At least six rooms seemed to branch out from the central hall, including the room Arden slept in last night and the bathroom where she had showered. She assumed that another door opened into the master bedroom.

Arden had no idea what the future held for her and Alex, or even if they had any future at all, but a woman could definitely fall in love with such a house.

"Did you manage to sleep at all?"

Arden jumped about a foot and almost dropped the pewter vase she'd picked up to admire.

She turned to face him, embarrassingly aware of how she looked to him. Her hair was damply curling around her shoulders and down her back, and her face was flushed and washed of all makeup. The shorts and thin T-shirt she wore must be absurdly revealing in the morning sun.

And, of all things, she stood in his hallway, handling one of his Colonial antiques.

She saw him take all this in, some points with a more interested eye than the others, and smile at her as if it were the most natural thing in the world that they should confront each other in such a way. Well, it surely was easier for him to think that; he was fully dressed and very much at home.

"More deeply than I thought," she answered truthfully. "And I guess you slept less deeply than the doctors feared. I forgot to check on you last night."

"I survived," he said.

He had, and managed to look as if nothing much was amiss in his life. He wore a long-sleeved fleece shirt, which must have been a trial to pull on over his head, but seemed to fit comfortably enough over the cast. It was red, which made his skin glow under his tan, and his hair seem even darker. There was a bruise over his lip, which Arden hadn't seen yesterday, but it didn't detract from his splendid smile, which somehow, she had seen a good deal.

It wasn't until she saw beads of moisture on his forehead that she realized his skin was ruddy and his hair darker because he'd just showered

"What did you do?" she asked. Taking the offensive seemed like a good defense in her present position. "Didn't the doctors say you couldn't get the cast wet?"

"So they did," he said, and gave a little grunting sound. "But I figure I'm going to sacrifice a hell of a lot to this little mishap, and I refuse to walk around stinking like the emergency room of a hospital for six weeks. It was a bath. It was a little difficult to manage at first, and I was almost tempted to ask for help with those plastic bags that are supposed to fit on over the cast, but I handled it myself, after all. Just for good measure, I kept my right arm out, dangling over the edge."

"And now?"

He didn't answer at first, and Arden wondered if it had something to do with this cozy confrontation in his house or her modeling his underwear. It was stupid of her, she knew, and yet she wanted to know if he was as interested in her as she was in him, and for reasons that had nothing to do with her cottage.

"Now? Well, it's remarkable what a little soap and water can do to your spirits. That, and the unexpected comforts of home."

"I need to get down to mine, by the way," Arden said, a little too quickly.

"There's no hurry, is there?" And then, in response to what must have seemed her look of suspicion, "Look, I went down hours ago, and made sure there wasn't anything we overlooked last night. The place looks like an abandoned battlefield, but is locked up and secure. You don't really want to deal with all that yourself, do you?"

"I've dealt with worse," she said. "I lost my job, my credibility in the industry. What's a few broken antiques next to that? Some people might say I did it myself, in a fit of pique."

"I don't even know what pique is," he said.

"Look it up. I'm sure it's very, very nasty." Arden's frustration was catching up with her again, and she took a deep breath. "Besides, I'd hate to keep you from your work."

Alex leaned against the doorframe of the bedroom she just vacated. "I think I'm going to have all the time in the world," he said slowly, deliberately.

****

Somewhere, deep in the house, his cell phone rang. Alex would have been happy to ignore it, but the sound was interruption enough. The moment, so fleeting, was gone. Arden, who seemed to be leaning in toward him, straightened and blinked, probably realizing how close she came to a little indiscretion. And since she didn't seem to like him too much, she would probably have one of those fits of pique at his expense.

"I better get that," he said.

"You're too late," she said, and sounded regretful.

"Then I'll call back. It might be the doctor, checking in to make sure I'm still alive."

"I've never known a doctor to care either way."

"Yeah," he said, sounding like an idiot. He pulled away from the door. "I better get that."

He knew she watched him as he walked down the hallway, wondering where he left his phone. Miranda suddenly appeared on the top step, with a sliver of silver in her mouth.

"Good girl," he said, wiping dog drool off his new and very expensive phone. He checked his call list and saw Anne's familiar phone number. Glancing back at Arden, he watched her disappear into the guest room.

"Hey Anne, what's up?" he said a moment later, into the phone. Miranda assumed he thanked her again and threw herself against his legs.

"I've been calling Arden all morning and she's not picking up her phone."

"I think she left it in the living room."

"And?" Anne said, "Where is she now? Where

84

are you? How do you know where she left it?"

Alex pulled the phone away from his ear and heard Anne quite clearly at a safe distance. He also heard the smirky implication in her tone.

"It's not what you're thinking. We just had a few problems yesterday, and Arden decided to spend the night here. No, it's not what you're thinking…"

Anne started yelling something, but Alex no longer paid attention. Instead he watched Arden slip out of the bedroom wrapped in a quilt. She glanced toward the staircase at the far end of the hall, but must have decided there was no chance she wouldn't be noticed. So she came toward him, the quilt pulling the sleeve of his T-shirt off her shoulder. He thought she intended to move right past him to make her escape, but instead took the phone out of his hand.

"Hi, Anne," she said. "Yes, it's a good thing I was here. I don't know what he thought he was doing twenty feet above the ground with a power saw. We spent a lovely afternoon at Norwell Hospital. Yes, you could say that. Yes," she repeated and laughed.

Alex reached for his phone, but Arden started down the stairs.

"Now let me tell you about the house. Yes, our house. Okay, cottage. Someone broke in. I think he came through the bedroom window, and left by the front door. There isn't a thing left untouched, no damn stone unturned. I haven't had the heart to face it yet this morning."

Alex waited impatiently, fidgeting with the buckle on his sling. "Tell her the police came."

"She already figured that out," Arden said, her lips away from the phone. "Do you know Bertram Wills?"

"Everyone knows Bertram Wills. He's Anne's lawyer and mine. I think he's everyone's lawyer."

"We have to get the inventory from him, Anne

says." Arden turned serious, listening very intently to her sister. "No, I'm sure he had nothing to do with it."

"Tell her I'm already on the case," Alex said quickly, and pulled the phone out of her fingers.

"Yeah, Anne. Don't worry, we'll take care of it. Talk to you soon." He fumbled for a moment, realizing for about the hundredth time this day how useful it was to have two working hands.

"Here, let me," Arden said softly, and pressed one of the tiny buttons on the phone. Her hair was no longer damp, but still carried the scent of his shampoo. She seemed ready to say something, but seemed confused.

"What is it?" he asked, pulling the quilt over her shoulder.

She shrugged and the quilt slipped again. She didn't seem to notice.

"Why did you ask for a copy of the inventory? Why would you even know about it?" she asked. "That seems to be a little beyond the scope of a caretaker."

"The cottage's inventory is legendary in Eastfield. If there was anyone at all who remained unaware of its existence, he would have been fully aware the night your Aunt Portia came to a Town Meeting and demanded to know who stole her Limoges teacup."

"Well, who stole it?" Arden asked. "Maybe that will help us find my thief."

He looked at her in disbelief and wondered if she was also knocked on the head yesterday. "How old do you think that thief would be right now? Do you think he's been waiting all these years just to come back for the matching saucer?"

"Very funny. And age doesn't mean a thing. They say eighty is the new..."

"Seventy-nine," he finished for her. "But it turns

out the cup wasn't stolen at all. The police found it under a pile of newspapers on the kitchen table. Portia used the table for storage, and took her meals at the kitchen counter."

She swallowed but didn't say anything.

"Which reminds me," Alex added. "Where do you take your meals? I could use a little breakfast."

"That sounds good. What do you have?'

"I think there's a bagel somewhere. And I probably have some cereal." He shrugged. "Didn't you go food shopping yesterday?"

"I did, but I wonder how you know that. Do you post spies in the bakery department?"

"The sushi chefs are on my payroll."

Arden looked as if she actually believed him. "Well, your information is correct. But are you forgetting that the robbers helped themselves in my kitchen?"

"We can go to Ludlum's, then. I would have preferred to avoid that, since I'm not in the mood to be interrupted every ten seconds by someone who wants to know what I've done with my arm."

Arden nodded thoughtfully, and a wisp of her dark hair fell over her forehead.

"Or what you're doing having breakfast with me," she said.

"You seem to have adjusted to life in Eastfield, Ms. Alexander. Congratulations."

"And to think I needed to escape from Boston, hoping for nothing more than privacy."

"Then you certainly came to the wrong place," he said. "I have a better idea. Let's pick up a few things in town, and go back to your cottage, where you can cut my bagel for me. And I can tell you all about your strange ancestors."

She glanced down at her draped garment and bare feet. He noticed she wore a silver toe ring. But when she looked up, she was smiling.

"I'm sure I must appear as strange as any of the rest of them this morning," she said, and laughed.

It was the first time he ever heard her laugh, and thought it strange in itself. Strange and very beautiful.

****

Sharing the burden of the break-in made the whole mess somewhat bearable. Arden and Alex entered her cottage through the front door, and she refused to look at the smashed pottery or ripped papers. Instead, she stepped over the rubbish, leading Alex along a path to her kitchen, where she deposited the shopping bags of groceries. She picked up a chair, checked its sturdiness, and pushed it to the table. As Alex sat down, intent on counting out the pieces of a very old chess set, she opened the refrigerator.

She was a long way from any sense of order, but it was very satisfying to organize the contents. When they finished breakfast, she would finish the rest of the refrigerator. An opened bottle of white wine lay on its side on the bottom, the thieves apparently taking a pass on Anne's French vintage, and would need to be cleaned up.

"Unless you're starving, I'm going to change out of these clothes."

Alex looked up from the chess pieces, all lined up in order of rank. "Take your time. There's enough to do here to keep me busy."

"Don't get too busy because I'll be right back. Promise me you won't break a wrist or something."

"That's very funny," he said, as she walked out of the room.

As she closed the bedroom door behind her, she realized she'd have to pick her wardrobe off the floor. The thief had had a field day in here, and the thought of a stranger rifling through her bras and panties was far more unsettling than the theft of family heirlooms. She pulled a blue bra off a lampshade, and a denim shirt from over a silk hibiscus. Several pairs of jeans were on the bottom of the closet, and as she walked toward them, the pile shifted and settled. Arden took another step forward, getting the same response. Beneath a twisted pants leg, a pair of eyes blinked.

"Alex!" she screamed, and heard him knock over his chair. In moments, he came up behind her, holding a paring knife in his left hand.

"Who's here?" he asked, pushing her aside. The room, despite its disarray, looked sweet and sunny.

"There's something under the jeans. Do you see? There are eyes watching us."

To Arden's surprise, Alex put the knife on the dresser and lowered himself to the floor. "Come here, girl."

The jeans lifted another eight inches and a small tailless cat arched her back and threw off the fabric. Then she walked to Alex and sat down on his lap.

"Her name is Glinda."

"Because she's a good witch?" Arden asked.

"Something like that. She was born at Garland, where Eleanor Zane lives, and someone must have thought it very clever." He leaned against the bed, where the thief had dumped a drawer full of lacy panties, and kneaded the fur on the back of the cat's neck.

"Should we bring her back to Eleanor?" Arden asked.

"Glinda's an independent little thing. She belonged to Margaret Brownlee, who used to live down the street. When Margaret, ah, left town, she left Glinda behind. The rest of us sort of adopted her, and she shows up in people's homes from time to time."

Arden knew there was a story here about

Margaret Brownlee, but she already had enough stories to write a book. "She got in through the broken window, I bet. Did she cut herself? Is she all right?"

The cat looked up into Alex's face, and he stared back at her. "She looks just fine to me. She must like your choice of clothes." He turned his head, and looked out over the sea of underwear. "I like them too."

"All right, that's enough. Both of you, out of here. Let me get dressed."

Arden helped Alex to his feet and for a moment she thought he would plead dizziness. But the cat, climbing onto his shoulder, made an honest man of him, and he steadied himself just before Arden pushed them out the door.

She dressed as if she had a train to catch, and as she ran a brush through her hair, she realized there was some truth in that image. She was only thirty-eight, but as friends married and had kids, and moved into houses and adopted pets, she had settled into solitary ways. She had her job, and an occasional date, but the train of domesticity had already left the station.

Yet here she was, with a single, good-looking man and a needy cat waiting in her kitchen, and a day's worth of housework to do. It was not the life she envisioned, but there was something very pleasant about the thought.

"I make an excellent omelet," she said as she walked into the kitchen a few minutes later. Miranda was now sitting beneath one of the chairs, looking a little enviously at Glinda.

"I make excellent toast," Alex said, and put Glinda down on the chair next to him.

"And what do the animals do? Can Miranda squeeze the orange juice? Will Glinda slice the bagels?"

Alex smiled, and the lines of stress that marked his face since the previous day disappeared. With his sling and mis-buttoned shirt, he looked rakish, and a lot better than anything Arden had studied for a long time.

"I'm sure they'll eat the bagels. Does that help?"

Arden shook her head and turned away to see if there were any pans still in the cabinet. She pulled one out, guessed it weighed about ten pounds, and started to scrub it out. From the looks of it, and the cobwebs around it, it hadn't been used since the Coolidge administration.

As Alex waited for the bagels to toast, he leaned against the tiled countertop.

"Glinda is yours if you'd like her. Margaret isn't coming back, and I worry about her."

"Is she ill?"

"Glinda? She looks fine to me. I think Debbie Siegel takes her to the vet every so often."

"I mean Margaret. Why isn't she coming back?"

"Oh, that. Well, she took some liberties with her neighbors. Including Evan Zane's aunt."

"That doesn't seem odd around here. Everyone in Eastfield seems to take liberties, even the pets." Arden gestured to the cat and dog seated at her kitchen table.

"Making themselves at home, sure. But not killing them. Margaret liked the antiques in other people's houses, and figured the easiest way to get at them was to bump off the neighbors. You understand why she won't be coming back anytime soon? Or why she had to leave Glinda behind?"

Were these the murders she already heard about? There was something absurdly quaint about the concept, she considered as she chopped onion, yellow pepper, and mushrooms.

"I don't understand why she didn't bump off Anne. This house is—or was—an antique showplace.

91

Or am I deluding myself? Is it all knock-off stuff from Target?"

The toaster popped open and Alex used a towel to extricate the bagels. "It's real enough. Maybe Anne wasn't around often enough for Margaret to get her in her sights. But she was dying to get into the house, and sometimes parked on the road and stared at the cottage. Would you like a bagel?"

Arden nodded as she thought about her sister's transient life, and how she resisted putting down any roots. She started to sauté the vegetables and turned to Alex. The bagel was inches from her lips.

Watching him, saying nothing, she took a bite.

Something shifted just then, something as subtle as Glinda's purring at the table, but it felt as shattering as their kiss, his body pressed at her side, his greeting an hour before. Arden looked at him over the toasted circlet. And knew he felt it also.

"Good. But a little too hot," she said.

"I was thinking the same thing." he said.

She opened her lips to take another bite, though of the bagel or of him, she didn't yet know, when the frying pan sputtered.

"Oh!" she said, and looked at a splattering of grease on her hand. She thrust it under the faucet as Alex turned on the cold water. "I better concentrate on one thing at a time."

"I'm finding it difficult to concentrate on anything," he said, holding her hand steadily under the stinging water.

Arden pulled away. "That's because you probably have a mild concussion. You'll return to your senses in a few days."

He didn't say anything, and Arden returned to the sizzling pan. She turned down the heat, and broke a few brown eggs into a measuring cup. Her hand hurt just enough to make holding the whisk a little awkward, but she focused on the task, rather than on the man beside her.

"Here we go," she said brightly, turning out the omelets onto the plates. Alex had backed off a bit, but still stood close enough to take a plate in his good hand and bring it to the table.

"I understand why you're upset," she said conversationally, sitting down with the second plate.

He looked at her in confusion.

"I mean, I understand what you must be facing, knowing you won't be able to work for weeks. Or, at least, work in the manner to which you're accustomed." She forked a piece of mushroom. "I'm going through the same thing myself. Not having a job, I mean."

Alex returned to his food.

"What will you do?" She tried again.

"Well, for starters, I'll show up here for breakfast every morning. This is pretty good."

"Don't count on it, Buddy. Unless you plan to take me out for dinner every night."

He looked up at her, and in the morning light, she saw several bruises on his cheek. "I suppose that could be arranged."

"I was just kidding," she said softly, but thought it would be a very fine plan indeed.

"I wasn't," he said quickly. "But what will you do?"

"I'm not sure. I haven't had that much time to think about it, but I'll start at The Thrifty Means. I have time to volunteer. And there seem to be so many smart women there, with so many connections, maybe I can do some networking." She wondered if she gave too much away. "What about you?"

"The Thrifty Means? I'm not sure they let men volunteer there." He slipped a bit of egg off his fork and fed it to Miranda. Glinda protested, and he did the same for her.

Just like a real family, Arden thought uncomfortably. If that could be said for a couple who just met a few days before, and fed pets instead of kids, surrounded by the wreckage of one's kitchen.

"Actually, I can do a lot of things, mostly catching up. I've promised to do some lectures around the country, but keep putting it off. There's a guy who wants to interview me for a book, though he's probably given up on me. I have mountains of paperwork to get to, and contracts to study and some things that have nothing to do with the art world. I'm pretty versatile, you know." He grinned.

"Do you ever take a vacation?" Arden asked.

"No. Do you?"

"Never."

"Do you think we should take advantage of our mutual bad luck and take one together? I haven't been to Rome in years. How about Paris? London?"

Arden could be packed to go in about fifteen minutes. But the familial conversation was making her delusional. This cottage in Eastfield was her vacation; she had come to get away from everything that made her miserable. And here she was, bantering with someone who might be more interested in her cottage than in her.

"How about Eastfield? It's all I can afford right now. And it has a certain appeal." Arden reached for a basket of fresh fruit and offered it to him.

"I'm glad to hear it. And come to think of it, I would have been packing to go to Cleveland right now, if I didn't have the accident. By contrast, Eastfield is paradise." He picked up a large red apple, probably not a coincidence.

As he munched on it, he leaned back on two legs of the rickety old chair. Perhaps he wasn't satisfied that yesterday's fall hadn't given him a concussion, and was giving it another shot. "All right. Let's stay around here."

"You can do whatever you'd like. I'm staying here as long as it takes to get another job. I'll send out resumes, volunteer at The Thrifty Means, and work on the inventory for the cottage. I may even do a little painting."

"Are you an artist, too?" he asked, coming down on all four legs. He seemed bothered by the possibility.

"Not one to give you any competition, if you're worried about it. I dabble a bit, that's all. I may want to touch up some of the damaged pieces here, like the painting in the living room."

"I wouldn't touch it," he said.

"But it's not your painting, is it? I can do with it as I please."

"No, you misunderstand me. I don't care if you throw darts at it. But my understanding is that there's a clause in the deed about the household goods. Bertram Wills will tell you more. It was your ancestor's intent that nothing in the house be moved from its place or changed."

Arden blinked, not sure she heard him correctly. "Well, I guess that plan's moot. This place looks like it's been hit by a cyclone. Everything, including the contents of the refrigerator, has been moved."

"We'll have to put it all back, as it was," he said reasonably.

Arden wasn't sure whether it was his calm assertion that he should have a part in the business, or the increasing strangeness of this discussion at her kitchen table, that made her lash out at him.

"I can handle it myself, thank you. Now that I'm here, I don't think I need you to act as caretaker. Do I owe you money for that, by the way?" She paused, realizing she probably went too far. "Anyway, who's going to complain if I move things around?"

"Victoria's ghost, I'm told."

Miranda made a little pleading noise, and he

stood up, a little awkwardly. "I guess I should be going. Miranda's used to a morning walk."

Arden had a feeling he was going to leave her with the dishes.

"Wouldn't Victoria have gone after the thieves, in that case?"

"I don't know. And you don't owe me money. Anne asked me to look after the place, and I do it as a favor, as a neighbor." He picked up his dishes with his one good hand, and wobbled them over to the sink, where he rinsed them. "Do I owe you money?"

"What on earth are you talking about?" Arden asked.

"I mean, for parking or things at the hospital. I know you're out of a job."

"I'm not that strapped for cash. I may not have enough for a Paris vacation, but I can manage five bucks for parking."

"Five bucks?" He whistled softly and both cat and dog stood at his feet, looking up at him. "The first time I broke my arm, it was only a dollar."

"Did you have someone drive you to the hospital then?" Arden asked, curious about the other women who might have been in his life.

"Yeah, my mother. And she stayed in my room all night, as I recall."

Arden said nothing, just watched him as he sauntered out of the kitchen, with Miranda at his heels and Glinda at hers. The man attracted females like the antiques in her cottage attracted dust, and at least one thief.

When Arden heard the front door close, she thought about the conversation, particularly Alex's warning about touching the mantel painting. But it was her painting now, and she didn't believe the spirits of her ancestors would blame her for trying to fix it up. Leaving the remaining dishes in the sink, she went into the living room. The Gainsborough look-alike was still hanging over the mantel, though the thief had taken a sharp tool to the edge of the wood, trying to pry it away. Splinters of wood were strewn on the mantel, and one of the fireplace tools was on the floor, where it had been abandoned. It looked like the thief had started to work on it, and decided it wasn't worth the effort.

Whatever it was, or whoever painted it, it still was a fine piece of Colonial craftsmanship, and quite unexpected in this modest cottage. Surely it would have been worth the effort to anyone needing to come into a little cash. Perhaps the women who lived here always had enough for their modest needs.

Arden shivered, though the air was far from cold. For the first time she realized she and Alex might have interrupted the thief in the middle of his work, and what might have happened if she came in alone. Or, if she was in the house when he decided to strike.

That didn't seem to make any sense at all.

The house had been practically abandoned for years, serving Anne on rare occasions, and Arden not at all. Judging by the amount of noise Alex made when he worked, someone could have put the whole cottage onto a truck and rumbled away down Old Tory Lane, without Alex hearing a sound. It just seemed too strange someone would have decided to rob the place while someone was living here, and might return at any minute.

Unless someone knew she'd be gone. And unless someone trashed the place not in spite of Arden's occupancy, but because of it. But that was just too strange to contemplate.

Chapter 6

"Cat hair on a sweater does not increase its value."
~Emma Grace Liddell (dealer in antique textiles)

Arden's welcome into The Thrifty Means was at once so friendly and so casual, that she wondered if they expected her. Eleanor Zane came forward holding a box of portrait miniatures, and Liza paused in her dusting to wave a cotton rag. Miriam Pell was at the front desk, discussing the weather with a customer.

"Ah, here's Arden right now," she said. "Arden, this is Emma Grace Liddell, who knows your sister. She sold her a few of the quilts on your beds."

"A pleasure to meet you," Arden said, and shook the older woman's hand. "The quilts are beautiful. I just assumed they had been in the house for years."

"Some of them were. They were kept in a wooden hope chest that's probably as old as the house itself. But some mice gnawed their way in through the bottom, and made themselves at home there. So Anne tried to replace them with quilts of a similar vintage."

"Two hundred years old? I'm surprised any of them survive," Arden said.

"The fabrics were heavier than we see in quilts nowadays. People used what they had on hand: brocades, woolens, thick cottons. I think the quilt in the pink bedroom has pieces of an American flag sewn in," Emma Grace said knowingly.

Arden paused, not sure which bedroom counted as the pink one.

"The one off the back hallway," Emma Grace said, reading her mind.

"Yes, of course. But isn't it illegal to cut up an American flag?" Eleanor asked. She put the box down on a weathered pine table, and picked up one of the miniatures.

"I suppose it is, but even the Eastfield police have more important things to do than pursue criminals wielding pinking shears. Besides, quilters don't usually ply their craft on the town green; they sew in the privacy of their own homes."

"I guess it's nice to have privacy in your own home," Arden said, wryly.

"Oh, yes! We heard all about it!" Liza said. "Are you all right? You must have been terrified!"

"I was," Arden said slowly, realizing if these women knew about the robbery, they must also know she spent the night in Alex's home.

"Was anything stolen?" Miriam asked.

Arden said nothing, because she simply didn't know. Until she saw the inventory, she couldn't say if a pair of candlesticks was missing, or a piece of Wedgwood, or a silver thimble. For all she knew, a chair could be gone, or a chest of drawers. But some sixth sense told her the intruders took nothing at all. The house had been invaded, vandalized, and cruelly used. The only thing no longer intact was her peace of mind.

"I hope the andirons are still there," Eleanor said. "I remember Anne showing them off one evening when she was trying to light a fire. My husband, Evan, told her the smoke might damage the painting over the mantel, so she gave it up. Is the painting still there?"

"It is. So are the andirons, now that I'm thinking about it. In fact, I'm not sure anything was taken at all. It seems odd, but I guess I should stop talking about the intruder as a robber."

"He robbed you of your welcome," Miriam said.

Arden smiled, as her troubles evaporated in the company of these women. "But you already welcomed me, so I've been quite at home."

"That reminds me," Eleanor interrupted the touchy-feely session. "One of these miniatures should be yours." She held out a small oval medallion.

"It's my cottage!" Arden said. "No, maybe not. I don't have a door there."

"I think you must have had one there at one time. There were some renovations done about fifty years ago, after the Great Flood. George Brook changed its course then. A bridge had to be relocated upstream, because it no longer spanned the water. And a lot of the houses along the banks were rebuilt, or shored up," Miriam explained and nodded, clearly remembering the scene.

"Anyway, I thought you'd like the miniature. It came in with a group of small paintings and sketches from Celia Cole's estate. She was a local artist and worked on commissions for just about everyone. I think these were intended to be sold as Christmas ornaments."

"Why wouldn't one of my ancestors have wanted them?"

"Oh, these were just knocked off for the tourist trade, for New Yorkers trying to create a country look in their brownstones. Celia could paint a dozen of these in a good afternoon."

"I guess they aren't worth that much to anyone, except me," Arden said and shrugged her shoulders.

"Everything has worth, if you wait long enough," Liza said knowingly. "Last week we sold a whole collection of ephemera, birthday cards from the nineteen-forties, and hand-made invitations to a Sweet Sixteen party. Miriam rescued them from the dump."

"So," Arden said, as if disarray and rummaging through garbage suddenly made volunteering a more desirable prospect, "when do I start?"

Eleanor smiled. "We knew you'd come back. We're only surprised it took you—what—three days? Come in the back with me, and I'll show you what we do, and how we do it."

"You'll never be able to get out of here," Miriam said.

"You won't believe how much you'll buy!" Liza said at precisely the same time.

Eleanor was already on her way through the labyrinth of furniture, linens, and dull silver. Arden followed her, resisting the temptation to examine everything in sight.

"Three days isn't a lot of time," Arden said defensively, when they sat down at either end of a weathered Ethan Allen table. Eleanor poured her a cup of tea, without asking.

"The water's hot. The kettle was whistling when you came through the door," Eleanor said. "You know Connecticut is well known for its tea companies."

"I didn't know, but I'm not surprised. I think the wall paper in the central hall of my cottage is original, and probably cut from the inside of tea crates."

"Yes, they did that during the China trade. Norwell was an important port. Not as important as Salem or New York, of course, but busy enough to ensure a steady stream of exotic items into the area. We see a lot of that in the old houses. Like yours."

Arden sipped her tea, appreciating the infusion of cranberries. She looked over her cup and Eleanor's shoulder to the shelves overloaded with merchandise.

"Are these things waiting to be appraised?" she asked.

"They are," Eleanor said. "Now that we're alone, please tell me what happened at Bradford."

Arden was surprised, for she didn't imagine she was called to the back for an official interview. After all, she only intended to be a volunteer here. And she hadn't pushed her way into the work room, but was invited to be here.

"Do you do this to all your potential volunteers? Or just the ones whose expertise you somehow distrust?" Arden asked.

Now Eleanor looked surprised. "I didn't mean to offend you. I'm only thinking about the credibility of our little business here. We're an Eastfield institution, started in the days when women primarily relied on us to upsize their kids' outgrown boots, or treat themselves to another set of pots or dishes. Through the years, our reputation changed, and grew."

"Do all your volunteers have industry credentials?" Arden persisted.

Eleanor picked up her tea cup and blew gently into the rising steam.

"Of course not," she said. "We welcome almost everyone who comes through the door and offers time and interest. But you're a different case."

"How so?"

"Well, you're famous, for starters. And we sought you out, which may ruffle the feathers of a few old-timers here. Don't let the casual nature and country ways of Eastfield fool you, my dear. We're a pretty elitist bunch. Snobbery abounds."

"Then I'm not sure I'll fit in."

"Oh, I'm sure you will." Eleanor sipped her tea and frowned. "I think you're like the cranberries in this tea:; a little tart, but good for us. You have a lot to offer."

"Because I'm famous?" Arden asked. "And wouldn't that actually be 'infamous?' "

Eleanor laughed, and someone poked her head through the door. Eleanor waved her off.

"How much do you actually know about what happened?" Arden asked.

"Only what we read in the papers. The *Eastfield Edition* ran a piece on it, because of the local connection. I think they just cut and pasted pieces of other articles, though. The real business of our town paper is to let us know how our high school sports teams are doing, and what our homes are worth. Your home has just gone up in value, I assume, because a picture of it ran on the front page."

"On the front page? Why on earth? My house has nothing to do with the story!"

Eleanor laughed again. "I guess neither Anne nor you were available for a photo shoot."

"No one asked," Arden said.

"Need I say more?"

"No, I get it," Arden said glumly. No wonder everyone seemed to know her business. The little cottage in the woods was front page news, an accessory to the fact. "What else would you like to know?"

"Were you right?"

Arden wasn't quite prepared for this question, because no one else seemed to care who was right or wrong in the incident. The Board of Trustees just wanted the story to die down. Her parents thought they were being comforting by telling her it was a lousy job after all. Anne just told her to move on, and would she need help in doing so?

"Yes, I was right. I had gotten a lead from an old acquaintance in Boston, someone who knew his stuff. He had been down in North Carolina, at the home of a university friend who had only moved there in the past few years. There was a pair of Paul Revere candlesticks on the mantel, real Paul Revere, made by the great man himself, and the friend was interested in selling them to pay off some debts. The house was a veritable gold mine, it seems, and there was a good deal else of interest, most of which came from the family's townhouse on Beacon Hill. Furniture, statuary, Canton china, silver, some paintings." Arden clicked off each category on her fingers, pausing on the last.

"On the wall, practically buried behind some draperies was a small portrait of a child. You know, it was one of those stiff paintings in which a five year old looks like a little old man."

"Are you going to tell me that this was a portrait of Lincoln or someone?"

"Someone, yes. But my friend wasn't so much interested in the subject as the painter."

Eleanor sucked in her breath, and squeaked, "Paul Revere?"

"Even better. Not a romantic horseman, thundering through all those Middlesex towns. But someone with pretty good credentials: inventor, writer, diplomat, among them."

"Franklin?"

"Who else?"

"I didn't know the old boy had it in him," Eleanor said. "But he's our own American Renaissance Man, so it makes perfect sense. Why not add painter to the list? He seemed to do everything else."

"Except ride through Lexington and Concord."

"I guess that would have been quite a journey from Philadelphia. How did his painting wind up in a home minutes away from the Massachusetts State House, in Beacon Hill? Or did it arrive separately in North Carolina?"

Arden paused before answered, noting Eleanor already seemed inclined to side with her. "I don't really know. But it's not so very strange; Franklin's parents are buried in the Old Burying Ground, about a half mile away. Franklin lived in Boston until he was seventeen."

"Did he paint? I wonder where he found the time."

"He vaguely alluded to some work he did, and Madison spoke very highly of his talent in that regard, but we simply didn't have the evidence to back it up."

"Until now. Until your friend found the painting."

Arden nodded. "So it seemed. I went down to North Carolina to see the canvas myself and spent the better part of last summer authenticating the find. It was good, very good, and I thought the proof inviolate. I recommended to the university to make a bid on the portrait, and produced the mountains of evidence I gathered. It was excessive, I admit, but we were going out on a limb for this one. It was to be the single biggest expenditure for the museum in the past twenty years."

"No one else went down with you to see it?"

"No one. At the time, I thought it was because my reputation and judgment were respected. But now, I'm not so sure." Arden spoke quietly, realizing for the first time she was able to speak of these things without experiencing physical pain. "I said that wrong. That is, now I am sure they really didn't respect my reputation and judgment. Now I think I might have been set up to take a fall."

Eleanor leaned forward on her elbows. "The plot thickens."

"Unfortunately," Arden said wryly. "And I still don't understand it. But I do know there wasn't a single person on our esteemed Board of Trustees or in the museum administration who could spare the time to look at the painting. But they found the time to dismiss me immediately when things seemed to go wrong."

"What happened?"

"We offered, were refused, and counter-offered a price significantly higher. And the painting was ours."

"And?"

"I wanted to go back to North Carolina to escort the painting back to Boston. But suddenly I was sent to examine the contents of an old house up in Marblehead, though any number of other people could have done that. My friend Peter was coming back to Boston soon, and the museum president asked him to be the courier for the painting, for a generous fee."

Arden rubbed her forehead, as the pain of those few days returned. "Peter arrived safely, as did the portrait. The only problem was, it wasn't the one I bought in September."

"Is Peter blind?" Eleanor asked. "Or just stupid?"

"I wish I could find humor enough in the situation to laugh. No, he isn't blind. And the painting that he delivered was very like the one I bought. Practically identical. But no Franklin. You could practically smell the turpentine on it."

"It was fraud, then."

"The Board of Trustees of Bradford thought so. They demanded I return the original painting at once, if it even existed."

"That's ridiculous. What would you have to gain by switching paintings on them? Or lying about the piece in the first place? There would be no point."

"Thank you for your vote of confidence; I said those very things at the hearing. But, in fact, I would have a great deal to gain if the fraud hadn't been uncovered. Money, for example. And a rise to prominence in my field, on my own merits." Arden looked down at the tea leaves in her cup, wishing she knew how to read her future. "There had always been some bad feelings, because I got the job over applicants who were older and had greater experience. I think they hired me because the budget was already tight and I probably settled for less. But I wanted that job so dearly."

Eleanor overlooked that comment, and instead asked, ""Who uncovered it? The fraud, I mean."

"I did. I spotted it right away."

"Arden!" Eleanor's cup clattered onto the saucer. "For goodness sakes! This gets more absurd by the minute! Why would you reveal your own fraud?"

"To throw the others off the scent, I suppose."

"My, but you are a clever woman, aren't you?" Eleanor said. "I think you're just whom we need at The Thrifty Means."

"So I pass the test, then?"

"What test? I recruited you, I wanted you even before you arrived in town."

"So what was all this about? Making me rehash that miserable nightmare?"

Eleanor looked a little sheepish. "Well, The Thrifty Means is the clearing house for most of the gossip in Eastfield, and I'm the manager of The Thrifty Means. My job wouldn't be in jeopardy if I mistook a potter's studio vase for a McCoy, but I would take some heat if I didn't know every detail of every item of gossip. I have obligations, you know."

Arden realized that coming from someone else, such words would be downright offensive. But Eleanor was on her side, right from the beginning, and it was hard to take her comments as anything other than as the humor she intended.

"I have another obligation," Eleanor added.

Arden glanced up, expecting to hear something about a trial period, or something of that sort.

"Yes?" she asked.

"I have an obligation to tell you that Alex Wingate broke up with someone last spring. He's available, but you'll face some competition from neighbors who will be stopping by to keep him company in his convalescence."

"They're welcome to him," Arden said and sighed. "He wants to buy my cottage for the retreat he's planning, and I believe that may be the only reason he has any interest in me."

"And that harem costume," Eleanor said.

"Will I ever live that down?" Arden asked.

"I doubt it."

****

An hour later, Arden sat on a stool that listed precariously to one side, but she seemed not to notice. Instead she squinted through a jeweler's loupe at something small and golden in her hand. Her long curling hair trailed down her back, twisting and turning like eddies in George Brook, and reflected glints of red and warm browns in the late afternoon sunshine. Though the shop was warm, she was wrapped in an old lacy shawl that made her look like a woman of another time, though not necessarily of another place.

She belonged in Eastfield; her presence in the old cottage felt as natural and familiar as the trees in each season, part of the order of things. It wasn't that Eastfield couldn't give up its own to the wider world, it was just that it seemed altogether right when the wanderers returned home. If only for a while, Old Tory Lane seemed whole again.

"Alex!" Eleanor Zane called out, and he turned to greet her. He saw Arden look up, nod distractedly, and return to her work.

"Hi, Eleanor," he said, trying to drum up some enthusiasm. Ellie was an old friend, but Alex had an objective in mind when he came through the door of The Thrifty Means. It had more to do with dinner at a nice restaurant than with chatting about the weather, Mr. Abbott's temperamental tractor, or worst of all, his damned broken wrist.

"How's your wrist?" she asked, and they soon had an audience.

"You know you should sleep with the cast raised on a pillow," said Miriam.

"No, let it hang off the edge of the bed. It'll strengthen your arm muscles," Liza said, and winked.

"Do you need help with anything?" Eleanor asked. "I can send Evan over later, when he's finished writing for the day."

Alex supposed that any man ought to feel good with three attractive women fussing over him, but he was more aware of one who was preoccupied, than the three who surrounded him.

"No, thanks, I think I'll be just fine. But I came in to see if you happen to have…ah…a crutch." As soon as he said it, he realized how stupid it sounded. But it was the first thing he thought of, and the damage was done.

"A crutch?" Eleanor asked in disbelief. "Did you hurt your leg as well?"

He glanced over to Arden, wondering how much he dared to stretch the truth.

"Well, I sort of twisted my knee when I fell, and now I'm having a little trouble getting up the stairs." That sounded convincing, even to himself.

Arden finally looked up, and studied his legs. He stepped behind a dry sink.

"I don't see how a crutch is going to help you, if you have a banister," Liza pointed out. "Wouldn't it be pretty much the same thing?"

"Perhaps Arden can give you a hand?" Eleanor asked. "Arden? What do you say?"

Arden brushed a cobweb off her brow and looked steadily at Eleanor, raising some question that went unspoken between them.

"Alex just stopped by," Eleanor said, as if Arden

hadn't been sitting ten feet away the whole time. "He needs a crutch to help him get around. But I thought you might be able to give him some help instead."

Arden raised a hand, shielding her brown eyes against the sun. "I think the crutch is more reliable. After all, I'll be coming to The Thrifty Means during the day and won't be around on Old Tory Lane all that much."

"Arden is one of our volunteers, now," Eleanor explained, as if excusing a rude child. "I intend to keep her busy."

"I'm busy now, in fact," Arden said.

Alex had nowhere left to go. He sat down on an upholstered chair, sending up a cloud of dust.

Miriam and Liza waved hands in front of their faces and Arden coughed.

"What are you doing?" he asked.

She finally looked directly at him, and put down whatever it was that held her interest. He realized that for the first time in their brief acquaintance she was actually doing something she loved, something she knew a great deal about. And he realized he was genuinely interested in what interested her.

"I'm looking at a set of hair brooches," she said, and held out her palm, where an odd piece of jewelry sat in her hand like a pearl in an oyster.

"Did women wear them in their hair?" he asked, curious. Behind him, someone laughed.

"No, they wore them over their hearts, because they contained the hair of someone loved and lost."

"Someone who died?"

"I doubt if women would have the same sentimental feelings about guys who abandoned them, or took up with other mistresses."

"I guess that would leave out a lot of the Wingate family," he said, under his breath. "Whose family are you looking at there?"

"This whole collection is from the South family. They have a whole range of hair color, and there is a sample from someone who might not have been part of the family,"

"How can you tell? DNA tests?"

She offered him the brooch in her hand. "I think this is sheep's wool."

"Do you think there was something kinky going on?" He reached for the pin, and let his fingers curl into her palm as he took it from her. She made a small noise and he looked into her eyes before turning his attention to the circlet of gold.

"Who can say? It must have been quite a challenge to be outré when you had five people sleeping in the same room. But perhaps this was only intended as a sign of affection for a small beast that provided food and warmth. A Connecticut winter would have been impossible to survive without warm woolens."

"And did you remember to pack your woolens, Ms. Alexander?" Alex closed his fist on the brooch, and again focused on her face. In the bright light streaming into the shop, he noticed a small scar partially obscured by her eyebrow. It disappeared when she raised her brow.

"I have lived in Boston, Mr. Wingate. I am very accustomed to seeking warmth on a cold winter day."

"Would you ever consider an alternative to a woolly sheep?" He leaned closed to her, vaguely aware when the brooch dropped onto the table.

"The Souths weren't really related to each other, you know," someone said behind him.

Alex straightened and remembered they had an audience.

"The Souths were Shakers. There was a small colony here in Eastfield in the late 1800s," said Miriam. She picked up the brooch. "They sought converts, people who would split up their family units and live within the laws of the colony."

"I almost forgot about that!" Arden said, a little too quickly. "There's a Shaker village in Pittsfield, Massachusetts as well. The South family probably lived in the southernmost dormitory."

"And David North's ancestors would have lived just opposite," Eleanor said. "He still works the old farm, off Shaker Heights Road."

"Well, that explains everything," Arden said.

"That explains all the different hair types," Alex corrected. It did not explain everything. It did not explain why he could not keep away from Arden Alexander, or why he felt the need to touch her every time they saw each other.

"Is David North still a Shaker?" Arden asked, turning in her seat to face Eleanor.

"I hope not," Eleanor answered. "Shakers are celibate and David's one of the best looking single guys in town. I'll introduce you one day soon."

"Thank you," Arden said with obvious pleasure.

"Thank you," Alex said with obvious sarcasm.

Arden turned back to look up at him, smiling with some wicked satisfaction. "Is there anything else you needed, Alex? Do you want a ride home? Or can you manage with your wrist?"

"I got here just fine, didn't I?" He knew he sounded like a high school kid, which pretty much summed up all his behavior when he was around this woman. "In fact, I wondered if you needed a ride back to Old Tory Lane."

"As you see, I got here just fine, as well. Your friend at the garage did a fine job on my car." She took the sheep brooch from Miriam's hand and replaced it in the display case. "The heat comes up very quickly, so I should have no trouble keeping warm during your long Connecticut winter. I don't think I need a thing."

Like the high school kid Alex was channeling, he

scowled and was tempted to kick something.

"Well, then," he said, pulling himself up. "I'll be off. There's plenty I can do, even with a broken wrist."

"I'm sure there is," Arden said. From anyone else, those words would have been an invitation.

****

The four women watched as Alex made his way through The Thrifty Means, out the door, and into his car in the parking lot.

"My goodness," Miriam said, and fanned herself with the day's copy of the *Eastfield Edition*. "Who needs a wool sweater? The two of you are probably the reason for global warming!"

"I think that's what Alex meant," Eleanor said dryly. "Why didn't you tell us it was like this between you? I wouldn't have brought up poor David North if I knew. I hope Alex doesn't go up to Shaker Heights Road to knock him off his tractor."

"There's nothing between us. If anything, it's just the familiarity that comes with being neighbors. Alex is about as hot as an old shoe." Arden stood up, thinking she had quite enough of this conversation. Besides, she remembered she left things out in the garden the other day and still hadn't cleaned things up.

"Alex is about as hot as the Fourth of July," Liza said.

"Or those silver candlesticks in the window," Eleanor murmured. "Did I tell you the police came by, and took some pictures? They think they belong to a family in Rowayton."

Miriam had some choice words about what the thief should have done with the candlesticks, and where, surprising Arden. But the temperament of The Thrifty Means thrived on the unexpected, and Arden felt she already contributed her fill for the day.

"Okay, ladies, I'm outta here," she said.

"Going back to Alex?" Liza asked.

"Going back to work in my garden. I heard we're getting frost tonight, and I still have bulbs in a bucket under a tree. I want to get them in the ground."

"If you left them sitting out in a bucket, the squirrels probably got to them first. What's ornamental for us is food for them. They'll bury them in your yard and if you're lucky, they'll forget about them and you'll have tulips coming up in all sorts of odd places in the spring." Eleanor smiled. "Trust me on this. We had a tulip come up in the charred remains of a little cottage on our property. And I know the former tenant was not a gardener."

"I heard he had a nice window garden," Liza said, and elbowed Miriam. "Didn't I hear something about weeds?"

"I think 'weed' would be more accurate. But the less said about that, the better," Eleanor said. "But that doesn't stop Lewis from looking around for Wayne's stash whenever he's home from college."

Miriam stepped away from Liza and said to Arden, "Eleanor has two sets of twins. The older ones are in college, and the little ones are just babies."

"Two husbands...what can I say?" Eleanor shrugged. "With Lewis and Leslie away at college, it's like having two families."

"I'd love to hear more," Arden said, and meant it. She wasn't especially interested in domestic matters, but wanted to understand how Eleanor Zane could manage two families, a career, and a major volunteering commitment. She, on the other hand, could barely remember to return her tools to the shed. "But I've got to go."

The women of The Thrifty Means waved her off with reminders to stop by whenever she had a chance. Liza settled down in the chair Arden vacated, to continue her work. Miriam greeted a newcomer at the door. And Eleanor just stood where she was, arms crossed, clearly relishing the action all around her.

Arden stepped out into the afternoon sunlight, guessing she had an hour or so before it became too dark to work outside. Then, she intended to cut up a salad for dinner, and spend the evening restoring some order to the cottage. It was a simple plan, and one she hoped she could manage without distraction.

She only needed Alex Wingate to stay in his own home, and leave hers alone.

****

The old flannel shirt was fast becoming her wardrobe item of choice. It was far too bulky to tuck into her waistband, so she left it flapping beneath her pea coat, providing some extra warmth. She found the thick canvas gardening gloves she discarded a few days before and a pair of Anne's duck boots. If Alex just happened to be looking out his window, and just happened to look down her way, he'd see a likely reject from the L.L. Bean catalogue, but a woman dressed for the part.

She closed her eyes for a moment, trying to remember what she had been doing, and where, when the horrifying sounds from the barn interrupted her agrarian pursuits a few days before. She was digging near the driveway, she recalled, and bent her new spade in half.

The strange moment of discovery, deferred, now filled her with a growing excitement. She had dug a fair-sized hole, large enough for Alex to stumble into while she backed her car out of the garage. She now remembered just where it was, where they were when she jumped from the car and pulled him to his feet.

Miranda was waiting for her near the garage,

115

but her owner was nowhere in sight. Carefully, Arden explored the ground with her toe, until the thick layer of leaves gave way, and caved into the hole she made days before. Miranda came forward, and sniffed at the damp earth, but it wasn't sufficiently interesting to keep her on her feet. She sat down again, unaware or indifferent to the fact she sat upon several daffodil bulbs.

As Arden reached for a hand rake, Glinda bounded over and jumped into the hole. Shaking her head, Arden began to wonder if this project was worth the effort. But something was down there, even if it proved no more exciting than a tree root or an old brick. She gently extricated the cat from the soil and kneeled on the ground, immediately feeling the cold damp seep through her jeans. Ignoring the discomfort, Arden started to poke at the softened soil that had fallen into the hole, and scraped it into a pile at her side. She caught her breath when she hit something hard, but realized it was nothing more than a good-sized stone, and tossed it in the direction of the stone wall. Miranda rose to her feet, stretched lazily, and trotted off after it.

Arden returned to her work, and immediately struck rock again. Whatever it was, it was not for tossing away. It was broad and flat, and when she shifted her position, the sun revealed the odd etchings she had only just noticed days before.

Arden worked quickly to widen the hole, anxious to determine the perimeters, and finally uncovered a squared off corner. The rock was broad and flat, set into the ground like a monument marker, a patio step, or a tomb.

The hand rake clattered to the ground between Arden's bent knees as she removed her gloves. She preferred not to look into the hole itself, and tried not to imagine the earthworms and other crawling things that made the soil their home. Instead she closed her eyes, and opened her mind to the sensations of the cool, moist soil, the rich odors of rotting organic materials, the sounds of her harmless nails scratching against the rock. Her hands were finally able to spread across the surface and she felt the patterns etched upon it. With her right hand, she unearthed the angle of a second corner and could just barely discern the shape of something beneath it.

"Are you digging a grave?"

Startled, Arden fell hard on her tush, and wished she wore heavier jeans.

"Where did you come from? I didn't hear you. And what difference is it to you what I'm doing?" she asked grouchily. "Besides, you asked me that question before, after you fell into it."

Alex shrugged, and Arden would have preferred not to notice how nicely his shirt stretched across his chest. She glanced down into the hole.

"I think I forgot that," he said. "But whatever you're doing, I can help."

She raised her head, looking pointedly at his cast.

He shrugged again, and took a deep breath, as if he knew the effect he had on her. "And I came down through your driveway. I think the gardeners must have blown away the leaves, so you didn't hear me."

"I don't have a gardener."

"Yeah, you do. Anne pays Mike to do the lawn in the summer, and the fall clean up."

"Why didn't he mention that when I picked out the bulbs?"

"Did you ask? This is Eastfield. People don't volunteer much information, unless pressed to the wall."

"That hasn't been my experience," Arden said tersely, suddenly impatient. "Anyway, I may not be much of a gardener, but I know which end of a bulb

117

faces up. So, if you don't mind, I've got this under control. You don't have to check up on me, you know. But thanks, neighbor."

Alex took that as an invitation to get down on his knees next to her. He smelled of pine and wood chips. "I'm not much of a gardener either, neighbor, but I know that hole is too deep for bulbs. You'll drown those poor onions."

"They're tulips."

"Even better. The deer will love them. But still, the hole is too deep. Our water table's pretty high, and your cottage sits on the lowest part of my...the property. The bulbs will just rot." Alex bent down to pick up a stick and whistled low to Miranda. The dog promptly dropped the stone she was drooling on, and wagged her tail. Alex stretched his arm back.

Arden closed her eyes. She imagined his arm settling across her shoulders and her own body leaning into his.

"Then it's an awful place for a graveyard," she said, giving up any pretense of secrecy.

Alex stopped short, the stick still in his grasp. An impatient Miranda barked, reminding him to finish what he had begun.

"What are you talking about?" he asked, flinging the stick over his shoulder. Arden watched it smack against an oak tree, ricochet back, and miss Glinda by inches. Miranda, saved the trek into the woods, wagged her tail happily, and took three steps to retrieve it. "I was only kidding. No one would bury a body in this wetland. You could guess what would happen."

"I would guess the body would soon fertilize the soil, but the gravestone would be just fine." Arden picked up a stone, and disappointed Miranda by dropping it like a plumb line into the hole. The sound of the impact seemed both eerie and solemnly insistent in the still air.

"What's down there, Arden?"

The sound of her name on his lips touched her like a caress. He pronounced it more like a Bostonian than a New Yorker, slipping neatly over the "r."

"Arden?" He said it again, and it took her a moment to realize it was with a sliver of impatience. But just a sliver. He watched her watching him and his head moved slightly forward, his light eyes cast downward at her lips.

"See for yourself," she whispered.

Cold air came between them as he turned away and sunk his good hand into the hole. His attention was all for whatever was buried in the earth, and Arden wasn't sure if she was relieved or disappointed.

Disappointed, she realized with an aching feeling.

"Do you have a flashlight handy? I think there's one in the laundry room, Or better yet, let's get this up if we can. I don't think it's too heavy," Alex spoke quickly, excitedly, as if he expected to find buried treasure. And, for all she knew, that might be exactly what lay below.

But Arden thought one of them ought to have a hold on reality. "Are you out of your mind? Isn't there a word for people who go digging up graves?"

"Yeah. Archaeologists. This thing wasn't put down here last week, you know. And I doubt if it's a grave anyway." He dropped closer to the hole, until his bent arm was buried up to the shoulder. He faced her, but wasn't actually looking at her, and she guessed he reasoned out some explanation for the stone in the ground. She was right. "Why would someone be put to rest here, when the parish churches were the first thing to go up in all these towns? Eastfield actually has two colonial churches, Congregational and Methodist. If you weren't accepted at either, you could be buried in Norwell, where the society was a little more cosmopolitan."

"You mean, where there were settlers of other religions," Arden said.

"That, and other things," Alex said, and cursed. He pulled out his hand, and blood ran down one fingernail to mingle with the crusted soil.

Arden gave him a clean tissue from her breast pocket. "If you don't watch it, you'll be sketching with a pencil held between your teeth. Let me dig it up."

"And ruin that manicure? Don't worry, I've got it." He pushed Miranda's head out of his way, and smiled. "I'm pretty sure it's a box of some sort, and too small to hold a body, unless someone buried his pet. I guess a cat wouldn't be allowed burial in a churchyard."

Arden patted Glinda's head and groaned. "Then please leave it. Let the poor thing rest in peace. It might be one of Glinda's ancestors."

"Let me have the spade, will you?" Even with the broken wrist, he seemed to be making progress. "It's definitely a box. But who buried it so deeply? The composting leaves of a hundred autumns wouldn't have brought it to this depth."

"Maybe it was buried when the garage was built?" Arden ventured a guess.

"In the forties? I remember reading an attachment to the original deed documenting the application and approval of the construction. There had to be an easement on the property. But I think if there was an existing grave on the site, it would have come to someone's attention." The last words were said into the hole as Alex pulled on the slab with his good hand. Arden didn't think it was a good time to ask why he was so interested in studying the deed to her property. When she said nothing, he looked up at her and said, "Help me get rid of this thing, will you?"

He shrugged his sling over his head, but he seemed stuck there, tied in a knot of his own making.

"Haven't yet got the hang of it, I guess?" she murmured, leaning toward him and reaching over his head. Without waiting for his arms to be freed, he dropped them over her shoulders, capturing her in his web.

She wanted him more than she even realized, and she had done little but think about him since she arrived in Eastfield. His lips closed over hers as he tentatively tasted her with his tongue, and she pressed against him, wanting more. Against her back, he pulled at the sling until he was free to hold her shoulders and then run his hand down the length of her arms. She felt the hard bulk of his cast, but he managed to warm her until she forgot about her damp knees, her cold cheeks, the reddened tip of her nose.

And then something in the air shifted, darkened, warmed, as if they kneeled on the ground in another season, at another time. She felt she had done this before, somehow, that they once came together like this, in the same place. She only just met him, and what she sensed was impossible.

She felt a sharp ache in her belly, neither of hunger nor indigestion.

"What?" Alex asked, against her lips.

"I...I'm not sure."

"You don't have to be sure of everything," he said, unaware of what she meant, other than the obvious. "Let's take it slow."

He drew away, and without his support, Arden thought she'd lose her balance. The sensation seemed apt; she most certainly lost her balance a moment ago, unable to conjure the memory to support her.

"We haven't met before, have we? At a party at Bradford or something like that?" Arden asked.

"I think I would have remembered, even if you chose to suppress it. It was only a kiss, Arden." He sounded eager to put it behind them, as casually as anything else between neighbors. One might borrow a rake, stop by with the paper, steal a kiss.

But it wasn't only a kiss, that much was certain. They shared a moment thawed from time, warming them in the sunshine of another day. The kiss brought it back.

"Do you want to do it again?" he asked, hopefully. She realized she stared at him, mesmerized by the experience.

"Not yet," she said softly, hesitating to stir up more ghosts. Eastfield was working a spell on her. How else could she explain what just happened? Why else would she feel such utter familiarity and ease with this man, unknown to her only weeks ago? And when had a simple kiss evoked such joy and contentment?

She continued to study him, and she saw the uncertainty in his usually confident expression. But she was equally uncertain. She was accustomed to meeting a date at a coffee shop, engaging in what passed for sophisticated conversation, and then going off for dinner and a show. And yet here she was, sitting on unraked leaves, her hair blown around her face, her fingers caked with soil, while an oversized dog and a tailless cat competed for this man's affections.

It was possibly the most romantic moment of her life.

Alex turned away first, found a stick and threw it clear across the driveway. Miranda kicked up a shower of dirt as she ran after it.

"I never realized gardening could be so much fun," Arden said softly.

Alex turned back to her and smiled. "If you think gardening is fun, you should try digging up a gravestone sometime. There's nothing quite like it."

Arden relaxed, grateful the moment had passed. "Well, it so happens I have a gravestone here. Or something like it. But I like what you do with your hands, so I think you should just leave this to me. I'd hate to have to wait until you heal from two broken wrists."

"It would take more than two broken wrists to keep me away from you, Ms. Alexander."

"I think you can call me Arden," she said, and put both her hands on her knees as she leaned toward him again. Something turned in her stomach, and faded.

"Are you all right?" he asked, concerned.

"It's the jeans, I think. I must be eating too well."

"Let's get some exercise, then." When she didn't move, he added, "By digging, I mean. Hand me the rake."

She did, and was content to watch him dig around in the dirt. At the moment, it felt about all the exercise she could handle.

"That's about it," he said after another ten minutes or so. "Why don't we each take a side?"

Arden edged forward on her knees until they were shoulder to shoulder. Thrown off balance when they leaned into the open grave, they pushed against each other and strained against the hold the Eastfield soil still had on their treasure. Arden was quite ready to call the whole thing off, when she felt the tension ease and the box finally come free of the earth. An avalanche of soil and pebbles rained down on the slab and buried their hands, but they didn't relinquish their hold until they were able to lay the box at their feet.

Arden spoke first, the first words between them

the whole time. "It is a gravestone," she said, breathing heavily. A wave of nausea passed over her. The stone slab was about a foot and a half long, about eight inches in height, and even before they brushed the rubble from its face, the letters and pictorial design emerged.

"There's the willow, and the date, and the name," she said, pointing out what must have been equally clear to Alex.

He moved his fingers across the surface, touching bits of soil and outlining the etches in the stone. For the first time she appreciated the artist he was, working with various materials, relying not only on his visual sense, but also on tactile impressions, feeling his way to an understanding of a creative problem. Not for the first time, she wondered what those fingers would feel like on her body.

He glanced at her. "Whoa You must be winded. Your cheeks are all red."

"I'm fine," she murmured, thoroughly embarrassed, even if he had no idea what she was thinking. For it was clear he was not thinking of her.

"It's not a willow," he said tersely, and bent back so the slab wouldn't fall into the shadow of his body. "It's a beech, or maybe an oak."

"Big difference," Arden said unhappily, suddenly hating the sight of the thing.

"Well, it is a big difference," he said thoughtfully. "You probably know more about this than I do, but I have never heard of any tree but a willow on early American funereal art."

"How do you know it's early American?" Arden asked a bit suspiciously, because, to be truthful, she wasn't sure of it herself. She had never seen anything like this.

Alex grinned smugly and moved his thumb off the lower part of the plaque.

"Seventeen seventy-four?" Arden asked. The date was inscribed in a graceful hand. "Well, then, you're absolutely right. But look at the name. I assume it's Spanish?"

" 'Quercus Chartula,' " Alex said softly, swallowing his vowels. There was something in his intonation that made Arden think that he had a certain degree of fluency. "It's a new one on me. If I didn't know better, and I probably don't, I'd say it was Latin. Isn't 'chartula' the word for 'treaty,' or 'map?' "

Arden looked at him with growing respect, one bolstered by the very intent look upon his face.

"I wouldn't know. To be honest, in my line of work, I've needed a working knowledge of French, and I only remember a bit of German from high school. I would have thought, in New England, that would have been sufficient," she said.

"So it would be. If you look at the names on the old tax registers for Eastfield and all the surrounding towns, you'll see a list that could have come off a London census. Oh, here and there is a Dutch or Swedish name..."

"Or Spanish?" Arden said. "He must be on the town registry."

She fingered the delicate etching on the stone, following the same path Alex's fingers took a few moments before.

"Or perhaps not," Arden added thoughtfully. "He might have been a servant, which could account for his being buried outside of consecrated ground. Or he might have been an illegal alien. Were there such people in those days?"

"I doubt it," Alex said and, with her help, turned the slab over. "But whoever he was, he wasn't buried here, and this isn't a grave."

"What is it? A shoebox? Of course it's a grave. He was probably cremated, poor soul."

"An urn on the mantel would have been more appropriate. Or they sent his remains back to Spain." Alex gently lowered the box on the ground before them, as Arden wiped her hands on her jeans. But this she did without thinking, for all her attention was on the box. It was a curious structure, carved completely out of solid rock but for the lid. And this was affixed with several metal hinges. Alex picked up the discarded sling from the ground and used it to brush off the encrusted soil and corrosion. "Let's open it, shall we? Though I think I'll need a hand—literally."

Arden reached out to help and then quickly withdrew her hand, when the fact of what they were about to do suddenly struck her.

"No," she said, stuffing her hands into the tight pockets of her jeans. "I don't want to see what's inside."

Alex grinned at her before returning his attention to the box. "It's a good thing Howard Carter didn't share your squeamishness before he broke into King Tut's tomb." He didn't say anything else for an interminable amount of time, as he worked determinedly over the latches, and manipulated the stone with his one good hand. Arden stood and withdrew to the side of the garage, undeniably curious even as she was repelled, and feeling just a bit selfish. She regretted her moment of prissiness, and told herself she would jump in to help Alex if he only asked again.

But he did not. With the same dexterity she admired before in him, his hand moved efficiently over the box, pulling and twisting and searching for the release. She knew when he found it by his grunt of satisfaction and the sudden relaxing of his tensely bunched shoulders. As she started forward, Alex opened the box and took a deep breath.

"Is it very horrible?" she asked,

"Even more horrible than I imagined," he said, though he looked disappointed. "The damned thing's empty."

He wiped the inside of the box with a corner of the sling and then studied what came off on the cloth.

"No ashes?" Arden asked. "No bone fragments?"

"Just a few splinters of wood. Aside from that, the thing's clean."

"Well, now that you've managed to smudge the evidence all over your sling, it ought to be clean." Arden stared into the cold gray surface of the stone box. "Then poor Quercus must be buried beneath it. This is just a head stone, and we ought to dig deeper."

"Aren't you the woman who couldn't bear to look into the box a few minutes ago? But now you're ready to dig up a man's bones?"

No, she wasn't ready for that, at all. But if a man was buried beside her driveway they—she—really ought to do something about it. Preferably, dig him up and rebury him somewhere else.

"I wish you could see your face," Alex said, and leaned closer.

Arden edged back. "I could call the gardeners. They like to dig things up. Even better, they like to fill things in. Maybe they'll plant a tree here."

"It's a bad place for a tree; the roots will work their way into the garage. But what do you want them to do with Quercus when they find him?"

Arden studied the position of the garage in relation to the hole in the ground. It was very possible the poor guy actually lay beneath the concrete foundation of the small structure.

"Pull him out from under the building, for one," she said at last. "And give him a decent burial. Perhaps there's still room for him in the graveyard at the Congregational Church on Oak Street. Then, at least, he would be with the souls he probably knew in life."

"It's an oak tree," Alex said firmly, apparently hearing only one word in all Arden said. He rubbed his hand over the slab again, but in that quick, sideways gesture one uses to take a rubbing.

"Who cares? I'm sure it didn't matter to Quercus if someone scratched an oak or a maple or poison sumac on his stone. He's been resting in eternal peace for over two hundred years."

"Probably not," Alex said, and put the box gently on the soft ground. "His rest would have been interrupted at least once, when they built the garage in the forties. I don't see how they could have avoided him when they dug the foundation. Nowadays, plans for construction would probably have to be scrapped. But back then, he probably delayed the builders by...well, I'd say at least a few hours."

"That's not funny," Arden said. "But if that's the case, there must be some record of it. After all, it must have been the biggest story to hit Eastfield in a year, unless someone's cow escaped from her pasture. A grave on someone's property would have even merited an article in the newspaper."

"It's unusual, but not unprecedented. People have found graves in the basements of their old houses, perhaps because of smallpox quarantine, or a long spell of frozen ground in the dead of winter. They didn't face zoning restrictions back then." Alex shrugged his sling higher onto his shoulder and grimaced. "Though they did in 1949."

Arden glanced up at him. "You just happen to know that?"

"The law, or the date?"

"Both, I suppose. But my parents might know about this as well. It's just the sort of thing that would have made for good conversation around the holiday dinner table. I'll call them later, and see what they recall."

"Where do they live?" Arden asked.

Alex looked at her, and blinked. He surely wasn't thinking about his parents at the moment. "Oh, they retired to South Carolina, to be closer to my brother and his family. For so-called rugged New Englanders, they were pretty anxious to escape our cold winters."

"Maybe they'll remember something. But I could just as easily ask some of the old-timers at The Thrifty Means. Unless someone found a set of bones, though, I doubt the story of a stone box would have been very memorable."

Alex said nothing, as he brushed bits of leaves and wood off his clothing.

"Your sling is filthy. Do you want help tying on a new one?" Arden asked.

"I don't think it would make that much of a difference, considering the rest of me," Alex said, and opened his arms for her examination. He smiled invitingly. Arden obliged him by savoring the sight of soil on his hands and face, the smudges on his shirt and jeans, and the sweat on his brow. She was probably a fitting partner for him at the moment.

"You never know," Arden said. "But if you'd like, I could retie this one. It looks like it's gotten tangled."

Though not as much as the tangle in which she found herself, she realized. The elusive voice of reason reminded her he was only interested in her cottage, she hardly knew him, and he was only being neighborly. But no matter what she told herself, she was drawn ever closer to him, entwining her life with his.

Arden stepped over the mysterious box and the hole from which they unearthed it. Since Alex hadn't answered her, she took his silence as acceptance, and stood face to face with him. He watched her in silence, doing nothing to help or hinder. She put her hands on his left shoulder, where the mesh was twisted and uneven, and unhooked the clasp. His arm stayed in place as she pulled the sling off, and she focused her attention on shaking the soil off the microfiber so it wouldn't rub off on his clothing or cast. Remembering the way in which the doctor applied the sling at the hospital, she bade him bend toward her, and gently caught his wrist in her free hand. She knew Alex watched her, and not her handiwork.

She didn't know what her expression revealed, but he mistook it for a different kind of worry.

"Don't worry, Sweetheart. We'll figure out this business of Quercus soon enough. And I'm reasonably sure his ghost doesn't haunt the place because we would have seen him already," Alex said encouragingly, and kissed the top of her head.

She sincerely doubted her own attractions if she could be this close to a man, practically pressed against his body, and all he could think of was a stone casket for someone long dead. Perhaps she imagined the desire in Alex's eyes, the raw earthiness of his unspoken invitation. Everything now—including his unexpected endearment—was cheerful and congenial. Arden stepped back, reached up, and retied the knot at his shoulder.

"There you go, as good as new!" she said, sounding as falsely optimistic as the nurses back at the hospital.

"Well, I wouldn't go so far as to say that," Alex said. "But it feels a lot better."

"I wish I felt a lot better," Arden admitted, though not willing to discuss why her heart raced like an engine. "I'd like to find an answer to this mystery about Quercus Chartula."

"We will. He probably was someone's pet dog,

and the tree his most prized possession to take along into the afterlife. They didn't have fire hydrants in those days, you know."

"That doesn't sound very romantic. Perhaps it's an old treasure chest, discarded and reburied after the builders took out the gold coins."

"Or a box for firewood. Hence the carved oak."

"Too practical for my taste. Perhaps it was a hope chest for a bride left at the altar, and she buried it, along with her disappointed hopes."

"I'm right. You are a romantic," he said.

"I…" Arden began, and closed her mouth. Once again, she stupidly walked into a trap.

"And I have the perfect place to take you," Alex said smoothly.

The bedroom in his beautiful white clapboard farmhouse?

"There's an inn just downriver, built at about the same time as my house. The food is great and they play live jazz in the evenings. Why don't we go there for dinner one night?"

"I…I'm not sure I…I think…" Arden knew perfectly well she sounded like an idiot, because that was precisely what she was. He was being neighborly and kind, and she was suspicious of everything he said or did. If he intended to make her an offer at the inn, it probably would be on the property, and the evening would end badly. There were other offers she would be happy to accept, and the evening might end rather remarkably.

"Look, it's just an evening out, not a big deal. Besides, I think I owe you one."

Arden cleared her throat. "For what? I made you dig up half my lawn, drive me into town, show me around."

"You took me to the hospital. And just helped me with my sling."

"Well, yes. I can see how shaking out a sling can

incur quite a debt of gratitude."

"It has. So, will you let me take you out?"

This sounded a bit more serious. "If that's all it takes, I shall have to do it more often," Arden said, trying to sound as cheerful as he.

His mood changed again, and he looked into her eyes. "Yes, I hope you will."

Chapter 7

"A town hall does not so much reflect the size of
the population as the scope of its ambition."
~*Hammond Riley (Eastfield Historian)*

Arden arrived in Eastfield thinking it was the
one place where she could find sanctuary from her
troubles. Now, she needed to get away from
Eastfield, at least for a few hours. She thought about
exploring the neighboring towns, or going to one of
the small historical society museums that dotted the
old roads. But she doubted she could keep her mind
on any of their local treasures when Quercus
Chartula's mysterious presence continued to
intrude. So, instead, she settled on one place where
she could lose herself in some quiet research, and
not likely meet anyone at all.

The Eastfield Town Hall was as definitively
New England as a straight-backed village matron on
her way to market, though not nearly as welcoming.
A few miles downriver and perched on a solid
promontory over the road that was built in the river
valley, it seemed haughtily indifferent to the stream
of modern-day traffic that passed beneath. Black
shutters and doors punctuated its gray granite
exterior, and a few metal plaques honored those who
served the country and died, those who served the
town and retired, and those who donated money to
support those who served.

Arden paused to read a few of these memorials,
and then walked her rusty bicycle to the rack at the
side of the building. She doubted anyone would

bother to steal it, or even venture to this small patch far from the parking lot.

The bike rack was adjacent to a well-marked herb garden. Even at this late stage of the season, the plants were lush and overgrown, and it was impossible to trespass without raising some scent of verbena, or mint, or chives. Those who drove up in their cars were denied this simple pleasure, and Arden felt rewarded by her decision to take in some exercise. She had a lot to work off, in any case.

A small signpost directed the townspeople to the appropriate entrances for their various, official purposes and Arden found her destination at the very bottom of the list: Town Records. Taxes, Permits, Voter Registration would all have to wait for other days, when the more mundane facts of existence needed to be reckoned with. Today, Arden wished to satisfy only herself.

She walked down a narrow staircase to the basement of the building and came into a large, irregularly shaped room. A handmade sign at the high counter indicated that the clerk was out to lunch, but that visitors could make themselves free with the records housed in the place. Any questions could be jotted down on a pad of paper and left for the clerk, who promised to call with an answer as soon as he or she had one.

Any concerns Arden might have had by intruding herself into the intimacies of Eastfield was dissipated by the casual and congenial way in which help was thus offered. Compared to the public records in Boston, to which one needed everything but a note from one's doctor to be admitted, this was like browsing through a family attic. She could have been anyone, looking for anything. She could have been intent on damage.

As she walked over to the wooden shelving that, she assumed, held the index, she realized the thought bothered her more than it ought. Anyone could have entered this place, tampered with records, or changed the roll. It was a veritable invitation to mischief or fraud.

She hoped Quercus Chartula hadn't any enemies.

Arden pulled out the long, heavy roll for 1949, not sure a reburial would be indicated on the record, but thinking it the easiest place to start. She lugged the awkward thing over to the closest table and opened it—probably the first one to do so in years.

As a record of life in Eastfield, it was fairly thorough and exacting. But then, with a population of 6,000, it was probably not a difficult thing to do. The postwar boom of new babies must have upped the total somewhat, but there were few comments along with the statistics, and Arden was left to draw her own conclusions.

The births of babies, the deaths among the elderly, the sales of houses were all among the everyday events that occurred that year, and each was duly noted. A penciled notation next to the record of death of one ten year old ascribed "polio" as the cause, and next to that of another child, "drowning." Forty-one houses, seven barns, and eighteen gardening sheds were built and permits were granted...

And yes, there it was. Absolutely straightforward and without any unusual note, "Portia Helena Alexander; Application to build garage to existing structure at 15 Old Tory Lane. Permit granted, April 14, 1949. Easement noted on title to property at 17 Old Tory Lane, May 1, 1949."

Portia was Arden's aunt, but she would have been a young woman in 1949, when the house belonged to her mother, Victoria Helena Alexander. But, Arden now recalled, Victoria died not many years after the war.

On a hunch, Arden flipped through the fragile pages to the record of deaths and found what she sought at once, surprised she passed right over it the first time.

"Alexander, Victoria Helena. d. natural causes January 2, 1949 at home of L.P. Riley. Burial provided by family."

One would hope so. And yet, Arden couldn't remember if she ever noticed her great-aunt's plot among the other Alexanders, Ardens, and various Shakespearean names at the family cemetery in Queens, New York, and wondered if Aunt Victoria remained, in a manner of speaking, in town. Perhaps the next stop should be the cemetery on Norwell Road.

Something else also occurred to her, and it cast Alex's words, about rearranging the furnishings, into a new light. Portia hadn't waited very long after her mother died to add a new structure to the exterior of the cottage. Wouldn't the construction of a garage be considered a greater offense against the memory of the departed than a rearrangement of the vases on the mantel? Arden couldn't help but wonder what sort of car Portia was driving at the time, and if her pride in it simply overrode her family obligations. Tory was barely cold in her grave when the groundbreaking occurred.

Arden returned to her more immediate problem and looked to see who broke ground and for what, in 1949. Here, the burials of each person were duly recorded, as were the sales of funerary plots in the several local graveyards. Just when Arden was about to give up on the possibilities of a specific mention made of reburials, her eye caught the notation of such an event, marked with a footnote further down the page. In 1949, it seemed, land was acquired for a new state highway going directly through Eastfield, and several old graves were disinterred and moved to safer locations. The displaced people—or what remained of them—were contemporaneous to her Mr. Chartula, and might have been his neighbors. But he was not included among them.

Arden put a hand to her head, and rubbed away the beginnings of a headache.

"The character line is pretty good, I think, but there's not much of a plot," came a voice from the door. Since there was no one else in the room, she presumed the speaker addressed her.

"As a matter of fact, I'm working on the plot right now," Arden said spontaneously and turned to see who had spoken. "The only problem is it's a cemetery plot."

"It's against the law, you know, to display any humor in the hallowed halls of the Records Office."

"That's funny. Since I arrived in Eastfield, people have been telling me what to do and what not to do, and no one ever mentioned it."

"Then I'm grateful they saved me something with which to start a conversation," said the man, smiling as he approached her. "And I see it worked."

He stood somewhat shorter than Alex Wingate, Arden thought, but just as solidly built and sturdy looking. He wore his crisp oxford shirt and gray suit well, though he looked like the sort of man who would prefer jeans to wool, and a sweater to a sports jacket. His hair was fair and straight and fashionably slicked down at the sides. His eyes, slightly magnified behind wire-framed glasses, were very dark. All in all, he was the best looking thing she had seen in hours. And if he knew his way around this place...

"I'm the Town Clerk," he said, and acknowledged the pleased response on her face. "I'm Hammond Riley."

"Hammond..?" Arden only paused because she

thought she just read the name Riley and wasn't sure where to place it. But Mr. Riley misunderstood her implied question.

"Hammond," he said distinctly. "Like the atlas. I was a natural to be the one to find my way around in this mess."

"Then you're just the man I need, Mr. Riley," said Arden happily, not caring how desperate she sounded. She pushed her own chair closer to the table so he could walk around her to an empty seat. "But I hesitated over the Riley part. I'm sure I've heard of another Riley."

"We're all over hereabouts," he answered easily as he sat down. He smelled faintly of cigar smoke. "There have been Rileys in town for centuries, and you'll find our name as common as dandelions along the road."

"Well, then it seems to me such a name gives you even better credentials to fill this position. You could probably tell me more about what I want to know than any book here."

He leaned closer, conspiratorially. "What do you want to know? If I don't have the answer, I probably could tell you where to find it."

Arden hesitated, though later she wouldn't be able to recall the instinct that made her do so. Hammond Riley seemed affable enough, and his invitation to help was not only kind, but also offered in his official capacity. He was a man who was trusted with the secrets of the town, and the sort to whom it would be easy to trust more personal ones. And yet, there was something in Arden's nature that made her hold back, something that was not yet ready to reveal the interesting find she and Alex made on Old Tory Lane.

"I'm trying to locate the record of one of my ancestors, who lived around the time of the Revolution. His name was Quercus Chartula, and I have reason to believe that he's buried somewhere in Eastfield." In fact, Arden had no reason to believe any of it, but it sounded perfectly reasonable.

"Chartula?" Riley's voice sounded a little on edge. "I know of the Alexanders, of course, the Winthrops and Wingates, and you even had a Trumbull there at one time. Don't look so surprised; it's just as you suggested. I may know your ancestors better than you do. After all, I'm paid to keep track of our families."

"I'm not surprised about your knowledge of the town, Mr. Riley. Only that you seem to know who I am, and I haven't even introduced myself yet."

A blush spread across his fair features, until he looked like a man who spent an unhealthy amount of time in the sun. He was looking down at the page, though, and so she couldn't read the expression in his eyes.

"I told you I'm well-connected here, Miss Alexander, and news travels fast. Especially when there's a new resident in town and she's one as pretty as you. It's bound to get you noticed." He cleared his throat and finally looked up at her. "I'm sorry if that sounds like an intrusion, but that's Eastfield for you. We tend to know who comes in, and make note of who leaves us."

But what if they're buried in a box in someone's driveway?

Arden smiled until she thought her face would crack. "Actually, in some ways I find that a comfort. I've only lived in the city, and it's easy to get lost there. Here in Eastfield, I'm beginning to feel quite settled. I suppose I'm relieved, though somewhat surprised, that recent events on Old Tory Lane didn't make the weekly paper."

"The Eastfield Edition," Riley murmured. "You mean the robbery, of course?"

"Yes, of course. You'd think it would have been

the biggest story in years."

Hammond Riley shrugged. "Well, we're rather proud of our serial killers, recreational drug dealers, and the sales of stolen merchandise."

Arden looked at him to see if he was kidding, and couldn't quite tell.

"Actually, my house wasn't technically robbed, because I don't think anything is missing. I suspect someone was looking for something, though I can't imagine what it could be."

"I heard about you from my cousin Mike," Mr. Riley said quickly, and Arden guessed that he wanted to change the subject. Of course, that made perfect sense; he had an interest in promoting a good image of Eastfield, and a mysterious break-in was not going to be an asset.

"Mike? The gardener?"

Mr. Riley laughed. "I think he'd be the first to remind you that he owns the nursery. But yes, that's Mike. He was very impressed with your interest in gardening. Your sister has always been content to have his crew take care of the land and gardens and, he guesses, wouldn't know a tulip from a rose. Mike admired your taste in...daffodils."

Something in the last hesitation made Arden believe Mr. Riley was about to say something else, and it had nothing to do with her elementary knowledge of botany.

"That's very nice of him, but I'm afraid my taste in daffodils is rather simplistic. I know what I like, and I know where I'd like to see them. But aside from that, I'm a novice. I shall have to rely on Mike's crew as much as my sister did. They've already been by..."

"I know."

Arden raised her brows in surprise. It was one thing to know the names of her ancestors or the general interests of the residents of the cottage. But so mundane a thing as knowing the gardening schedule on a small and insignificant property would seem to be carrying the neighborly spirit a little to extremes.

"Well, then, Mr. Riley. You've proven you're just the person to help me out in my ancestral search." Arden's voice was a little too high, a little too cheerful. "You know everything else about me. What can you tell me about Quercus Chartula?"

The dark eyes looked puzzled behind the thick lenses. "Nothing yet. Did you say he was here during the Revolution?"

"So I believe."

"Then why are you looking at the nineteen fifties book?"

"Oh." Arden said loftily. She didn't want to say anything about the stone box. "I was just curious to see when my Aunt Portia inherited the property. I didn't know when my great-aunt Victoria died and was curious."

It sounded pretty lame, even to herself, but Hammond Riley looked satisfied. He smiled broadly and patted her hand with cool, dry fingers.

"Well, let's see what we can find in the seventeen hundreds. Eastfield was part of Norwell then, and was not listed as a separate parish until 1802. But most of the records have been brought up from the Norwell Town Hall, at least, what was left of them." He stood and went purposefully over to the wall of narrower shelves, where the books were each sealed in a case of plastic.

Arden kicked back her chair and followed him. "Do you mean they've disintegrated over time? Were some of them lost?"

"'Disintegrate' is the wrong word. I think incinerate is more accurate. When the British came across the Sound from Long Island, they marched right through Norwell and burned a path as they went along. The old Norwell Town Hall, the Gunnery, the public house, and dozens of homes were destroyed. Most of the official records were safe up here in Eastfield, but not all of them survived."

"Here in Eastfield? Was that because the town was far enough away from the Sound?"

"Remember, we weren't a separate town yet. No. This is where the Loyalists gathered together. They weren't all that popular in the area and believed they would find safety in numbers."

"And the Loyalists were the..."

"Tories," he answered quickly, confirming what she already knew. "Old Tory Lane was named later, to commemorate the location of their meeting house."

"Do you mean they built a hall, something like this?"

"I mean they met in the parlor of Matthew Bowen's farmhouse, just down the road from you. Munitions were stored in the barn."

"I see," Arden said thoughtfully, and pointed to the book in Mr. Riley's hands. "Is that one of the original records?"

He carefully pulled off the casing and put it back on the shelf. "It is indeed. If you look right here, you can see the seal of the crown. It looks like some someone tried to scratch it off—small wonder about that—but you can see still the outline. And King George's name is right there."

Arden nodded, absurdly excited. There was no reason why all this should amaze her, since she'd been dealing with antiques and old artifacts all her professional life. But she was connected to this book, in a direct linear path across the centuries, and it now gave her a part of herself previously missing.

"Chartula, did you say? An odd name." Mr. Riley pulled off his glasses, and stuffed them into his breast pocket. His nose had marks where the frames rested, but he looked quite appealing. He also looked younger than she had thought him at first, and was probably no more than thirty. "Do you suppose it's Spanish or Portuguese?"

"Alex Wingate says it's Latinate, so it could be either," Arden said, and regretted her words at once. She hadn't intended to bring Alex into the conversation, hadn't wanted to say anything at all about their growing relationship, or the fact that they already discussed the name of Quercus Chartula.

"Mr. Wingate? I'm not surprised. Your neighbor seems to have a penchant for insinuating himself into everyone's business, even if it couldn't possibly concern him," Mr. Riley said coolly. "He also makes a point of meeting every attractive young woman who moves to town."

Arden realized the man intended his remark to do double duty, as a rebuke to Alex Wingate and as a compliment to her. It accomplished neither.

"As I practically live in his backyard, he could hardly avoid the acquaintance, Mr. Riley," she said softly.

"Well, here we are in 1769," Mr. Riley said gruffly. "Did your mysterious ancestor live here then?"

"I really don't know. I only suspect he died in 1774." She peered over his arm at the tiny lettering scrawled in even lines across the page, trying not to touch him.

"And how do you know that? I'm not trying to be a snoop. It just seems to me that you must be basing your information on something you've read or heard, and it would be helpful to know what it is."

"Nothing, really. I think it was a listing in the...ah...family bible."

"I see," said Hammond Riley, and sucked on his lower lip. "Well, here's your old Trumbull relation, another Victoria. The cottage has a long history of spinsterhood, you know."

"What do you mean?" she asked.

"Well, until the most recent Victoria's time, the cottage was always an extra structure on the larger estate. And, it seems, the single sister or widowed mother was usually allowed to stay there. The large house was owned by Trumbulls during the revolution, and for whatever reasons, Victoria Trumbull was consigned to the cottage. I suspect they were quite novel among their neighbors."

"What do you mean?" she asked again.

"Ah, Miss Alexander, despite your excellent lineage, you're not really a Connecticut Yankee. If you lived here all your life, you would know the Trumbulls are to Connecticut what the Adamses are to Massachusetts. Jonathan Trumbull was the only British colonial governor who supported the patriots, and we're told his descendants all followed suit. But one or two might have dissented, as is the way in all families. Perhaps Victoria Trumbull was relegated to the cottage because she held unpopular opinions."

"And Quercus Chartula?"

"I have no idea. Honest. I've never heard the name, and I don't see anything like it here. Seventeen seventy-four, did you say? I don't see any record of his death."

"Could he have been a servant, or even a slave?"

"There were very few slaveholders locally, but plenty of servants. Even so, he would be listed here if he had died. I wonder..."

"Yes?"

"You don't suppose your illustrious ancestor took herself a Latin lover, do you? That might explain her banishment to the cottage."

Arden thought it might, but it wouldn't explain why or how she had buried him in her back yard. Unless...

"When did she die?" Arden asked. Perhaps her relatives did the job for her.

"Let's see now..." Mr. Riley flipped the pages forward. "There she is, in 1818. In the Congregational Cemetery."

"And there's no sign of a Quercus Chartula anywhere?" Arden was frustrated by what were, literally, dead ends.

"Let's see now..." Mr. Riley repeated. It must be his stock phrase for all the requests people made of him in this office. Realizing this, Arden now wondered if his interest was not at all personal, and she needn't take any of his words as an affront. She edged closer until they stood shoulder to shoulder, and together they ran down the names of people and places, of taxes and burials, of everything mundane that went on while a revolution stopped at their doorjambs.

"Here's a Quentin Charles," Mr. Riley noted and pointed with the tip of his pencil to a notation on a page. Quentin Charles was a blacksmith, who died of an accident in his shop in 1779."

"I don't think he's the same man," Arden said.

"Well, it's the closest thing we have. Do you want to go further?" Nothing changed in his moderate tone, but Arden now wondered if she was wrong, and everything was, in fact, personal.

"Perhaps I will, but not today. I've already taken up too much of your time."

"I don't think so. In fact, I'm thinking that I might want you to take up more of my time. Are you doing anything on Sunday?"

She was right, a small consolation that felt immensely gratifying. She might be a stranger in the strange land of Eastfield, but her instincts knew their way around without a road map.

"Is the office open then?" she asked sweetly.

He laughed, and she realized how likable he

was.

"No, it is not. This is Eastfield, where you can't even buy a drink on Sunday. I was thinking something unofficial. Are you interested in antiques?"

"Antiques?" Arden squeaked. Surely he baited her; everyone in town seemed to know what she did before arriving in Eastfield.

Hammond Riley shrugged. "Well, I just thought you might be interested. You know, since you have so much old stuff in your cottage, you may want to see what's on the local market. There's a large fair on Sunday, in Chatwell. Would you like to go with me? We could have dinner afterward, or see a movie."

Maybe he really didn't know what she did, and here was just a straightforward invitation for a date. Alex just took for granted she would be around, waiting for him to suggest something. But Hammond Riley seemed to understand the protocol of modern dating still existed.

"I'd love to, Mr. Riley. It sounds like fun."

"You'll have to call me Hammond. Everyone else does. The town already has a Hamilton, who's known as Hammy."

"Well, I suppose you ought to be grateful for that, Hammond. Anyway, I'd be delighted." She looked at him, and recognized his pleasure at her response. "What time should I be ready?"

"Is one o'clock convenient? Or is that too early?"

"You must think me very lazy, if you can ask that," she said, teasingly.

He shrugged. "I just didn't know if you'd be out late on Saturday night."

He didn't have to spell it out for her. "No, I won't be. I'll be up and ready for you. And, of course, you know where I live."

"Of course," he repeated. "I won't be the first

Riley to have called at the cottage."

Arden smiled at that, now thinking it very comforting to live in such a place as Eastfield. She gathered up her papers and handbag, and with another few words of parting, left the office and climbed the stairs up into the sunshine.

It wasn't until she started to roll her bike down the road that she remembered where she had seen the reference to the Riley name before. It had been so immediate it should have been obvious, except that it hadn't made much of an impression on her at the time.

Her great-aunt Victoria had been dutifully buried by her family, as the record went. But on January 2, 1949, she had died in the house of L.P. Riley.

****

Back on Old Tory Lane, Alex Wingate waited for her in the driveway. He sat on a large stone near the road, plucking away at the rough edges of his plaster cast, and looked up as she swerved around him on her bike.

Arden dismounted, waved at him, and started up the few steps to the side door.

"I've been worried about you," he called out, and rose from his seat. "When I noticed the car but didn't see you around, I wondered where you were."

Arden wondered how someone wearing muddy boots, a thickly cabled sweater, and smelling of fish could manage to look so damn appealing. Standing a few steps above him, they were almost eye-to-eye when he came up to her, and she noticed a swelling from a bug bite on his cheekbone. "I could have been out for a walk or gotten a lift into town. I might have been riding my bike. I could even have been out on a date." She paused, waiting for him to rise to the bait. But he didn't look the least concerned. "And I might ask where you've been. You look like the Gloucester

147

fisherman."

"The Eastfield fisherman. We're a tamer variety."

"You've been fishing? You've actually been fishing?"

"You don't have to act like I wouldn't know how to go about it. I'm sure I could manage to rustle up dinner for us, if you wouldn't mind gutting and scaling the catch, picking out the bones, cutting off the head..."

"Thanks, but no thanks. I'd rather buy a fillet at the market." Arden had no idea what sort of fish swam in the brook, but guessed catfish were pretty common. "So what did you catch?"

"A couple of tires, a rusty bucket, and an excellent assortment of beer cans. It was an outstanding day."

"It sounds like it. Maybe you can bring in those cans to the recycling center and use the nickels to buy a tuna sandwich at Ludlum's."

"Maybe two, if you'd like to join me. Then we can really go out on the town, and bring this junk to the dump. It's already in the truck."

"You're serious about this?" Arden asked.

"About the tuna sandwiches? Well, you can have anything you want, really."

"No, I mean about fishing. You really went fishing, and pulled up all this stuff?"

"No, but I really went into George Brook and dragged the garbage out before it went further downstream. I don't know who's using our waterway as a private dump, but I'd like to get my hands on him."

Arden glanced down at his hands, and saw the water stain spreading across his plaster cast.

"You're not supposed to get your wrist wet, or the cast might disintegrate."

"If only it were that easy. It's stronger than you

think." For emphasis, he banged his arm against the side of the cottage and grimaced. "If you stayed around, you could have reminded me to keep it dry, or wrapped me up in plastic."

Arden didn't allow her imagination to explore that possibility. "If you came with me you could have gone to Town Hall and filed a complaint about the polluters."

"Is that where you were?"

"I was. In the Records office."

Alex started picking at the edge of his cast again. "Did you find out anything?"

"As a matter of fact, I did. I found out that the Registrar's a very pleasant, very agreeable sort of person who knows an incredible amount about our local history. He's very generous, too. He's going to help me find out more about poor Quercus Chartula."

"Are you talking about Hammond Riley? I should have known it wouldn't take him long to find you."

"He didn't find me. I found him, by walking right into his office."

"Don't trust him, Arden," Alex said gruffly, and added something under his breath. "There was some story about him, I don't remember what."

"Well, then I'm sure we'll get along just fine. There's a story about me too, remember? I'm not considered trustworthy either."

"You already explained what happened," Alex said tersely, and looked up from his cast. His face was so red the insect bite was no longer visible. "Someone set you up."

"That makes things even worse. I've lost my reputation over something that's not even my fault. I may never work in my field again, and it's not even my own fault." She kicked one of the cans he retrieved from the brook.

"Maybe I can help. I have some connections," he said, as he picked up the can.

"You're good at picking up other people's garbage," she said bitterly, "but this mess is my own."

He laughed, which bothered her more than it should. "I don't think the two situations can really be compared..."

"You're right," Arden said quietly. "But still, I'll handle things on my own. I always have."

Miranda sauntered over and shook out her wet fur, showering them both. Alex laughed as he held up his hands, but Arden took the moment's advantage to escape from both of them, stamping the dried mud off her shoes as she sought refuge in her cottage.

Chapter 8

"Grandma's attic may be filled with treasures.
But you may get tangled up in cobwebs
before you find them."
~Dierdre Doherty (volunteer since 1977)

It wasn't until Hammond Riley pulled into the vast parking lot in Chatwell on Sunday afternoon that Arden fully appreciated the scope of the event they were attending. Her weeks in quiet Eastfield predisposed her to envision a small barn, a few local vendors, perhaps a lemonade stand. But it seemed that here, as elsewhere in New England, antiques were big business, and the Chatwell Antiques Fair presented an opportunity to purchase highly respectable acquisitions. When she was a museum employee, Arden was so high up on the ladder of purchase and sales it was rare for her to attend such functions. Most likely, though, some of the dealers with whom she had done business would be here or in places like this throughout the country.

But she was no longer a museum employee, was no longer accountable to anything but her own tastes and very slim checkbook, and therefore earned the well-deserved privilege of doing nothing more than simply enjoying herself. Hammond, free from the dull responsibilities of the Eastfield Town Hall, proved amusing and witty, solicitous in a very old-fashioned kind of way, and surprisingly knowledgeable about the furniture and artifacts they examined through the long afternoon. Arden shrugged off Alex's dampening blanket of innuendo against him, and decided she liked Hammond Riley very much.

Therefore, when she decided to buy a lovely Victorian dressing table, she felt more concerned he would think she was taking advantage of his good nature, than that her long-dead aunt would turn over in her grave at the insult done to her carefully arranged cottage. Like most Victorian pieces, it was large and heavy, and like most modern cars, Hammond's was barely roomy enough to allow them to take it with them. But they enlisted the help of the dealer who sold it to them, and, like the last piece in a large puzzle, the table managed to be wedged in between the seats.

"It has the mark of a Hartford cabinet maker, did you notice?" Hammond asked, when the dealer walked away, counting his money. Hammond pulled a stiff white handkerchief from his pocket and dabbed at his brow. Arden had a brief image of Alex wiping dust and grime from his face with a sweep of the arm of his flannel shirt, and shook her head to dispel it.

Hammond misunderstood the gesture and went on. "Well, I didn't want to say anything in front of Mr. Ledyard M. Winfield, Antiques, back there, but the hallmark was right under my nose when I was pushing the thing into the car. It was made by Samuels, in 1870."

"I guessed it," Arden said. "They always worked in oak."

"It was plentiful in the area, you know. It's one of the state symbols.One of the most famous oaks is associated with Connecticut's prototype of the Constitution."

Arden hardly heard him as a thought occurred to her. "I didn't realize it was so popular. I wonder if it ever replaced more traditional trees in art. Did local artists put the oak in the Garden of Eden?

Or..." She caught herself, realizing how enthusiastic she sounded about a common tree. Calmly, she added, "Might stonecutters have carved it on local tombstones?"

Hammond eyed her more carefully than such a simple comment might have merited. "It's an interesting theory. But I can't say they did."

"Oh, well," Arden said dismissively, and turned back to look at her new table through the smoky back windows of his car, "it was just a thought."

"An interesting one, though," Hammond said lightly. "Do you want to talk about it over dinner?"

"I can think of a dozen other things I'd like to talk about. But the dinner part sounds great, if it's my treat. You've been so nice to me today. "

Hammond seemed to think so too, because he didn't dispute it. They climbed into the now cramped front seat of his car—cramped because the table necessitated moving the seats all the way forward—and very carefully left the huge lot of the Chatwell Antiques Fair.

It was just dusk when Hammond pulled his car up into the driveway on Old Tory Lane. Arden already developed the habit, by unfortunate experience , of doing a quick visual inspection of the cottage and grounds before she dared to step out of the car, and was relieved to see everything looked peaceful and just as she had left it.

"The back door?" Hammond asked. The question surprised her because when he had picked her up she had been waiting on the stone wall at the bottom of the drive, out of the view of the windows on the hill. She didn't think Hammond knew her home well enough to guess which door would be more convenient. But if it was only a guess, he guessed well.

"That's probably best. We'll have to negotiate some uneven steps, but the door is modern and wider than the one in front."

"Let's do it then. I'll pull around to the back, and we'll try our luck."

Arden gave him a grateful glance. It really was a lot to ask of a man she hardly knew. Who else would have been willing to play the part of professional mover on their very first date? Of course, there was one who had treated her to an afternoon at a hospital emergency room, so perhaps this was just the way Eastfield men did things.

The real question was, what did Eastfield women do? And more to the point, should she invite Hammond Riley to stay for a drink after their job was done?

"This was a lot easier with three people, Arden," Hammond said with a grunt and she realized he was already out of the car and starting to pull the oversized table toward him. "We may need help."

Arden was beside him in a minute, and instantly apologetic.

"I'm so sorry, Hammond. This is really my headache, isn't it? And here I am making you do all the work."

"Well, if we can't get it out of the back seat, I expect it'll be my headache. I wonder if we can find someone to help us?"

"I've only met a couple of my neighbors. Mr. Ward is too elderly for this. The people in the brown house are away for the weekend. They asked me to take in their mail. And I'm not sure I want to ask any favors of Alex Wingate."

"I thought he broke his arm. I doubt if he'd be much help," said Hammond, and nodded as if there was some personal history behind the words. Certainly, the antagonism was mutual.

Arden was curious. "It's his wrist and fingers, but he's managing fairly well, I think," she said. "He has one good arm, and two good shoulders."

Hammond gave her a look that made her instantly regret her words, and then gave a very determined push against the dressing table. Arden guessed this was going to be a two-person job and if she didn't keep her mouth closed, Hammond Riley was going to abandon his good-natured instincts. She braced her knees against the weight of the antique piece, but as she did so, she couldn't resist a glance up toward the barn and Alex's property.

She wondered what he was doing.

Her glance wavered along the graceful lines of the stone walls, the orange and gold leafy trees and the autumn flowers, to the large structure of the barn, and was surprised to see the wide doors were open.

Where was he?

It took Hammond a moment to realize he wasn't getting any help from her, and another before he followed her gaze up the hill.

"Damn," he said, surprising Arden. "I forget you're living in this fishbowl of a house. Do you ever get any privacy?"

Not really, thought Arden, but said, "I haven't really anything to hide."

"That's good, because we're being painted in the act."

Arden blinked and realized what she thought was a fluttering bird was Alex's hand holding a paintbrush, moving across a canvas. He might have been painting her cottage.

"I didn't realize Alex was interested in what went on down here."

"I bet he wasn't until you moved here," said Hammond. "But why don't you call him down to help out?"

Arden knew they needed a hand, but also knew she did not want to be standing between these two when they got together. She had no idea what their issues were, but didn't want to be yet another. When she said nothing, Hammond cupped his hands to his mouth, which surely wasn't necessary in the short distance separating them, and yelled out. "Alex! Can you help us with this? We've got a heavy piece of furniture here."

Alex said nothing, but held up his plaster-encased arm with an air of triumph. Knowing his physical limitations, Arden knew there was also a certain amount of pain involved.

"Damn," said Hammond again and on a sudden spurt of adrenalin, hauled the entire piece right out of the car. Arden acted quickly, and grappled with the heavy edge of it to prevent it from falling down upon him.

"What is it with you two?" she asked, once the piece was steady on the ground. "You get all ruffled every time I mention his name. And I'm not doing that to annoy you.He's one of the few people I know in this town, so it's hardly surprising his name comes up in conversation."

"And have you mentioned my name to him?" Hammond asked, and his dark eyes narrowed as if he were waiting for a blow.

Arden hesitated, knowing if she said she didn't mention his name, it would be a blow to his self-esteem. But she also didn't want to reveal what Alex said, or even that he had said anything at all. There was a lot going on that she didn't understand, and she wasn't yet sure on which side of the fence the tree would fall. So she did the cowardly thing and lied.

"I did. I told him how helpful you had been to me when I came down to Town Hall."

"He knows what you've been researching?" he asked, and when Arden nodded, muttered something rude under his breath. Arden turned away, allowing him to think she was offended, but in reality, she looked up to see if Alex was listening to them. It was impossible to tell; he just continued painting. Or whatever it was he was doing to the canvas.

"Forgive me, Arden, I'm forgetting myself. It's just that guy makes me so angry. His family is no better than anyone else's, but he's trying to have everything done his own way. He has no respect for the old timers, and is offering to buy up their land before they're in their grave. It shows you what he knows about Eastfield," he added derisively.

"He probably knows more than I do," Arden reminded him.

"Well, yes, that's true. But your people have always respected the property. This place hasn't changed for generations and things are just as they should be. Wingate isn't happy to keep things as they are. He's rebuilding, expanding, and doing things he shouldn't."

Arden glanced back up the hill. She didn't see Alex as a bad boy, but the thought was intriguing.

"If he owns the place, why shouldn't he do whatever he wants? Really, Hammond, if it doesn't bother his neighbors, why should it bother you?" She decided not to reveal that it bothered her enough to bring her to town to ward off his advances to buy the Alexander sisters out.

Hammond looked her over carefully, and placed both his elbows on her antique dressing table. His expression changed to a slow and easy smile and Arden was old enough and smart enough to know his thoughts.

"I guess you could just say that I'm feeling a little territorial," he said and, of course, she knew it had nothing to do with the house or land. Arden felt herself blushing under the light sunburn she had gotten that afternoon in Chatwell, and looked away.

Up on the hill Alex rose to his feet. He held his crooked arm at shoulder height, and either stared at his canvas or at them. In either case, he looked like he just put the final flourish to his canvas.

****

After positioning the dressing table in Arden's bedroom, Hammond surprised her by asking if she would mind taking a rain check on dinner. He offered no explanation, but she could see he was exhausted, and his wrinkled shirt had a smudge of furniture wax along one sleeve. Feeling he deserved something after the lovely day he had planned for her, and for his backbreaking efforts in navigating the table through the door and into the house, she asked if he would just like to stay for a while. He did, and accepted a mug of hot chocolate, some cookies she picked up at the market, and a comfortable chair in the living room.

They spoke about many things, continuing some of their earlier discussions, but the subjects of Quercus Chartula and Alex Wingate were carefully avoided. Hammond's eyes darted around the room, so that Arden thought he nervously anticipated the entrance of her neighbor, but he seemed more interested in her antiques and the simple design of the room.

Finally, he stood, and brought his glass and plate to the kitchen sink in a very familiar and domestic manner. Arden followed, nearly tripping over him when he suddenly turned back toward her.

He caught her by her shoulders, steadying her. But he held her just a bit too long, and he leaned in too closely.

"It was a beautiful day," he said, and it seemed a very solemn pronouncement.

When Arden nodded, he kissed her on her forehead, and pulled her into an embrace. It might have been a gesture of friendship, nothing more, but Arden sensed it was a friendship with very specific rules, and one demanding exclusive rights.

"We'll see each other soon," he said into her ear.

"At Town Hall? I'm sure we will," Arden answered lightly, and pulled away.

"I mean at dinner. After all, I promised. When are you free?"

As Arden hadn't a single thing written on her calendar, she could have suggested any day and any time. But she didn't want Hammond to know how very available she was.

"I think Friday is good," she said, after a few moments.

"I'll pick you up at eight then," he said. "Maybe we'll catch a movie afterward. Or I'll give you a private tour of the Historical Society?" He winked.

"I haven't been to a movie in ages. That sounds terrific," Arden said, with somewhat more enthusiasm than she actually felt.

Arden waited until the headlights of his car disappeared down Old Tory Lane before she reached for her sweater on the hook near the back door and stalked out of her house. She could think of ten wicked things she'd like to do to Alex , and several of them involved his damn easel. Fishbowl, indeed. He had no business watching her at any time, least of all when she was returning from a date with Hammond Riley.

"Are you still out here? Or did you have to go inside and search for your binoculars?" she called indignantly into the woods, but was only answered by the banging of a loose shutter. She set her sights where Alex sat before, perched on a little outcropping of rock, but could see nothing in the deep shadows. His house was absolutely dark, but she saw Glinda standing in the open door of the barn. Still working, was he? She hoped to find him lying on the floor again, perhaps with his legs broken this time. Wrapping her cardigan around her, she stomped across his graveled yard.

As she approached the barn, she could hear movement within, and the familiar sound of a classic rock song. The light flickered, suggesting he was moving back and forth in front of it, and once or twice he joined in with the song's chorus.

It was too bad she intended to kill him, because he had a fairly good baritone voice. She knocked once, but pushed her way in before giving him a chance to respond.

Alex's back was to her, and he was busy closing up his cans of paint. It couldn't have been an easy job, not with his wrist still hurting and bandaged, but the relaxed set of his shoulders suggested he was taking it at his own pace, and reasonably pleased with the results. He wore a white cotton shirt that fit snugly over the muscles of his arms and across his back, and well-worn khakis splattered with paint.

"I wondered when you'd get up here," he said casually, without turning around, and Arden caught her breath. She assumed he heard her, but then noticed a small mirror above the sink where he worked and realized she had been in his view for several minutes. It didn't help her mood that he ignored her until now, and seemed more interested in his task.

"Why didn't you just come down? You would have been able to join right in and hear everything we said and see everything we did."

He turned around then, and leaned against the sink. "I think I saw as much as I want."

"That's called voyeurism, isn't it?"

"I don't think so. I spent the day painting. I had no way of knowing the two of you would show up when you did. I wanted to take advantage of the last half hour of sunlight."

"And so, you also decided to take advantage of me?"

160

"No," he said. "I would never take advantage of you."

Arden felt the color rise in her face and she pulled the sweater so tightly around her she heard the shoulder seam give way. This conversation was not going at all the way she expected, and it didn't help when Alex's hair fell over his brow in a way she found particularly endearing. She had to look at something else, and turning just to the right, she found it.

It was her cottage, as it might look in the spring, when the world was fresh with promise. Yellow daffodils dotted the path, and a spade was propped alongside the garage. The curtains in the windows looked lacy and crisp—did he know she just ironed them the day before?—and the charming asymmetry of the structure looked like an architect planned the whole thing. Arden doubted she could ever forget the look of this place, but here was a picture that could make her feel at home, wherever she lived.

"Do you like it?" he asked, as if he was a student and not an accomplished artist.

"I think it's wonderful. I think you're..." she stopped, stopping before she said too much.

"What?" he asked, and moved away from the sink.

"Very talented," she said, idiotically.

"Thank you," he answered, unbearably polite. "It's good to have validation every once in a while."

She laughed, though the sound was a little hollow. "I'm sure you can sell it for a lot of money. That would be validation, wouldn't it?"

"I'd rather give it to you."

"But why? I already have the house, after all," she said, reminding him of the fact.

"You can have the damn painting and the house," he said irritably. "I just want you."

It was impossible for her to look at the painting

now, or, indeed, to find interest in anything other than the fact that he walked toward her, unbuttoning his shirt as he did so. He barely paused to release the sling and pull the sleeve off his crooked arm, before tossing the shirt over an unused easel.

"I didn't want paint to get all over your pretty sweater," he explained, utterly practical and logical while Arden thought she was dreaming. He took the last step between them.

"Why didn't you ask me to take it off?" she asked, as she pressed her palm against his bare chest, feeling the rapid thumping of his heart and the springy hair on his warm skin.

"Because you never do what I want you to do," he whispered.

"What if we both want to do the same thing?" she asked, but really answering the one great question remaining between them.

Though they now knew each other a week longer than when they kissed before, the last days had been a sort of estrangement, a separation interrupting the racing course of their relationship. For Arden, it felt a period marked by alternating realities of reasonable indifference, and intense longing. She and Alex were thrown together by circumstances closer than those usually experienced by a woman and a man in the first tentative steps of a relationship. As a result, Arden felt that she knew him a lot better than she should—and not as well as she'd like.

But here was her chance to change that.

Alex tried to capture Arden's hands in the tight place between their bodies, but she would not be so contained, nor did she imagine that he really wanted her to be. Her fingers found his warm and sensitive skin just above the horrible cast, and felt his muscles tightening as she caressed the smooth flesh in the crook of his elbow. As his good arm came around her shoulder, enveloping them both in the scents of turpentine and soap and themselves, Arden's hand moved to the ridge of his collarbone, rubbed raw by the weight of the sling.

"I wish I could take away the pain, that I knew something about healing," she said, as her lips pressed against his chest.

"If you gave me any more of your sweet medicine, I might become intoxicated," he said, as his lips roamed across her forehead to the tip of her ear. "And I'm known in town as a very upstanding citizen."

"That's not what Hammond Riley tells me. In fact, he thinks I should keep my distance from you."

"He said that, did he? The little mole."

Arden laughed, though Alex was doing remarkable things with his lips while his good hand struggled with her shirt buttons. "A little mole! I never heard anyone called that before."

"That's because you haven't lived long in Eastfield. The little buggers tunnel under the ground and eat whatever looks tasty to them. They're probably feasting on those delectable daffodil bulbs you just planted." Alex released the last button and spread the edges of her shirt apart. "There's no greater pest."

Arden put her head back and closed her eyes as Alex's lips caressed the curve of her breast above her bra. "He's not so bad. But it's true that I met him in the basement of Town Hall, where he's squirreled away all sorts of interesting information."

"Don't mix the wildlife metaphors, my dear Ms. Alexander."

"He definitely wasn't wild, if that's what you want to know." Arden's hands cupped the back of his head and she held on for dear life.

"I just want to know what he feasted on," Alex

said as his hands settled on her hips.

"Do you think you're getting leftovers?"

"I think we're doing far too much talking," Alex said as he claimed her lips and gave her no opportunity to say anything at all.

But she didn't need words to tell him how much she wanted him, wanted this, since she could scarcely put two rational thoughts together since the day she met him. She wanted to despise him, for his interference and for his assumptions and for owning the land that should be hers. But when a man appears in every blessed waking dream and paints a picture of your beloved cottage and brings you to a hospital emergency room for your first date together, detestation dries up like a puddle in the sun.

Suddenly Arden realized Alex was walking her backward and then gently pushing her down against something soft and lumpy. The couch, of course. She saw it here in his barn, strewn with sketches and note pads.

"We have two homes," she murmured, removing some papers from beneath her backside. "With beds."

"We have almost no clothes on," Alex answered, and set about finishing the task of undressing her. "This might be just the evening the Eastfield birdwatchers will decide to hike through the woods, looking for a rare pigeon."

Arden reached for his belt. "I wouldn't want to disappoint them."

"I wouldn't want to disappoint you." He caught his breath as she pulled his zipper down and he wriggled out of his khakis.

"I don't think that's possible," she said, looking at him, as she settled back into the cushions.

He remained just above her, poised somewhat awkwardly because of his heavy cast, and his breathing was rough and shallow.

"Alex?" she asked gently.

He closed his eyes and she couldn't imagine what he was thinking at a time like this.

"Is everything…?"

He reached over the back of the couch and Arden heard a drawer open. He fumbled for a moment, and gave a sound of satisfaction as he held up a small sealed package of protection.

"Boy Scouts are always prepared," he said, taking care of business.

He hovered over her, studying her body as he might one of his canvases, savoring, admiring, perhaps finding some fault. Not wanting him to find any, she reached for him, her arms circling around his neck, pulling him down to her. They came together in one shattering moment of clarity, in which nothing else mattered, nothing else existed, but the two of them.

Some time later, she turned and curved her back against his body, and his hands came around her to cup her breasts. They were still uncovered and the air in the great room was cool, but Arden snuggled into the source of heat. He ignited once again.

"You are definitely not a Boy Scout," she murmured, and they said nothing else for the remainder of the long, dark, divine night.

Chapter 9

"Don't buy anything until you can see it
in the light of day."
~Dorris Hartley (discerning customer since 1980)

Arden knew exactly where she was the moment she awakened, suffering none of the disorientation and discomfort usually associated with opening one's eyes in a strange bed. Somehow, there seemed nothing at all strange about the dawn of this new day, nor in the slumberous and delicious peace that had settled over her. She felt as if she had been waking up for years with Alex in her bed.

Or on his couch.

Arden turned her head slightly to better see him, and the warm, regular breaths that had been blowing against her ear were now on her cheek. He shifted slightly in his sleep, giving no sign that he knew the day had already started without them, or that he had any intention of awakening.

She wondered if he remembered she slept with him, but then reasoned that though he might be asleep, he was not dead. Their warm bodies nestled against each other under the thin quilt, and his good hand rested in the small of her back. One rough-haired knee tickled her thigh and her hands were pressed against his broad chest. Arden wryly considered how he had started their lovemaking by removing his shirt on the pretext that its paint-splattered surface would stain her clothing, but that he hadn't bothered to consider the rest of him. She now saw the speckling of green paint near his collarbone and above his nipple, and a few white streaks in the dark hair that tumbled over his brow. These were the colors of her house, she realized, and by now, they were probably neatly tattooed on her body, wherever she pressed against him.

Thinking about her own body proved to be a mistake, for she became acutely aware of a particular necessity, and she wondered how complete were the facilities in Alex's renovated barn. She glanced over his shoulder and saw an open door that looked promising. Somewhat less promising was her ability to extricate herself from his embrace without awakening him.

Arden pulled herself up and climbed over his slumberous body, carefully avoiding any pressure on his ungainly cast. Alex muttered something, and pulled the quilt over his bare shoulder, leaving Arden completely exposed to the cool morning air. She rubbed her hands against her goose-bumped flesh as she looked for something with which to cover herself and settled for Alex's shirt. As she wrapped herself into the stiff fabric, she breathed in the scent of turpentine, oil paint, and her lover.

She was grateful he was considerate to his guests, because the bathroom in the barn would have been a comfortable addition to any home. It not only contained the requisites, but housed a redwood hot tub under a large open skylight. She wondered whom else he entertained here in the past.

Arden turned away and gasped, not recognizing herself in the large mirror framed on one wall. Here she was as she never knew herself, a stranger who looked vaguely familiar and might be someone she'd like to come to know.

The woman in the oversized and unbuttoned flannel shirt stared at her with heavy-lidded eyes and cheeks reddened by contact with her lover's beard. Her wildly curling hair spilled over her shoulders, a small tortoiseshell barrette was caught in a tangle just below her ear. Her lips were parted and a smudge of green paint on her chin added to her look of wild abandon.

She was not likely to be confused with the businesslike young woman who, until recently, earned her living in the basement of a university museum. That woman was all sense, and here was her foil in sensibility. This beauty was earthy, in harmony with the woodlands visible through the small window, at home in a barn erected by the first farmers along George Brook.

Arden wiggled the barrette out of her curls and tried to pin up her hair with it, though the pile on top of her head looked nothing so much as a bird's nest.

She stepped out of the bathroom, glancing at the long, sleeping form on the couch before she detoured past his desk. Her curiosity was now thoroughly aroused, and with it came a remembrance of something she glimpsed on the day of his accident. Things had happened so quickly after that, she nearly forgot the sketches he drew of her when they scarcely knew each other.

But there they were, just as she had seen them when she rifled through his things, desperately trying to help him on that day. Lying among his letters and bills, weighted down with a fan of soft artist's pencils, were the portraits. She did not need to ask the woman in the mirror what Alex saw when he looked at Arden; he already answered her questions.

He had seen things in her that until this morning, she wouldn't have suspected were there. There was the sensuousness so newly revealed, here suggested by soft strokes about the chin and lips and a delicacy about her half-closed eyes. She looked dreamy, as if she was in a far-off time or place, and her hair was loose, as it had been on the morning they met. A week ago, Arden would have dismissed these sketches as the work of a hopeless sentimentalist, but she recognized the artist's model in the new light of day, and love.

"They're not very good," came a husky voice from the couch. "I couldn't get the model to sit still for me."

Arden turned around, and the sketches fluttered to the floor. Alex had pulled himself up on the couch, and the quilt was down around his waist. It looked as if something branded him on his cheek, and she realized he bore the imprint of her barrette.

"I would think you'd have more confidence in yourself by now. I've heard rumors that you're supposed to be pretty good." She folded the open edges of his shirt over her breast. "Besides, you never asked."

His good hand came up to grind the remnants of sleep from his gray eyes. He blinked at her and asked, slowly, "Asked what?"

"Asked her to sit still. It might have been a new experience for her."

Alex didn't say anything at first and it was several moments before Arden realized that he was no longer looking at her face, but his interested gaze was focused somewhat lower down. She didn't have to look down herself to realize his shirt barely covered her and that it did nothing for her belated sense of modesty.

But it must have been doing something to Alex. She saw him swallow whatever it was that he might have said, and ask, instead, "Would she come over here now if I asked her to? If I said please?"

Arden dropped his shirt from her shoulders and allowed it to fall upon the sketches. The answer, as well he knew, could be a simple one, but there was always a lot to be said for style and taste. As an artist, he would scarcely be unfamiliar with undraped women. And so, her modesty was abandoned as she came to where he still sat, on their narrow couch.

****

The next time Arden awoke, it was to the feel of fingers running through her tangled hair and the sound of her barrette dropping to the floor. She nestled closer against Alex's warm chest, but the light hair near his nipple tickled her nose and she sneezed.

"I hope you're not allergic to me," he mused, and pushed her hair off her face.

"To penicillin and to cashews, but not to you," she said, her voice muffled. "I thought I demonstrated that already."

"No, not really. I still need convincing. I wonder if we might try..."

Arden pulled herself out if his arms and arched her back. "As much as I'd be willing to try just about anything you suggest, I think I need to recover. I'm not exactly used to this kind of exercise." A bone cracked in her neck.

"Exercise? Is that what you call it?" Alex threw off the quilt, uncovering them both.

"I suppose that's what I will call it when the women of The Thrifty Means ask why I'm walking around like a cripple. I promised I'd help out this afternoon, and they're bound to notice. They seem to notice everything else." She glanced down at his body, and hoped some things managed to remain private in Eastfield.

"In that case, I suppose we should do something about the green paint on your nose." He stood up, faced the sun shining through the eastern windows and stretched his arms wide. "What do you say to a relaxing soak in my hot tub, and a quick shower? It's guaranteed to heal whatever ails you. And I'll join you, just in case."

"Just in case of what?"

"Just in case you're in the mood for more exercise."

****

Alex stretched out in the steamy warmth of the hot tub, his cast thrust awkwardly on the bench behind him, and his toes touched Arden's thigh on the opposite seat. She sighed contentedly, and sank deeper into the water, but did not open her eyes.

"This is heaven," she said, after several moments. "I could stay here forever."

He hadn't thought about that possibility until this very moment. Everything he did to and with her since her arrival at the cottage was motivated by his desire to finally consolidate the properties, to convince Anne and Arden that they really didn't need or want the place, and that he would be happy to take it off their hands. A house was like a string of pearls; without contact with a warm body, it would crack and fade, and finally become useless. Alex had a use for the place, a damned good one.

But at the moment, he could only think that a string of pearls around Arden's neck would give her the look of a mermaid.

"I was just thinking the same thing," he lied. "I mean about the 'heaven' part. But someone's bound to come looking for us sooner or later. Eastfield looks out for its own."

"A little too well, perhaps. I wasn't here a day when the women of The Thrifty Means stopped by. And you came right after," Arden said. She found his toes in the water and started to massage them, running her fingers along the lines of his nails and pausing at each roughened callous. She pressed her palm into the ball of his foot and the effect was surprisingly erotic. Where did she learn that little technique?

171

"I would have been at your door earlier, but I thought I'd give you time to get dressed," he said tightly.

She opened her eyes and stared at him, a half smile on her lips. Her amusement was well-placed, after all, they knew each other only a few weeks and already managed to shed every inhibition. Arden's hand abandoned his foot, but his moment of regret vanished as her fingers began to walk a trail up the length of his leg. As they traveled she leaned forward, until her breasts pressed against his legs.

He sucked in his breath when her fingers reached their destination and with his good hand, he pulled her onto his lap. The spa water bubbled around them, lifting, tickling, reflecting the colors of the Portuguese tiles that lined the walls. Alex nestled his nose in Arden's damp, sweet smelling hair. He designed this bathroom, and the barn that rose all around it, but he had not realized it was heaven until she was here with him.

"We can't stay here forever," he said against her ear. "I've got to leave."

"If you're going into town, wait for me and I'll hitch a ride with you. I'll walk back home this afternoon."

"I'd drive you anywhere you'd like, but I'm not going into town. I have to go up to Boston."

"Oh?" was all she said, but he could feel her body stiffen as she edged off his lap.

"I have some business to take care of," he said.

"Are you checking out the post season action at Fenway?" she asked sweetly, even as she pulled away from him. "Walking the Freedom Trail?"

She returned to her side of the hot tub and ducked deeper into the water so he could see nothing below her chin.

"I have business in Boston," he repeated. "I'll spend the day there."

"I see. Well, I'll be quite busy here in town. There's The Thrifty Means, of course. And I expect I'll see Hammond Riley again. I owe him a dinner, for helping me with the dressing table."

Whatever remained of Alex's good humor disappeared at once. It was foolish and stupid, but he couldn't bear the thought of that lout hanging around with Arden, sitting too closely, artlessly touching her.

"You don't owe him anything. That's the point of being neighborly. You help others, and don't expect anything in return." The fact that he was now lecturing her was made even more ridiculous by the fact that he and his neighbor were sitting naked, in a hot tub.

"Of course," Arden said reasonably. "But the other point of being neighborly is showing gratitude when its least expected. I'm sure Hammond asked me out with nothing selfish in mind."

"I wouldn't be too sure of that," Alex muttered under his breath. He popped some of the bubbles with his finger.

Arden looked at him, and smiled again in that knowing way she had. "I suppose all you've done since I arrived has been entirely altruistic? Nothing selfish in mind?"

Alex splashed out of the water, thoroughly dousing his damned cast. "What have those nosy women been telling you?" He stood up before her, and he was briefly satisfied that she seemed more interested in studying him than in their conversation. She remained seated on the bench of the hot tub, gazing immodestly up at him.

"Are you talking about my new friends?" she asked. And then she looked up at the ceiling, submerging herself so that her dangling earrings danced in the water. " Or are you just worried about Hammond?" she asked.

Of course he was. He thought Hammond was an idiot, but if he told her so, she would think he was just plain jealous. And she would be right.

"It's not Hammond," he hedged. "What about the guy who came in and trashed your cottage? What if he comes back?"

"Oh" said Arden again. "I haven't given that a thought at all. And what about Quercus Chartula? I've abandoned him altogether, poor fellow."

"Well, whatever else we find out about old Quercus, we know he's not the one who trashed the place." Alex sat down on the redwood bench and reached for an old bath towel. He wished he anticipated the company of his beautiful neighbor, for he might have found one not covered in dried paint.

But at least the terrycloth didn't smell of Miranda's wet fur. He rubbed his hair as best as he could with one useless hand, and handed the towel to Arden.

She held it aloft like a flag of surrender, and stood up into it, wrapping herself in one graceful movement. When she eased herself out of the hot tub, she shook out her hair, splashing him.

"Perhaps he's a ghost," she said.

"Who?" he asked, too preoccupied with the cleavage revealed by her slipping towel.

She gave a gesture of impatience, entirely justified. "Quercus. Maybe he's buried somewhere else on the property and his ghost is haunting the place, pining for a proper burial."

"And do you think the stone box is a proper place for a burial? It's big enough to just about manage to be a reliquary, able to contain one or two choice parts of his body."

"What do you consider choice parts of a body?" Arden asked. She looked quite serious.

But then, so was Alex. "I can think of a few," he

said. "I suppose it would depend on what he died of."

"Like a broken heart, for love?"

"Or a gangrenous leg, during the Revolution?"

Arden made an expression of disgust, which at first Alex thought had to do with the subject of blood poisoning. But then he realized he was wrong; she was displeased with his rotten, unromantic soul.

"Perhaps his right hand, with which he wrote letters to his beloved, far across the sea?" she said, and walked out of the bathroom.

Naked and damp, he followed her into the chill of the great room of the barn. Arden was already rummaging through the pile of their discarded clothing and threw a T-shirt and boxer shorts at him. He managed to get his shorts on, but the cotton shirt caught in his wet hair.

"Do you think he died for love?" he asked when his head finally emerged from the trap. He was surprised to realize Arden had come close, and probably helped him manage the business.

"Yes," she said softly. "Or died in love. Such a tragedy, to be separated from the one you love. He killed himself in despair, and unable to be buried in sanctified ground, they buried him in the garden, along with the pet hamsters and goldfish."

Alex leaned over and kissed her. Her lips tasted faintly like the chlorine of the hot tub. "They didn't have pet hamsters in colonial times. They were too busy with their chickens and pigs, and ate anything that wasn't human."

"That's enough to ruin my appetite for breakfast."

"And I'm only going to Boston," he said. The minute he said it, he knew he made a mistake. She spoke of tragedy, of separation of lovers, and despair. They had one spectacular night together, but he had no right to elevate their own drama to one of tragedy. He didn't even know if she left a lover behind when she sought refuge in Eastfield.

She turned her back to him, suddenly modest, and let the towel fall. She pulled on her shirt, which brushed against her upper legs, concealing everything interesting. Her lean fingers combed through her hair as she bent to retrieve her jeans.

"And I'm going to The Thrifty Means," she said, as if his departure now meant nothing to her. She had already pulled up her jeans when she paused and picked up a scrap of pink lace. Since it didn't look like any of the cloths he used to clean his brushes, he guessed it was her panties. "I'm not worried about ghosts, or thieves or Hammond Riley. In fact, by the time I meet him for dinner, I expect I'll have my appetite back. Do you have a place to recommend?"

"For what?" he asked roughly.

Arden just cocked her head and stared at him. She ran her tongue over her lips and he wondered if she could taste him.

"Tony's Grill," he said. "You meet all the best people there."

"Then Tony's Grill it is. I'll ask for a quiet, dark corner."

"You do that, Babe." He walked past her, to one of his experiments in metalwork. The sculpture was about eight feet high and resembled a tree, except when you looked closely and saw that it was actually the figure of a man. A man who just now had Arden's bra draped around his neck. Alex unwrapped it, trying to remember which of them flung it here last night, and returned it to Arden.

"You might find this useful," he said.

She took it out of his hands and tucked it into her shirt pocket, like a handkerchief.

"Perhaps I will," she said. "Though you never know what could happen in dark corners."

****

176

"You're going to Tony's?" Eleanor said from a ladder in the window of The Thrifty Means. She adjusted a pashmina around the shoulders of an old mannequin but didn't seem satisfied with the result. "I thought you liked the guy."

A young woman stepped between Eleanor and Arden. "Is that pashmina for sale?" she asked.

"Yes it is. It's a silk blend and $10." Eleanor said hopefully as she handed it to the potential customer.

The woman held it up to the light, possibly looking for moth holes. "I'll take it. Do you have any in blue?"

"It ain't Macy's," someone called from the desk.

Eleanor looked like she was about to laugh, but answered the customer as if, indeed, she stood in a fine department store and not a thrift shop in a small town. "Try us again. We never know what we'll get in."

The woman nodded and shrugged. "I came in for a tea pot and I'm leaving with a pashmina."

"That's reasonable," said Liza, at the desk. "Eleanor here came in to find a book, and left with a husband."

Arden laughed. "And all I'm looking for is advice."

"Well, that comes cheap," Eleanor said, as Liza walked away with the customer. "We don't make a profit on it, but there's lots to go around. Did you want to ask about a nice restaurant?"

"Won't Tony's be okay? I have a recommendation."

"Tony's is fine if you like drunken brawls, grease, and going to the hospital for food poisoning. I wouldn't go inside if my car broke down in their driveway. Who recommended it, Wayne Durant? No, Wayne's still in prison." She picked up a pink cardigan and glanced at the dress in the window. "If you want a romantic night out, I suggest L'Avignon.

It worked for me."

"I'm not really thinking romantically."

"You poor girl. Is something wrong with you? Alex Wingate is the hottest guy in town."

Arden looked down and breathed deeply. She already knew Alex Wingate's approximate temperature, and was afraid he might incinerate her.

"Alex is in Boston. I'm taking Hammond Riley out to dinner."

"Ah, now you're talking about the coolest guy in town. And I don't mean that he wears leather and fashionable shades. He's all business and serious study. We think the decaying town records have gotten to him."

"I should think people might say the same thing of the women of The Thrifty Means," Arden said, opening her hands to the merchandise surrounding them. "A person could get lost in here, buried under all this stuff."

Eleanor stepped down off her ladder, but remained in the window, higher than everyone else. "We haven't lost a volunteer yet. At least, not in that way."

"We have asked some people to leave," Liza said thoughtfully, counting on one finger. "There was one woman who seemed to be operating her own business out of the shop."

"And some volunteers have moved, or moved on, or, you know," added Miriam, whom Arden also recognized from the welcoming visit.

"Died," Liza said bluntly, ticking off two, three and four on her fingers.

"And then we had a volunteer who murdered old ladies," Miriam said. "Though I hope that was a singular hobby."

Eleanor jumped off the window step and dusted some lint off her brown turtleneck sweater. "It's very bad for business to refer to Mrs. Brownlee that way. Let's just say she hastened some people to their inevitable conclusion, my husband's aunt included."

"Mrs. Margaret Brownlee?" Arden asked.

"Goodness, yes," Eleanor said. "Please don't tell us she went after your sister, trying to smother her with a pillow. Margaret was dying to get hold of the things in your cottage. But Anne would have fought her off and pushed her into George Brook."

"I'm trying to think what Anne said, but I'm sure she would have mentioned an attack on her life. Anyway, Anne doesn't qualify as an old lady. And if her plastic surgeon is good, she never will." Arden tried to recall where she heard Mrs. Brownlee's name before, and gently spun an old globe while she did so. "I think Anne might have mentioned that Mrs. Brownlee was interested in buying a few pieces in the house, but she wasn't going to do anything until I had a look around."

"And did you? Did Anne sell anything to her?"

Arden blushed and put her palm on the globe to stop its spinning. "No, I'm really embarrassed to say that I never came down here, not until I arrived some weeks ago. There was always one thing or another, and I would be busy when Anne came to Eastfield, or I had some excuse. Now I regret it, of course."

Miriam beamed. "Because Eastfield is such a lovely place?"

Arden smiled. "Yes, there is that, of course. But also because there really are a lot of wonderful things in the cottage. I understand things haven't changed much in a few hundred years, as the property passed from one woman in the family to the next."

"Just women?" Eleanor asked. "I'm sorry if I'm being too personal."

Arden shook her head. "No, you're not. It's a

strange thing, but the place just passes through the line of women in the Alexander family."

"Are men allowed in the house?" Liza asked. "I mean, it would be a little awkward if they're forbidden."

Arden thought of Alex in her house, his hair just brushing the low doorframes, his hands on her things, his body settling down onto her narrow mattress.

"Stop blushing, my dear," said Miriam. "I just don't know how you would keep Alex out,"

"I wasn't thinking about Alex," Arden lied. "But we...I did come across something very strange."

Arden realized she had an audience, not just of the volunteers but also the customers. She hesitated, not knowing if she should reveal any secrets. But whatever mysteries there might be had started many years before, and this might be an excellent forum for uncovering some truths.

"I found a box buried in the ground. It's a stone casket, decorated with a large spreading tree and has a name inscribed on top. It's a foreign name, Quercus Chartula, and I thought he might be Portuguese. There were settlers from Portugal here in the colonies, weren't there?"

"There were," Eleanor said. "They were engaged in the local shipping businesses, and there still are many descendants in the area. But Chartula doesn't ring any bells for me."

"Dare I ask," Miriam said, and looked as if she just ate something distasteful. "Was there anything inside?"

"Bones and things like that?" Liza asked.

"Nothing. Just a few splinters of wood." Arden realized she left out an important piece of information. "But it isn't the size of a coffin. If it contained human remains, it would be a reliquary. As it is, I don't know what to think."

"Do you want to bring it in?" Eleanor asked. "Between all of us, someone could figure it out."

"Though remember we had that metal thing a few years ago. We thought it was a hat rack, until someone told us it was an antique toaster," Miriam said.

"And we had a freeze dried cat." Liza murmured.

"The less said on that, the better," Eleanor said quickly. "Why don't we get back to work? Liza, there's a trunk that was delivered this morning from an estate sale down on Milkweed Lane. Do you want to sort through it with Arden and show her how we price and label things?"

"Arden?" Liza looked at her, smiling. "Are you ready to get dirty?"

"I spend half my time digging in the garden and..."

"And the other half?" Liza asked, sweetly.

Arden smiled. "The other half thinking dirty things. So, where do we start?" She began to roll up her sleeves.

Liza led her through the crowded shop, past shelves of books, and racks of vintage clothing, and old furniture stacked one upon the other.

"How do you keep track of everything here?"

Liza laughed. "Well, that's when the fun begins, because we hardly have space for anything. Since Eleanor became manager of The Thrifty Means, we've been moving merchandise around so things always look fresh. But when Mrs. B. was manager, things stayed in one place for years and years until no one remembered how or when they came to be in the shop. And given Mrs. B.'s extracurricular hobbies, there may well have been a body or two stuffed in an armoire."

Arden paused to turn over a Wedgwood plate. "I'm very curious about all that. All of you keep throwing out little comments, enough to make me

181

think there's a big story here."

"There's a crack in that plate," Liza said, and pulled her away. "Well, the big story was pretty much hushed up in town, and now it's an old story. We're all relieved that Eleanor was willing to take over the running of the shop and keep everything going, even when she needed time off to have the twins."

"She has two sets of twins?"

"Yes, one with each husband, and each a boy and girl pair. She's a busy woman."

"And yet here she is, all the time," Arden said. "I, on the other hand, have nothing going on in my life. No husband, no kids, no job. I don't even have a pet, unless you count a little cat named Glinda who showed up one day."

"Oh, good. I wondered what became of Glinda. In any case, you have us now. And The Thrifty Means is a lot more than just a place to volunteer and shop and make money for charities. You have friends, and you'll be networking. You may find a job through a connection here, or someone who wants to give up a pet. Eleanor adopted a parakeet that came in one afternoon." Liza offered all this information in the manner of a tour guide. "But I think you already managed to find a guy without our help."

Arden met Liza's gaze, hoping to deflect the rumors with an effort at denial.

"Really, he's very nice, but I hardly know him. And he hardly ever seems to leave the basement of Town Hall."

"You're not fooling me, you know. When Alex Wingate spends an hour away from his commissions, he's smitten by something or someone." Liza pulled a couple of stools out from beneath a table and set them in front of an old, battered trunk. Luggage stickers were plastered on the leather lid and the metal clasps and hinges were rusted and dented.

"He broke his wrist, you know. He can hardly get anything done these days, and I'm probably nothing more than a diversion for him," Arden explained even as she hoped it wasn't actually the truth.

Liza smiled as she pulled open the trunk's lid.

The two women stared silently into the store of dozens of small items, each wrapped in yellowed, fragile newspaper. The interior of the trunk was papered in printed patterns of the Orient, glued to resemble nothing so much as a patchwork quilt. Some water damage was evident just beneath the lid, but neither mold nor insects had corrupted the careful packaging efforts of someone who valued whatever the trunk contained.

"In *The Scarlet Letter* Hawthorne writes about finding Hester's A in a collection of old things," Arden said softly.

"Is that what you're expecting?" Liza said, and laughed. "More likely, we'll unwrap some homemade Christmas ornaments that a kid made in kindergarten."

But Arden would not be deterred. "But everything, even trivial, has a story to it. Hawthorne claims to have found the story of *The Scarlet Letter* in that attic room of the Custom House in Salem. But what if we find things that have no story? It's up to us to figure it out, isn't it?"

"Oh, boy. Eleanor has already gotten to you, hasn't she? We come across mysteries every day here, and never figure most of them out. The facts are just buried in the past."

Arden thought someone touched her shoulder, but Liza's hands were already lifting the first tidy little bundle. "Just the same, I would love to find out something about Quercus Chartula and whatever was buried in my garden. Even if it turns out that the box held rat poison or something."

"Put on those gloves if you like," Liza said, gesturing with her chin to a storage rack. She unfolded the newspaper slowly, as if peeling petals from a rose. The fine paper crumbled in her hand, but one piece of print revealed the date 1887.

"It's a baby bowl," Arden said. The porcelain bowl was decorated with the letters of the alphabet on its perimeter and a picture of a small child holding a dog in the center. The bottom was encased in lead into which a small tube was inserted, looking somewhat like a chimney stack. "How very clever. You would put hot water into the tube to heat the lead well. That way, the bowl would stay warm while the baby was eating."

"And the mother could burn her fingers on the hot metal," Liza said. "Or the baby would get lead poisoning by eating continuously from the same bowl."

"That would be the least of the poor fellow's worries. Without antibiotics, proper sanitation, safe foods, and with candles burning within reach on the table, is it any wonder so many babies died before their first birthday? At least, in this case, the food didn't touch the lead, so there's one less worry."

"One less worry for the mother who could very well die giving birth to his younger brother?"

Arden shook her head. "We are pretty grim, aren't we?"

"Realistic, I would say," Liza answered as she unwrapped a tiny double handled cup. "Not quite a match, but very sweet."

"And here's a little dress. Of course, that could be for a boy or girl. Boys had long hair and wore dresses and lace until they were six or seven." Arden unfolded a delicate scrap of fabric, brown with age and starch. She sniffed the fabric and imagined the strange milky scent of baby. "I wonder…"

"If the baby survived?" Liza anticipated her.

184

"Here's a little pair of ice skates and a rabbit muffler, so we can stop being so morbid. The little guy made it."

"I wonder if Quercus did not. Now that I think about it, the box I found is large enough to hold a small child, a baby."

Liza shook her head. "There were cemeteries in Eastfield since the 1600s. The baby would have been buried in consecrated ground."

Arden felt sick, not so much for the fact her lovely garden might have been an old graveyard, but rather that an innocent baby might have been denied eternal peace.

"Not if the mother was unmarried. Perhaps no one knew she was pregnant and when the baby died she buried it secretly and close by." Arden sighed and unwrapped a daguerreotype of the homeliest child she ever saw. The dog next to his chair, however, was very cute.

"You're forgetting one thing," Liza said, brushing slivers of newsprint into a neat pile. "You don't have the body. A baby is not going to just disappear from a coffin."

Suddenly it was easier to breath, even in the dusty confines of the back room of the shop.

"You're right. It's probably just a box. With a tree carved on it." With tentative fingers she unrolled a scroll of paper that looked like some sort of proclamation. "Just like this, in fact."

Liza glanced at the document, a commendation from the state's governor to one Hiram Adams of Eastfield. "It looks like an oak tree. We've got a million of them. Ah…but here's something we don't often have!"

Their patience in unpacking was rewarded when Arden uncovered a samovar, ungainly but painted in an array of colors. The blues had faded to purple and the yellows to white, but the red pigment remained bright and vivid. The inside of the large pot had not fared as well, and it hardly seemed worthwhile for anyone to scrub out the rust in order to make a good cup of tea. Still, the elegant antique would be a conversation piece in any Eastfield dining room.

"My grandmother brought hers from Russia. She left my Aunt Bella behind, but wouldn't be parted from her samovar," Liza mused.

"Well, I guess they had no idea what they'd find in the New World. And to be fair, there aren't a lot of these around. Eastfield is not exactly a cosmopolitan place now, so I imagine it was pretty provincial in the 1800s." Arden stood and stretched her legs. "Whose stuff is this, anyway?"

Liza answered by pressing a button on the intercom unit on the desk. "Eleanor? Where did all this junk, I mean treasure, come from?"

Eleanor answered by coming through the door. "It was in an attic on Milkweed Lane, next door to where I used to live. The Walkers, who have been there for twenty years, never bothered to open it, and wanted to sell it along with a lot of other stuff before they moved. I gently persuaded them to donate a lot of their stuff here. The trunk was in the house when they bought it."

Arden sat back down. "I suppose I would be a happier woman if I could just keep my nose out of things, like they did. But I dig up a box and can't sleep until I figure the whole thing out. You probably think I'm obsessive."

"Dear girl, at The Thrifty Means, it's our stock in trade. We obsess over pricing an item $10 or $12. We worry about having too much merchandise and too little. We agonize about throwing things away," Eleanor said and picked up the leaded bowl. "This, however, we don't have to worry about. We'll price it at $75 and put it in the window. I give it a day to sell."

"If it sells that quickly, you've priced it too low," Liza said. "I say, price it at $100 and let's see what happens."

Arden laughed as she listened to the interchange between the two women. They were smart and witty, and completely in their element. A few weeks ago she would have envied it, but now realized she was a part of this unique community.

"What if I want to buy it?" she asked

Eleanor looked amused. "Why, then it's $150. Just for you."

"Such a deal," Liza murmured.

"Okay, I'll take it," Arden said.

"No, please, I'm kidding. It's yours for $75. Volunteers usually get first dibs," Eleanor said, putting it into Arden's hands.

Arden ran her fingers over the gray lead, finding nicks and dents in the soft metal. She wondered about the mother who washed this, the baby who used it. She had no use for such a thing and scarcely knew where to find a place for it in her crowded cottage. But as the lead warmed in her hands, she felt it somehow belonged to her, a new member of the Eastfield community.

"Then working here must be a dangerous thing. How do you all manage to control yourselves? I may buy everything in the trunk," Arden said.

Eleanor put her hands behind her back, as if preventing herself from picking up another object. "We're our own best customers," she said. "And this is a very successful little enterprise."

"Hear! Hear!" came a voice from the door. The three women turned to see Hammond Riley, looking very formal in his suit and tie.

"Hardly leaves the basement of Town Hall, hmmm?" murmured Liza. "I guess there's something here to make him crawl out of his cave."

Arden pushed against her arm but said nothing.

She smiled at the man and thought he would be appealing to most women. He was reasonably attractive and an excellent dresser and had what seemed to be a good job. And yet there was something about Hammond Riley, a lifelong resident of Eastfield, that made one think that here was a man not quite at home in his world. Here, at The Thrifty Means, he looked downright uncomfortable.

"How are you, Hammond? Are you looking for something special?" Eleanor asked, always polite, always professional.

"You could say that," he answered. But Arden, believing she was the object of that little attempt at humor, expected him to acknowledge her with a smile or, at least, a glance her way. Instead, he picked some imaginary lint off his dark sleeve and straightened his tie. "I wondered if Arden would like to go for a walk along the river."

Still he did not meet her eyes.

"I'm busy, Hammond," she said. "Are you free later this afternoon?"

"Oh, we could spare her now," Liza said, pushing her back. "We were just talking about lead bowls and dead babies."

"We were talking about nothing at all," Arden said quickly. She couldn't say why, but she preferred not to reveal to Hammond that she was looking elsewhere for the answer to her Quercus Chartula mystery.

"That's why she can go with you. We're talking about nothing at all," Liza said. "Go ahead, Arden. I'll clean up this mess, and you can buy the bowl later."

"Thank you, Liza. That's very kind of you." Arden turned her back on Hammond and made a face at Liza.

"Are the two of you going out to lunch?" Eleanor asked. "If you're going to Ludlum's, would you bring me back a Caesar salad?"

Arden nodded, hearing the subtle message. They were not going to Tony's Grill. And although Eleanor had suggested L'Avignon earlier, she now thought the old diner was good enough for Hammond, poor fellow.

"Sounds good," Hammond said and finally looked at Arden. She could have been any casual acquaintance, and not a particularly interesting one at that. But perhaps she wasn't being fair to him. Was she seeing what she wanted to see, in contrasting him with Alex Wingate?

****

Hammond Riley looked and spoke like a gentleman, a holdover from a more gracious time. He let her off at the door at Ludlum's when it started to drizzle on their way to the diner, mildly protested Arden's insistence on paying for their burgers, and thanked her for the pleasure of her company. Though it was warm and even stuffy at Ludlum's, his jacket remained on, and his fingers often sought the knot of his tie, as if to reaffirm that nothing dared slip loose. They talked about antiques, new house construction in Eastfield, rising property values. Quercus Chartula came up just once, and Arden realized she need not have been on edge about bringing him in on the mystery. He seemed indifferent to the whole business.

Unfortunately, she was indifferent to him.

She played her part. But nothing he said or did made her think she'd want to spend more time with him or share any additional confidences. When she picked up Eleanor's Caesar salad at the register, she paid for that, and Hammond dutifully returned her to The Thrifty Means, where the women were far more interested in a donation of musical instruments than in her outing.

She needed to escape.

She went home first, checked that all was well, and left the bowl on the kitchen table. Then she walked up to Alex's house, where Glinda slept on the front steps, and Miranda was patiently waiting within. Alex had left her his key and instructions on the care of his dog while he was up in Boston, and it seemed like a good time to take their daily walk.

Though the sky was gray, it was no longer raining, and so they went down Old Tory Lane, until it ended at a crook of George Brook. Miranda chased a few ducks and found a tennis ball among the rocks and got thoroughly filthy in the water. She shook herself out, splattering mud and dead leaves on Arden and started back down along the trail.

Arden followed, raising an umbrella when it started to drizzle again.

Things were moving too quickly, she decided. She had come to Eastfield to figure everything out, to decide what she was going to do next, to consider places she might apply for a job. So far, she spent most of her time with a man and his dog, another man who was probably wasting the time spent on her, and at a thrift shop filled with engaging things, most of which were human. It was all the fault of The Thrifty Means, she decided. If Eleanor and her friends had not arrived on Arden's very first morning in town, Arden might have had time to build the walls of a sanctuary around her cottage. She might have remained hidden, even from Alex.

Miranda ran past the cottage, up the path to Alex's house, until Arden called her back.

"You're staying with me tonight, Babe. I know you miss him. I miss him too." Arden looked around her, wondering if anyone heard her say it aloud. The road was quiet but for the pattering of rain on the leaves and the distant music of the river. Miranda returned to Arden's side and rubbed her wet fur against her leg. "He'll be back tomorrow."

She studied her cottage, looking for anything out of place, as was now her habit. She wouldn't admit it to anyone, but she did feel less safe without Alex nearby, looking down from his lofty farmhouse perched on a ledge of New England shale. Where did her stubborn independence, her need to seek her own counsel, go? Whatever remained was here, in this small sanctuary, filled with the musty history of her family's women.

Miranda ran through the open door and, for good measure, rolled her wet body around in one of the antique scatter rugs. Arden walked past her into the kitchen and opened one of the cans of dog food Alex left for her care. Miranda jumped onto the seat of one of the pine ladderback chairs and waited patiently to be served at the table. Glinda, who had disappeared while they were out, suddenly jumped onto another seat.

Alex did know how to treat a lady, it seemed. It was not for Arden to remind Miranda and Glinda that they were not human. Instead, she spread newspaper on the table, and carefully set down the bowl. Miranda cocked her head, as if wondering if Arden would join her, but Arden just patted her on the head and walked to the window.

She ought to go up to the farmhouse and collect Alex's mail, but decided it could wait. For now, she just wanted to turn inward, here in her cottage, and savor whatever peace it offered.

Ignoring the blinking light of her answering machine, she left Miranda in the kitchen and walked out into the living room. At one time, it would have been the center of the house, perhaps its only room. Now, a wingback sofa stood in front of the massive hearth that dominated one wall. The beehive oven was open, and a display of glass paperweights filled the space where once all the baking was efficiently accomplished. Arden's ancestors didn't need silly modern conveniences like thermometers to gauge the heat; a woman would just thrust her clenched fist into the arched opening and know if her loaves would neatly rise or burn to a crisp. If her hand burned to a crisp, she would pause to smear lard over her knuckles, and then continue with her business—undoubtedly with several babies crying at the table.

Arden ran her fingers over the narrow trestle table, and all its grooves and knotholes. She imagined it in place in front of the hearth, and in a moment of vision saw a woman and a baby sitting there. On the table was a piece of charcoal and a rough sketch of the infant.

She blinked and they were gone. An old framed photograph was on the table, and she thought her grandmother was one of the several people who posed for it in front of the hearth many years before. The hearth, if not her grandmother, was immediately recognizable because it looked like nothing had changed in all this time.

Arden turned to compare the photograph with the present scene. The same pieces of pewter still sat on the rough mantelpiece, crowded together because they were not arranged for decoration but for utility. Arden reached up to examine the bowls, the forks, the pierced lantern that would illuminate the way to the outhouse on a dark and windy night, the peal used to remove baked goods from the oven. But even as she handled the implements, her eyes were on the small painting fixed to the wall, a thing of beauty but no practical purpose.

The men or women who broke into her cottage had noticed it as well. The marks of a tool, perhaps a crowbar, still scarred the edges, as she had not bothered to repair it since the day of the intrusion. Arden wondered if the wall would have to be dismantled before the painting could be removed from its place.

Miranda's nails clicked across the bare wood floor and she barked once when she reached Arden's side.

"What do you say, girl? Do you think it's a Gainsborough? A masterpiece that managed to find its way out of an English country house and wind up in a Connecticut backwater town?"

Miranda barked again.

"Well, I don't care what you say, it sure looks like a Gainsborough."

Miranda stared solemnly into her eyes.

"Oh, I'm sorry. Eastfield is not a backwater. You're so right."

Miranda continued to look at her as if she were an idiot, which certainly seemed the case when Arden realized someone was knocking at the door. She crossed the room with the dog at her heels, and she was suddenly grateful for the illusion of protection.

"Mike!" she said as she opened the door. Glinda scampered through, right between his legs. "Was I expecting you? Or were you looking for Alex? He's up in Boston today."

"I know," he said bluntly.

Arden looked at him with surprise and a bit of suspicion.

"Hammond came over to the nursery after the two of you had lunch. I hope I didn't catch you at a bad time?"

Arden relaxed. "No, I was just admiring my Gainsborough."

"Is that a brand of jewelry or something?"

Eastfield was definitely a backwater.

"Gainsborough was an English painter, mostly of landscapes and portraits. I have a small piece in the living room, which can't possibly be authentic, and yet looks close enough to be the real thing.

Someone must have copied it from a photo."

"Did they now?" The New England inflected voice was only mildly curious. "Well, I'd like to see it sometime, especially if it has some good-looking plants."

Arden laughed, thinking everyone had their own vision of perfection. "You could come in and see it now, if you'd like."

"No, ma'am! I make it a rule not to tread through people's houses in my work clothes. You'd need a month to clean up after me. Some other time, maybe."

"Well." Arden said, and then waited for him. He still hadn't explained what he was doing here.

It took him a moment to catch on, and then he seemed to notice a book he held in his hand.

"Well," he echoed. "I needed to talk business, which had best be done outside."

"All right. But what about?" Arden grabbed her sweater from the peg near the door and walked past him, closing the door. She was near the garage before he answered.

"Your sister asked about putting in some shade trees around here. A couple near the brook. Maybe one alongside the drive, by the road. It's a noisy and messy job, so I thought it's best done when you weren't in the house. I wanted to know when you might be in town, maybe working all day at The Thrifty Means."

Arden didn't answer at first, wondering why on earth this wasn't done in all the months the cottage had been deserted. When had Anne asked for this? But then, seeing the earnest expression in Mike's eyes, she assumed that there was some perfectly logical answer. Perhaps new trees can't be planted until the fall, or until the ground is marshy, or the sunlight less intense. She honestly knew nothing about it.

"Okay, I suppose that would be fine. I'll be at the shop all day on Monday."

"I was hoping you'd say something like that. So now I just need you to pick the trees."

"Oh." She knew nothing about that either. "What did you have in mind?"

As she suspected, Mike had a lot of things in mind. He raised the book—a large, soft-covered thing—and started thumbing through the pages. There was soil on his hands and in his nails, but the book already bore the stains of years of good use.

"Here's a dogwood, a native tree. That's nice down by the brook. You know what that looks like, in the spring? You'll love it."

"If I'm here in the spring," she pointed out. He looked up from the book with an expression of surprise, as if she could not be anywhere else. That seemed to be a common perception in this town.

"Yes, that looks lovely," she said.

"And maybe a willow, or two? They soak up the water here, but the water table is so high, there's enough to go around."

Arden looked in the book at the photograph of a mature willow, and decided that in order for her to witness the growth of a sapling to full fruition, she'd need to be here for many, many springs. She nodded.

"And down on the drive, how about an oak? A real Connecticut Yankee? I love those babies..."

Arden finally surrendered, and took the book from his soiled fingers to see what an oak looked like. She ought to know, but couldn't say with any certainty.

The photo showed a lovely tree, a solitary figure on a well-mowed lawn. Defiantly, majestically, it spread its branches in its summer glory. Arden would have been satisfied on appearance alone, but as Mike looked so expectant, she dutifully read the description of the tree in the gardening journal.

"Yes, that would be fine," she said, and meant it.

"I'll have my men get them in the ground on Monday, unless we have heavy rain. But assuming all goes well you won't recognize the place when you come home."

"Well, please tell them not to go as far as all that. I still have trouble finding my way around town as it is."

Mike laughed and started down the walkway toward his truck.

"Mike, wait! What is all this going to cost?"

Walking backward on the irregular path, he shrugged. "Don't worry. I love working on old properties. You never know what you're going to find."

"Well, unless you find a pot of money, I need to know what this is going to cost."

"I meant we might have to dig through ledge or other hard rock. But we'll make a deal if we do," he said, which was no answer at all.

Chapter 10

"Something was always cooking
in the hearth of a colonial home."
~*Lynn Davidson (volunteer since 1984)*

A few hours later, Alex pulled into his gravel driveway. His house was dark, though lampposts flickered behind blowing leaves and branches. Down the hill, through the trees, he saw Arden's lights in the cottage and he felt an unexpected lift of pleasure. After all his years of independence, there was something comforting about coming home to someone. Even if that someone did not live in his house. Yet.

He got out of the car and paused a moment to smell the cool, humid breeze of the early autumn. Whistling, he started down the path until he came to Arden's back door. He listened for a moment, to hear any sounds of activity, and decided he would not awaken her if he knocked on the door.

She opened on the first knock.

"I could have been an ax murderer."

"Do you know what kind of ruckus your car tires make in the driveway? Besides, I have Miranda for protection," she said. Behind her, his dog was sound asleep on an oval rag rug.

"I trained her well, I see."

"Thank you for that, because I decided I'm going to keep her. I like having her around."

"And she obviously likes being around. It looks like she could care less that I'm back." Alex hesitated, no longer certain of anything. "I hope you also like having me around."

"Oh yes I do," Arden said and put her arms around his neck. "Welcome back."

He kissed her gently, savoring the moment. Passion banked was sweeter than the wild bonfires that sparked so easily. They waltzed away from the door and into her living room, which smelled of warm bread and wet dog. Behind him, the wind slammed the door shut, and a moment later Miranda was pushing between them.

"Aren't you curious to know what I did in Boston?" he asked.

"It could wait," Arden said against his lips. "Would you like some coffee? I picked up the 'Eastfield Blend' at Ludlum's today."

Alex gently moved her to arm's length. "I hope your Thrifty Means ladies didn't tell you to buy it as the best way to a man's heart. The chef makes it out of mud and spices it up with a touch of battery fluid."

"It sounds like you've used that line before. And as a matter of fact, a man suggested I buy it. So not everyone shares your opinion."

"I guess it depends on the man." He studied her and realized she was probably ready for bed, in her Red Sox T-shirt and plaid boxers. Sweetness aside, he was ready for bed as well. "But if you wore your harem costume, I bet we'd be in agreement on some things."

Arden pulled out of his arms. He loved it when she blushed, and wonder how often he could make her do so. "That's Anne's costume and it was very rude of you to even notice it."

"I noticed it the same way you notice when I pull into my driveway. You just can't help these things when you're neighbors."

"Sure. Neighbors with binoculars," she said wryly. "Anyway, would you like tea instead? I'll save my Eastfield Blend for someone who appreciates it."

Alex had a feeling he knew who that person might be.

"That sounds good. Do you have any bagels or something? I haven't eaten since lunch." He noticed her expression of slight annoyance and vowed to remember that while he might feel like he was home, this wasn't his home, and he had no business asking a woman to rustle up some food when the kitchen was already closed for the night. "Anyway, even if you're not curious about my day, I'd like to know about yours. Who was the man who recommended the coffee? Someone you bumped into at Ludlum's?"

Arden was on her way to the kitchen, Miranda at her heels. That was unfortunate because the large dog somewhat obstructed the view of Arden in boxer shorts.

"Someone I had lunch with at Ludlum's," she said over her shoulder.

Damn. He went out of town for one day and that idiot Hammond Riley jumped right in to take his place.

"The Thrifty Means ladies didn't like your suggestion, so we went to Ludlum's instead. Hammond thought it was great."

"Hammond Riley is a jerk."

"That sounds very mature," she said slowly, though she didn't bother to dispute his assessment. "But, really, what can one expect of someone who watches women with his binoculars?"

"I didn't have binoculars," he answered in a low voice, but she was already running water at the sink and didn't hear him. He waited until she lit the old gas stove and turned back to face him. He sat down at the table and changed his tactics. "Okay, so I hope you had a nice time with Hammond. He's a great fellow, full of town wisdom and advice for anyone fool, ah, smart enough to listen."

"And gossip. Don't forget gossip. The man should really be volunteering at The Thrifty Means."

"The man should really be putting the town's paper files onto a computer, so we don't lose our local history when he ignites the place with one of his cigarette butts. No, I'm sorry, I shouldn't have said that. He's terrific, old Hammond. What did you two talk about? The tax code of 1947? The fierce campaign for First Selectman in 1971?"

Arden stood at the open refrigerator door, studying him. "You really are a pill, do you know that?" she asked, and pulled out something that looked like a pie.

It was not. It was a quiche, or half of one, and looked like it was stuffed with spinach and onions. His stomach growled, and Miranda watched the plate with as much interest as he did.

"Bagels or something would be fine," he said.

"I don't have bagels. I have a quiche. Do you want it or not?"

God, she was sweet.

"You won't ask me twice. I hope you don't mind if I finish it." She set the whole plate before him with a fork and knife. "I thought you didn't cook."

"Making a quiche doesn't require a lot of skill. Anyway, Miranda helped me."

"Hmmm," he said, already digging in. "I wonder why she's never made it for me up at the farmhouse."

"Perhaps she was pissed off because you asked her about every squirrel she chased that day or who recommended doggie bites to her."

Arden waited until the water boiled, pulled a couple of mugs out of the dish rack, and sat down across from him at the table. She opened a small tin, revealing an assortment of tea bags, and selected chamomile.

"So, what did you do in Boston today?" she asked, after she took her first sip.

He knew this question was coming, and he should have simply lied about where he spent the day. She would not have cared if he went to Hartford, or Albany, or Providence. But he found it harder and harder to keep his wits when he was around her, and this morning, when they were naked in the hot tub, all his sense went down the drain. Nothing was going quite as he planned. Before Arden arrived in Eastfield, he decided he was going to make a move on the property, but somehow made a move on her instead.

"I had a meeting with the president of Bradford University."

Arden cleared her throat and looked down at her cup of boiling tea. He pushed his chair a little further away from the table.

"This better not have anything at all to do with me," she said. "My relationship with Bradford is none of your business."

"Of course it has to do with you. But I have a relationship with them also, and I thought I might find out what happened with your recent acquisition."

"Why?" she demanded. "So they might hire me back and I'd leave Eastfield? Do you think I don't know that you want this place, that you wish I'd never come in the first place? Well, I have bad news for you. They won't hire me back. The ship has already sailed. Even if they find out where the switch was made, and by whom, the museum is already closed, I've been fired and I'm never going back."

He was surprised to see her so angry, and even more that she still saw him as her enemy. He had no one to blame but himself for that. He should have met her in the driveway on the first day, and made her an offer on the property, and everything would have been neat and clean and uncomplicated.

But the moment he saw her, everything became complicated.

He took a bite of the quiche and choked on what might have been a piece of eggshell. "I don't want you to go back there either. You can stay in the cottage or hitch a tent on Town Green or live in a houseboat on George Brook. You can move in with Hammond Riley, for all I care. But I thought I might find out what happened with that painting, and why they didn't do a proper investigation."

"And the answer?" She reached across the table, took a piece of crust off his plate, and ate it. "What did John have to say?"

"He said you were the best curator they ever had."

"That's big of him. I guess that's why they hesitated all of five minutes before they decided to fire me and close the museum."

"Did it occur to you that they might have used the scandal as an excuse to close the museum?" Alex said. "And forget what I said about moving in with Hammond Riley."

"Forget Hammond Riley." She leaned toward him, her hands pressed against the table. "Did John say that? Were those his words?"

"No," Alex admitted. "But he admits everything was coming down at the same time. The Board of Trustees was on his case to save money, and then the scandal erupted and he took advantage of a bad situation. He fired eight people and reduced his overhead. He saved hundreds of thousands of dollars a year with that move, and can use the space for classrooms."

"My feeling is that a museum is a classroom."

"I agree one hundred percent. That's my philosophy for an artist's retreat here in Eastfield.

There will be exhibition space, studios, artists-in-residence."

"Ah, now it's out in the open. This is what you want. This is why you want the cottage from us. It'll be in the way of some boxy dormitory or something like that."

"Your cottage is in the way of nothing. All I ever did was ask your sister to allow me first dibs if you and she decide to sell the place. It's your house and I'm not going to pressure you." Alex shrugged and thought perhaps his skills at lying had not altogether atrophied. Before she came, he had every intention of pressuring her.

"That's not what Hammond Riley thinks. And Anne must have been even a little bit worried if she thought it would be a good idea for me to come down from Boston and live here." Her voice grew quieter at the end of the sentence, as if she was thinking it through. She stared at him with what looked like suspicion. "And you are planning an artist's retreat."

"So kill me."

"You are tempting me, you really are." She picked up a knife but used it to stir her tea.

He let out a deep breath. "I offered John a plan to set up a foundation to help support both the reopening of a museum at Bradford and the creation of the retreat here in Eastfield. Other universities can be a part of the same consortium. The problem we all face is that donors like to give works of art to museums and universities. That's great, but those works have to be insured and cared for, and usually come with a proviso that they can't be sold. So a museum has to make money elsewhere. I thought we might open a string of galleries across the country, and feature the work of new, promising artists. The galleries would be run as nonprofit corporations, and a percentage of the sales of the works would help finance all the agencies in the consortium."

He had her interest now. He watched the display of expressions across her face, registering surprise, pleasure, intrigue.

"It's expensive to open galleries."

"I have money," he said, and regretted his words at once. If he intended to bargain on a price for the cottage, it was a poor strategy to boast about his finances. "Even after buying up half of Eastfield, as some people say. Besides, I could use the tax write-off."

"Could this work?" she asked. She didn't seem that interested in his money.

He shrugged his shoulders. "I have no idea. I plan to examine some nonprofit business models, including that of The Thrifty Means. They've made over a million dollars over the years, and it all goes to charity."

"It's not quite the same thing," she pointed out.

"Well, that's just it. Nothing is going to be quite the same thing. That's why I hope it will work." He took the last bite of quiche and wondered if she had more in the refrigerator. He didn't think it was a good idea to ask her.

"You'll need people to run those galleries," she said, and tipped her chair back.

"I have some connections in the field," he said slowly. "And in the neighborhood."

And somehow, absurdly, he sensed that he was on the road to forgiveness.

She blushed and avoided his eyes. Alex watched her for several moments while he grinned like a fool, and then decided to have some mercy on her.

"So, what did you and Hammond talk about, besides me?"

"You," she said. "But I had a far more interesting discussion with his cousin about trees."

"You mean, like the things that grow outside?"

She looked at him with impatience that he

entirely deserved. "Did you think I meant coat trees?"

"Well, it could have been family trees. We're big on that in Eastfield." He tried his tea, which was tepid by now. But then, compared with what they had been talking about, so was the topic of conversation.

"He asked me about putting in some new trees around the place, and wanted me to choose them. I know nothing about trees, but some of them looked nice."

"I'll bet. But is this something you want? Or is he just drumming up some business? Mike could sell poison ivy if he had a mind to do it."

"It seems like it was already arranged with Anne."

"She never said a word to me," Alex said, wondering why he should be so suspicious of the guy. Mike wouldn't forego the good business he did in this town by being dishonest with one of his customers.

"Well, in any case, there'll be a few more trees on the property by next week. They'll blend into the landscape because I picked out the most ordinary things: a dogwood, a willow, and an oak. He showed me the pictures in a book."

"You're a real city girl, aren't you? You really had to see pictures of the darn things?"

"Well, yes," she said defensively. "I read through the descriptions, of course."

"Of course." They sat companionably drinking their tea, while Miranda snored under the table and Glinda played with the fringes of an old afghan. Alex wondered if he overstayed his welcome, if he should wash the dishes, or if he should just spend the night in the cottage. He hoped for option three.

Suddenly, Arden sat up her chair, and rubbed her hand across her forehead.

"Quercus Chartula," she said, more to herself, than to him.

Alex groaned. "Not that guy again. Did Hammond figure out who he is?"

"No, not Hammond. Mike told me, though indirectly." She was excited, her thoughts were running into themselves. "Quercus Chartula isn't a person. It's not a name. At least, not of a man. I just saw it written this afternoon, and didn't even realize what I was looking at!"

He said nothing, waiting for something to make sense. Again, he watched the myriad expressions cross her face and made a mental note to play poker with her. He would win hands down, every time.

"It's a tree. I'm sure it is. 'Quercus' is the species name for an oak tree."

Arden stood so quickly, her chair fell back behind her. She twisted to catch it before it hit the floor, not wanting to break it, or wake Miranda. Alex continued to watch her as he had since he walked through her door and she wasn't sure if he was seeing her, or was lost in thought.

"Alex," she said, and he seemed to snap out of his reverie. "It makes perfect sense. We were on the wrong track all this time and getting all hot under the collar thinking some poor soul was buried in my back yard. But now it turns out that our box is nothing more than a garden marker. I should have been searching the records to find out who was the botanist in the family tree, rather than who had an illegitimate Portuguese baby."

"This isn't nearly as exciting. And it is pretty elaborate for a garden marker. We may have a botanist in the family, but these weren't exactly public grounds. Who cared what was growing here or there?"

His words, so casually tossed off, nevertheless reminded her that as they got closer and closer to the trunk of the family tree, they shared a common ancestry here in Eastfield.

"Well, you never know. Even Luther Burbank could have had his start in the back garden," Arden said, though she thought their gardener would have had to be a woman. And a hardy one at that. "You yourself pointed out that the tree on the box wasn't particularly funerary. It must have stood on that spot, and one of my ancestors chose to mark it with a plaque. *Quercus Chartula*. Oak Tree. Big deal." Arden laughed ruefully. "The joke's on us."

"If it's a joke, then it's not a very funny one. And it's not a marker or a plaque, which someone would have made out of wood, anyway. It's a box. Something was in it."

It was a good thing they hadn't had anything more potent than chamomile tea to drink, because Arden was intoxicated just on possibility.

"Seeds? Perhaps brought from a garden in England? From the original Eastfield?"

"Maybe something bigger than that," he said, cryptically and stood. He took the plate to the sink and turned on the faucet.

"Leave that, Alex. I'll do it in the morning. What do you mean by 'bigger?' Branches or something like that?"

"Nothing so common. I wonder if this Quercus Chartula was the Holy Grail for our Yankee ancestors."

"Do you mean a religious symbol?" Arden was genuinely confused.

"What was more precious than religion in the new world?"

Now she got it. Or so she thought. "A land deed?"

"No, their liberty."

She stepped close to him, until they were just inches apart. "Tell me Alex. I can't bear this anymore."

"Neither can I," he said and kissed her again, long and hard. Ordinarily, this would have been an excellent way to end their discussion, but Arden couldn't leave it here. After several minutes, she pushed against his chest, and looked up at his eyes. "Listen, I think I may have part of the puzzle figured out," he explained.

"You're having a very good day today, aren't you?"

"One of the best," he said, and grinned. "Do you remember when I said that I thought that Chartula was Latin for map or something like that? It's so obvious it should have hit me at once. Well, it might have, if other things hadn't hit me harder."

She blushed and said, "You hit the floor, not the other way around."

"Whatever," he said. "Enough of that. But what if Quercus Chartula is our Charter Oak, and the picture engraved on the box is an actual sketch?"

"Forgive me. I hope you don't revoke my citizenship. But what the heck is the Charter Oak?"

"And you call yourself a daughter of Connecticut!"

"Actually, I don't call myself that at all. But you'll have to call yourself an ambulance if you don't tell me what I want to know."

"Okay, let me see if I have the story right." He released her and leaned against the kitchen counter. "You've heard Connecticut called the Constitution State?"

"Yes. It must be for the battleship." Arden hadn't ever thought about it, but it seemed reasonable.

"It isn't. The USS Constitution is in Boston Harbor, not far from Bunker Hill. You should know that. Here, the Constitution refers to the fact that the colony of Connecticut had its own independent, codified laws for some time before the Philadelphia convention. In fact, the Declaration of Independence wasn't even proclaimed in Connecticut, because by the middle of June, in 1776, the governor had already issued one just like it. One of the towns, Mansfield, I think, had declared itself independent two years before."

"Then why does Massachusetts get all the credit for the start of the revolution?"

"They're much more colorful. They have Paul Revere, and a tea party, a massacre, and the Minutemen. In Connecticut we have a tree, and the story dates back long before the revolution."

"We have Nathan Hale," Arden pointed out.

"That didn't work out so well," Alex mused. "But we still had the tree, a hundred years before the revolution. One of the provincial governors convinced James II that all of New England should become a royal dominion. They convened a council in Hartford and the colonial charter was supposed to be turned over to one of the king's men. But just at the critical moment—and here it does get colorful—the candles blew out and the charter was stolen. It wasn't recovered until James II went out of business, so to speak. And then the charter was conveniently located."

"In an old oak tree." Arden wasn't asking it. "That's the Charter Oak."

"It is. And the charter remained the governing law of Connecticut, until after the revolution."

Arden applauded, which Miranda took as a signal that a snack was waiting. She sat at Arden's feet and raised her front paws.

"Good girl." Alex said approvingly.

Arden gave her a sliver of crust. "Good boy, I ought to say. Where on earth did you pick up all that? On Wikipedia?"

"As a matter of fact, I think your lover boy told

me all about it while I was trying to listen to the Eastfield Jazz Concert last summer. He sure knows how to show a fella a good time. But at least it's come in useful."

"Am I hearing this right? Are you saying the two of you were on a date?"

"It's a long story."

Arden made a face at him. "Okay, smart guy. If the charter was stowed away in a tree in Hartford, why is there a box in its honor in my back yard?"

Alex shrugged. "Hammond probably knows, and isn't telling. Maybe one of your illustrious ancestors snapped off a few branches from the memorable tree and kept it as a souvenir. This is America, after all. People pay for dirt from the old Yankee Stadium."

"So they do," Arden said thoughtfully. "But that makes it very unlikely it would have been buried in the ground. Anyone who actually owned a few of those sacred branches would mount them over the mantel, and probably march them up and down Main Street on the Fourth of July. And if those branches broke or rotted away, he'd probably just go into his own backyard and snap off a few more..."

"Which all means that our little coffin must have held something else."

Alex frowned and Arden realized he was as confused by it all as was she. His little history lesson had carried them out to sea on a high tide, but now they seemed adrift.

"Well?" she asked. "Where do we go next?"

"L'Avignon, I think. Tomorrow night?"

Arden looked up and met his light gray eyes. There was just the faintest touch of blue in them and a shade of humor. "If this is part of your plan to seduce me into selling you my cottage you can save some money and take me to Ludlum's instead. My answer will still be the same."

"Can we forget about the cottage, and I'll just

seduce you instead?" he asked solemnly.

For once, she had no answer. He must already realize she would do anything at all with him, with or without dinner at an elegant restaurant.

"I think the occasion calls for something a little finer than our local diner," he added.

"What is the occasion?" she asked. He managed to muddle her thoughts so easily, she didn't even remember what they were talking about.

He smiled and she blushed again, self conscious under his scrutiny.

"We managed to solve a little mystery. That's cause for celebration. So L'Avignon it is. If it's a nice night, we can row over."

"Down George Brook?"

"Down the Norwell River. It's not exactly the Grand Canal in Venice, but it has a certain charm."

So did he. Arden felt it the moment they met, but resisted imagining any of it would be turned in her direction. She had suffered too many disappointments to dare hope for too much. But he was already her neighbor, her friend and her lover. Why was she so skittish about the notion that he could be her date, charming her and flirting?

"That sounds lovely," she said politely. "How should I dress?"

He looked at her in such a way she thought he might say, "In nothing at all," but the practical Eastfielder intruded. "Warmly. It gets cool at night, especially on the river."

****

She took his advice. When he arrived at her front door, he was greeted by both Arden and Miranda. His loyal dog had been somewhat less loyal lately, preferring the society in the little cottage to his own.

And he could see why.

Arden wore neatly fitted black slacks and a pink

furry sweater which he supposed was cashmere or something like that. More to the point, it had a deep V of a neckline, punctuated by a beaded necklace. The largest bead, a pale heart shaped stone, rested between her breasts. Her dark hair fell over her shoulders, curling at the ends.

"You're on time," she said, reaching for something on the coat tree.

He supposed he ought to help her, but he was too interested watching her move, twisting her body as she wrapped a dark woolen shawl over her shoulders, obscuring the view. The fresh scent of cedar embraced them both for a moment and he marveled that what was repugnant to moths could be so attractive to people.

"I didn't have far to travel," he said stupidly, like a kid on his first date. The only thing he was missing was a rose corsage in a box to bring him back to high school and the junior prom.

She studied him for a moment, probably wondering why she was going out with a tongue-tied idiot, and then reached for a small black tote bag on a nearby chest.

Miranda watched every move and was panting. At least he had the presence of mind not to pant.

"Is that a goody bag for Miranda? They'll give you one in the restaurant," he said.

"Miranda has been on a healthy diet since coming here. No escargot or crème brulee for her. And I don't want you spoiling her appetite with the junk food you've been eating." Arden bent down to whisper something in Miranda's ear, and Alex swore his dog was laughing at him. "I have shoes in my bag. I couldn't see getting into a rowboat with heels on, and don't want to have dinner in the nicest restaurant in town wearing work boots."

She kissed the top of Miranda's head, and then urged Alex out the door, so she could lock up.

"You don't have to leave the light on for her. She can see well in the dark."

"I'm leaving the lights on, and my car in the driveway. Between that, and a barking dog, and a cat who's always underfoot, everything should be quite safe."

He took her arm to help her along the dark path. "You know the break-in was a rare event. There are only a couple of burglaries a year in Eastfield, and the likelihood of lightning striking the same house twice is almost nil."

There, he sounded like himself again, practical and sane.

"I know that. But that's why I think I'm going to be victimized again. This was not a random break in. With all the lovely houses, including yours, why would anyone bother with an old cottage in the woods? And why now, when the place has been standing empty for years?"

"You've been thinking about this," he said quietly.

"I've been thinking about little else," she said tersely.

They walked on for several minutes in silence, taking care not to break an ankle.

"No, that's not true," she said suddenly, and a little too loudly. Her words echoed in the woods around them. "I've been thinking about you."

The high school boy inside Alex Wingate was mightily pleased about this. The man was feeling pretty good as well.

"What have you been thinking about?" he dared to ask. He wasn't altogether sure he wanted to know.

"I wonder what has kept you in a little town like Eastfield for all your life. You're a successful artist, you could have a studio in Paris, in Milan, anywhere you want. Did something happen in your past that has kept you here?"

Alex's small canoe, overturned on the bank, made a cozy shelter for wildlife, but he checked it out this afternoon, to make sure they wouldn't disturb a nesting animal beneath it. With his bad wrist, it was a difficult business to upright the boat, but Arden put down her bag and helped. They shimmied the craft into the water until it was settled on the gentle current.

"Are you sure about this?" she asked.

"Are you worried? I can still paddle with a broken wrist. And I think the trip will be worth it."

Alex steadied the boat as Arden stepped onto the center seat, and then accepted a paddle from her before seating himself in front of her. He pushed off from the shore and realized his mistake almost immediately.

"It hurts, doesn't it?" Arden asked, though it was clear she already knew the answer.

"Like hell," he said, and put the dripping paddle on the floor at his feet. "I think it's the angle."

She picked up the paddle. "I think it's just plain New England stubbornness. You could have chosen another day to impress me, and taken the car today. You manage that all right, I notice." He was about to warn her about approaching rocks, but she steered clear of them. "But never mind. I went to summer camp in Maine. I know how to do this."

Alex pivoted in his seat, so that he faced her. His legs were too long for the short bay, so he settled them on either side of her, gently touching her thighs.

"You'll get wet," she said softly.

"I went to summer camp in Vermont. I'm used to getting wet."

She smiled, but her eyes looked over his shoulder as she steered the canoe down the gently flowing river.

"How will I know when we're there?" she asked.

"The river widens into a pond, and there's a small landing for rowboats and canoes at the restaurant. If we go any further, we'll be over the waterfall." He hoped she'd just let the current take them to the restaurant, to prolong the journey. He felt contented, a very rare thing. "I'll tell you when you get there."

"You're not looking at the river, you're looking at me," she said.

"I'll see the reflection in your eyes," he said, and was rewarded with a smile. "And I've known this river all my life.

"It's my past that's kept me here," he continued. She looked startled. "Remember, you asked why I stay here? Well, this is the one place that holds me, that always feels like home. My parents moved to New York before heading South, but most of their things stayed here in the house. I'm comfortable here."

"Yes, I guessed it. You have enough room to do whatever you'd like. You have friends and Miranda. You belong here."

"I feel it all the time. But I'd like more."

"Is that the restaurant up ahead? I see lights," Arden said quickly, purposely stopping him. She was smart to do that. He wasn't even sure what he was about to say, or how whatever it was might be received. He knew her for a matter of weeks, treated her like an old friend, and they were out on their first real date. The only thing of which he was certain is that he never wanted her to leave this town, his property, his life.

"I'm going to come in on the left side of the dock. Is that okay?"

He finally turned his head, looking over his shoulder.

"Yeah, that's fine. It looks like we're expected." Jack, a local college student who sometimes helped

Alex move heavy works and supplies, stood on the dock, watching them. His short white jacket was unbuttoned and the cap he wore was slightly askew.

"Welcome, Monsieur. May I help Madame come on shore?" Jack bowed a little too deeply, so his cap fell off. Alex caught it in his good hand, and gave it back.

"Practice your French on someone else, Jack. The lady isn't impressed."

"How do you know?" Arden whispered as she stepped over the seat and took Jack's waiting hand. He helped her onto the deck, where she stood, straightening her slacks.

"Okay, Alex," Jack said, ignoring her. "In that case, don't order the steak. Three people already sent it back to the kitchen. But the salmon is great tonight, with some kind of mustard something."

"Arden, meet Jack Liddell, gourmand extraordinaire. Jack, this is Arden Alexander, Anne's sister."

"And you must be Emma Grace's grandson?" she asked.

"Nephew," Jack answered. "She's inside, having a drink."

"Jacques?" A voice called from the back door of the restaurant, the steam and smoke obscuring the speaker.

"That's David, the new chef. He's used to working in a fancy Baltimore harbor restaurant and hates this old kitchen. Remember to compliment him on the food, or he'll come out into the dining room with a meat cleaver." Jack put his cap back on his head. "Gotta run. I'll tie up the canoe in a few minutes."

"Charming place," Arden murmured.

"It is," Alex protested. "It's an old inn, and powder kegs were secretly stored here during the revolution."

"No, I mean it. It is charming," Arden said apologetically. "I don't think I've ever taken a boat to dinner before. It's lovely."

"Haven't you been to Venice?"

"You sound as if it's around the corner, Alex. No, not all of us can afford to take the Grand Tour. I'll have to content myself with the Norwell River instead of the Grand Canal."

"Or the Seine. But I think you'll find the food here is as good as anything you'll get in Paris. Aside from the steak, I guess."

"I'll take your word on it."

"Maybe you'll soon get the chance to see it for yourself. Paris, I mean, and not the steak."

Alex led her through the small garden, past the enclosed plot that still had a few vegetables and herbs on spindly stems, and around to the front of L'Avignon. There was a back door for the convenience of those who arrived by the river, but it opened into a dark hallway. The main entrance was intended to impress, bringing one directly into the elegant porch that had served the inn for centuries. And Alex wanted to impress Arden Alexander.

"You forget my situation, Alex," she said, as they climbed the stone stairway. "I have no job, no prospects and no money except what I've saved over the past few years. I can barely afford my apartment in Boston, let alone travel to Paris or Venice. I came to Eastfield to figure out what to do, in a place where I don't have to do a damned thing."

Alex smiled, thinking of all the ways he might fill the hours for her, in Eastfield and elsewhere.

Arden mistook his smile for one of amusement. "I know what you're thinking and it's not funny. Things will settle down here and I'll finally be able to sit in the rocker by the window and read a good mystery novel."

"Or write one," he added.

Arden looked at him in surprise. "Whatever made you say that? Just because I have a literary family doesn't mean I can string two words together."

"Eastfield has always been a haven for artists and writers. The solitude suits us here, and we're close to our agents and editors in New York. And as far as stringing together a few words, I've read your monographs on eighteenth century painted pottery and thought they were very good."

Before she could respond, he led her through the door into the candlelit foyer.

"Hello, Alex," said the maitre d' from her place at the wooden podium. Leslie Styles rubbed her breasts against the leather-bound menus as she stepped forward to greet him. She didn't seem to notice Arden. "I saw you on the reservation list, and I wondered whom you were bringing this time."

"The last time I brought my mother, didn't I?" he asked. He glanced down at Arden, but she seemed more interested in the building's old beams than in this conversation. "I believe it was her birthday."

Leslie laughed. "Then I would say she grows younger by each year. She looked to be about thirty."

"Thanks, Les. I'll be sure to pass that on. She'll be delighted to hear it," Alex said, reaching for Arden's arm. Leslie waited for him to introduce her, but he decided he didn't care to. Let her find out through the usual Eastfield networks, if it mattered to her. He and Leslie spent one night together over ten years ago and he refused to believe one lapse in judgment could matter to either of them. "Is our table ready?"

Her eyes half closed, so he couldn't read her expression. "Of course. Follow me."

Leslie brought them to the table he requested, by the bay window, and waited while he politely seated Arden. When she handed him the menu, she allowed her hand to brush against his chest. He looked across at Arden, but she seemed very intent on the menu.

"She's very lovely," Arden said when Leslie walked away, not looking up from the menu.

"She's very lonely," he corrected. "She's been married three or four times, and has entertained any number of men in between. She has a bit of a reputation in Eastfield."

Arden finally dropped the menu. "Is there anyone in Eastfield without a reputation? Is there anyone who is absolutely nobody? Is it even possible?"

Their waiter came to the table to recite the day's specials. Alex looked at him, recalling he dropped out of college years ago but refused to go into the family's lumber business when he came back to town. It was rumored he was building a space ship in the family's back yard.

Yes, everyone in Eastfield had a bit of a reputation.

Alex asked the rocket scientist to bring a bottle of wine and Arden nodded somewhat distractedly.

"Aside from myself, of course," she murmured when they were alone again, and picked up the menu.

"Yourself, what?" he asked, completely lost.

"I'm nobody, aren't I? But as I say, that's what I tell myself I came here for, to live out of the limelight, with no pressure, or anyone to bother me."

"It sounds like it's not what you expected, being a hermit. Are you not happy here?"

"That's just it. I'm almost too happy. And what am I doing? Volunteering at The Thrifty Means. Planting bulbs in the garden. Driving injured men to the hospital."

"How many men have you been driving to the hospital?"

"Just you," she said, and finally smiled. Alex's words caught in his throat, just looking at her. For the first time in his life, he realized the truth of romantic ballads; as they said, he had been waiting forever for her to come into his life.

Their waiter came back with the wine and dutifully poured it for Alex to sample. Alex supposed it was fine, but considered himself no expert. In fact, for all his flings and more serious relationships in the past, he still felt about as sophisticated as a burger and fries.

"Are you ready to order?"

They were, and both ordered the salmon.

"Jack...I mean, Jacques told you to order it?" the waiter asked. "I think the guy gets a kickback on every recommendation."

"You see?" Alex said to Arden after the waiter left, "it is just like Paris."

Chapter 11

"What do we do when two people
want the same thing in the shop?
We pray we get in another item just like it.
Or we just let them fight it out in the parking lot."
~*Eleanor Gilmartin Zane (volunteer since 1990)*

The food was Paris via Greenwich Village via Eastfield, and was delicious.

Arden, who had been perfectly satisfied with sandwiches from the Market, and her own culinary creations, fully appreciated what had been missing in her life. And the food was only part of it.

She had worked for years to earn her credentials and her place in the world. She was determined to pull herself up again. And yet, how might her life be different if she tied her star to such a man as Alex Wingate? Would she forever be a shadow in his wake? Or would she have a partner, someone to support her interests and ambitions, and allow her to let down her guard just once in a while? How would it be to be nobody, paired with somebody?

"So, what's the problem?" Alex asked. He was studying little brown sugar cubes artfully arranged on a silver server, and Arden wondered if he found something that didn't belong on them. "If you like it here in Eastfield, and have lots of things to do, why are you unhappy?"

"I'm not unhappy. I'm just impatient, I suppose. I want to move on with my life and get back to the things I love."

Something flickered in his light eyes and she

guessed it had to do with the renewed hope he might buy her cottage. But how would he respond if she told him that perhaps the things she loved were to be found in Eastfield? Would that give him hope of a different sort? Would it matter to him?

"Look, I can't expect you to understand, you who have everything you want. Your house, your roots are here, your career, this community that seems to love you. You have it all."

Alex pushed the tray of sugar cubes across the table, but Arden liked her tea straight up. She picked up the small serving fork and started to construct a little wall of the cubes. Tomorrow, someone in town would undoubtedly remark that the Alexander girl played with her food. But that would come tomorrow. Just now, she wanted to avoid looking into Alex's eyes.

"I don't have it all," he said quietly. "You have some of the things I have, including being part of a community in which you have deep, deep roots. Eastfield is your home, too. But I've recently been thinking that it isn't enough for me."

When he didn't say anything else, she looked up. His hands were cupped over the lukewarm coffee, but he was studying her, waiting for her to notice him.

"Are you waiting for a distinguished award, something to acknowledge the best work of your career?" she asked. It seemed a possibility, though she doubted it.

"I don't intend for my paintings or sculptures to be my best work. I was thinking of marriage and children."

"Oh," Arden said, and the wall of sugar toppled.

"Why are you so surprised? Is it disbelief?" He reached for the pincers, and started to build again. The sugar cubes were now crumbling, but he seemed determined to right everything. "The property has

222

been in the family for centuries, used and loved by each generation. How can I let it stop with me? But there's more, though it's not as noble. Do you think I want to spend the next forty years of my life coming home to an empty house? Or to whomever happens to be living with me at the moment?"

"You're forty?" she asked, though she already knew that from his license and from Liza Silver, who had the goods on everyone.

He smiled so broadly, the waiter chose the opportunity to come to their table and ask, "Is everything *bien*, sir?"

Alex sat back on the chair, still smiling. "I'm not sure it is. Mademoiselle thinks I'm too *vieux* for her."

At the next table, a woman who looked vaguely familiar squinted at them. The waiter shrugged, his French vocabulary already exhausted.

"I do not," Arden whispered, leaning forward. "Though I'm only thirty-eight."

"Then I think we're perfect for each other," Alex said.

Arden caught her breath, thinking things were happening too fast, too soon. But what could she expect from a friendship that started on the very first morning in Eastfield, even earlier if she counted his spying on her the night before? She already knew Alex better than any other man of her acquaintance, not counting her relatives. Their first date had none of the awkwardness one expected; they were as comfortable together as an old married couple.

"Because we're nearly the same age?" she said tartly. "And probably watched the same sitcoms when we were kids?"

"Because I like coming home to you."

"Aren't you taking the cottage affair a little too literally? I thought the point was that the women in the family could always have a place to go, to call their own." She was being stubborn, she knew. But how could she acquiesce to something thrust on her so suddenly? She wanted time, she wanted to get her priorities in order and act on them. She wanted her cottage.

But she wanted him too.

Something in her face must have revealed herself, because his expression suddenly changed as well. He looked annoyed.

"Well, look who's here," someone said. "I knew you two would get around to dinner at L'Avignon."

Arden looked up into Hammond's unsmiling face.

"It's a lovely place, isn't it?" Arden asked cheerfully.

"I didn't see either of your cars in the parking lot," Hammond said, sounding suspicious.

"Not that it's any business of yours, but we came by canoe," Alex said. "And by the way, how old are you?"

"Not that it's any business of yours, but I'm thirty-seven."

"*Tres jeune,*" Alex said, under his breath.

"What was that?" Hammond asked angrily.

"Try the juice," Alex said smoothly. He looked around and waved at one or two people in the restaurant. "Are you eating solo tonight?"

"I'm not eating here. I came to pick up Leslie when she finishes her shift, and we're going out."

"I'm not surprised. She's a lovely girl," Alex said and nodded.

"You should know, Wingate," Hammond said, watching Arden to make sure she understood the full implication of that. Though it seemed odd when it was so obvious he knew the woman just as well.

"I do. She let us know what was available when she showed us to our seats."

"Are you planning to go to the antiques show again, Hammond?" Arden asked quickly, just barely getting her words out, in her haste.

The sentence hung among them for several minutes, while the men glared at each other and Arden wished herself anywhere else on the whole wide earth.

Leslie suddenly came between them, hugging the menus, her skirt hugging her hips. Apparently unable to help himself, Hammond hugged her.

"Hammond! Not now, I'm working," Leslie protested, pushing him off her. Awkwardly, he stepped back to make way for the diners she was leading.

"Arden! How good to see you."

Arden looked up to smile at Eleanor Zane, in a very lovely blue dress that might have been in the window of The Thrifty Means earlier in the week. Arden had tried it on herself.

"Eleanor! I'm surprised to see you here," Arden said, before realizing how stupid the words were.

But Eleanor must have been used to it. "Oh, just because everyone teases us about living at The Thrifty Means doesn't mean we actually do. Somehow, I manage to do lots of things. Though for tonight, I only had to manage to find a babysitter willing to come out on a week night."

"And willing to babysit for twins," said the man at her side, his hand settled on Eleanor's waist.

Eleanor leaned against him and said, "Arden, this is my husband, Evan Zane."

"How do you do?" Arden said, extending her hand. "Your name seems familiar."

"Evan's a celebrity in the teen world," Alex said.

"Are you in a band or something?" Arden asked, ignoring Hammond's snort of derision.

"Nothing so exciting. I write student guides, short and sweet, on historical subjects. Though Ellie and I are now collaborating on a definitive history of Eastfield that's definitely not short. We thought we'd be finished with it a year or so ago, but everyone we interview somehow opens the door to a story we hadn't heard before."

"And we have to include it in the book, of course," Eleanor added.

"And we haven't even finished all our interviews," Evan said, looking at Alex.

Alex held up his hands in mock surrender. "I know, I know. I promise we'll find the time to do it. But now that Arden's here, you'll want to include her as well."

"Do you see what I mean?" Evan said, and smiled. "This may turn out to be a life-long project."

"You won't hear any complaints from me," murmured Eleanor.

"But I know nothing at all about Eastfield," Arden protested. "I barely knew my Aunt Portia, and never even came here for a visit. There must be stories behind the paintings and pots in the house, but I don't know them."

"I do."

They all turned and looked past Evan Zane, to where Hammond still stood, his hands in his pockets as he rocked back and forth.

"And how is that?" Alex asked quietly. Arden heard the undercurrent of challenge, possibly of threat.

Hammond shrugged. "No big surprise. The Rileys and the Alexanders go way back. Friends, neighbors, cousins, business associates, partners in crime..."

Arden decided to cut him off right there. "Are you telling me we might be cousins?" The idea settled on her even more uncomfortably than kinship with Alex Wingate. In both cases, she preferred a distant relationship, though for different reasons.

Hammond shrugged again, this time with a

worldly air. "Aren't we all? Just glance at the names on each branch of any Eastfield family tree and you'll see the intersection of all the families here since Colonial times. The Rileys and Alexanders. The Hammonds and Zanes. The Brownlees and Liddells. Margaret Brownlee, who used to manage The Thrifty Means, was married to a Durant."

"And we all know how that turned out," Evan said, and Eleanor gave him a little push.

"Is there an Eastfield family tree?" Arden asked earnestly, ignoring the comments around her. "Is it at the Historical Society?"

"There's a sampler there, done in 1857. It's valuable but not very useful in the town genealogy, especially since Miss Polly Stoughton, aged 8, neglected to include last names." Hammond made it sound as if the little girl of long ago deliberately thwarted him in his efforts. "If there's a family tree somewhere, it's probably etched on a gravestone. And the tree would almost certainly be an oak."

"Like the one Arden..." Eleanor began.

"I think your table's waiting, Evan," Alex said. And, in fact, Leslie looked bored. Though from impatience to seat them, or frustrated for lack of attention, it was hard to say. "Why don't the four of us get together one evening, and figure out which of us can make the greater claim to ousting the Native Americans from their lands? I'm sure it will make all of us wish we all came to town recently and bought condos, instead of inheriting old wood farmhouses."

Hammond opened his mouth to say something, but Evan cut him off.

"Sounds like a plan. I'll bring my recorder and you can tell us all about your corner of Eastfield, and its history." Behind him, Eleanor sighed.

"Enjoy your dinner," Alex said and waved them off. His gesture managed to include Hammond, as well.

Arden watched them all walk off through the sea of tables and chairs, and turned her attention to her dessert. The cheesecake was dissolving into a pool of syrup and the raspberries looked a little sodden.

"I suppose you're grateful that Hammond's not a 'kissin' cousin," she said.

"I'm grateful for us both," Alex said. "This coffee is cold."

"Though probably not as cold as the reception you gave Hammond. What is it about the guy you don't like? He really is a nice guy. Not very exciting, but a nice guy." Arden said as she played with her raspberries.

"Is that what you're looking for? A nice guy?" Alex asked.

She put down her fork and looked at him. He managed to make the words sound contemptuous, and yet he surely knew he was a nice guy himself. Was that so very bad?

"I'm a nice girl," she said instead. "I did everything I could to make my parents proud, I took a job that interested me in a field I know a lot about. I worked hard and made some wise investments, I listened to those who would teach me, and ignored those who would steer me wrong, I had several respectable boyfriends, and a pleasant apartment near the Charles River. I gave money to charities. I remember birthdays and anniversaries, and make my own greeting cards."

Alex's eyes didn't waver from hers as the waiter came with fresh cups of hot coffee.

"And what do I have in return?" she asked, wishing she didn't sound so self-pitying. "I'm living in an old musty cottage with an unpredictable heating system. My car is being eaten by rodents. I'm rummaging through other people's junk, trying to find something worthwhile to price for sale. I'm getting older by the hour and I don't have a job and I don't know how long those wise investments are going to keep me going."

"I'm trying to help you," Alex said and handed her a linen napkin. Arden wiped her cheeks in frustration. "You must remember that book about bad things happening to good people?"

Arden answered with a sniff.

"Anyway, you saved my life, so you have my gratitude," Alex said, lingering on the last word. "And maybe someday you'll think that coming to Eastfield is the best thing that ever happened to you, instead of the worst."

"You are not helping right now, Alex," she said. "When I first arrived I continued to hope that I'd get a call, and someone would tell me it was all a mistake and I should come back. But now I think I will have to sell my apartment, and pack up everything and put my furniture in storage. There's no going back."

"Then let's go forward."

A large bowl of fresh fruit arrived at their table, though Arden didn't recall they'd ordered it. But the sweet scent of freshly picked apples and pears had more appeal than the lavishly prepared desserts that languished on their plates. Arden picked up a red Macintosh apple and studied it for a moment before bringing it to her lips. Suddenly she changed her mind and offered it to Alex instead. He took a bite and then caught her wrist in his hand and kissed her fingers.

"There. Now you're an official Eastfield bad girl," he said.

"Like Leslie?" Arden asked softly.

"Leslie makes the rest of us look like amateurs. But let's say that letting a man kiss you in a restaurant is putting you on the road to perdition." Alex grinned like a fool. "Now, how does that feel?"

"Scarcely enough to imagine the town elders will make me wear a scarlet letter. But I refuse to be punished alone, like poor Hester Prynne. What can I do to entice you down the same path?" Her tears had evaporated and she dared to imagine he could be right about coming to Eastfield.

"I can think of a few things, though none I would care to share with the audience here."

"Do you mean because Hammond Riley has been glowering at us since he sat down at the bar?"

"That, and Eleanor Zane watching us over her bifocals. She protects the women of The Thrifty Means, you know."

"I thought as much," Arden murmured. "And yet I suspect if I stood on your porch, wondering whether I dare enter your home at the cost of my reputation, she'd push me through the door."

"God, I love the women of The Thrifty Means," he said, and released her wrist. "And this restaurant. Though not necessarily in that order."

"Why were you and Eleanor not an item?" Arden asked, and then realized her mistake. "Or were you?"

"I confess the woman tempted me. Evan Zane wasn't around, and neither was her ex-husband. But I wasn't ready to take on a family, prete-a-porter with teen-aged twins. Then Evan came back to Eastfield, and it seemed as if they had been waiting for each other all their lives."

Arden thought of a dozen things she might say, but they all presumed too much of him and what the future might hold. Whatever it was, she doubted people would someday say of them that they had been waiting for each other all their lives. Such things were too rare, too precious, to devalue with a cliché.

"Do you think it will be chilly canoeing up the river this late in the evening?" she asked.

It certainly was a non-sequitor, irrelevant to the topic at hand. But studying her, his fork poised near his open lips, Alex seemed to understand what she was asking and why she asked it.

"I am willing to abandon this delicious black lava cake at L'Avignon if it means you have something sweet planned on Old Tory Lane."

Arden looked down at her plate, immensely impatient with the raspberries that remained there. "I can't say how sweet it is, but I believe it will satisfy your appetite," she said.

Alex put his fork down and pushed his plate aside.

"And mine," she added.

****

Miranda woke Arden up early, excited by some noise just beyond the periphery of Arden's consciousness. Arden opened her eyes and squinted at the alarm clock on the Shaker table next to Alex's bed. It was 8 a.m., not an ungodly hour, but one far too early to arise on a damp and foggy day.

On a day such as this, she didn't at all miss the exhausting regularity of an office job.

On a day such as this, with Alex's arm holding her naked body against his, she was prepared to believe the truth of the clichés uttered last night in the restaurant. If this was a dream, she didn't want to awaken.

But Miranda had other ideas. She pawed at the bedroom door and dared to give one high-pitched bark.

"I should have guessed she'd be jealous," Alex murmured in Arden's ear, and licked the outline of her lobe. "I can't say that I blame her. We gave her quite an eyeful last night."

A moment later, he was back asleep, snoring softly. Miranda came over to the edge of the bed and tapped Arden's hand that was sticking out from beneath the blanket. Arden began to extricate her body from her lover's arms, and gasped at the assault of cold and damp air on her skin. She bent down to retrieve an oversized flannel shirt from the floor. Comfortably enfolded in Alex's embracing scent, she followed Miranda down the stairs to the front door, where Glinda stood guard like an ancient sphinx.

The noise grew louder when Arden opened the door, and seemed to come from the vicinity of her cottage. A stiff breeze brought down a flurry of red leaves, and Arden walked through them until she had a better vision of the landscape below her.

Mike's men were at work in her garden, the steady rhythm of the backhoe punctuated by the staccato of picks and shovels. These were country noises, and these men kept country hours. Which meant it would be impossible for her to return to her cottage without them knowing she had not spent the night in her own bedroom. Unless she went off the path and quietly went in the back door.

No, she would not. She had left Bradford under a cloud, vacating her office after hours, and in the company of a security guard. But no one would unjustly oust her from her cottage, nor judge her decisions. She would just brazen it out, alone.

But even her bravery had certain limits. She would not give Mike's men a free show, sauntering past them in Alex's flannel shirt and with her bird's nest of a hair style.

Miranda came out of the woods and barked a greeting, as if she hadn't already seen Arden a minute earlier. Arden patted her head somewhat absent-mindedly, realizing that she and Alex were already headed down a path on which they could not return. No matter what they imagined about their freedom to make choices, they could no sooner find their way back than if they sprinkled breadcrumbs behind them. They could only go forward. And if things didn't work out, one of them would move on.

It would have to be her, Arden supposed. And yet, she liked living in Eastfield very much.

Miranda was already pawing Alex's front door by the time Arden followed her to the steps of the outside porch. Alex, wearing nothing more than boxer shorts and his cast, opened the door to the chilly air and stepped out as Miranda swept past him into the house.

"You'd better get back indoors, unless you want to give Mike's men a show," Arden said as she stepped into his arms.

"They won't even notice me while you're showing them some cleavage," he said. "I think I like this shirt better on you than on me."

"I'm sure you do, but I'm going to change back into yesterday's clothes. I'm not going to march through the woods in a flannel shirt."

"That's a pity," Alex said. "Please remember to close your curtains, as well. Mike hires his guys for their muscles, not for their moral fiber."

"You're a fine one to talk," Arden said, as she ducked out of his arms, and followed Miranda into the house.

"Is it my fault your sister never used the curtains on her windows?"

Arden turned around, knowing he was right behind her. "You didn't have to look."

He smiled then, and she knew what was coming, and that she practically asked for it.

"Oh, yes, I did. I couldn't do anything else. Once I spotted that harem girl through my window, I knew my days of stargazing on a clear autumn night were over. There's enough here to keep me tethered to the earth," he said.

Arden sighed. "That's very romantic, you know."

"I know," he said. "But is it irresistible?"

Arden thought it very well might be, but remembered the path they were treading, and wanted to slow their pace. He leaned toward her, and she pressed back against him.

"I guess not," he said, still smiling. "But I'll settle for romantic right now."

"And I'll settle for a bagel and cream cheese, which is not romantic at all."

"But, very, very good, just the same."

****

After breakfast, Arden dressed for the walk down to the cottage. Alex offered to accompany her, but she thought his appearance would just be overkill to what the workers would already suppose.

"Morning, Arden!" Mike called out. She looked around and realized he was the one on the backhoe. The other men paused in their work and studied her as she walked past them. "I knocked at the door, and figured you were either a sound sleeper, or out bright and early."

Arden stepped over some uplifted slate tiles as she approached him.

"Both, as it turns out," she said. "How's the work going? Did you find anything exciting?"

"A couple of old horseshoes and bits of glass. The old cistern is just past the bed of mums."

Arden glanced over the yellow and orange blooms, and was startled to see a rock foundation that looked just like that of a tomb. But then, she already knew it was a tricky business to make snap judgments on the identification of items long buried.

"No gravestones?" she asked, a little recklessly.

Mike hesitated, as if he had to think about it. "Have you seen ghosts? Any signs of mischief?"

"The only mischief I've seen seems to be from the human sort. I doubt my colonial ancestors would dump out my drawers and trash my living room."

"Well, we didn't spot anyone this morning,"

Mike said.

"That's good. I guess I have my own security force while you're working here."

"No one I don't know will get through," Mike reassured her.

But as she waved him off and started toward the cottage, she realized he hadn't reassured her at all. Surely he didn't mean that literally? Did he think letting those he knew pass through was acceptable?

The door was locked when Arden turned her key, and it held fast as she pushed her shoulder against it. It finally yielded to her pressure, but did not close easily behind her. It was the dampness, she supposed, making the old oak swell to fit tightly against the frame. It was a seasonal hazard.

She entered a sweet-smelling greenhouse of warmth, so different from the empty chill that greeted her on her arrival weeks before. With the windows closed and the morning sun beating down on the slate roof, the cottage had captured the soul of these rare days before winter, as garden herbs dried in the kitchen window and the spicy scents of pumpkin pie lingered in the still air.

She wandered through the rooms, drawing the curtains in each, and pausing to finger some of the little treasures that graced every shelf and tabletop. Satisfied that everything was in its place, she started to unbutton her black slacks and pull her cashmere sweater over her head. As she tossed back her unbrushed hair, her eyes lit upon the painting over the mantel.

It really was a fine little painting, a perfect companion piece to the season. The keenly executed farm workers plied their trade as Mike's men did just outside their door, using garden tools that hadn't changed in generations. In both cases, the men toiled to guarantee a future harvest, though the men in the painting did not have the luxury of

235

shopping in a supermarket if things did not work out so well.

Alex had offered to touch up the damaged edges of the wood, and yet there was something to be said for following Victoria's wishes, and just leave the painting as it was, with scratch marks as permanent testimony to the mystery of the break in. There was no reason for anyone to touch it, repair it, or even identify it. Let it stand as it was, part of the history of the cottage.

Arden mused for several moments, quite pleased with her resolution, when she realized someone had, in fact, touched it, very recently. Something had changed since she left the cottage last night for her canoe trip downriver, and it was so subtle she would not have even been aware of it under normal circumstances. But yesterday evening, unaccountably nervous about her date with Alex, she burned off some energy by dusting and polishing the mantelpiece.

There on the white wall, within inches of the frame of the painting, was the distinct pattern of fingerprints. Left by a hand larger than her own.

****

Alex saw Arden approach his house, and was glad he managed to shower and dress, rather than give in to temptation and go back to bed. He was exhausted. Arden, who matched him in last night's adventures, looked awake and efficient, and ready for business.

She knocked on the door. Miranda didn't even bother to bark, but looked at him expectantly.

"Did you forget something?" he asked as he opened the door. "Because I thought about a few possibilities we haven't yet explored."

She tried not to smile, but was unsuccessful.

"I'm sure you have, but I don't want the good people of Eastfield to blame me for killing you when you collapse of a heart attack."

"You are a romantic, after all." He kissed her as she walked past him. She wore a black suede jacket and herringbone slacks, and boots with heels that would be covered in mud in an hour.

"A bit formal for an afternoon at The Thrifty Means?" he asked.

"I called and gave my apologies to Eleanor. By the way, Evan asked her to pass on the message that he thinks you have more luck than you deserve."

"He must be talking about the commission in New York," Alex murmured.

"Yes, I'm sure that's it." Arden made a little sniffing noise, either intentionally or because she had an allergy. "But I'm heading back up to Boston."

He just stared at her, not sure what to make of the announcement. Had he scared her off?

"I know you were just there, but do you want to come along for the ride?" she added, and all his irrational worries evaporated.

"Hell, I'll even drive, if you'd like. But what are we doing? If you're planning to spend the day shopping in Harvard Square, I'll take back that offer."

"You don't have to take it back, I'm not going shopping. From now on all my shopping is restricted to what I can find at The Thrifty Means. I intend to be very loyal, and I'm told the volunteers are their own best customers. Besides, I'm broke."

Alex's feelings of a couple of moments ago did a complete reversal. If she intended to remain a loyal volunteer she'd be staying around for a while. He just hoped he had more to do with it than the bargains at a thrift shop.

"Women in Eastfield are a hardy bunch," he said. "You'll be able to manage just fine on wild fruit and berries and make your own clothes from wool you weave yourself."

She shot him a look, which he supposed he deserved.

"And I'll take you out to L'Avignon once in a while." He saw that she was readying a retort. "So what are we doing in Boston?"

"I called my friend Larry at the Museum of Fine Arts, in the Early American Department. He was my thesis adviser, and we often consulted with each other about things we came across. I'd like to talk to him about the Gainsborough."

"Larry Palmer?" Alex asked. How was Larry Palmer old enough to be Arden's thesis adviser? Was he fifteen when he got his PhD?

"Yes. Do you know him?" she asked, though the answer was already obvious.

"Are you sure I won't be in the way? If you're old friends and all?" Alex asked, like an idiot.

Arden smiled, in that way she had that suggested she knew why he was acting like an idiot.

"Okay, I'll just stay out of the way," he said, but fully intended to stand between them if Palmer got too close to her. "What time are we leaving?"

"As soon as we can pack some things. Within the hour, I hope."

"Does that mean you want to stay overnight? Let me call someone to look after Miranda and Glinda. I suppose we'll need a hotel room?"

"I have an apartment on Beacon Hill," Arden reminded him.

"No wonder you're broke," Alex said, snapping the phone shut.

"You don't have to give me that look. It's a very little place."

"Like your cottage?"

"Much, much smaller. Just big enough for a bed and a refrigerator." She closed her eyes as if envisioning it for the first time. "Okay, and a couch and recliner and table and pots and pans. There's even a bathroom."

"Is there room enough for me?"

"There's even room enough for Miranda. But it might not be a bad idea for the person who looks after her to check our houses while we're gone."

Alex heard the concern in her voice. "Do you have reason to be worried again?"

"I think I do. I looked at the Gainsborough, and there were fingerprints on the wall around it. I don't recall seeing them before."

"Fingerprints? We must be dealing with the stupidest burglar in the world. Even a five-year-old kid knows to put on gloves before a break in."

"A five-year-old kid who watches crime dramas."

"Any five-year-old kid. And any adult, for that matter. Even a dunce like Hammond Riley."

Arden looked at him steadily for a few moments. There was something different in her appearance, something beyond her stylish outfit and look of determination. She looked not merely ready to conquer the world, but as if she had already done so, and merely added gratification to gratification.

"Do you think all this is the doing of Hammond Riley?" she said at last.

"Well," Alex said, careful to choose his words, "if we have fingerprints, there's one way to find out."

Arden took a step back and looked down at a small sculpture he created out of a single piece of marble when he was in his teens. He thought the work rather respectable at the time, but now he could think of a hundred better uses for that lovely white carrerra, mined from a quarry in Italy. Arden picked up the piece, and it seemed amateurish next to the elegant beauty of her long fingers.

"Not now, not yet. If it's Hammond we'll be able to catch him in the act. I'd rather do that than try to steal a wine glass during a dinner party and test for fingerprints, or something nutty like that," she said.

"When we're ready to make our move, we'll find him at Town Hall," she said.

Though Alex had no such scruples about busting the guy at any place and at any time, he was happy to make any move at all with Arden in his company. He took a deep breath. "Why don't you run down and pack up your things, and lock up the house? I'll drive around to pick you up as soon as I'm all set with Miranda."

****

A half hour later, they were on the Merritt Parkway, heading northeast. The early morning traffic had dissipated with the damp fog, and there were few cars to interfere with Alex's speeding pace.

"So," he said, "did Larry ever marry? Wasn't he out in San Francisco for a while?"

Arden turned to study his profile, remembering how she traced the slope of his nose with her finger last night.

"He was, but came back for a woman. It's a very romantic story."

"If it involves you, I don't want to know about it," he said. "Besides, I don't think he's your type."

"Who exactly is my type, Mr. Wingate?"

He didn't hesitate a second. "Well, me, of course."

She had a feeling he was absolutely right. For once, she felt content to let someone else drive the engine of her mission, of her quest. Not very long ago, she would have asserted her independence in her own name and in the names of women everywhere. But just now she was perfectly content—even gratified—to have his company and accept his lead.

"We might stop off in Hartford on the way back," he said, filling the space of her silence. "There must be something in the state archives about the Charter Oak."

240

"Larry grew up in Hartford and is a local history buff. I want to pick his brains and the titles in his library about our little box. We'll be killing two birds with one stone."

"Good pun. Do you think the two things are related?"

"I don't see how that's possible," Arden answered, having already considered it. "Old oak trees and a rare and beautiful little painting. I wonder if it's an oak tree in the foreground, perhaps the original Charter Oak."

"It looks like a beech to me."

"You know the difference? What do you know about trees?"

He shrugged. "I grew up here. I could probably identify five different types of maples, as well. It's what we country boys do."

"That's not the only thing, I noticed," Arden said, and watched him smile.

"Besides," he added, "the Charter Oak was next to the meeting house, at the center of colonial life in Hartford. The scene in the painting is out in the fields, far from any buildings or evidence of commerce. Hartford wasn't a city then, but it already was a pretty hopping town."

"Like Eastfield?" Arden asked.

"If our town leaders have their way, Eastfield will never be more hopping than it is right now. The most exciting thing to happen in months was your arrival. And possibly a recent delivery of rusty old pots to The Thrifty Means."

Arden say back in her seat, reading the occasional road sign along the Merritt Parkway, and noticing how the trees seem to shed more of their autumn leaves the further northeast they went. It would be winter soon, and then the holidays, which meant that, realistically, she wouldn't be starting a new job until the New Year. A potential move, though still some months away, was somehow no longer reassuring.

"At least the women of The Thrifty Means gave me a proper greeting. I can't say as much for whoever broke into my house. But the more I think about it, the more likely it seems that the cottage was broken into because I was there."

"Or not, for the afternoon," Alex said. "Remember, we were at the hospital."

"I'm not likely to forget. But what did I bring to Eastfield that anyone would want?"

"You," Alex said.

Arden didn't rise to the compliment. "But I wasn't there, and someone would have realized that right away. It's not as if he had to upturn chairs on the chance that I was hiding beneath them."

"But what if someone—let's call him 'Hammond'—thought he could play the hero by solving the mystery of the break in for you. You'd be very impressed, wouldn't you?"

"If you're suggesting I'd sleep with him out of gratitude..."

"I'm suggesting he might think you would sleep with him out of gratitude. Hammond isn't very sophisticated. The world is divided into good and bad guys for him, and good guys get rewarded by the damsel in distress."

Arden sighed, and waited to answer until they went over a bridge spanning one of Connecticut's many beautiful rivers. Even from this height, Arden saw the branches of trees reflected in the deep waters.

"I hope I'm not that pathetic, am I?" she asked.

"Never. Needy, sometimes, but never pathetic,"

"Thanks," she said sarcastically and was ready to dispute him when she recalled her very first morning in town, when her car didn't start. Well, her only excuse had to be that she was tired, cold, and under a great deal of stress. Maybe she was a tad needy.

"He would need to produce a bad guy, though," she said at last.

Alex said nothing, and just continued to watch the road.

"That is, if that break in was part of a stupid scheme, there would still have to be a bad guy, and that person would be arrested and charged. Hammond wouldn't get anyone to do that."

"No, not even Mike would be enough of a moron to do that," Alex said.

"You really don't like them, do you?" Arden asked, though she already knew the answer.

"I'm not crazy about any of the Rileys. They insinuate themselves into people's lives, looking for gossip like old biddies sitting in their windows, watching their neighbors go by. Mike takes a more active role, showing up on people's doorsteps ready to work at their house, though they never called him to come over."

Arden realized that was precisely what Mike did to her. And she just bought it, believing he had been hired by Anne, and somehow everything was already settled. She just trusted him on that.

"And Hammond? He doesn't seem to go anywhere."

Alex glanced at her with something like pity, probably thinking she was pathetic, after all. "Hammond goes everywhere without leaving Town Hall. He knows how much we owe in taxes, the size of our mortgages, the complaints we've filed against our neighbors. He sits down there in his windowless cell and sketches family trees and reminds people of old property disputes. He probably knew you were coming to town even before I did."

"Did you know?" Arden asked, surprised.

"Anne called me to air out the house, and get it

ready for you."

"Thank you."

"Yeah," he acknowledged. "No problem."

"Tell me more about the Rileys," Arden prodded.

"The Rileys seemed to be the only people your Aunt Portia would talk to in her old age. She was frail and a little suspicious of everyone, but the Rileys always seemed to be going in and out her door."

Arden's cell phone rang, but she ignored it.

"Did you know her?" she asked.

"I could hardly avoid it. We lived next door. She used to bring over home-baked pies and garden vegetables, none of which my mother seemed to recognize. Old Portia once mistook squash for a cucumber and, well, the less said on that, the better. But as she grew older, the garden went to seed and she stopped baking. Whatever she was doing with the Riley family had nothing to do with the culinary arts."

"Did she ever talk to you?" Arden asked. "Did she ever tell you anything interesting about the property or the things she owned?"

"I was a kid, Arden."

"But you said you knew her."

"Not well enough to hear how her great-great-grandmother buried her Portuguese lover in the garden next to the garage." Alex paused. "But I used to go down and shovel her walkway in the winter. Sometimes she'd invite me in for hot chocolate when I was done."

"I don't think the cottage would have been a comfortable place for a child."

"She treated me as if she were a museum guard and I a rambunctious child. But I was old enough to know better than to leave puddles on the old floorboards or fingerprints on the wall. Your old Aunt Portia was fastidious, the sort of woman who would make up her bed even if she only had to go to the bathroom in the middle of the night. I think she stayed like that until the end."

"But you said the garden went to seed."

"That came years later. The inside remained orderly, but the outside looked like a war zone. Mike was supposed to be looking after the place but after a while, it fell to ruin. The cottage needed painting, the driveway was rutted, there were holes dug all over the place."

"Holes? What kind of holes? In the garden?"

"The place looked like a school for gravediggers."

"Why didn't you tell me this before? Especially after we found Quercus Chartula? I would think it might be relevant."

"To be honest, I haven't thought about it in years. And at the time, it barely registered. I was starting my own career, and negotiated with my parents to buy the property. I was having the barn renovated into my studio. That's when your garage was rebuilt."

"My garage?"

"Well, as long as I was keeping the local contractors in business, I thought it made sense to ask them to do something nice for an elderly lady. I asked Portia's permission, of course, and paid for the lumber, but the carpenters rebuilt it for free. Mike was very angry at the whole business."

"Why should it matter to him?" Arden felt they were close to something, but couldn't figure out what it was, or what it would mean.

"He had some bullshit argument about the garage taking up too much space in the garden. Not that he was doing much to earn his monthly retainer. I think he felt like he owned the place. He probably still does."

"I don't even own the place," Arden said a little helplessly.

245

"It's a little sticky, isn't it? Well, I can think of one way to straighten out the land deed. The two properties can fall under sole ownership..."

Arden held up her hand to stop him. "Don't count on it, Alex. Even if I move on, I'm not planning on selling the cottage to you."

"Who's talking about selling?"

His eyes met hers for only a moment, but everything was said.

"Watch the road," Arden whispered. "Don't let everything end before it's even started."

If they weren't in a car, speeding toward Boston, his words might have released a dam of emotions. But sitting as they were, Arden somehow believed she sounded cool and confident. And perhaps it was time to change the subject.

"Where is Aunt Portia buried?" Arden said. "Eleanor thought she might be in Eastfield Cemetery, but I couldn't find her there. I found lots of Alexanders and Wingates, but no Portia more recent than the eighteen fifties. The groundskeeper was very nice and helpful and told me that he thought she might be up in Danbury."

"No, she's here in town. She never left in her lifetime, so she certainly would not have been buried surrounded by strangers in another town. We'll just have to look a little harder."

"So you knew she was there all along?"

"I haven't been trying to hide things from you, if that's what you're thinking. I haven't thought about Portia or her garage or that cemetery in years. But I remember there was much ado about the grave site and someone else was disinterred. Portia wanted to be laid to rest next to a Victoria ancestor, though don't ask me why. The first Victoria has been dead for two hundred years and I don't even know if she's a relation."

Chapter 12

"In our work, we always have the answers for everything, even if we have to make them up."
~Harriet Helmsley (volunteer since 2003)

"Arden! I can't believe you hooked up with old Alex! Now I wish I'd introduced the two of you years ago." Lawrence Palmer gripped Arden by her shoulders, and kissed her European-style, on both cheeks. And then, in more the manner of an American klutz, allowed his wire-framed glasses to slip off his nose and into the neckline of her blouse.

Arden dipped her hand into the hollow between her breasts and retrieved them for him.

"Alex is my next door neighbor, Larry. Eastfield is a lovely town and my little cottage is heaven."

"Filled with antiques, I suppose." There was a note of longing in his voice, as if the vast collection of the museum was not sufficient to intrigue him. "Don't let Alex here convince you to refurnish with modern design."

"I would think you'd want that, Larry. Then Arden would have to buy all new furniture and pack up everything as a donation to the museum." Alex picked up a pewter candlestick with a twisted handle. "But don't get your hopes up. The cottage is full of treasures and I'm hoping that all of them stay there."

Larry looked from one to the other, at once understanding Alex's implication. "Well, good luck to both of you."

"Thank you, Larry," Arden said softly, accepting

his assumptions and Alex's promise.

"So, what do you need me for?" Larry asked a little gruffly. "What's this about a Gainsborough in your living room?"

"I'm sure it's not a Gainsborough, though it's a pretty good imitation. The person who did it was a master craftsman, a fine artist. It's been hanging there for years, but Anne wouldn't have noticed or cared, and I don't know enough about my aunt to guess if she even wondered about it."

Alex took his cue. "The woman couldn't tell a Picasso from a DaVinci, so I doubt she gave it a second thought. Though, to be fair, I've been in and out of the cottage for years, and never thought about it either."

"I have a picture of it here," Arden said, and opened a portfolio on Larry's cluttered desk.

"Why didn't you just bring it up to Boston? Unless you were afraid that it would be destroyed in a car crash," Larry said. "I've driven with Alex, you know."

"Good point," murmured Arden. "I would have to think twice about carrying any irreplaceable artwork with me. But actually, the painting isn't just hanging over the fireplace. It's attached to the wall and can't be pried off without doing some damage. Someone's already tried, and recently."

"Maybe the painting isn't as valuable as what's behind it."

"And maybe the painting is covering termite damage in the wood." Alex said.

"If it is, then you'd better pry it off, and quickly. Termites aren't particular about what's on the wood they eat, just as long as it's wood," Larry said.

"There's no rush. The last termites to dine on Arden's cottage were there in the 1850's," Alex said wryly. But Larry wasn't listening.

"This is a beautiful painting," he said in a low

voice. He picked up Arden's photograph and angled it for better light. "But from this print, I can't tell if you copied it out of a magazine or changed the coloration. And as you well know, anyone can doctor up a photograph and misrepresent the real goods."

When Arden didn't answer, Larry realized what he said, and apologized.

"Don't bother, Larry. My reputation is already shot. And for what? That painting in South Carolina was nothing to this. If this is what I think it is."

"I can't say. Let's see what we can discover. But if we don't have luck today, let me hold on to this, and dig deeper. I promise I'll make it my priority."

"Still worried about the termites?" Alex asked. He already settled himself behind Larry's desk and was thumbing through a large book.

Larry looked surprised, and glanced at her. She pretended to study a blown glass paperweight. "No, still worried about Arden, no matter what you've promised her."

****

Some time later, the three friends sat in the window of a small café, enjoying warm drinks and the passing landscape of pedestrians on Newberry Street. The hour was late for lunch, so they had the additional advantage of privacy.

Alex was disappointed they had not uncovered anything remarkable in their search through old papers and limited access sites on Larry's computer, but he was satisfied that his old friend would do his best for them.

"But there's another puzzle we'd like to discuss with you," he said to Larry, after he was sure they all finished eating. He took a sip of his coffee, and gestured to the waitress for a refill. "There's some business about the Charter Oak."

"What do you need to know?" Larry asked.

"Everything," Alex and Arden said at once,

which prompted a recitation that could make one believe Larry memorized textbooks for pleasure. He gave them a version of the old story that was pretty much what Alex remembered from Hammond's impromptu lecture. But then things became more personal.

"The Trumbulls and the Wadsworths played important roles, as you might expect," Larry said. "Jonathan Trumbull was the colonial governor, but supported the patriots and issued a declaration of independence two weeks before the other one was adopted in Philadelphia. And it was a Joseph Wadsworth who secreted away the colonial charter back in the days of King James. But there's no evidence these Trumbulls and Wadsworths had any direct connection to the Eastfield branch of the family, except for one little tidbit."

Arden and Alex leaned forward as Larry paused to take a bite into his apple pie. "I have a letter in the archives that mentions a Trumbull cousin removed himself from revolutionary Hartford to the more sympathetic loyalties of Fairfield County. The letter is undated, which is an odd thing in itself. But where and when this happened could have been incriminating evidence, depending on the shifting tides of the war."

"It could be Eastfield," Arden murmured. "My cottage is on Old Tory Lane."

Alex glanced at her face, illuminated in the afternoon light. He wanted her to find her answers, but hopes rested on such slivers of evidence, unlikely to amount to anything substantial.

"Where is the Charter?" he asked. He fingered his paper napkin, damp and soiled and ready to be consigned to the garbage bin. What chance did a sheet of parchment have over centuries? "And where is the Oak?"

Larry sat back and grinned. "The Charter is in

the state archives. I could probably pull a few strings so you can see it for yourself. As for the old tree, it must have fallen down a hundred years ago or more. There's a monument marker—a big, ugly granite shaft—to mark its place. You can detour on the way back to Connecticut and check it out."

Alex sensed Arden's excitement, but knew she was setting herself up for disappointment. What would a granite marker possibly reveal to them? For that matter, what advantage would they have for seeing the great document? But perhaps the story was more involved than was generally known.

"I'm not as interested in what the thing looks like as much as where it's been," Alex said. "Was it ever stolen—aside from that first time—and brought somewhere else? Are there copies?"

Larry looked at him speculatively and nodded. A man in his profession did not get advancements because of his good humor, but because of his keen intuition.

"All right, be honest with me. What have the two of you found? The Charter itself? Where was it?"

Alex knew they had already given too much away, and on very little more than several pointed questions. Larry's immediate assessment of the situation seemed to be confirmation that their little find in Eastfield might be connected to a larger, more dramatic truth than one would otherwise believe.

Arden glanced at Alex, caught his nod, and told their story.

"No," she sighed, sounding disappointed. "Not the Charter. I found something buried in my yard, dated 1774, that may have been a receptacle for the Charter, but nothing else. For all I know, it may have held a few sacred branches of the Oak, or a couple of acorns. We hoped you could tell us more."

Arden pulled out her cell phone, and showed

Larry the screen. "It's not all that clear, but I think you can make it out."

Larry turned his back to the window and hunched over the phone. Alex thought he might be guarding their secret, but then realized the man was trying to block out the sun's reflection.

"I don't know," he said, and Arden sighed. Alex realized his hopes were almost as high.

"What do you mean, you don't know? Who else would know if you don't?" Alex asked.

Larry shrugged.

"I don't know," he repeated. "I've never seen anything like this. I suppose it might have contained a copy, though none have ever turned up before. But that doesn't mean they aren't out there. Didn't someone find a Declaration of Independence in his attic a few years ago?"

"Yes," Arden said. "I saw that in Philadelphia when it went on display. And someone found Lincoln's signature in the flyleaf of a book bought for a quarter at a flea market. These things do happen, but I think it would be nothing short of remarkable if a copy of the Connecticut colonial charter came into my hands. Remember, Larry, all I've found is a box. If there was anything of value in it at any time, it was cleaned out years ago."

Larry reached behind him and pulled on his jacket. Alex reached for the billfold, guessing this interview was at an end.

But Larry was still thinking ahead of them. "And put somewhere else? What would someone do with a document like that? Not burn it, let's hope. Return it to the Crown? Not very likely. But, perhaps, store it somewhere else. Are there any good hiding places on your property?"

"About a million of them. But someone went through half the possibilities when he ransacked the place a few weeks ago."

"You were robbed?"

"I don't know," Arden said. "I have no idea if anything was taken. And my sister is just as clueless."

"We're suspicious of the fact the break-in occurred only after Arden arrived in town. The place has stood empty for years, but within days of her arrival, someone trashed the place," Alex explained.

"Maybe he was interested in something Arden owns, and it has nothing to do with the house."

"My rings and necklaces were left on the top of my bureau. There were some diamonds there, but nothing was taken."

Alex looked at her speculatively, wondering who bought her diamonds and when.

"Why do you think it has anything to do with the Charter Oak?" Larry asked, probably already knowing the answer to the diamond question, at least.

"Why do you think it doesn't?" Arden asked, and laughed. "Quercus Chartula, a date, and an engraving of an oak tree. What were we to think?"

"Exactly what you did think. After all, why shouldn't you have a national treasure lying about the house? Maybe it's wedged behind a mirror, or lining a shelf in a closet. Stranger things have happened, and it sounds perfectly reasonable."

"Just as I thought," Arden said.

Alex looked at her in surprise, and she laughed out loud.

****

Larry left them on Newberry Street, standing in the middle of the sidewalk as waves of pedestrians bustled past them. Bright sunlight reflected off rows of large plate windows, displaying paintings and pottery and fashionable and extremely expensive clothes. Before her dismissal from Bradford, Arden enjoyed many pleasurable hours here, enjoying the scene and spending her weekly paycheck. Now she found the crowd annoying and wished she was back in her flannels and loafers on Old Tory Lane.

"Do you miss it?" Alex asked, locking her arm in his. His cast felt clammy and showed signs of wear; it would soon be time to have it removed.

"Not as much as I thought," she admitted. "When I first came to Eastfield, I thought it was the other side of Beyond, and couldn't imagine how I'd manage."

They started walking in the direction of her apartment, close to the Common. A stiff cold wind rolled off the Charles River, and Arden nestled closer to Alex's side.

"And now you find it bearable because you're in pursuit of a national treasure?"

They continued to walk into the wind, heads down and scarves flapping behind them.

"You have a very high opinion of yourself, don't you?" she asked, and laughed again, realizing he had no idea what she was talking about.

****

Hartford, Connecticut, a grand and sprawling city on the banks of the Connecticut River, was midway on their southwest route back home. As important as the Charter Oak monument might be to their investigation, it didn't merit a listing on their car's GPS system. After they stopped at two gas stations to ask directions, and were met with blank stares, they stopped at the Mark Twain House, figuring that those connected to one historic site might know the location of another. They did.

"Let's come back here some day," Arden said. "The house is beautiful."

Alex nodded. "We'll also visit next door, where the Beechers lived. Hartford still has shining examples of its Victorian elegance."

As they drove through increasingly congested

streets toward the heart of the old city, Arden mused about Alex's ready acceptance of their future, one busy with journeys and plans together. "There it is," Alex said, and pointed his finger under Arden's nose to where a rather austere monument stood on a street corner. "That's your *Quercus Chartula*, in petrified form. I have a feeling the original tree must have been more impressive."

Arden thought of the wide-boughed oak on the cover of her box and nodded. "Could we get out?" she asked, but Alex already found a parking spot and pulled up to the curb.

The Charter Oak monument stood on a street corner, at the end of a line of stately brick homes. It was a busy place, and dozens of people brushed past Arden as she bent to read the inscription. She wondered if it had been like this when Joseph Wadsworth first did his daring deed and brought the charter to safety here. Had it been his private joke that the document should be hidden where the city's populace would pass it unknowingly every day of their lives? Or had he searched out a quiet place, a less-traveled path in town? A place that in the seventeenth century might have been something like Old Tory Lane was now. Arden's gaze, narrowed against the late afternoon sunlight, moved up the long shaft of granite.

"A masculine kind of thing, I'd say," said Alex wryly, standing a few feet away.

"I was just thinking the same thing," Arden said over her shoulder. "Also, the original tree must have been so much more impressive. Wadsworth would have realized the symbolism of putting the charter in a living, spreading thing. The town fathers in..." She fingered the dark stone as she read the date, "...1856...weren't quite so astute. They were probably thinking more about themselves and their own power."

"Are you implying they weren't living? They were, and probably spreading as well. But I see your point," Alex said. "And remember, it was a man's world."

"It still is," said Arden. She straightened and turned to look at him. "You know, the case isn't closed on Bradford," Alex said. "I think there's a good chance you'll be reinstated."

"I doubt it. The case seemed very much closed when they asked me to clear out my desk and leave. I was accused, tried, and found guilty, on the basis of everyone's testimony but my own." Arden stuffed her cold hands in her jacket pockets. "Under those circumstances, why would I want to go back? And to what? I appreciate your intervention, but I have moved on."

"To Eastfield."

She hesitated. "For now."

Alex leaned forward, his expression inscrutable. What whatever he was about to say was preempted by the blasting of two car horns, as their drivers battled it out for a parking spot. Alex and Arden watched the drama for several moments before he spoke again. "Do you know Peter Clarke is in some sort of trouble?"

Arden was certain this was not what Alex was about to say, and she was certain that she could care less about Peter Clarke. His duplicity on the matter of the misattributed painting could not be forgotten, or forgiven.

"Peter? No." Arden stepped across the pavement, to Alex's side. "What has he done? Or, should I say, what do people say he's done?"

"I don't know the details, but I received a text message while we were back in Boston, having lunch. He was negotiating with a Japanese buyer for a piece at Bradford. I think it was Church's 'Rain Maker.'"

Arden looked up and down the street, in the habit of speaking of such things in secret. "But that's impossible. It's part of the permanent collection. Peter knows better than anyone else that it can't be sold."

Alex smiled and pulled Arden's arm through his. "Let's go home," he said. "Unless you want to buy a postcard of the Charter Oak or something?"

Arden let herself be led away, back to the warm refuge of Alex's car.

"Tell me more about Peter," she said, after he started the engine.

"He contacted the buyer and started negotiations. He claims the sale will put the museum back on its feet, but he neglected to tell the university of his plans. A decision like that requires the vote of the Board of Trustees."

"Of course. They are a very astute group, ready to question and find out the truth of the business for themselves," Arden said bitterly.

"They are a lazy group, prepared to believe the loudest person in the group," Alex corrected. "Remember, I've had to deal with them as well. But I think I've managed to stir things up a bit."

"You have? What do you have to do with Peter Clarke?" Arden's eyes were fixed on the monument as Alex drove slowly past it.

"Nothing. But when I was up there, I managed to apply a little pressure in a few vulnerable places. It didn't take them long; someone uncovered this little business within hours."

"The sale of a painting by Church is not a little business."

"That's my point," Alex said. He paused at an intersection, deciphering the many directional signs, some of which seemed to contradict. Nodding to himself, he set them on the course to Eastfield, to home.

****

Though tired from the two days spent in Boston and Hartford, Arden showed up at The Thrifty Means when the doors opened the next morning. She hadn't been in the shop for a few days, and the landscape had predictably changed in unpredictable ways. A cabinet of Shaker design now stood where an upholstered love seat had been in the window earlier in the week . A large display of books was pushed back against the wall to make room for Halloween costumes. And someone decorated the shelves with sprays of honeysuckle and ivy. The familiar scents of lemon oil and dust were enhanced by something spicy.

"Emma Grace baked pumpkin tarts," Eleanor said, as she went around the shop, turning on lights and repositioning some of the wares. "She delivered them to the shop early this morning, before we opened."

Arden recognized the scent of nutmeg and cinnamon, very appealing after her bland breakfast of toast and butter.

"They smell good, but I'm not sure I ever saw a pumpkin tart."

Liza stood at the counter, playing with the knob on the shop's ancient radio. "You may not have recognized it as a pumpkin tart. It would have looked like the heel of a shoe. And tasted as good."

"Liza!" Eleanor admonished, though she laughed.

"I think they taste fine," said a young girl, who suddenly appeared behind the front desk.

"This is Jocelyn Gold, one of our student volunteers," Eleanor said. "We're always glad to find someone who has the patience to untangle necklaces and chains."

"Do you want me to help you find a better radio station, Liza?' Jocelyn asked.

A piece by David Ives, dramatic clashes overwhelming the static, came through the radio. Liza turned to Jocelyn and stepped back, letting the girl try her luck.

"Well. We're told that cinnamon has healing powers, so the tarts have some value, at least." Liza left her place from behind the sales desk and picked up a dusty pot. "I wonder if they'll work as polishing cloths."

"They're not greasy enough," Eleanor said, and looked at Arden. "I'm serious, you know. People used to use biscuits and buns to polish their shoes and shine their pewter."

"Oh, I'm sure you're serious. You invited me to volunteer here by appealing to my ego, and telling me you needed my expertise. But I haven't done anything remarkable, except learn a lot from all of you. I'm still an amateur here," said Arden.

"We're all amateurs. Women who have worked at The Thrifty Means for fifty years are still amateurs," Eleanor said, the pride evident in her voice. "But we manage to do very, very well."

"So I've noticed," Arden said quietly. Though Eleanor was talking about the shop and the donations it was able to allocate to charity, Arden thought of other things. The women, and girls, who volunteered seemed to take life with good humor and grace, and met their challenges with the help of others. They were friends, counselors, helpers, and a community. They knew when people were ill, and when someone needed a hand. They were smart and educated, but a big part of their world centered on this small corner of Eastfield.

"And speaking of serious," Eleanor began.

Arden blinked, and returned to the present. Had they been speaking of serious things? She remembered the pumpkin tarts, and polished shoes.

"What's happening with you and Alex Wingate?

I heard you went off together a couple of days ago."

"I suppose it will make headlines in *The Eastfield Edition*. Well, I hope they get the facts right. Alex and I went up to Boston, stayed over, and stopped in Hartford on the way back down. That's it. Nothing serious, and nothing to gossip about." Arden realized she sounded defensive. "We're just friends."

"Like you're friends with Hammond Riley?"

Arden knew what friendship was, and what would be considered more than friendship. Her relationship with Alex was so different from anything she experienced before, she didn't dare give a name to it. But whatever it was, she guessed he was as confused as she. And while that was the case, the two of them needed to work it out together, without the advice of the women of The Thrifty Means, no matter how good their intentions.

"Yes," she lied.

"Fine," said Eleanor. "Hammond was in here yesterday, looking for you."

"I guess he didn't get the bulletin about my trip to Boston."

The two women studied each other for several moments while Arden wondered how they managed to tie themselves into this little knot. Did Eleanor feel she was responsible for the lives of all her volunteers? Had Alex asked her to pick at Arden for some confession of how she felt about him? Had Hammond? If so, she preferred to believe the former.

"We got something in yesterday that might interest you," Eleanor said, breaking the ice that had formed between them.

"The picture?" Liza chimed in.

"An early American painting?" Arden asked, grateful for the diversion.

"Nothing so valuable, but something of greater interest to you, I think," said Eleanor. "It's a photograph that came in with some cartons of stuff from the Mayfield estate. Miss Lucia Mayfield lived in town for all of her ninety-three years. There were a few souvenirs in the cartons that suggest she may have left town once or twice to take a trip. She was born here, lived here, worked here, and died in the house her grandfather built in 1856."

"And she never married?" Arden asked, not sure if the title was one of respect, or indicative of the woman's marital status.

"She never married, and never had kids. The house and land are going to the town, to be used as a public park. Some of her money is going to the cat shelter, but even if they built a hotel, there wouldn't be enough room for all the cats roaming around the property." Eleanor paused as the door opened and a man came through, dragging a leather trunk.

"Here's another load," he said. "Mostly clothes, I think. But anything you can get for them will be appreciated."

"Of course, Nick," Eleanor said, and waited until he moved past them to the back of the shop. "And the things in the house and the barn are coming here, to help raise money for the cats."

"Antique clothing will do very well," Arden said.

Eleanor looked to be sure Nick was out of range. "If the things in the trunk are like what we received yesterday, we'll have to throw them out. Poor Lucia's cats must have become a little complacent, and mice have gotten into everything."

Nick walked back past them, and gave a little wave. "I'll be back in a few hours."

"Thanks, Nick. And we'll do our best to find some homes for the cats." Eleanor waved back.

"Would you like a cat, or ten?" she asked Arden.

"What do they look like? Are they healthy?"

"They're healthy and gorgeous," Eleanor said. "They're Maine coons. Their thick coats probably saved them in the winter. Lucia warmed the place with a few strategically placed space heaters."

"Let me think about it," Arden said.

"Alex is not allergic to cats," Liza said. "And Miranda gets along fine with them."

"I hope Glinda won't mind. She seems to have settled herself in the cottage," Arden said, trying to be noncommittal and not succeeding.

"We'll go over there later, and you can have your pick," Eleanor said. "But first, come and see this."

Arden followed her to the back room, now piled high with boxes and trunks. A few faded quilts were laid out on the tables, their colors obscured by the layer of cat fur embedded in the cotton fibers. Everything smelled musty. Arden knew if she stayed for any amount of time in the room, she would smell musty herself.

Eleanor gently went through a series of framed photographs, carefully avoiding contact with the nails that secured the prints in their frames, and shards of glass that dropped to the table. She nodded when she came to a large group portrait, and put it into Arden's hands.

The sitting was composed of all women, all in black, all staring so rigidly at the camera they might have been mannequins. But they were real enough, and a closer look revealed some flashes of individuality among the black chintz and lace. Eight women sat in a row in the foreground, and the ten who stood behind them looked grimmer, perhaps for standing while the photographer positioned everything just right.

Even so, one woman must have turned at the last minute, so her face was little more than a blur. Another held a spade in her lap, though could not possibly intend to garden in her costume. One held up a piece of paper that was impossible to read. And another cradled a box. Leafless trees loomed behind them all.

"Is this the Society of Schoolmistresses for Eastfield, or something like that?"

"Let us hope not," Eleanor said. "For they don't look like they would have tolerated so much as a sneeze in the classroom."

"The founding sisters of The Thrifty Means?" Arden guessed again. "They look like they would have been lots of fun to be around."

"Oh, I'm sure they were," Eleanor said. "I believe this is the Ladies' Burial Society. Look where they took the photo."

Arden positioned the print out of the fluorescent glare of the overhead lights and held it closer to her face.

"My goodness. They're standing in a cemetery, aren't they? Please don't tell me that this crew dug the graves."

"I hope not, though I'm sure they were capable of it. No, more likely, they washed the body, comforted the widow, took care of the children. They probably made a collection to provide food and assistance for the family, which means they actually may have been founders of a tradition that later became our shop."

"I think you might have warned me, before I volunteered, that I might be washing the bodies of the dead," Arden said.

"We don't wash their bodies, only their glassware and china." Eleanor said quickly. "Actually, I'm talking about our care of the needy in the town."

"I'm only teasing, Eleanor. I know how much good you all do, and manage to look a lot more cheerful about it than this coven. But it is a wonderful photograph, all the same. Perhaps you should keep it, instead of selling it?"

"Perhaps we should, though the descendents of some of these women may be interested in buying it.

263

You might be yourself. That's your Aunt Portia sitting second on the left."

"How on earth do you know that?" Arden asked.

"Intuition," Eleanor said, "and a handwritten list of names on the back."

"Cheater!" Arden laughed, but focused on the large, frowning woman tightly sandwiched between two companions. She was the one who held the box, and her elbows jutted out into their sides. "She looks like Anne."

"I thought so, too. That is, if Anne ever frowned long enough for a photographer to catch it on film."

"That's because she believes she's always on the stage, always giving a great show for whoever happens to pass by. But I'm her sister. I've seen her frown." Arden took the photo out into the shop itself, where the light was better. "Not like this, though. Aunt Portia could be the poster child for their burial society."

"Death surrounded them in those days. The date on the back is 1904, and who knows how many of them would live to see 1905?"

"Do we have a magnifying glass?" Arden asked, but Eleanor was already passing it to her. She studied the portrait of her aunt, the clothes she wore, and what she held. She knew Eleanor watched her closely. "Do we know which cemetery they're standing in?"

"I believe we do. Do you see that monument there? It belongs to the Liddell family. I remember seeing it when Emma Grace buried her husband."

"Oh, I'm sorry to hear that."

"She wasn't," said Eleanor. "Would you like to go there?"

"To the cemetery? When?"

"Let's go now. Lisa and Jocelyn will look after things, and a few more volunteers are due to show up soon. We'll look around up there, and then go over to check out the cats at the Mayfield place. Nick wants to get them all adopted by the winter."

"There isn't much time," Arden said.

"My point exactly. Let's go," said Eleanor. "Take the photo and we'll be able to figure out the very spot where they posed for that. Not that I think it's a treasure map or anything."

"But you never know," said Arden.

****

Arden had marveled at how much the past remained with the residents of the modern town of Eastfield, and its oldest cemetery was a veritable shrine to that history. It was completely untainted by the technological, electrified world around it. A deeply rutted road snaked its way up the hillside, around boulders that stood in its path and the occasional headstone that must have been set in place before the road was marked out. The wind met no resistance here, and the sun made little gain against the stark, cold landscape.

"It's lovely in the summer," Eleanor said, guessing Arden's thoughts. "I was sitting on that bench over there when I decided to marry Evan."

Arden looked at her in surprise. "I'm sure there are many more romantic spots in town."

"Evan's home is among them. But I wasn't looking for romance. I was looking for a reason, and there's nothing to remind you of the goodness of life as when you're surrounded by the whispers of the dead."

"You know people here," Arden said.

"I do. Several came here long before their time."

Arden supposed she, too, was looking for reasons, but they had to be her reasons. She wondered what stories Eleanor had to tell, and decided they would wait for another time, another place.

"Is there a church here?"

"There was a church here, but it burned down in the 1700s. By then, other churches had been built in town, and I suppose there was never enough money to rebuild. So the church sold the property to the town, and this has been a secular cemetery ever since. That's why a Burial Society was needed."

Arden wrapped her jacket closer to her body. "Does it still exist?"

"I suppose you're hoping that you're not an honorary member?"

"Something like that."

"Don't worry. The last member of the society was Aphrodite Jones who died several years ago, but not before ceding the property to the Historical Society. They administer it now, as a historic site."

"So there are no more burials?"

"There are. I was at a funeral here not long ago. And you'll be happy to know all descendents of the original society may have a plot here for free."

"That's very comforting."

"Alex is a descendent also."

"Of course. We're cousins, after all."

"What? Twenty times removed, or something like that?" Eleanor asked.

"Something like that."

But Eleanor already walked ahead, away from the car, and up a footpath. Arden followed her until the path crested the hill, and a tall monument appeared above the tree line.

"There it is," Eleanor said unnecessarily. "The Liddells are also descendents."

"Why am I not surprised?" Arden asked. "Isn't everyone?"

Eleanor grinned. "I'm not. That's why I had to marry Evan, so I could finally become an official townie. It's a position of distinction."

"You have more right to the title than I do, you know." Arden hesitated and looked around her. "I think this is where they took the photo," she said.

Eleanor retraced her steps and stood beside her, on a fallen gravestone. "Yes, I think you're right. All these graves were not yet here, and the trees have grown, but this seems to be the place."

"I think everything's grown. Has anyone weeded the place recently?"

"Probably not since the summer. There aren't too many visitors these days."

They stood alone on the hillside, looking around them. Here and there, a bouquet of dried flowers marked a grave, and a few tattered flags remained from the patriotic holidays of the spring and summer. Crows watched them from the bare branches of the trees.

"Where are the Trumbulls?" Arden asked.

"I don't actually know, but I recall a gravestone with a quote from Shakespeare. It's the one about abjuring rough magic, from *The Tempest*. Given your family's theatrical tastes, I suppose we might start there," Eleanor said.

"I think the theatrics came from my mother's side of the family," Arden said.

"And yet your aunt was named Portia," Eleanor pointed out. "Come, I think it's over here."

They waded through tall and spiky blades of winter grass, off the path and beyond a stand of ancient trees. Arden paused to read one or two of the stones, and pull up weeds from the tiny lambs marking the graves of children, all unnamed. Everyone who would have known these people were now themselves dead and families had moved away, or passed into obscurity. Eleanor paused and looked around her, clearly at a loss.

But Arden somehow knew where to go.

She walked to Victoria Trumbull's grave as certain of her destination as if there had been a path to lead her there. A tangle of climbing roses, now dead and faded on the vine, a fallen branch from a nearby tree, a broken headstone of a neighboring grave were no deterrent as Arden made her way to the pale granite shaft near the south wall of the graveyard. And there Victoria waited for her.

The stone was plain, without ornamentation, the letters starkly etched to give no information other than a name and the dates of birth and death. There was some sadness in this, and Arden was surprised to find herself moved to tears. Victoria was a relative, a resident of Eastfield, a cousin of the venerable Wingates. And yet, while all the other graves were marked by references to "wife of" or "beloved mother," Victoria Trumbull was an island, entirely of herself.

Arden kneeled in the tall grasses and started to pull the weeds away from the stone. If no one else had come in all these years, perhaps this small gesture would let the community know someone still cared. And in the spring, if she still remained in Eastfield, Arden would bring flowers from the garden, possibly the daffodils she only recently planted.

Eleanor coughed, and Arden was a little embarrassed by what she must look like, kneeling here and crying at the grave of a stranger. She stood up and bumped against the gravestone at her ancestor's feet and, grateful for its support, decided to clear the grass away from that one, as well. When her fingers brushed against the incision of an apex, she guessed she found another Victoria, a relative buried long before anyone's memory. This stone was darker, thinner, and its lettering practically effaced by the elements and by time. But Arden's fingers decisively moved over the letters of "Victoria," and then a name equally familiar.

Arden pulled a clinging stem of ivy off the grave and angled her body so that more sun would fall on the flat slab. Here was another Victoria Trumbull.

"What have you found?" Eleanor asked. "Are we in the right section?"

"We seem to be in the Victoria Trumbull section," Arden said. "I wonder how many there are of them?"

"Well, it's a good solid name in New England," Eleanor said. "Not quite Revere, but very honorable, just the same. Like the Wingates and the Alexanders."

"Do we have a few moments? I've got to see who's here."

"Let me help, or I'll freeze to death," Eleanor said, and started to brush leaves off a fallen stone.

Arden got to work. She pulled up weeds from some of the other nearby graves as names and dates came into view, symbolizing nothing but the transience of human life. There was a space next to the older Victorias which Arden might have disregarded altogether if she hadn't spotted the smallest bit of stone glinting in the waning sunlight. Thinking it a remaining shard from a broken stone, Arden dutifully separated the grass to reveal the eroded form of yet another little lamb.

Arden must have made some small sound, because Eleanor was at her side at once.

"Oh, a baby," she sighed. "I wonder whose it was?"

"There's no name, no date." The child who slept beneath the lamb could have belonged to either Victoria Trumbull, or to neither. And without a marker, or the testimony of anyone who might remember, the poor thing was forever consigned to obscurity. Arden was certain she hadn't ever seen a baby photo among the family relics, but she suddenly envisioned an infant in swaddling clothes, dark eyelashes resting on her pale cheeks, a rosebud mouth with lips slightly parted. Arden's own reddened cheeks were cold as her tears froze on her skin, and she briefly wondered if coming to Eastfield somehow stifled the cool voice of reason that hitherto spoke to her for all of her adult life.

This place got to her; that much was certain. She stood up, her knees damp and a little stiff, and brushed clumps of moss from her wool slacks. Not yet willing to contemplate her future, she would gather none of it, and remain a rolling stone. The two Victorias and the estimable Trumbulls and the long-dead child would never know she had come to visit this day. Nor would the one who lay beyond the child, or the many others making a ribbon of graves across the rocky landscape.

But who was buried beyond the child? Curious, Arden stepped over the lamb, setting loose the seeds from a milkweed pod. She pushed away the tall grass and ran her fingers over the letters on the weathered stone.

"Who is it?" Eleanor asked, and Arden jumped about a foot.

"I'm sorry. I forgot you were there," she answered. "But it looks like we have Joseph Wadsworth here."

"And more compelling two hundred years after his death than I am, apparently. Well, Wadsworth is another of those names in Connecticut. They're all over the place. Especially up in Hartford."

"I know. I've been to their Athenaeum. But why is this one here, in rural Eastfield? And why next to a baby and my two Victorias?

"Oh, are they your Victorias now?" Eleanor grinned as she brushed feathery milkweed seeds off her dark jacket.

"They must be, as no one else seems to claim them." But even as she said the words, Arden knew one of her ancestors had been claimed, even if the connection was not officially acknowledged. Why else would a man and a woman rest in eternal peace next to a child? That they did not share a name was no guarantee of a chaste relationship, as well she knew. And if the townspeople and the church frowned upon promiscuity, public sentiment was merely a deterrent, and not a doctrine.

"Did you say the church burned down here? Was the cemetery desanctified? Is that the right word?"

"Deconsecrated, perhaps?" Eleanor asked. "I have no idea."

Together, they walked down the hill carefully, avoiding the patches of glassy smooth ice.

"Wait, I do have an idea. I haven't thought about this in years. But there is a section in the cemetery of the Methodist church for people who have been reinterred. I heard, years ago, that coffins had been dug up in Norwell, and brought by formal procession to be reburied in sanctified ground. The whole town turned out for it, rather like people along a parade route."

"Dear God, but that's a horrible image. What condition must those coffins have been in?"

"It's not the physical condition that matters, but the state of the soul. Or so I'm told. But here in Connecticut, we haven't been bothered by such metaphysical matters."

"Why do you say that? The old Puritans found fertile soil here. Eastfield is still a dry town. The Blue Laws are still enforced on Sundays."

"Oh, yes. But you can bury your grandma right next to the grave of your golden lab under your front lawn. You can't buy a beer on Sunday, but people can be buried anywhere at all. Except in wetlands."

"Because of the decomposition of the body?"

"Because it might interfere with the mating cycle of spring peepers. Around here, you can't plant a tree in wetlands without written permission and the payment of a bribe."

"I see," said Arden, though she wasn't sure that she did.

"But you want to know if an unmarried couple who made a baby can be buried in this cemetery," Eleanor said, getting them back on track. They reached her car, which had been warming like a greenhouse in the sun.

When they were settled comfortably into the heat of the leather seats, Arden asked, "I suppose we can find church records of the burials. Will we have to get permission to examine them?"

Eleanor started the engine. "It's all waiting for us at the Historical Society, in dozens of shoeboxes waiting to be sorted out. I told you the Society was ceded the deed some years ago, and got the records as a bonus. The volunteers might not see it as much of a bonus, though, as there's always tons of work to do there."

"And I suppose you're a volunteer?" Arden asked.

"Please. They would scarcely let me through the door if I wasn't married to Evan Zane. Again, being a descendent of one of the original families has its privileges. Before we were married, Evan took me to a Society fundraiser and some people were absolutely scandalized."

"But they'll surely let me in?" Arden asked in a small voice. She was pretty sure she didn't want to be associated with such small-mindedness and blatant discrimination.

"And so they will, you lucky girl. But in this case, you needn't worry. I have some connections there myself."

Chapter 13

"We never know what's going to crawl out of a box.
And once in a while, it bites us."
~*Annabel Bishop (volunteer since 1981)*

When Eleanor turned into a narrow drive off
Norwell Road, Arden realized she had no idea the
Historical Society was located here. The property
was clearly once a private estate, as mature trees,
now bare, lined the drive and stone walls created
terraces on the hillside. She expected to see a
farmhouse like Alex's, but instead a stone fortress-
like building came into view. Hand painted signs
directing visitors to a blacksmith shop, a farm, and
an apple orchard were mounted on the old maples.

"Is that one of your connections over there?"
Arden asked. Someone with whom she was
intimately acquainted stood with his back to them,
contemplating something in the garden.

"Oh, is that Alex?" Eleanor asked. "I had no idea
he was planning to be here. But we'll get him to help
us out. I'm sure his broken wrist won't prevent him
from going through some papers."

"His broken wrist doesn't seem to prevent him
from doing anything at all," Arden said tartly, but
when Eleanor looked questioningly at her, she
smiled. "We manage just fine."

"I thought so." Eleanor parked next to the spot
reserved for handicapped drivers, from which Alex's
Jeep was conspicuously absent. By the time they got
out of the car, Alex stood at the hood.

"What brings you here?" he asked, not bothering

273

to hide his pleasure.

"Your relatives," Eleanor said and brushed something off his shoulder. If he noticed, he paid no attention, as his eyes were on Arden as she came around to the driver's side of the car. "And hers."

"We came to look over the burial records for Victoria Trumbull and Joseph Wadsworth. And possibly another person as well."

"And I came to look over the garden for a good site for a sculpture. Next summer will be the Society's one hundredth anniversary." Alex looked down, realized he was stamping down some herbs, and stepped onto the flagstone path. "I'm supposed to create the 'Spirit of Eastfield' or something like that. I'm looking for inspiration."

"Well, maybe you'll find it in the library. When you get tired of standing out here in the cold, join us. We'll be the ones surrounded by decomposing paper and cardboard boxes."

"It sounds like The Thrifty Means," Alex said.

"Well, let's just say it feels like home," Eleanor said, and pulled Arden toward the open door of the stone house. Arden looked back to where Alex stood and she knew he would join them soon.

Eleanor introduced Arden to Shannon MacRae, a tall, efficient-looking woman with reading glasses poised on the very tip of her nose. She explained what they intended to do, and Shannon offered her approval with a gesture of despair. "I wish you well, but it could take years to get through that stuff. Goodness knows what kind of filing system was popular in the nineteenth century, but you wonder why no one in Eastfield hit upon the idea of an alphabetical listing."

"Do you have a site plan?" Arden asked.

"No, that would be a little too easy. What we have are monographs, little bits of oral history that someone decided to transcribe into notebooks.

Wherever there is mention of a person buried in the cemetery, someone has starred the name in red. I hope it's ink, but DNA tests might reveal the names are written in the blood of the deceased."

"Thanks for sharing that, Shannon. Can we work in the library?" Eleanor asked. "We need enough room for three of us."

"Oh, you've enlisted Alex Wingate's help? Maybe he'll find his inspiration there."

Eleanor glanced at Arden. "I'm sure he will," she said.

****

The library was, in fact, a closet only slightly larger than Arden's car. Its contents spilled out into the foyer of the second floor of the museum and onto a round table surrounded by a few folding chairs.

"What was this place, anyway?" Arden asked.

Eleanor looked around, as if seeing it for the first time. "Perhaps a dressing room? Or a baby's nursery?"

"I mean, this building. Was it someone's house?"

"Oh, yes. The Campbells lived here since the seventeen hundreds. After their home burned down a few times, they rebuilt in stone. They weren't farmers, though. They owned the mercantile, the building that is now the Eastfield Market. All the Campbells are gone, now, and they left their home to the town about thirty-five years ago."

"But the Historical Society is a hundred years old," Arden pointed out.

"So we're told. Before they acquired this place, everything was crammed into the basement of Town Hall."

"Instead of being crammed into here," came a voice from the stairway.

Arden and Eleanor looked up to watch Alex approach, filling the space at the top of the stairs.

"Well, that didn't take long. I think I'll go see if

Shannon needs a hand," said Eleanor.

"No, really, Eleanor, we'll make enough room for all of us here," Arden said.

Eleanor looked from Arden to Alex. "This is your family's business, and it may turn out to be none of mine. It's hard to imagine, but there are probably a few secrets left in Eastfield."

Alex waited until they heard her footsteps on the floorboards down below. "There might be, but our relationship isn't one of them."

"Well, I knew that from the beginning," Arden said and raised her chin as he bent down to kiss her. "We never had a chance at any privacy."

"We'll do our best," he said cheerfully, and unfolded two of the metal chairs. "What are we looking for, by the way?"

"Anything at all about Victoria and Joseph, and the possibility they were married, or intended to be married. I think they had a baby."

"How old were they?" Alex asked, as he read the hand written labels on the cartons around them. "Maybe they were very young."

"Do you think they were teenage sweethearts?" Arden looked at the boxes stacked on her side of the foyer and pulled one out.

"I wonder if they are brother and sister, and the child between them another sibling who died years before."

"Oh!" Arden said, surprised she didn't think of it herself, and then reconsidered. "No, I doubt it. They have different last names."

"They could have different fathers. Or Victoria might have married a Trumbull when she was little more than a kid. Their families might have buried them together."

"So this is your way of telling me this search might be harder than we thought?"

It wasn't. Someone had already stashed the files

of Eastfield's earliest history on the top of a cabinet supported on one side by a thick phone book. Alex and Arden sat quietly in their dusty sanctuary created by the ephemera and carefully sorted through fragile papers and small artifacts.

"Someone ought to take better care to preserve these papers, or everything will be lost," Arden said.

"They can't afford to pay for another full time staff person, and the interns who come down from the high school don't stay long enough to learn how to do it properly," Alex said. "I believe they're waiting for someone new to come to town, who's both motivated and experienced."

Arden paused, her hand on what appeared to be a faded bill of sale for a dump rake, and met his eyes.

"Of course, The Thrifty Means has gotten you first. But just in case things don't work out there, you may wish to consider putting in some time at the Historical Society." He looked into his carton.

"But like the high school kids, I may not be here long enough to do the job," Arden said, wondering what he might have to say to that.

"Perhaps you will," he said, still not meeting her eyes.

"And even if I do, I will have to find a real job, one that will allow me to support myself in this pricey little town."

That got him. He looked up and smiled as if he knew some secret of which she was unaware.

"Perhaps you won't," he said succinctly, but conveyed a world of meaning.

He looked back down into the carton and surprised Arden by pulling out a scroll. She imagined he had been simply avoiding her when he looked into the box. But now he flattened it on the small square of table that remained uncluttered and murmured something under his breath.

"What do you have there?" Arden asked. "Is it something about the Trumbulls or the Wadsworths?"

"Both," Alex answered, and shifted his seat so that the light fell directly on the scroll. "Some of this we already know. Jonathan Trumbull, the colonial governor, supported the revolutionaries and Joseph Wadsworth was the fellow who stashed away the colonial charter way back in the days of King James. There's nothing to connect them, aside from the fact their stories appear in the same paragraph. And here's that Eastfield connection, just like Larry said. A Trumbull cousin removed himself from the enemy camp in Hartford to the—and I quote—'congenial and loyal environs of Eastfield near the city of Norwell, taking his possessions with him.' "

"Well, of course he took his possessions with him. If he had to get out of Hartford before an angry mob found him fishing along the banks of the Connecticut River, or something of that sort, he probably packed up everything he had." Arden shrugged. "It may have amounted to nothing more than a cartload."

"That's right. So if it's that obvious, why mention it?"

Arden realized her head ached. The dust and close quarters contributed to her pain, to be sure, but she also recognized the mind-bending challenges of deciphering a mystery with very little to go on.

"Perhaps the chronicler mentioned it because there might have been incriminating evidence among his possessions?" She ventured a guess.

"And perhaps it was known by neighbors in Eastfield that that incriminating evidence was now to be found somewhere in our wooded acres. If the townspeople were Loyalists, such a thing might be fiercely protected."

"And buried next to my house in a stone casket? They would do better than that, I think. Does the author of your scroll say anything about it?" Arden reached for the paper.

Alex handed it over, his fingers brushing hers. "If you're looking for an announcement that the sacred Charter is now on display at the town meeting hall, you're going to be disappointed. We don't even know what the hell we're looking for."

"It must have to do with Quercus Chartula," Arden said with more conviction than she felt. "What else do we have? A box, an engraving of an oak tree, and a date."

Alex didn't answer, and pulled another carton off the cabinet. He seemed determined to find something, and Arden didn't have the heart to discourage him, especially as he had determinedly taken up her mission. She looked over the tiny scripted letters of the scroll, seeing nothing.

"This box is mislabeled," Alex said suddenly. He held up a leather bound book and as he thumbed through it, Arden could make out tinted etchings on many of the pages. "This book was published in 1885."

"It looks like an art book."

"It is, on the great English painters in the Royal Academy." He fingered the other papers in the box with his good hand. "Maybe it was just thrown in here by accident. Everything else seems to be from the colonial period."

Arden's headache vanished in a moment. If she knew anything about her field of study, it was that there usually were reasons when something was done "by accident."

"Is there a Table of Contents? Is there anything about Gainsborough or *The Harvest Wagon*?"

"Why don't you look for that," Alex said as he handed her the book, "while I check to see how much Miss Abigail Warren paid for a goat in 1769."

Arden didn't bother to answer, but began

studying the book. It was an expensive edition, published in Boston. She checked for signatures in the flyleaf and slips of paper ticked between the pages. She tapped the binding, to discern anything irregular about the stitching. And she looked through the pages for anything, even the slightest reference to a companion piece to *The Harvest Wagon*.

There was nothing, not on that, nor any indication any of Gainsborough's much-admired works were sold in the colonies before the Revolution. Of course, by 1771, he was commanding fairly high prices for his paintings in England, and those likely to buy his works abroad most likely lived in New York or Boston or Hartford, but certainly not in Eastfield.

Arden looked past Alex's shoulder, out the narrow window, and realized it was beginning to get dark. This time of day seemed to her a magic hour, when townspeople returned from whatever concerned them during the day, to Eastfield's solitude and peace, to its sanity and order. It was hard to imagine such a place to be a setting for political intrigue two hundred years before. What better place to hide something, or retire into obscurity?

Is that what Alex offered her, if in fact his oblique comments were intended to be a promise? Would she shelve her professional life and spend her days as the partner of a famous man? Or would she work with him and create the artists' retreat he vaguely spoke about, while volunteering her spare hours for the betterment of the community?

A knock on the wall broke her reverie, and Arden looked around, confused.

"It's almost closing time," Alex said. "I guess we haven't found anything that can't be put off for a while?"

"No, there's nothing here. Just a nice book about nice paintings, undoubtedly written by a nice man." Arden sighed, sorry it didn't contain a nice reproduction of the painting over her hearth.

"Then how about a nice dinner?"

"If nice means Ludlum's, I'm good to go. They won't mind if we bring in a few spiders, would they?"

"All the better. Spiders eat roaches, don't they?" Alex asked and gently replaced his papers in the cardboard box. By doing so, he was able to avoid Arden's look of horror.

****

If there were any ingredients in Arden's hamburger other than those listed, they didn't preclude her from getting a good night's sleep. She tumbled into bed soon after Alex left her off in her driveway, and dreamed of farming and oak trees and fishing in the Connecticut River, and Alex Wingate. She might well have continued dreaming through the day, when she was awakened by someone singing, off-key, outside her bedroom window. Someone was working in her garden, scraping against stone.

She stretched as thoroughly as she could in her narrow twin bed, and opened her eyes. Outside her window, a fierce flurry of snowflakes danced against a gray sky.

She jumped out of bed. Alex must have caught her movement in the glass because he stopped shoveling her walkway and waved a gloved hand at her. She ran to the door, not caring about her wrinkled tee or her hair curling like a mad halo around her head.

"What are you doing out here?" she cried out into the snowstorm, her voice eerily echoing in the silent woods. "You're going to hurt your wrist!"

Alex walked through four inches of unshoveled snow and used her doormat to remove clumped ice from his boots. He used his teeth to pull off his left glove, and reached out to finger one of those curls, in his thoughtful, quietly observant way. She wondered if his daily experiences were stored in a creative reservoir for some future use.

"You're going to get cold out here," he said, though he didn't relinquish his hold.

Arden was so warm she was surprised her hair wasn't on fire. "If you had just given me a little time, I would have come out and shoveled my own walk. And I would have dressed for the occasion," she said.

"It is an occasion," he said. "That's why I'm shoveling your walk, so you can come with me."

"Back to the Historical Society?"

"Even better. Back to the hospital."

Now she felt her body go cold and she shivered. "What's the matter? Did you hurt yourself again?"

She looked at him carefully, trying to discern signs of pain but he looked almost too healthy. His dark hair was damp with sweat and stood out in little spiky edges around his ears and neck; the melting snowflakes glistened and disappeared. His down vest hung from a nearby tree branch, and he seemed comfortable enough in an old blue chambray shirt.

"I never felt better," he said, and she believed him. "We're going back to the hospital so they can crack open my shell."

"Well, you certainly don't need me," she said, and pulled him into the warm cottage. "You've already proved you can drive very well by yourself, and once they take the cast off, it'll be a cinch."

He nodded, though he suddenly looked less sure of the day's outcome.

"What? Do you have reason to believe things won't go well?" she asked.

"You never know about these things, I'm told," he said in a low voice.

"Oh, doctors are always leaving the door ajar, just in case things don't work out perfectly. But you had a clean break, you've been mostly good about taking care of it, and you're fairly young. It'll be fine."

"So, you won't come with me?"

"Do you want me to come with you?"

"Isn't that where this conversation started?"

Arden looked at him, utterly familiar with his face and body, his moods and motives. That he was an accomplished artist seemed the least interesting thing about him, just a footnote to the whole man.

"I think this conversation really started on the day you coerced me to take you to the hospital, when an ambulance would have been much more efficient. And, undoubtedly, wiser." She pulled his face down to her level and kissed him.

He stayed where he was, the melting snow on his shirt and gloves dripped onto the doormat.

"I don't recall coercing you into doing anything. It's not my style." He pressed a cold cheek against her forehead. "I thought you would want to do the neighborly thing."

"Is that what all this has been about?" Arden sighed.

"No," he answered succinctly. "I assure you, if Lilianna Durant was my neighbor, I would have sooner walked to Norwell than ask for her help."

"Who is Lilianna Durant?"

"Ask your friend Eleanor about Lilianna. I think Evan practically had to use a forklift to get the old witch out of the house before he married Eleanor."

"She's a relative?"

"She was the long-time companion of his aunt. Make of that what you will."

"I see," Arden said. "This town continually surprises me. It seems so conservative, so traditional in most ways. And then something is revealed that is just the opposite."

"Eastfield's untraditional types are a long part of the town tradition. After all, the extremely unpopular Loyalists found a safe haven here. Artists, actors and musicians have populated the place for generations. And people of different religions and races were settled here before the Civil War. It's a good place."

"I wonder what it was like for Victoria Trumbull and Joseph Wadsworth." Arden really wondered about that little lamb who slept between them.

"I wonder why we're having a history lesson in your foyer when we have an appointment with the surgeon in a half hour," Alex said, a little gruffly. "Unless you want to show up in your T-shirt."

When had "I" become "we?" Arden stepped back from him and looked up at his face. Perhaps it was time she trusted him, and allowed herself to believe that not all his decisions were based on getting her to sell him the cottage. She ought to admit that somehow she and Alex were a pair since that wretched encounter in his barn, when she pulled him up from the floor and led him down to her garage. And then pulled him up again when he fell into the hole she dug for her promise of spring flowers. Those bulbs might not have been the grandest things planted that day.

"Give me ten minutes to shower and dress," she said softly. "And don't walk on my pine floors with those wet boots."

****

Alex stayed just where she left him, savoring the warmth of her cottage and the lingering caress of her forehead against his thawing cheek. Anne never liked it here, and her sojourns to Eastfield seemed nothing more than an obligatory return to her family's rugged past, and possibly to make sure he hadn't burned down the place in her long absence.

284

As a result, he told himself he wasn't entirely selfish to believe this cottage could be his, and he would be doing the Alexander sisters a favor by buying it. After all, as he already owned the land beneath it, where would they ever find another buyer? And how could he guess that Arden was not another indifferent traveler, passing through history—both his and the town's? Everything seemed so simple, until she arrived.

But after her first morning, Arden proved herself a real Eastfielder. She embraced the land, the seasons, the quirky attributes of her ancient cottage. And best of all, she embraced him.

He spent years attending parties as the resident eligible bachelor, and casually had affairs with a number of equally eligible women. He always found some excuse to break it off, move on, and retreat to his sanctuary in the Eastfield woods. Sometimes he wondered if there was something lacking in his own character.

But on the day he looked down the hill and caught a flash of color and light in the open windows of the cottage, he knew the only thing he lacked was her. She could have been a horror, for all he knew, but when she glared up at him from the confines of her stalled car, he recognized the face of the one he had been looking for. She was beautiful, as no woman had ever been beautiful before.

"I just need to find my keys," Arden said as she rushed back into the room.

And she was always on time, he added to himself.

"You don't need your keys. We'll take my car," he said. "It has better traction in the snow."

She paused to look at him. Her hair was wet and slick against her scalp, and left a circular stain of dampness along the shoulders of her turtleneck sweater. Without stepping off the mat, he pulled her fleece jacket off the coat tree next to the door, and held it out for her to walk right into.

"You'll need a hat," he said.

"I have a hat," she said impatiently. "What I need are my keys."

God, he loved her.

"We won't be gone that long. Just leave everything as it is."

"And we know how that worked out before," she said. "We were at the hospital that time, too."

"So we were," he mused, leaning over to sniff her shampooed hair. She smelled like summer. "It seems like a million years ago, and not six weeks."

"I'm sure the Eastfield police will take a million years to solve the crime." She put her hand in her jacket pocket and he heard the unmistakable sound of jingling keys. Her mood improved in an instant. "But they undoubtedly have more pressing cases, like tracking down people who park in the handicapped spot at the Market."

"And stopping drivers going five miles over the speed limit on Norwell Road. Which might be me, if we don't get out of here soon," he said. He opened the door and stepped out into the frosty air, drawing in deep breaths as Arden locked the door behind them.

He handed his own keys to her as they entered his garage. Her initial look of surprise changed to satisfaction as she buckled up and backed out into the driveway. The plow guy had already come through, leaving ridges of frozen terrain and a mountain of snow that surely would remain on the side of the garage until early April.

"I asked him to do your driveway as well," Alex said.

"How did you know I didn't hire my own guy?"

"If you did, we'll let them joust it out with shovels in front of your garage door."

"Well, that will surely deter any thieves."

"That, and the fact they may already have what they wanted," he said as they turned onto Norwell Road.

"What did they want?" Arden asked, distractedly. "How many times have I asked that question in six weeks?"

"Something," Alex said, confidently. "They wanted something."

"Well, I know what I want," Arden said.

"What might that be?" Alex straightened in his seat, even more confident.

"I want to know who Joseph Wadsworth was," she said, cautiously passing a mail truck.

This was not the answer Alex was expecting, though he wasn't surprised to know she was dreaming about a dead man when he hoped she was dreaming about him.

"We already know who he was. He hid the damned charter from the English."

"A Joseph Wadsworth did that, to be sure. But you know who I mean. I'm bothered by the one born about a hundred years later. He died in 1801, and they buried him with Victoria and a baby. Why? I dreamt about the cemetery yesterday and woke up realizing they are buried in a corner of the site, though surrounded by a lot of people."

"Maybe it was the place set aside for sinners?" Alex asked. "I imagine it would be very crowded there. I hope they saved a place for me."

Arden glanced at him. "Eleanor told me there's always a place for the descendants of the original Eastfielders. Are you afraid they'll make an exception in your case?"

"Almost certainly," he said happily.

Arden did not look nearly as amused. "She also told me the place was disaffiliated from the church a very long time ago. Maybe the townspeople were

287

reluctant to let old habits fall by the wayside. If Tory and Joe weren't married, their families might have succumbed to some local pressure."

"You're assuming a lot, aren't you?" Alex asked.

"Do you mean, by calling them Tory and Joe?" Arden grinned as she glanced into the rear view mirror.

"No, I mean by assuming that they might have been a couple, or that the baby was theirs. We didn't find anything at the Historical Society to prove that."

Arden was silent for some minutes, though he wasn't sure if it was because she was navigating her way through traffic or thinking about their ancestors, buried beneath the snow.

"I am relying on my instincts on this, and nearly everything else. We may never understand why a stone box was buried, or why there's an extraordinary painting fastened to my wall, or why someone ransacked my house, or why Tory and Joe have different last names. But the only way I ever make sense of anything is by creating a narrative, a story that holds everything together. Tory and Joe have a story; I just haven't figured it out yet."

"Or made it up?" Alex asked and caught her scowling at him. "Okay, I'll give it a try. Victoria Trumbull and Joseph Wadsworth were caught in a sudden snowstorm and sought shelter in a little stone cottage. One thing led to another, and nine months later, she had a baby."

Alex, more than willing to abandon the subject and try to solicit the last moments of her pity for his broken wrist, hoped that would put an end to it. But, of course, Arden was not yet ready to let it go.

"Why didn't she just marry him?"

"The usual reasons, I support. Perhaps he had a girl in every port. Maybe he was considered objectionable by her family."

"Perhaps the Trumbulls and the Wadsworths were the Capulets and the Montagues of their own time? That might have been the start of the family's interest in Shakespeare."

"What were the Capulets and Montagues fighting about, anyway?" Alex asked, forgetting about his wretched wrist.

"I don't really know. They were powerful families. Perhaps there was some political intrigue? It was a volatile time."

"As was the time when our own hero and heroine lived," Alex said softly, thinking over his own words very carefully. "Eastfield was a hot bed of Loyalist sympathies. Joseph Wadsworth, if truly a namesake to the more famous one, might have been a regular activist, a revolutionary of the first order. If Victoria loved him, her family might have disowned her or banished her, as Romeo was banished."

"Well, that's a good story. But Romeo killed someone before he was banished."

"And Victoria might have been pregnant, which might have been the greater offense to the family name."

"But surely they would not have closed the door on her; her family could not have been so cruel."

"Why not?" Alex asked, enjoying himself immensely. "Families still do that sort of thing today, if a child is considered beyond redemption. Besides, they might have assumed she'd go to her lover for protection, no matter how reprehensible they thought him."

"And these are our common ancestors. Perhaps the kindest thing we can say about them is that they left us some very valuable real estate." Arden frowned as she was reminded of the truth. "Well, you were left the real estate and a farmhouse and a barn. I was left a cottage the size of your living room."

"Which has been passed down from one generation of women to the next, as curious a thing as ever existed. It's also a pretty clunky easement on my own deed, though at such time when there are no longer female heirs to Victoria Trumbull's line, the owner of my property inherits the cottage."

Arden tapped her fingers on the steering wheel while she waited for a light to change. He wasn't sure why she was impatient; by his own reckoning they had all of three minutes to spare.

"That would be a pity, I think," she said. "The cottage must have served as a refuge for these two hundred years, a place where a solitary woman might go to find solace. Or herself, as the case might be."

"Or separate herself from a family who no longer accepted her?" Alex realized this narrative thing was more fun than he imagined. "Perhaps, in their rugged society of early Eastfield, banished meant living a hundred yards away from their front door in a cottage of her own?"

Arden turned to him in surprise, her dark brows arched like punctuation points on her brow. The driver behind them jammed on his horn, as if trying to wake the dead.

But they already awakened the dead. A story had taken hold while they rode along the old country path that was now Norwell Road, with its traffic lights and impatient drivers, and Victoria and Joseph now seemed more real to him than any ghosts he invoked in the old farmhouse.

Arden turned the corner a bit too sharply and the car fishtailed to the right.

"Here we are," she said, as the stark edifice of the hospital loomed above them.

It took Alex a moment to remember why they had come.

They were both quietly lost in their own thoughts as they entered the surgeon's exam room, a sign he interpreted as their unease with the procedure.

After he spent five minutes explaining what he was about to do, Alex made a gesture of impatience. "Why don't you just do it already?" he asked irritably.

"Is your husband always so grouchy?" the surgeon asked, reaching for a cast saw.

Though intrigued by the device, Alex was more curious by the expression on Arden's face. Six weeks ago, the assumption about their relationship rattled her; today she seemed to accept it.

"You can hardly blame him, since he's had a great excuse to do nothing for all this time. Now he'll have to go back to work," she said. Alex supposed it was as good a story as the one they just concocted.

"I bet you're looking forward to that," the surgeon said as the blade sliced open the plaster.

"No, actually," Arden said. "The past six weeks have been wonderful."

Predictably, the cast was off in less time than it took to tell about it. Alex looked down at the strange white thing that appeared to be attached to his arm, and finally recognized his hand in the rubble of the plaster. He braced himself for pain as he flexed his wrist, but aside from a little stiffness, everything felt fine.

"This is your time to ask if you can now play the violin," the surgeon said. "That's supposed to be a joke."

"Can I now sculpt?" Alex asked, earnestly.

"That's a new one," the surgeon said, and laughed. "Sure, go ahead."

He was still laughing as Arden and Alex gathered their things and escaped.

Chapter 14

"A good snow buries the mistakes of the fall."
~*Mike Riley (Owner of Rosy Outlook Nursery)*

Hours later, they sat at the table in the cottage, sharing an omelet Arden hurriedly put together , and a fruity wine Alex claimed was made from grapes grown along the river. Neither the food nor the drink was half-bad.

Miranda, sitting under the table, approved of the omelet or at least what parts of it went flying onto the kitchen floor. Alex was not yet adept at managing a knife and a fork.

"I think you were better at this when you had a broken wrist. At least, I don't remember having to duck from flying pieces of food," Arden said. "Do you want me to cut it for you?"

"You can't blame me for this," Alex said. He held up his knife, which was slightly bent. "How can you cut anything?"

"I seem to be managing just fine," Arden said, and shrugged. They'd known each other six weeks or so, and they already sounded like they were married for years. "Anyway, this is part of my inheritance."

"I think you're allowed to throw out bent knives and broken forks," he said as a piece of meat slipped off the table. Glinda edged ahead of Miranda and caught it before it hit the floor.

"I'm not taking any chances, or I'll be buried in a corner of the cemetery with murderers and thieves. I'm glad the ghost of Victoria didn't come knocking when I washed the curtains."

"Maybe she chased away the intruder when he trashed the place. That mess would have had her turning in her grave."

Arden smiled over her glass of wine. "Things looked pretty quiet when I was at the cemetery with Eleanor. But I wonder, would all the household items be included with the sale of the cottage? If someone like you were to buy it, that is."

"I haven't thought about it, but I suppose they would."

"And why would a new owner feel any sense of obligation to hold on to this stuff? I'm tempted to pack most of it up and bring it down to The Thrifty Means." Arden ran her finger over a chip in her wineglass. "What would stop me other than a guilty conscience?"

"Nothing. We already know it's a nutty stipulation that wouldn't hold up in court."

"So what's the point of including it in the will? It can only be enforced by years of habit, and will be negated when the place is finally sold. Why would Victoria restrict the creative impulses of so many generations of women?"

"Because she was crazy, living here by herself in the woods?" He looked across the table and caught Arden's expression of indignation. "No, I'm sure that's not it. Maybe she just wanted everything to stay in the family."

"Maybe she was hiding something."

"Maybe we already found the hiding place and it was empty."

"You're talking about the stone box. But it wasn't in the house. There's something else here, meant for Victoria's heirs to find. And whoever broke in six weeks ago and trashed the place somehow knew about it." Arden sat back in her seat and crossed her arms, watching for his reaction.

"Well, don't look at me. I was with you at the

293

time."

"How do I know you didn't hire someone?"

"And break my wrist at the appointed time, so I could get you out of the house? That would be quite a plan." He rose from his seat, flattened his hands on the small table, and leaned toward her. "You're starting to sound as nutty as your Aunt Portia."

Arden stood on her side of the small table and mimicked his pose. "It's part of my inheritance. We're hopeless romantics, you know."

"Not so hopeless, perhaps." He leaned farther over the remainders of their meal, as did she, until their lips met.

The sweet wine tasted better on him than in the glass, and the barrier between them made her impatient. Slowly, without parting her lips from his, she moved around the perimeter of the table, as they came closer together. His arms came around hers and the lightness of his touch, without the bulky weight of the cast, made her shiver.

"What would Victoria say about this?" he asked, as his lips paused over the tip of her nose.

Arden sighed, moving her hands up the length of his body to meet at his neck. "I have a feeling you're not the first man to explore the contents of the cottage."

"And find the hidden treasure? I don't know what the other guys wanted, but I can now die a contented man." He picked her up and onto the tiled counter and she wrapped her legs around him. She laughed and made a small sound of pleasure. And whatever else needed to be said waited, along with the dishes, until the morning.

****

It was still snowing at dawn. The dark skies and absence of any school buses lumbering down Old Tory Lane made a perfect excuse to stay in bed. Alex made that decision when he opened one eye and decided that whatever remained of his energy would be better spent exploring Arden's sleeping body. She said something in her sleep and turned to him, finding his shoulder a warm but hard pillow. He closed his eye.

Outside, the wind howled under the eaves of the roof and battered a loose shutter. Sleet splattered against the window and the aged furnace sputtered and fired in the basement beneath their bed.

But it was the cottage itself that spoke to him, gently reminding him that other men slept in this bed, in this sanctuary of women. Alex moved slightly, so as not to disturb Arden, and stared at the ceiling. Pine strips made a checkerboard of the plaster and here and there, patched sections revealed previous repairs. Perhaps the roof leaked, or an animal gnawed its way out of the dark attic. When had he last been up in the attic? How thick were the walls, the space between the floors? A woman could hide anything in even so small a place as the cottage, and keep her secret from the men in her life.

If he had something to hide, he would make a trapdoor in the ceiling or in the pine floor with its oversized boards. But where would a woman hide her valuables? If she wasn't handy herself, she'd have to hire someone to build her a secret niche. That meant that someone else would share the secret, someone she would necessarily trust.

But if she had a hidden trapdoor, why would it be necessary to forbid any attempt to move things about? Perhaps, like Poe's purloined letter, the answer was in plain sight.

"This mattress is so lumpy," Arden complained. Her eyes were still closed.

"That's not the mattress, Princess, it's my shoulder," he said, though he thought she was already back asleep. That got him thinking about the mattress and if anything was sewn into it. But he could feel the springs in this one—especially the one drilling into his hip—and guessed the original horsehair model had been thrown out years ago. Hadn't he read about a woman who surprised her mother with a new mattress and sent a million dollars and the old one to the town dump?

Whatever was hidden, whatever might have once been of value, might be buried under a hundred years of refuse at the town dump.

But it would have to wait a while longer, as Arden fingers were walking across his chest and dipped under the quilt.

****

"What are we doing today?" Arden asked some time later. They were still in bed and the storm was raging just as fiercely outside, but the storm within had abated and they were both exhausted and exhilarated. She wondered if she presumed too much by her question, but they just spent the night together, after all. And it was a habit to which she could get very accustomed.

With a short bark, Miranda announced the first order of business, and Arden realized the poor lab had been in the bedroom with them all night. Wordlessly, Alex pulled himself out of bed, leaving a warm spot where his body had been. As Arden moved over, he pulled an afghan off a quilt rack, and wrapped himself in it as he made his way to the door. Arden heard his footsteps, and the clicking of Miranda's paws, across the wood floor, through the kitchen, and the metallic click of the bolt on the back door. Miranda barked as she ran outside—she was probably desperate—and did her business very quickly. A few moments later, the door closed and Alex seemed to be complaining about something.

"There's snow all over the place," he grumbled as he got back into bed, pushing her over.

"That's what happens when it snows," Arden said, pushing back.

"I mean, inside the house." Miranda pattered back into the room and shook herself out for good measure. Alex held up the quilt like a shield, and Arden folded herself up against the blast of cold air.

"I've been thinking," he said, when he tucked the quilt back around them.

"So have I," she said. "But you go first."

"Okay, for starters, tell me if you could cut a trapdoor in the floor."

"You mean, me personally? And a trapdoor with hinges and a latch and maybe a little stairway going down into the basement?"

"That's fancier than I imagined, but, yeah. That would work."

"No."

"That's it? Just 'no?' "

"What more can I say? I never took shop class or anything. If you recall, I barely could figure out how to turn off your damned chain saw when you had the accident."

"So you would have to hire someone to install one for you. Just as I thought."

"Why? Are you looking for some extra work? I also have a leaky toilet you might want to check out."

"A bathroom would be a perfect place to hide something, now that I think of it. No one ever looks there."

Arden waited to answer while they listened to a snowplow roar up Old Tory Lane.

"The intruders did," she said. "When we came home that day, the lid was off the toilet and the contents of the medicine cabinet were strewn all over the floor."

"I wonder if they found what they wanted."

"Yes...rusty razor blades and outdated aspirin. I

hope they're happy with the loot." She ran a hand under her head and spread her hair on the pillow. Alex reached for a curly tendril and ran it back and forth beneath his nose. "So you've been thinking about good hiding places."

"That, and other things. What have you been thinking about?" he said.

Arden took a deep breath.

"I think there's a copy of the old colonial charter here, on this property, probably in the house. Victoria Trumbull was somehow connected to the scapegrace Joseph Wadsworth, who was related to the Wadsworth who hid a copy of it in the old oak. Victoria kept it in the stone box, but then moved it for safekeeping sometime after 1774. Wherever she put it, she wanted to ensure it would not be moved from its place, so she made it a term of the inheritance that nothing would ever be moved."

Alex let out his breath. "Well, that's pretty succinct. Do you have anything, other than a vivid imagination, to make you think this is true?"

"It's just a feeling. It sort of came to me before I went to sleep."

He turned his head sharply to look down at her, and she smiled. "Well, it wasn't the only thing."

"I'm glad to hear that." Alex stretched his long body, and Arden realized he would have been more comfortable if they had spent the night in his larger bed. "Now tell me why they buried the box, if nothing was in it."

Arden said nothing for a long time, until Alex nudged her. She cleared her throat. "I think it was a coffin for their baby, Victoria's and Joseph's. When the baby died, the cemetery land was still consecrated, so he couldn't be buried there. But later, when the church burned down and was never rebuilt, it was possible to reinter the body, and let it rest between them."

"And rebury an empty coffin? I'm not sure that theory would hold up to any scrutiny."

"So let's leave that for now," Arden said. "Something is hidden in this house. I can just feel it."

And the odd thing was, she really thought she could.

"Well that answers your question, doesn't it? We'll spend the day looking for we-know-not-what in we-know-not-where."

"I was hoping you'd say that," she said, looking forward to the challenge, especially as it meant a day with no one but Alex Wingate for company.

"And while we're at it, I'll fix your leaky toilet."

Goodness, could Heaven be any better than this?

"I was hoping you'd say that, too," she added.

After sharing a shower, Arden's bottle of herbal shampoo, and the one large-sized towel, they shared a box of cereal and milk for breakfast. Alex dashed up the hill to his house with Miranda at his heels, but was back down, in a clean flannel shirt and brown corduroy slacks, before Arden finished the dishes.

"What do you have there?" she asked, when he pulled a large manila envelope from under his shirt.

"Almost everything your sister gave me pertaining to the cottage. It's mostly receipts for work done, and a few blueprints, but you never know what could be handy. And, before you ask, there's nothing about a charter or an oak or a stone coffin."

"That would be too easy," Arden murmured. "Well, do we divide and conquer? Why don't we start in the two bedrooms? The light is brightest there now, even in the snow, and then we can move into the living room in the afternoon."

"It practically is the afternoon, but I see your point. If you start in the master bedroom—I guess I should say the mistress bedroom—I'll fix the toilet and then catch up in the other room. Unless the voice that came to you directs you to a double wall or something."

"It wasn't that specific," Arden said tartly, though she knew Alex was prepared to follow her instincts. It was a measure either of his trust, or of an absurd willingness to please her. She hoped it might be both.

They were busy in their separate rooms for over an hour when Arden paused in her exploration. She had already tapped every inch of the floorboards and pulled a collection of old junk out of the hope chest and drawers. Outside, the wind was still howling and the snow was already at the height of the stone wall. The plow came by periodically with a sander in its wake. The occasional glare of headlights in the window suggested that some of her neighbors ventured out, even in the storm.

A few rooms away, Alex was busy soldering bathroom pipes and making a mess of the place. Miranda sat on the floor outside the bathroom, ever watchful that he might happen to pull a steak out of his pocket.

Arden heard a tapping, which she assumed to be coming from the bathroom. But then she heard it again, and realized it came from the other direction, past the living room.

She opened the front door, letting in a shower of snow and Hammond Riley.

"Hammond! Is everything all right?" she asked, reaching for his hat when he took it off his head. He bent and kissed her on the cheek with icy lips.

She stepped backward and repeated herself. "Is everything all right?"

"Of course. I was just worried about you. I haven't seen you in days, and I thought you might be unwell. And with this storm and all, I thought you would appreciate a peace offering. I have some bread and rolls and chicken salad here." He handed her a shopping bag and unwrapped his scarf from around his neck.

"I have a phone," she said, and then realized how ungenerous she sounded. The man had just risked his life in a snowstorm, for goodness sakes. He brought her food. He was worried about her.

It was just that it was a very small cottage to share with two large men.

"Come in, of course," she said. "But what brought you out in the first place? The roads must be awful."

"They're not so bad," he said, slipping out of his coat. "I went to work as usual. But Town Hall is locked up and closed for the day."

"But why didn't someone let you know before you left your house? Shouldn't they put it on the website or call in to the radio station?"

Hammond shrugged his shoulders, dislodging some more snow. "I didn't check. But then I went to the Market and picked up the groceries. I thought we might share some lunch."

"That's a lovely idea," Arden said, wondering how she should announce Alex's presence. "Come into the kitchen."

Behind her, she heard Miranda's clicking nails on the floor, and Hammond looked over her shoulder. She saw his surprise and then his very obvious displeasure.

"Wingate. I didn't know you were here," he said.

"Riley," Alex said a little nastily. "I usually hang out a red necktie to announce my presence, but wasn't in the mood to go out into the snow. You are a hardier man than I if you drove all the way here in this storm."

"I was hoping for Arden's company. Just the two of us."

"It just goes to show that you can't always get

301

what you hoped for." Alex came up behind Arden and put his arm around her shoulders. "But at least we know we have similar interests."

Hammond made a rude noise that suggested otherwise.

Alex wiggled his fingers. "Notice anything new?"

Hammond looked around the cottage with a curiosity that defeated the purpose of Alex's attempt to get his attention.

"I like the new draperies. They're a good idea since you never know who's going to be looking through your windows."

"Or knocking at the door," Alex said. "You did knock at the door, didn't you?"

"He did, Alex," said Arden, a bit impatient with their steady stream of insults. She ducked out of the shelter of his arm and started toward the kitchen, not caring who followed her.

They both did, of course.

"I guess you're trying to tell me that your cast is off," Hammond said. "You should have shut up about it, and I would have offered to shovel her walkway."

Arden turned around and held up her hands. "Stop this, both of you. I'm capable of shoveling my own walkway. If you want to be really useful, you can both make sandwiches while I wash up."

She let the two of them walk past her, Miranda at their heels, with her nose against the shopping bag. Then Arden went in the opposite direction, to find solace in the wreckage of her bathroom.

****

Alex eyed Hammond warily, distrusting his humanitarian motives and wondering what really brought him out in this storm. He was reluctant to let the man out of his sight as he opened the refrigerator and pulled out some drinks.

"Coffee's good for me," Hammond said companionably, and started to unpack his groceries.

"I'm not sure how to work this machine," Alex said, fidgeting with the dials.

"I would have thought you'd be right at home, old man," said Hammond, pushing him aside and nimbly setting up the program. "I understand you spend a lot of time here."

"Shows what a lot you know. Anyone will tell you that Arden spends most of her time up at my house."

"So it's working out very nice for you, isn't it?" Hammond said, still pulling out containers and wrapped packages from the bag. It looked like he intended to stay for a long time.

"I would say it's working out for both of us," Alex said. "We're become good friends."

Hammond looked disbelievingly into the shopping bag, perhaps wondering if he overlooked a few pounds of roast beef. Without looking up, he said, very casually, "I wasn't thinking so much of your personal relationship, but about acquiring this cottage."

Alex now knew he had every reason to be wary of Hammond Riley. "Why would I care about the cottage? I have enough room up at the farmhouse for everything I want, including a wife. And kids," he added, in a particularly pleasant afterthought. He pulled some mismatched plates out of the cabinet, including one that celebrated the marriage of Prince Charles and Lady Diana Spencer. He doubted if Victoria Trumbull would spin in her grave if this bit of kitsch went out to The Thrifty Means.

"In all these years, there's never been an alliance between the owners of this land and the inhabitants of Victoria's cottage, though it would have been the simplest way to get rid of that codicil in the old deed. Right now you have the inconvenience of having something on your property that doesn't actually belong to you. It's highly unusual," Hammond said.

"It's also unusual for someone who is not at all connected to this business to be so concerned. What the hell does it matter to you what's on my land, or what I do with it?" Or who's on my land and what I do to her, he might have added.

"Intellectual curiosity, I suppose." Hammond arranged the containers on the table in careful rows, confirming why he was so well suited to the job of town registrar. He fussed about every detail. "If Arden decides to move up to the farmhouse with you, what do you think will happen to the cottage?"

"Maybe we'll burn it down."

"No!" Hammond said, dropping a container of potato salad.

"Just kidding," Alex said. "I wondered what you'd have to say about that." And, in fact, Hammond Riley just said a great deal. He knew there was something in this house, something of value that went beyond the antique timbers and sagging glass in the windowpanes. His next words confirmed it.

"I thought, if you made this house available, I would be willing to rent it."

"Don't you already have a place?"

"I rent it from Mike. It's convenient to town but too close to the train tracks. I like it here, near George Brook."

"Yeah, I like it here too." If Hammond rented from Arden, he would be far from the tracks but too close to them. "But I don't think it's going to be available for rent any time soon."

"What?" asked Arden, coming into the kitchen.

"This cottage," said Hammond.

"The Market," said Alex at the same time.

"I see," said Arden, though she clearly did not. She looked at the array of food on the table. "Well, thank you, Hammond, this looks great. Why don't we fill our plates and eat in the living room, where the chairs are more comfortable."

"That sounds great," Alex said without enthusiasm.

"I also made the coffee," Hammond said and glowered at Alex.

Arden opened her mouth but closed it without saying anything. Instead, she picked up the royal plate and covered the blessed couple with chicken salad and a couple of slices of pumpernickel rye.

****

"So, what are you folks doing?" Hammond asked conversationally.

"Eating lunch," Alex grumbled, though he seemed to be doing a very fine job of it. Arden thought she might entice him to the cottage more often if she became a better customer of the Market.

He looked at her and she blushed, realizing he already was enticed, and by a good deal more than chicken salad. His eyes caught the light of the lamp behind her, and promised her something sweet for dessert.

"We're doing repairs and housecleaning," Arden said. It was pretty close to the truth, and had the advantage of discouraging Hammond from staying around.

Hammond put down his half-eaten sandwich and looked around the quaint and cozy room.

"Yes, I can see this place needs a lot of attention. I'm happy to stay and help."

Arden thought quickly, trying to think of a way to get him out of her cottage, gracefully and politely. His offering of food, which they were devouring as if they had been starving, seemed calculated to ward off an early exit. And the snow hadn't let up in the least. Only a grinch would send a man back out into the storm.

"I think the fireplace damper needs some work,"

305

she said sincerely, coming up with a task nearly as awful as soldering the pipes of her toilet. "The place gets smoky when I light a fire."

"And you wouldn't want to get soot on any of the antiques you have here."

Alex cleared his throat, and Arden didn't have to look at him to realize her mistake. Hammond seemed not only willing but eager to work in the vicinity of her fireplace.

"If you have a flashlight and a screwdriver, I'll get started on that after lunch," Hammond said. "In fact, the two of you can go on with whatever you were doing, and I'll clean up lunch before I get started here."

"I'll work here too, to keep you company," Arden said, unwilling to leave him alone.

But that seemed to be a mistake as well, as he looked triumphantly at Alex. "We'll leave you to finish up in the bathroom. Don't hurt your wrist turning a wrench, though, or you'll really be out of commission."

"I've managed to get a lot done in six weeks, in case you haven't noticed," Alex said, and stood. He dusted off a few crumbs, but left the remains of his lunch on his plate. "You'll get that, won't you, Hammond?"

Arden watched him stomp out of the room, and liked what she saw. She had come to know him with the awkward cast on his wrist, and now appreciated how fluidly he moved for a big man, and how well he negotiated the tight spaces in a cottage with ceilings that were only seven feet high.

"He's rude, isn't he?" Hammond asked, already reaching for Alex's plate.

Indeed he was, though it was in her service and she was prepared to forgive him nearly anything.

"I think he's anxious to get back to his work," she murmured.

"Well, why doesn't he, instead of hanging around here with you and procrastinating?"

Whatever else was true about her relationship with Alex, procrastination was not a word she'd use. She wondered if he recognized something in her at their first meeting, as she now could admit she did in him. Some things, such as his interest in acquiring her cottage and working closely with the president of Bradford University, remained between them, but with each day they grew more trivial in import. She didn't consider herself romantic, and therefore would never profess belief in "love at first sight." But if not love, there was something equally potent, and perhaps more mysterious, at work.

"Because I asked him to help me, Hammond. The good people of Eastfield always tell me how neighborly you all are. Can't a neighbor ask something of another without arousing any suspicion?"

Arden happily realized she put this in the best possible terms. After all, Hammond used this as his own excuse when he came through her door bearing gifts, but with the flimsiest of excuses.

He nodded and smiled, as if he liked the sound of her explanation.

"Right you are. If you just show me where you keep your tools, I'll get started on the fireplace. With any luck, we'll have a good fire going in a little while."

"Thank you, Hammond," Arden said sweetly. "And don't mind Alex, I'll clean up our dishes."

It was the second time in only a few hours she did this most domestic of tasks, and the water stung her dry hands. But having two men at work in her house had some rewards, and she took her time in the kitchen. After carefully drying her hands and the dishes, and rubbing in yet another dollop of hand cream, she walked out into the living room, and instantly regretted her leisure.

Hammond, as it turned out, stayed where he was. However, the rusty damper was either fixed or held little interest for him as his attention was focused on the mantel. He stood on a stool, fingering the edge of the painting, examining the marks left by the crowbar. If she hadn't already suspected, Arden now knew why he had come out to catch her unawares in the middle of a snowstorm.

"Do you like it?" Arden asked, announcing her presence. She walked across the room, but stayed a little distance from her guest.

"You have to admit it's a little masterpiece," said Hammond, almost begrudgingly. "Most mantel paintings around here are extremely primitive, but my guess is this is English, since no one in the colonies was doing work of this quality. What does the *artiste* say about it?" With his thumb, he gestured toward the bathroom.

It was an odd question, since she, herself, was the resident expert on colonial art. But Hammond so easily dismissed her in his overriding resentment of Alex.

"Alex has kindly offered to touch it up for me. The scratches you see are very recent damage left by my mysterious burglar."

"Oh, yeah, I forgot about that. Did you ever find out if anything is missing?" Hammond continued to look at the painting as he spoke. Very quietly, he added, "Do the police suspect anyone?"

Arden felt a chill, and clutched her cardigan across her breast. Perhaps the damper remained open.

"The police think it might have been kids, looking for valuables to sell for easy cash. I know they didn't take my jewelry or laptop, and the only other things I can think of are the antiques. I'm not sure kids would recognize the value of Norwell redware or a whale oil lamp." She stopped, unwilling to reveal too much. "But I have my suspicions as well."

He glanced down at her, and suddenly the cheerful façade was cracked. He looked like a stranger.

"About what was stolen?"

"No, not about that. I don't have a reliable inventory of the house, just some pages of notes and some brief descriptions. There's nothing about the painting at all. So, you see, it could have been painted by an itinerant artist, passing through from New York to Boston."

"I have the inventory," he said, and hopped off the stool.

Arden took a step back. "Why on earth would you have one?"

He laughed without humor. "Oh, it's not mine, of course. I only meant there's a copy, dated 1801, in the record of deeds at Town Hall. Along with the unusual terms of Victoria Trumbull's will, is a detailed record of the contents of the cottage, down to the number of lanterns for the outhouse. I could make you a copy, if you'd like."

Arden reflected that he also could have made a copy for himself, or anyone else he chose.

"Why didn't you ever mention this to me? You even let me burrow through the archives without mentioning a word."

"You were looking for a person, weren't you?" he shrugged. "People come in looking for lots of things."

"And you're the keeper of all that information," said Arden, trying not to sound accusatory. "That's quite a responsibility."

Though she didn't hear a sound, Arden felt Alex come into the room behind her.

"It is," Hammond said. "It's why I show up for work every day, even in a snowstorm. And I never take a vacation."

"You probably could use one," Alex said. He walked past Arden to stand closer to Hammond. "You had one today, and decided to work anyway."

"Having lunch with a friend is not exactly work," said Hammond, his slight very obvious and intentional.

"But fixing a damper can be a real bear. How are you doing with it, by the way?"

Hammond looked confused for a moment. "Oh, I forgot all about it. The painting here distracted me."

Alex folded his arms and studied the painting. "Yes, it is a little beauty."

"I can take it down and fix it up, if Arden would like that."

"We've got it covered. Arden would like you to fix her damper."

Arden raised both hands. "Arden can speak for herself." Having said that, she quickly needed to think of something she actually wanted to say. "I say we forget about the paintings and the inventory and the damper, and play a game of cards."

Alex was merely surprised, but Hammond looked horrified.

Arden was very pleased with herself when, after playing a couple of uneventful rounds of rummy, Hammond folded his cards and announced his need to check that the driveway to Town Hall was sufficiently plowed.

****

They listened to the sounds of his retreating muffler as his car skidded down Old Tory Lane.

"Well, that was pleasant," Arden sighed. "At least he left enough chicken salad for dinner."

"What inventory?" Alex asked, dealing out the cards for two.

Arden looked uncomprehendingly at him.

"You said something about the painting and the

310

damper and the inventory. What inventory?"

Arden had to think about that for a moment. "Oh! He told me there's a complete inventory of the contents of the cottage, filed somewhere with our original deed." Alex studied his cards and then folded them and scooped up hers as well. "What did you do that for? Did you deal yourself a bad hand?"

"I'm tired of playing cards. And I'm tired of that weasel knowing more about our business than we do ourselves." Alex looked restless as he tapped his fingers on the table. "Let's go out for a walk."

Miranda came running into the room.

"She understands everything we say, doesn't she?" asked Arden.

"She does, which is why I have to be careful what I say to you, so she doesn't get too jealous." Alex leaned over and whispered in Arden's ear.

Arden giggled and pushed him away. "Yes, I think it's a good time for a walk, so you can cool down."

He stood up and pulled her to her feet and into his arms. "Tell me you don't care for Hammond Riley," he said.

"I must be doing an awful job if you can even imagine that I do. He can't even fix a damper."

"Damn it, I was hoping he could. This means I probably have to do it now."

"After our walk," she said, pulling him toward the coat tree. "Then we'll need a good fire to warm our toes."

Their weather gear was simply defined: as many layers as possible of as many wool garments as they owned. Looking like snowmen within minutes of stepping outside, they set out toward the river, away from any possibility of an accident between a snowplow and an elderly dog.

Though this was Arden's first snowstorm in Eastfield, she had the same sense of the place as she did on occasional quiet afternoons through the autumn. With the road behind them, and almost no evidence of modern civilization, she could imagine what the place was like for the first settlers. Native Americans harvested the first crops here and made their way throughout New England along rivers, and irregular paths that later were paved over. The Dutch and the English followed those paths and, undeterred by winter days, decided to stay, as well.

Cities grew up along the coast and on larger inland waterways, but a place like Eastfield could keep its character and its old ways and its old families. Its only natural resources were the beauties of the land itself.

"Do you like it here?" Alex asked.

"It's beautiful," she said, pausing to pick up a plastic bag that must have blown over from a neighbor's yard. "At the moment, I feel like saying that I could stay here forever, but I wouldn't want you to think I'm another Hammond Riley."

Alex said something rude under his breath. "Hammond doesn't stay here because it's beautiful, but because he has no idea there's a world out there. He's not alone in that. Some people never get out, never leave the place where they were born."

"Well, look at us." Arden stopped in her tracks, and realized she didn't want to study herself too closely. The snowman look wasn't all that flattering. "We're living in houses that have belonged to our families forever."

Alex took her arm and helped her over the stone wall on the river bank. Before them, the blue water pushed through ice and frozen branches, breaking through clumps of leaves.

"We come back home to our houses," Alex corrected her. "And I think Eastfield is better appreciated when we know what's out there in the world."

Nothing more needed to be said about their afternoon visitor. Arden nearly forgot him, instead imagining this place in another century, on a day such as this. She had a sudden vision of a woman, bundled in a wool blanket, dipping a bucket through a hole in the ice.

"I think the cottage has always been a refuge. For other women, and for me. Maybe that's what old Victoria had in mind for the place." When Miranda put her snout in the water, Alex whistled softly. "Even Anne found some comfort here when she was between shows, or men."

"Did she ever tell you that?" Alex asked.

Arden felt a stab at her heart. Could her sister have had more than a friendly relationship with Alex? "That she found comfort here in between men?"

He laughed, which reassured her completely. "I don't think she's ever between men, at least not for more than an hour or so. I can't even remember the names of all the guys she brought here. No, I was thinking about her level of comfort. I'm not sure your sister is happy unless she's exposed to all the world, playing the role of her life."

"You're right. She and I are nothing alike."

He said nothing at first, and Arden guessed it was because he couldn't think of anything to say. Her sister was a celebrity, and quite beautiful and—as he just said himself—nearly irresistible to men.

"You are not. A private life, with its secrets and quiet pleasures, is a much finer thing. Anne would never go out into a snowstorm, you know."

Arden slipped under his arm, though she was not in the least bit cold. "Not even with you for protection?"

"Not even with an army for protection," he said, and kissed her. Not far away, Arden heard the scrape of metal and a splash of water.

Chapter 15

"We use our window display to show off our best
things, and hope to draw in new customers."
~*Margaret Brownlee (founding volunteer of
The Thrifty Means, recently and forcibly retired)*

Arden sat in her living room surrounded by the
remains of the lovely day, and watched Alex as he
slept on the old horsehair couch. He had shoveled
her walk and worked hard on her bathroom pipes,
navigated a persistent Hammond Riley away from
her painting and out the door, and hiked through the
deepening snow. But she guessed it was their
lovemaking, energetic and glorious, that finally
exhausted him.

She ought to sleep as well, though there was
scarcely room left for her on the couch. Instead, she
was perfectly at peace with herself and her current
circumstances, tucked under a quilt and nestled in
an old upholstered chair.

She loved this place, she realized. Her arrival
here now seemed the reward for a fiercely ambitious
career of making a name for herself in a field she
loved. But it turned out the name was worth nothing
against the power plays of others, and what she once
desired no longer pulled her. Eastfield pulled her
now, as well as her longing for a home and a life
apart from a crowded office in a museum. Here there
were possibilities; just because they didn't play out
on a world stage did not make them less noble. She
still had ambition and creative energy and desire.
She had a place of her own, and friends to cheer her.

She had Alex Wingate.

He shifted on the couch and his hair fell against the pillow. She wanted to believe she didn't mistake his regard for her, and his promises about a life they might share. But she had been burned before and besides, she hardly knew him.

She didn't know how long she had been sitting like that, studying him and thinking about the sort of life she might have with him when she realized his light gray eyes were open and watching her. His hand rose beneath the crocheted afghan, until he realized he was trapped by the way it was wrapped around him. He pulled it down from within, as his neck, then shoulders, then chest were revealed.

"I guess I was more tired than I thought," he said, as if he needed to apologize.

"I'm tired too," Arden said. "I've just been sitting here, thinking."

"About what?" he asked, sounding suspicious.

She sighed, wondering if she would regret her words, as she somehow regretted so many other things. Then she remembered the doctor at Norwell Hospital, over-thinking the process of extricating a man from his cast, and realized she should go directly for the power tool.

"I love you," she said. When he didn't say anything, she said it again. "I love you."

"Well, that makes everything easier, I suppose. I love you too, as you must know by now. I think I fell in love with you the first day I saw you."

"Not in that ridiculous harem costume," she protested, feeling a giddiness unlike anything she ever felt before.

"I was thinking about when you were stuck in your car, thinking I was a stalker. I'm glad you didn't whack me with that brake lock you keep under the front seat." He sat up, and the afghan slipped down to his waist. She noticed the whorls of dark hair on his chest were not symmetrical. "But I guess the better story for our grandchildren will be that skimpy costume. Bless your sister Anne for her eccentric taste in wardrobe."

"I really prefer that story not get around," Arden said.

"And what are you going to do to stop me from repeating it?" he asked. "How persuasive are you?"

She doubted she was as persuasive as he was. When he stretched his arms out, revealing just about everything else, she dropped her own blanket onto the chair and stood to join him in his warm cocoon on her couch.

"Now, what would you like me to do?" she asked, as she fingered his lips.

He nipped her fingers, and answered her by deed and not by word.

****

"Are you awake?" Alex asked some time later. If he was merely exhausted before, he was completely spent now. He still considered himself a young man, but he thought days such as this with Arden might kill him. Of course, it would be a glorious way to go.

He twisted his neck somewhat awkwardly to look down at her, and was relieved to see she was still breathing. Her lips were slightly parted in a smile and he wondered what she dreamt about. Even Joseph Wadsworth couldn't make her that happy.

"I'm awake, sort of," she said in a voice so low he thought he imagined it. "But I never want to move from this spot." Her hand moved up his spine to the back of his neck and he shivered, though he had never felt warmer in his life.

"We'll be more comfortable in a bed. I know where to find one. I'll even carry you there if you're too tired."

"Oh, you're good. But I bet that's what they all

say."

He supposed they did. But hers was the only opinion that now mattered, and he wanted to be the only one to hear those words from her. He shifted slightly beneath her and sat up so she was now in his lap with a bulky knot of yarn between them. He pulled it out and rose somewhat awkwardly, with Arden still in his arms.

Her eyes opened in alarm as her hands met behind his neck and tugged his head down.

"I can walk myself, if I can only find my legs. Really, Alex, this isn't necessary."

"It's my pleasure," he said, as he knocked over a lamp.

"Oh, please!" she said, and giggled. Now he staggered about more for effect than for need. At his feet, Miranda scrambled to get out their way and hid beneath the coffee table.

"To the pink bedroom?" he asked. "I'm beginning to like those faded pink roses."

"They're carnations," she said, still laughing. "We Eastfield women have very simple tastes, and roses are quite an extravagance."

"I'll have to remember that," he said, and caught her before she fell right out of his arms.

Arden pulled herself closer against him and had just begun to explore a part of his anatomy he didn't think about too often when the phone rang.

"Leave it," she said, and he was tempted to do so. "The machine will pick up."

But then he thought about what he'd like to be doing with her in the next hour or so, and did not want Hammond Riley coming to her rescue if he thought she was unable to get to the phone. Or, in bed with Alex Wingate. So he brought her to the phone, and dipped her body low enough so she could pick up the receiver. He thought his back would break.

"Eleanor, what happened?" she cried. "Oh no! Of course not. We'll be right over." Her large eyes met his. "Yes, I'll bring Alex. He'll be happy to help. And besides, I think he'd prefer to drive me over in this storm. Don't worry, I'll be able to get hold of him quickly."

"Very quickly," he said, into the receiver, and earned a stern look from Arden.

"Give us fifteen minutes," Arden said. "Maybe a little longer, if we get stuck somewhere."

As she spoke, Alex looked over her tousled head toward the carnations in the bedroom. Right now, he'd even take stinkweed over roses, if they didn't have to leave the cottage. But he knew there was no hope for it and slowly lowered Arden to her feet. She stumbled a little, and he caught her by her shoulders.

"I hope you don't mind that I volunteered you to help us," she said, looking a bit worried.

"There's no rest for the weary at The Thrifty Means," he said. "What happened? Did someone die and leave the shop all her treasures, just as long as you pick them up in a snowstorm at nine at night?"

"If only," Arden said. "There's an emergency, Eleanor said. She's calling most of the younger women to see who can help. A plow slid in the parking lot and crashed through the window of the shop."

As far as Alex knew, there was only one person who did the plowing in Eastfield Center.

"Was anyone hurt?" he asked.

"I don't think so. Mike Riley was driving, and he's the one who called Eleanor."

"Well, if old Mike was careless enough to drive into a storefront, he can get some plywood and board up the place. Can't this wait until morning?"

Arden looked at him beseechingly, and he had the feeling it would be like this for all his life. He didn't think he could say no to her, ever.

"That's just the thing," she said. "He was able to back out of the window, but when he did, the plow pulled out some cases and merchandise. It's a mess, and the snow is still falling." She pushed her hair behind her ears and he noticed she was missing one of her pearl studs. He glanced back at the path they took across her living room.

"If you don't want to do this, Alex, I can drive down myself," she said, mistaking his moment of distraction. "I just feel I have to help out."

He turned back to her and smiled. "No, I love this idea. Who wouldn't want to leave a cozy cottage to drive along treacherous roads to save a collection of old junk?"

"Well, if that's the way you feel," she said, ignoring his sarcasm, "I'm grateful to have your help."

****

The women of The Thrifty Means were grateful as well. Several men Alex knew were already there with their wives and Arden sensed the emergency outing had taken on the spirit of a party.

"There's wine in the back," Miriam Pell said, waving through the shattered window.

"Thank you for coming," Eleanor called out, as she bent over a broken table. Her husband Evan walked past her, pulling a stack of books on a sled. Alex went over to help him when the runners bumped up against the small curb, and Arden looked to see how she might be helpful.

"Do you want to get a flashlight?" Liza asked her. "That crushed square of metal over there is our cashbox, and there might be a few hundred dollars quickly being buried in the snow."

"Alex and I brought a few flashlights, in case anyone else needs one," Arden answered. "But where's the plow, and Mike Riley?"

"He left the scene of the crime," a man answered. "I guess he figured we can clean up after him, and he can continue to milk the town for overtime."

"Don't mind my husband," Liza said. "Mike Riley is a perfectly nice guy. Mark, this is my friend Arden, who lives on Old Tory Lane."

Someone thrust a box into Arden's arms before she would answer. She looked up to see Janet Sterling, a woman she had, up to this moment, considered frail.

"These papers are all wet. Bring them in, and try to dry them with paper towels," she commanded. "And don't smear any of the writing."

Arden thought she might be more useful elsewhere, but a job that would bring her into the dry shop and to a seat was hard to resist. She took the box as she nodded her acquiescence, and moved through the ravaged shop on her way to the back room. The place was as cold indoors as out, but the one harbor of warmth might be the place reserved for sorting and pricing the merchandise they received.

Within a few moments, she knew she had seen this merchandise before. She loosened her scarf as she stared down into the files of old photos and postcards, letters and certificates. Everything was wet, and if she delayed much longer, the drying pages would stick together, and render all this ephemera useless.

She just finished spreading out towels and Lucite sheets to prevent the papers from wrinkling when she heard the sound of hammering. As the plywood went up on the front windows, the sound of the howling wind diminished, and finally was gone. It seemed like only a few moments passed before she began to feel warmer, and slipped off her jacket.

"That was fast," she said, when Alex sauntered

into the back room. "There's hot chocolate, if you'd like."

He propped a massive cast iron pan against the wall. "It wasn't so fast," he said, irritably. "It took us nearly an hour to remove the shards of glass so we could get that plywood up. I think I hurt my wrist."

That got her attention, but he reassured her by lifting his arm and flexing his hand. "That's enough for me for tonight," he said. "Unless you'd like me to give you a hand with these papers. I think I can manage this, even in my weakened state."

"Thank you," was all she said, and handed him a packet.

He watched as she worked and then followed suit. As if she needed another reason to appreciate him, she considered there was always something to be said for a man who didn't require an instruction book to do the obvious. They worked in silence, while other volunteers whisked in and out of the room, retrieving supplies, or delivered more damaged goods. But after a while, Arden realized he had stopped.

"What do you have there?" she asked.

"I remember seeing this many years ago," he said, smoothing the edges of a photo as he set it down on a towel. "It wasn't significant then, but I find it very interesting now."

Arden leaned on the table to get closer. She had seen one very much like it, though in a different setting. It was another group photo of old Eastfielders including her Aunt Portia. She wondered why no one already purchased it, as some of the women were surely mothers or grandmothers of volunteers at The Thrifty Means. Given the age of some of the volunteers, it was even possible they posed for this themselves.

"What do you find interesting?" she asked. "That clothes in Eastfield never seem to go out of style? I'm sure I've seen that boiled wool jacket on someone in the last few weeks."

"Nothing goes to waste in this town; there's a reason why this shop has been so successful. But that's not what I mean," he said. "Look where they are."

Arden studied the picture, overlooking the lineup of unsmiling gray faces. "They might be in a house, because there's the edge of a wool rug and you can see the pine floor. I see a window. And, oh! This is my cottage."

Alex nodded sagely and pulled the flashlight out of his pocket. "What does that look like to you? That box over Martha Washington's head?" He shone the flashlight on the print.

"Their clothes aren't as timeless as all that," Arden said. "They're not so much Martha Washingtons as Eleanor Roosevelts. But that looks like a shadow box where the painting is now."

"No, I think the painting is there."

Arden looked at him in confusion, and for want of anything more appropriate, found a jeweler's loupe in the desk drawer. She studied the blurry, water stained square in the picture.

"You're right. It looks like the painting is actually the backboard of the frame. You can see the trees and the wagon behind the glasses in the shadow box. But why would anyone want to hide a Gainsborough?"

"Why would anyone want to hide a nice little painting done by a talented amateur, you mean. Someone must have noticed the backboard colors while she was dusting the glasses or cleaning off the mantel, and removed the frame and shelves."

"Sometime after this picture was taken," said Arden and turned the photo over, "in 1938. Maybe the crow bar damage came at that time, when they separated the frame from the painting."

"No, that's recent enough. I would have noticed those marks before."

"And yet you didn't notice anything about the painting, until I came here," Arden said.

"I didn't notice a lot of things until you came here," Alex said, and held out his hand to her.

"How are you two doing?" said Emma Grace, gruffly behind them. "Keeping warm back here?" She stomped the snow off her boots.

"You could say that," said Alex. "Say, Emma Grace. What do you know about this photo?"

"Everyone has a copy of that one," she said, brushing off the snow on her collar, and him. "What do you want to know? That's my aunt right there, in that fine woolen shawl. I wear it often, myself."

Arden caught Alex's glance, and smiled.

"What was the occasion, Emma Grace? It doesn't really look like a party."

"Anything but. These women were about to commit themselves to years of hard labor."

"Where they planning on building a railroad or something?" Alex asked, and Arden kicked him under the table.

"Even worse. They were about to start the Eastfield Historical Association. They vowed to collect everything they could about the history of the town and gather as many artifacts as they could. That's also when The Thrifty Means was founded, you know."

"No, I didn't," Arden said. "Was that a coincidence?"

"Of course not. People starting bringing all their junk to a barn on Pine Ridge, and the things that weren't worth saving went to The Thrifty Means. There's been a good working relationship between the two groups of women ever since."

Arden looked down at the severe faces. "Why are there only women?"

323

Emma Grace shrugged. "The men claimed they were looking to the future, and had enough to do without worrying about saving old letters and rusted tools. In those days, antiques weren't valued as they are now. Why would anyone keep a hand-punched lantern when you could have electricity in every room? Of course, they were being very short-sighted."

"And why did they meet in the cottage on Old Tory Lane?" Arden asked.

Emma Grace slipped off her glasses and held the photo very close to her face. "Is that where they are? But of course, it makes sense. That's your Aunt Portia, who wanted to get the whole thing started. She had very little to contribute but her time. Since she didn't have a family, she had a lot of time. She used to go around in her old Dodge, picking up things from houses all over town. She once got into an argument with someone who donated a highboy chest, though he wanted to keep the drawer knobs. Goodness, those were the days."

"That story must have made headlines in *The Eastfield Edition*," Alex muttered.

"Yes, I believe it did," Emma Grace sighed.

"Did Portia contribute nothing from the cottage?"

"I don't believe so, though the other women were probably salivating over her collection. That's why they look so glum, I always thought." She put the print down on the table and made a face.

"Do you know who they are?" Arden asked.

"Some of the other prints have names written on the bottom. But I know a few of these women. That's Lilianna Durant and her cousin Margaret Brownlee. Margaret's passed on now, which is a fortunate thing. Here's our own Mim Pell, next to your Aunt Portia." Emma Grace fingered each portrait in turn pausing longer on those she did not know. She came to one face and tapped it several times. "And here's someone familiar. That's Nancy Riley, Hammond and Mike's aunt. She and your Aunt Portia were very tight friends."

****

At the first traffic stop, Alex took his hands off the steering wheel and flexed his fingers.

"Are you hurting?" Arden asked softly. He turned to glance down at her but the night was dark and he couldn't see her expression.

"I'm just tired," he said. "But we'll be back home soon. I wonder if you'd like to come up to the farmhouse. The bed is bigger."

"I'm so exhausted, I could sleep right here in the back seat."

"Along with the flashlights and my tools? I think we can do better than that," he said. The light changed to green and he pulled onto Norwell Road, which looked like it hadn't been plowed in hours.

"I'm sure my theory is all wrong about the painting," Arden said. "I know I was all excited about the possibilities, but they're just so unlikely. If someone removed a frame from the painting seventy years ago, she would have noticed if something was hiding behind it. The rule about not moving or getting rid of things may have been more of a suggestion than a restriction."

"Then you probably won't get arrested if you throw out a broken fork."

"Still, why risk it?" she asked, and he heard the smile in her voice.

He drove along slowly and carefully, feeling only a modicum of relief when he saw a plow pulling out of Old Tory Lane.

"That was Mike," he said. "I'm surprised he's already making progress on the back roads."

When Arden didn't answer, he thought she might already be asleep. He wondered if she needed anything at the cottage, but decided it could wait until morning. Like her, he felt he could doze off just about anywhere, though preferably after he parked the Jeep. They would be at the farmhouse in minutes.

"We forgot to leave on the lights in the cottage," Arden said, as they passed her driveway.

"I thought we left on the lamp in the living room," he said, uneasily. But it was absurd to worry about such things on a night like this. "Maybe the bulb blew."

Arden seemed satisfied. "I hope I'm allowed to change light bulbs in the house."

"I'm not a lawyer, but I would guess that if your aunt was able to tamper with a fixed frame, you can change light bulbs."

"The real mystery is not why they removed the frame, but why the picture was covered in the first place. Even if it isn't worth anything, it's far prettier than some pine shelves and cheap glasses."

"I think we've got to stop talking about it and do something," Alex said. "If we manage to wake up tomorrow morning, let's tackle your little Gainsborough."

"I'm sure it's worthless."

"If it is, so much the better. We'll never have to worry about it, and I can do a little touch-up paint job on the edges without tampering with the work of a master. If you like, we can even move it to your bedroom. Or ours, some day."

He glanced across at her and the light reflecting off the snow cast a dreamy glow on her smiling face.

****

When Arden finally awoke, she wasn't sure what day it was or why she wasn't in her own bed, and realized this was getting to be a habit. A good habit. She turned, and accidentally elbowed Alex in his stomach. He muttered something under his breath, and pulled the blanket over his head, nearly burying her as well. She groped her way back to the surface, trying not to disturb him again.

It still snowed, but without the intensity of the day before. Weak sunshine glittered on the covered tree boughs outside the large picture window in Alex's bedroom and icicles hung from the roof. She slipped out of bed, pulled on one of Alex's worn flannel shirts, and walked to the window.

It was a grand view, in any season. The bare trees and old stone walls punctuated the sloping woodlands and George Brook, far below, wound like a silver ribbon through the tapestry of the landscape. To the right, the meadows that had once been farmed fanned out from the barn. To the left, the old road led into town. And before her, as exposed as it had been for over two hundred years, was the cottage. She resented having Alex as an audience the first night she spent in Eastfield, but now she realized she could hardly blame him. The owners of the farmhouse had surely watched the comings and goings of the owners of the cottage for many years.

"Anything interesting going on out there?" asked a muffled voice.

"Yes, the circus has come to town," Arden answered clearly.

"Well, it can't be as interesting as the usual show I get from that window," he said, and then groaned when she went back to the bed and sat on him. "Okay, I'm getting up."

They shared a shower, a couple of bagels and a pot of coffee before pulling on their boots and opening the door. Miranda was out in a flash, and heading directly to the cottage.

"I guess I have her well trained," Alex reflected. "And she's a creature of habit. Either that, or she's forgotten you're standing right here, and is eager to go down and see you. I know just how she feels."

"Have you also forgotten that I'm standing right here?" Arden asked.

"That will never happen," he assured her and kissed her on the forehead. "But let's go down, just to make sure."

They followed Miranda's tracks through the snow, to where they merged with other, larger, footsteps in front of the cottage. Arden hesitated to admit to finding suspicious deeds everywhere she went, so she remained silent as she looked across at Alex to see what he was thinking. A muscle in his jaw was flexing, but he said nothing, even as she opened the front door.

Though the day was bright enough, Arden walked over to the lamp in the living room and turned on the switch. The light went on immediately, and still they said nothing to each other. Alex seemed particularly interested in a small puddle of water by the doormat. Then he pulled off his boots and his jacket and headed toward the bathroom. Arden heard water running and tapping on pipes, before he returned to the living room with his tools.

"Everything looks fine in there," he said, pulling up a wooden chair to the fireplace. "Now, let's see what's doing here."

He didn't ask for help, but Arden wasn't taking any chances. She left her jacket hanging over a heating grate in the floor and came to stand next to him in front of the fireplace.

For something that had remained so staunchly in its place for so many years, the painting separated from the wall very easily. Alex used a screwdriver to pry it from its place and eased out the tiny nails by hand. He sneezed several times when the dust went flying, and asked for a tissue. But only moments passed before he was able to hand the picture to Arden.

"We should have done that years ago," he said.

Arden was only interested in the treasure he gave her. The painting was on several dark pieces of wood totaling the size and weight of a school composition book. Tiny holes around the perimeter marked the points where the shadow box had been affixed and deeper scars on the right side revealed the handiwork of her mysterious burglar.

"It's a neat little thing," he said, jumping off the chair. "It's not the sort of thing I'd expect from an English master. The painting is exquisite, but the wood looks like a few scraps that must been lying around the place, cobbled together with rusty nails. It might have been damaged at one time by a leak from the chimney. See where the stain runs? And the paint is of a different color on the edge. Old Victoria or one of your other ancestors painted the wall around it, but left your painting in position."

"But I've seen works like this," said Arden thoughtfully, as she ran her finger over the edge. "Local colonial artists painted on wood because it was more readily available than canvas, and sturdier. But usually, when there were two boards joined together, they were flush against each other. This looks as if there's a space between the painting and backboards, something..."

She looked up at Alex. "It can't be."

"It can," he said, and took it from her. He sat down on the rug in front of the fireplace, and pulled the screwdriver from his back pocket. Slowly, he separated the layers of wood, as Arden watched wordlessly. "And here it is."

A sliver of yellowed parchment slipped through the widening crack.

"It can't be," Arden said again. "It was just a dream I had. It didn't really make sense."

"It still doesn't make sense. And for all we know,

this is someone's shopping list."

"You know it's not," Arden said, tempted to take the painting out of his hands.

He paused and looked at her, sitting across from him with her hands open. "I think you deserve the honors, even if it is a shopping list."

Her acceptance of the painting and the screwdriver would have been a lot more dignified if she somehow managed to keep her hands from shaking, and if she had been able to manipulate the tool with two hands as easily as he did with one. After several moments, Alex's warm, steady hand closed over hers, and he directed her, so that she might drive the tool. Finally, and with a regrettable splintering of the wood, the backboard fell away, bringing with it the whole of the parchment they only glimpsed moments before.

Arden heard a whisper of sound and looked up. But there was only the fireplace over Alex's shoulder.

"One mystery is solved, and another begins," Alex said, as he carefully spread the parchment on the table between them. "If this is what we both think it is, the earth won't spin off its axis, and Connecticut citizens won't find themselves now free of the yoke of a colonial power. This is now a personal history and the questions that remain are, how did a copy of Connecticut's centuries-old charter came to be in a little cottage in Eastfield, and who hid it above the hearth?"

Arden reached out a tentative hand and turned the document over, revealing the faded script of another century and the crumbling seal of a king whose indifferent descendant had let the vast lands of America slip from his grasp. And Arden knew, as surely as if the words had been spoken, that the first of her ancestors who had come into possession of this document had become empowered by it, and wished for it to remain with the property, as a continuing legacy of strength for all the women who would follow her.

"Quercus Chartula," Arden murmured. "This is what the box contained. Someone removed it and hid it above the mantel and then buried the box." It didn't quite make sense.

"Not necessarily," said Alex thoughtfully. They were his first words in a while, and his voice cracked with emotion. He picked up a shard of wood that had fallen by the way, and turned it over to its painted side. "Didn't you tell me that Mike Riley admired the trees and flowers on the landscape, and that you thought it amusing that his scope of vision was so limited? Well, so was ours. Look at this; here is the same tree that's etched on the box. The spreading oak that's now only a ghost up in Hartford. The old Charter Oak is alive and well in Arden Alexander's living room."

Alex's tone was light, but it was a momentous statement. Between them, artist and historian, on the ancient wooden floorboards, was a document of liberty, used as an instrument of defiance, and preserved as a source of empowerment. It was a perfect, dignified moment, marred only by the sound of snowplows liberating Eastfield residents from their homes.

"What do we do next?" Arden asked.

"How about shoveling the walk?"

Arden smiled, thinking how this new chapter in their lives began with the very same deed the day before. But it seemed that everything now changed and any hopes she might have harbored of settling into comfortable obscurity in Eastfield were now dashed.

"How about reading this to make sure it isn't a shopping list or a bill of sale? We want to be sure of ourselves before giving it over to the state."

Alex looked thoughtful. "Consider your options before you do anything. It's generous to hand it over to the state, but you could probably sell the document for a good deal of money. You'll want to talk to Anne, I think, and probably the Historical Society. Your friend Larry Palmer could link you up with the right people in Hartford. And then there are practical matters of insurance coverage and the need to consult independent appraisers." His eyes met hers.

"I know what you're thinking. People will recognize my name from the Bradford debacle and presume this is another fake. But don't you add some credibility to this find? I should be grateful you're with me." She reconsidered her words, realizing his reputation was the last thing she ought to consider. "I *am* grateful you're with me."

Alex winked and said, "Always."

It was as good a promise as any she ever received. They leaned over the document, their foreheads touching, and read the words that were so sacred to their ancestors.

Finally satisfied they had not uncovered a bill of sale for a porcelain chamber pot, and still tingling with excitement, Arden stood and stretched her arms over her head. Though she had showered, she still wore the clothes she threw on yesterday, when they went out on the rescue mission to The Thrifty Means. Alex was still intent on the reading, using the edge of a magazine as a placeholder, and seemed not to notice her. It was an excellent time to get into some fresh clothing.

Arden walked out of the room, toward her bedroom, savoring the wonder of their discovery, and replaying the events in her mind. Everything would fall into place, into a new chapter of the narrative history of Eastfield, except for the unbidden bit of intuition that told her what they would find, and where. That made no sense at all, unless one accounted for pockets of memory emptying their contents in the warm, dry winter air. It might not make a plausible story for the newspapers, but it would be wonderful to tell their grandchildren some day.

Arden paused against the frame of her bedroom door, thinking the excitement completely went to her head. She was losing her mind. Or, to put a better spin on it, she was simply getting a little too ahead of herself. Perhaps a lot ahead of herself.

She came into the room, and smoothed down the hastily made bed. In her closet, she found a soft flannel shirt and well-worn jeans. She didn't expect a news crew to show up on the doorstep today, though she didn't doubt they would be here some day soon. As she buttoned her shirt, she thought she heard the front door open, and assumed Miranda had her own business to attend. Glancing at the wall mirror, darkened with age, Arden ran her fingers through her tangled hair and dabbed on a bit of lip-gloss. She felt terrific.

"Whom do we call first?" she sang out gaily as she came through the bedroom door and back into the living room. A fresh breeze ruffled some papers on the coffee table, and seemed to come from the direction of the kitchen. Surely Alex hadn't left without saying a word to her?

Arden went through the kitchen door, repeating her question.

"Whom do we call..."

But her voice trailed off when Alex's light eyes met hers, and she saw his warning there.

"Try the police," he said tersely, and turned his head to face the intruders in the cottage kitchen.

Chapter 16

"So much merchandise leaves The Thrifty Means
each day. Most of it sells,
and some of it is donated to charity.
But then, there are the things that mysteriously
disappear with women wearing large capes
and men with big pockets."
~*Janet Sterling (volunteer since 1938)*

Alex saw the confusion in Arden's eyes replaced by panic. Her right hand settled on her neck and her left hand cupped her right elbow. At any other time, the gesture would appear casual, but he had the sense she was arming herself. For that, she had good reason.

"Stay away from him. I want to keep the two of you as far away as possible," Hammond Riley said tersely and a little desperately. He stood between them, in front of the sink, and his eyes shifted from one to the other.

"Hammond!" Arden said. "What on earth are you doing here?" Her voice sounded hoarse, and was as welcoming as a bucket of cold water. She took a few steps closer.

"Listen to what he says, Miss Alexander. We don't want to see anyone hurt," said Mike Riley in very sensible tones, but the pruning shears in his hands were held in such a way it was impossible to imagine them as anything but a weapon. Alex had a sudden sickening image of the blades cutting through flesh, and teetered unsteadily on his feet.

"Leave her alone," he said, with more courage

than he felt. It was hard to argue with a man who was crazy or murderous, or both. "She has nothing to do with this. Take what you want and get the hell out of here."

Hammond laughed, a giddy, feminine sort of sound.

"That's easy to say, Wingate, but not so easily done. What we want is highly identifiable and pretty unique. There could only be a few copies left in the whole world, and this one hasn't seen the light of day in a few hundred years. It was buried away by a senile old lady who hadn't the sense to advertise for a bidder. You have the very thing we want, but we don't think we'll depend on the two of you keeping quiet about it. So we're making no promises about nobody getting hurt. Besides," and here he looked Alex up and down with a critical eye, "I'd like to see you hurt real bad."

Alex flinched and realized the punch Mike gave him at the door was probably already a nasty-looking bruise. Behind his back, he clenched his fist, waiting for a chance to get even.

"This is ridiculous, Hammond," Arden said. "What do we have here that you could possibly want?"

The only ridiculous thing was that the Charter was open on the table in front of them all.

Mike snorted and poked his cousin in the back with the shears. "I think you know just what Hammond's talking about, Miss Alexander. And if you had given him what he wanted in the first place, we wouldn't have to go through this trouble with the second thing," Mike said, leaving little doubt to his meaning.

Arden's face burned, and she seemed to be studying the broomstick in the corner. Alex hoped she didn't do anything stupid. At least, not until he did something stupid first.

335

The moment she grabbed the broomstick, Alex kicked over the pine table, letting the Charter slip to the floor. Using the table as a battering ram, Alex pushed Hammond Riley against the sink, trying to break his back, at the very least.

He might have succeeded if Arden's warrior instincts were a little keener. But Mike jumped over an upturned chair, and grabbed her arms, pulling them behind her back. The broomstick hit Alex on the head, before clattering to the wood floor. He threw the table against Hammond, but probably suffered as much damage by reinjuring his wrist, which hurt like hell.

Arden kicked Mike in the shin. "Oh, take the damned thing, the two of you! We weren't going to sell it to anyone. It belongs in a museum, or in the state archives, though it couldn't matter to anyone, except historians. What were you going to do? Return it to Queen Elizabeth? Sell it to a foreign bidder? Hide it over your own mantel for all eternity? Take it. Just get out of my house and out of my sight!"

Mike laughed, and Alex knew he was right about the crazy part. "Just take it? After all the trouble we had finding it? Not on your life." The cruel hands tightened on Arden's arm and Alex heard a bone crack.

"How did you know it even existed?" Alex asked conversationally. He had lots of practice with crazy after all, he dealt with artists all the time. He caught Arden's expression, and realized she was just furious and likely to strike back at all of them this time.

Outside, up in the driveway at his farmhouse, came the sound of spraying gravel. No one else seemed to notice.

"We didn't," admitted Mike, breathing heavily into Arden's ear. He still grasped the pruning shears and teased the ends of her hair with them. "We knew that old Portia Alexander mentioned a valuable document that was in her family for years and..."

"Why?" asked Alex, now genuinely curious. "Why would she have mentioned it?"

"The witch was a friend of the family. She died in the Riley house," Hammond said.

"Did one of you kill her?" Arden asked, and was rewarded with a pull on her arms. Alex got close this time, but the shears were now turned on him.

"The old lady collapsed in the living room, and babbled on about some oak tree and hidden paper. She said it was hidden where no one could find it because it was very valuable. That's all we knew. Our aunt told us everything before she died herself. That was two years ago." Mike lowered the shears slightly. Even for someone as accustomed to using them as he, it must have been a considerable weight to maintain.

"So you decided to break into my house, and see if you could find out what it was without entirely destroying the place. You came close, though. And then one of you came back when we went to Boston. You left your fingerprints on the wall above the mantel," Arden said quietly. "Again, you were close."

"We wanted to get at it while you were away," Hammond said. "We're not used to this kind of thing, Arden."

He might have been talking about cooking his own breakfast. But as he spoke, in normal tones, his guard seemed to be slipping. Hammond cocked his head at the sound of something that sounded like crying in the wind. The sound was other-worldly, so far removed from the grim reality of the scene in the cottage.

"Why did you wait for Arden to get to Eastfield in the first place?" Alex asked, hoping to disarm him.

"The cottage was practically abandoned for years, and then all of a sudden Arden showed up and you're in business? What's the deal?"

Hammond snorted, as if he were reasoning with an idiot. He looked at his cousin and nodded his head.

"We were biding our time," Mike said. "We had no idea where to look, and would have bought the house when it came on the market, just so that we'd be able to take it apart, piece by piece. Anne wasn't the type to poke around, so we weren't worried about her. But as soon as her damned sister arrives, she starts digging in the dirt."

"Is that the reason you asked me out, Hammond?" Arden said, sounding utterly dejected. Alex wasn't sure what game she was playing, but he had the feeling things were about to get more difficult than they already were.

"No!" Hammond protested. Perhaps chivalry was not yet dead, but inasmuch as Mike held Arden captive with a pruning shears, it was in its final throes.

"Shut up," said Mike, to all of them, and ran the blade slowly up Arden's neck. "The first thing you're doing is digging around in the yard. Then you show up in Town Hall, reading the old records. We know who you are, the job you had at Bradford. And to us, lady, you spell trouble."

"So what are you going to do about it?" Arden said, nastily.

There was a dead and heavy silence in the room, during which Alex imagined every horrible possibility.

Then footsteps stomped on the mat at the kitchen door, and the sounds of the crying grew even louder. The back door squeaked open and slammed close almost at once.

"Alexander Wingate! What are doing in Arden's

kitchen when your poor dog is crying out in the snow?" Emma Grace Liddell removed her hat and shook it out, apparently indifferent to the overturned table and broken glassware. Miranda looked at Hammond and happily shook her tail.

"Arden! Get out of the way!" Alex shouted, and seized the moment. He jumped the startled Mike Riley, pulling him off Arden, who staggered back against a case of cookbooks. The shears dropped straight downward, nearly slicing off Mike's booted toe, and landed with enough force so that they stood rigidly out of the wooden floor. As Mike jumped back from the sudden danger, Alex pinned him back against the wall, punching him with a strength derived from the adrenaline rush, and regardless of the fact he probably broke his wrist again. When Mike finally fell to the floor, Alex grabbed the shears and turned to help Arden.

But she was managing fine without him, it seemed. She was on Hammond's back, riding him like a rodeo cowboy, kicking and biting. Alex reached for a can of coffee, thinking he'd knock Hammond in the head, but Emma Grace got there before him, with a Staffordshire dog. Her aim was excellent. She smashed it over Hammond's head and he fell like a stone, taking Arden down with him.

Applause broke out in the tiny kitchen, and he realized Emma Grace wasn't the only visitor they had today. Eleanor and Miriam shared the small doormat, melted snow pooling around them. Alex pulled Arden to her feet and bowed to their applause, though he knew they shared the limelight with the ladies of The Thrifty Means.

Behind him, Hammond Riley groaned.

In front of him, Emma Grace Liddell made a similar sound.

"Did he hurt you, Mrs. Liddell?" Alex asked.

"In the worst way possible," she said. "What

have I done? My mother gave Portia that Staffordshire ages ago. It is worth hundreds of dollars by now. It *was* worth hundreds of dollars." She shrugged her shoulders several times and marched straight into the arms of her friends, where she started to sob.

Whether it was for the possibility that she might have been killed in Portia's old kitchen, or for the irreplaceable china dog, he couldn't say. And when Arden came up behind him and settled herself under his shoulder, he realized he didn't care.

****

The police arrived at the cottage with a great deal of style, crashing in the screen door and slipping on the wet floor. By then, Hammond and Mike were tied back-to-back with old nylon stockings Arden found in the drawers of the spare room, and the ladies of The Thrifty Means were taking tea in the living room.

Alex clutched his arm to his side, trying to block out the pain, but he knew there would be another trip to Norwell Hospital.

"Hammond, is that you?" one of the officers asked. He prodded the man with his boot.

"This has all been a misunderstanding, Pete," Mike said, looking up. Alex was pleased to see he looked a lot worse than he did himself.

"Mike? You, too? What's going on?"

"Hammond's right. This is a misunderstanding. We came over to see if Miss Alexander needed help, and her friends attacked us."

One of the men saw the shears on the kitchen counter and kneeled down to inspect the fresh hole in the kitchen floor. "Were you planning to do a little gardening?" he asked.

"Aside from anything else, he broke a very valuable Staffordshire dog," Emma Grace said, and wiped a tear from her eye.

"And tried to kill us," Alex added. "I'm not sure which is the greater offense in Eastfield."

The oldest officer looked very severe. "I also received a report of a dog left out in the snow."

Miranda wagged her tail, and barked.

"These two men broke into my home and tried to kill us, officer," Arden said in a plaintive voice, as she brushed aside her hair to reveal a line of blood down the side of her neck. Emma Grace cried out, causing Miranda to scamper away. "This was not a neighborly visit."

"You should get that checked out, Miss," the policeman said. "Did you do this, Mike?"

"It was an accident!" Mike cried out, and struggled against the pantyhose that bound him to his brooding cousin.

The officer looked down at the floor, at the shattered glass and china, at the deadly shears, at the overturned chairs. Alex watched in disbelief, nearly certain the officer would agree with Mike, for no other reason than the Riley family history in Eastfield. Justice was not always served, as it was sometimes crowded out by tradition and respect and a keen desire to make certain that what happens in Eastfield stays in Eastfield.

"I can't say for sure, Mike," said the officer, "but it doesn't look like it. I think you and Hammond ought to come down to the station with us. Miss Alexander can give us her statement now."

Alex gave a sigh of relief, catching Arden's attention.

"It will have to be quickly done, though, as I think we have to get Mr. Wingate to the hospital," she said. He thought he was acting pretty cool, so he didn't know how she guessed he was in so much pain. "Look at his wrist. It's broken again."

"It's okay," Alex said cheerfully, not wanting to give Hammond and Mike the slightest reason for

341

celebration. "Or it will be once I get it fixed up again. Don't worry. I'm getting used to this kind of thing. Happens all the time."

Arden looked at him as if he were an idiot, as he supposed he was.

"Clearly he has a concussion," she said, authoritatively, taking charge. "I've seen this before. I would like an ambulance, please. Can you arrange that?"

The police pulled Mike and Hammond to their feet and cut away the nylon bonds. The one named Pete shook his head as he pulled handcuffs out of his pocket. "There will be a wait, on account of all the road accidents in the snow. I can put in the call, though."

"Don't bother," Arden said. "I'll just take him myself. My car could find its way to Norwell Hospital without me."

"We'll take him," Eleanor said, reaching for her jacket.

"No, this is my responsibility," Arden said firmly, without looking at him.

He was not concussed, and he rather liked the sound of that.

Ten minutes later, they were alone in the cottage, once again surrounded by the wreckage of her property. Arden picked up the Charter from where it had slipped under the pie rack and gently blew on it to dust it off.

"Such a small thing to cause so much trouble," she murmured.

"It's part of history. People died for what the Charter represented," Alex said. She had already helped him into his jacket, and he was standing patiently by the back door.

"But we could have died too. And for what? You said it yourself; no one's liberty is in peril now." Arden glanced around the kitchen and saw a

342

pressure cooker high on a shelf. It was old and sturdy, and at least as inconspicuous as an old oak tree. When she opened it, she realized someone had used it as a hiding place in the past.

"What do you have there?" Alex asked.

"It looks like a sapphire ring. Oh, and here's a string of pearls. And some tissue paper."

"The famed family jewels," Alex said wryly. "We'll have to do a bit better than that."

Arden said nothing for a few moments, and then looked up at him. It was absurd to discuss these things now, when he was obviously in pain, and waiting to be delivered to Norwell Hospital. But he seemed as unwilling as she to let the moment go.

"Of course someone's liberty is in peril," he spoke first. "Mine. That seemed to bother Hammond more than not getting his hands on the Charter. It puts a whole new perspective on things for me, as I thought nothing was tempting enough to get him out of the basement of Town Hall."

Arden pulled a wool hat down over her ears, feeling the smart of her cut. "I have a feeling I'm not all that tempting at the moment."

And then, seeing the light in Alex's eyes, "Oh, no. We are going to the hospital. Don't even think about doing anything else."

She put out bowls of water and food for Miranda and Glinda, who was probably hiding under a bed somewhere, and picked up the car keys. Alex obligingly followed her out to the car without saying a word, but she certainly knew he was thinking about doing something else.

****

The most exciting thing about their trip to and from Norwell Hospital was the trip itself, as Arden had to navigate around snowdrifts and plows, and a few wrecked cars. The hospital experience was one to which they were familiar, and they were even greeted by a few staff members who recognized them. No one dared to make any comments about two broken wrists in two months, though the attending physician mentioned that it was not a recommended strategy for healing. Alex merely looked resigned and somewhat bored.

A few hours later, back in the cottage, Arden and Alex sat at the kitchen table, sharing a potluck dinner that didn't seem to be all that lucky. The leftovers from Hammond's feast were still in the refrigerator, but they seemed so distasteful, Arden didn't even want to touch the wax paper wrapping. Not tempted by the meatballs and pasta set out on the table, Arden thought she might have better luck with the pot part of the dinner. She stood up.

Alex, intent on his meal, reached for seconds. With her help, he had changed into a gray shirt that very nearly matched the color of his eyes, but was now ruined because they had to cut open the sleeve to accommodate his new plaster cast. His hand rested on his lap beneath the table, and he had taken a couple of stitches for a cut on his forehead. But otherwise, he looked perfectly healthy. And clearly, his appetite was not affected by the events of the day.

Arden went to the shelf and pulled down the pressure cooker. Missing its thermostat, it was unlikely anyone would accidentally cook up the Charter for an evening's meal, but she was relieved to find it inside, just the same. The lovely old ring and yellowed pearls were also as she left them, and she brought her impromptu strong box to the table.

"You may want to check the other pots in the kitchen," Alex said, after gulping down about a gallon of mineral water. "I've heard that Portia never had a bank account and she must have hid her money somewhere. We already know it's not beneath her mattress."

"Nor is it in a stone box in the garden." Arden pulled out the tissue paper in the bottom of the pot. "There is something here, though."

Two strange looking bills fluttered to the table.

Alex reached across the table to retrieve one and studied it for several minutes. "These are silver certificates," he said. "Here's a ten."

"Is it worth a lot of money?"

"Probably twenty dollars, but I don't really know. Unlike your aunt, you do have a bank account, and they could probably help you down there."

"Well, that's a start. And here are some stock certificates from the Civil War, unfortunately issued by the Confederacy."

"Not a good investment," Alex said. "But undoubtedly in keeping with your family's rebellious history."

"It's your family too, as I recall. But what is this?"

"It looks like a letter," Alex said, though she had figured that part out for herself. "If you're not going to finish your spaghetti…"

"Help yourself," Arden said. "And it is a letter, addressed to Portia."

Once she started reading, however, she realized the missive, scripted in a small, cramped hand, was written as much for her, as for her aunt. It was unsigned, but the author wrote with some authority, and the narrative was the story of the Trumbull women.

"It starts with Victoria Trumbull," she said, thinking out loud.

"What does?"

"The story that the letter records. I can't make it all out, but it starts with the Trumbull family here in Eastfield. They were Tories."

"The whole Eastfield branch of the family were

Tories," Alex reminded her, as he put her empty plate on top of his.

"Victoria was not. She took up with some man who had been in collusion with Nathan Hale, I think, and that was to the shame of her family. Her brother banished her to the cottage on the property."

"Was that man a Wadsworth?" Alex asked, sitting back in his seat. It creaked ominously.

Arden's hand was shaking so badly, she placed the letter on the table. "It does not say. Only that he came down from Hartford to see her."

"If it was Wadsworth, they must have shared something other than a few good times. That would explain the little lamb between their graves."

"But why didn't he just marry her?" Arden asked.

"Maybe he was already married. Or maybe he just lacked incentive."

"Would her honor not count for anything?"

"The poor wretch was already banished. What difference would an illegitimate child and a secret lover make?"

Arden fumed. "If you really think that's funny, I will break your—"

The phone rang, and the sound was unusual enough so that Arden looked around her in surprise before she identified the source of the interruption.

"Let it ring," Alex advised.

But she already had her hand on the phone. "It might be the police."

It was not.

"Larry! How are you?" Arden said loudly enough for Alex to hear. "I was going to call you tomorrow. I have such a surprise—."

Larry interrupted her before she finished the sentence.

"I hope it's better than the one I have for you," he said.

"This doesn't sound very promising. Please don't tell me that my painting was a kindergarten art project."

"Oh, it's a lot better than that." Larry cleared his throat. "How's the weather down there?"

Arden sat down on an old pine chair and knew that her old friend was not calling to inquire about the snow on her lawn. "This is not about the weather. This is about the Gainsborough."

"It's not a Gainsborough," Larry said, and before Arden could breathe a sigh of disappointment, he quickly added, "But."

"Tell me everything."

"You know I will," Larry said, unable to keep the excitement out of his voice. "It seems the master had under his tutelage a certain recalcitrant young man who got fed up with begging patronage from the aristocracy and took off for America, looking for better opportunities."

"And did he find them?" Arden asked softly, tired of the whole business. Alex came to stand over her, leaning in the doorway.

"I believe he did. My friend at the Tate was only able to tell me that he took up with the Trumbulls for a while, who also had artists in the family. But our man grew tired of earning poor workman's wages, so he opened shop as an artist's agent. He tried to pass off some of his own paintings as Gainsboroughs, claiming he brought them over from England."

"But the Trumbulls would have known the difference, wouldn't they?"

"Would they? Artists aren't always the best judge of other people's work," Larry said, and added, "Is Alex standing right there?"

"Yes, he is," Arden said, and smiled. "But this painting is good enough to fool anyone, even someone who is very cautious because she has been

347

burned by experience. It's an excellent little piece."

"So what is it doing in a little cottage in Eastfield, aside from attracting termites? I would like to recommend a few museums that might be interested, even in a fake Gainsborough. It has age, and I believe we can now give it provenance."

"Thank you, Larry, but Alex and I will take it from here. It's not that I don't appreciate everything you've done. But I've got to talk it over with Anne, and perhaps some of the other people in town." Arden paused, knowing she sounded ungracious. She looked up at Alex, who was still watching her intently, and spoke as much for his benefit as for Larry's.

"I have a theory about the painting and how it came to be here. It starts with the first Victoria Trumbull who, for whatever reasons, was banished to this small cottage on the family farm. 'Banished' might be too strong a word, for though she lived apart, they were able to watch everything she did."

She put her finger to Alex's lips when he laughed at that.

"I think Victoria had a child with her lover who, for whatever reasons, couldn't give her his name, or take her away from Eastfield. But he gave her something of value that she could redeem for currency if she needed to escape or set out on her own with their baby."

"The painting would not have been worth that much in their own time," Larry reminded her.

"Ah, but that's where my surprise comes in," Arden said. "What would a copy of the Charter be worth?"

She waited to hear the sound of the phone dropping, but Larry exercised remarkable restraint.

"You have it?" he asked.

"I do. It was behind the painting, set against the mantel. It's in excellent condition. At the moment, it's in better condition than I am." Arden tried to ignore Alex's expression, telling her what kind of condition he thought she was in.

"Where is it? Is it safe?" Larry asked in some agitation.

"Very. It's in an aluminum pressure cooker."

"What the hell's a pressure cooker?"

"Something I've been living in since I arrived in Eastfield. But somehow, I now feel that everything's turned out remarkably well."

"I suppose you're referring to Alex Wingate," Larry said.

"Yes, and other things."

"Well, sure. You're a rich woman now."

Arden looked around at her tiny cottage, filled with the memories of so many women who sought shelter here, at the treasures they dusted and polished and preserved for over two hundred years, and at Alex Wingate, whose family so intimately intersected with her own.

"I suppose I am," she said.

****

Alex, feeling uncomfortable once he realized Arden was discussing him with her old friend, walked away and started setting things to right in the cottage. He picked up the wooden slats of the old painting and realized they fit together as neatly as a jigsaw puzzle when gravity pushed one layer down upon the next. He considered it wasn't so different from the discreet and somewhat mysterious pieces of the puzzle he and Arden had encountered since she arrived on Old Tory Lane. While it was true that they might never fully understand what they found here, everything somehow connected to something else. The stone coffin revealed the connection to an old document, and the Rileys connected to Portia Alexander. Arden came to the cottage because of a scandal related to an old painting, and the Rileys' dirty prints were all over another old painting that kept the Charter hidden and safe for so many years. And then there was The Thrifty Means, where photos and family history came home to rest, like hibernating creatures before the long, cold winter. If Eleanor and her friends had not drawn Arden out of her refuge and into the bright lights of the shop, items of deep and enduring interest might well have been passed over for another generation to discover.

"A penny for them?" Arden asked, and Alex looked up in surprise. He was so wrapped up in those thoughts, he didn't even realize she'd hung up on Larry Palmer.

"The pieces of your little painting fit together like a puzzle," he said, and showed her how he held them together.

"So, if Mike and Hammond were clever, they might have disassembled the painting, taken the Charter, and put the whole thing together without anyone knowing."

"If they were clever," Alex said. "But of course everyone would know because they would cart it around the country, appear on a dozen talk shows, tweet from their special appearance at the White House, and then sell it to the highest bidder."

"Is that what you think I should do? I have to talk to Anne, of course, but she'll probably go along with whatever I want."

"What do you want?" Alex walked toward her, very slowly, so as to not rush her in anything she decided. He realized that, like Anne, he was willing to go along with whatever Arden wanted.

"Larry thought I might sell it for a lot of money."

"But?" Alex saw the doubt on her face.

"But I'm torn. On one hand, the Charter, an old document of that sort, is beyond price. I'd like to donate it to the state archives or to a museum, where it properly belongs. On the other hand, I believe Joseph Wadsworth may have given it to his Victoria for safekeeping, as an insurance policy to be drawn in a time of need. It would guarantee her independence."

Alex slipped his arm over her shoulder and kissed her forehead.

"Is that what you want? Or do you think you can manage to find some independence as my partner? I've bought up property all over Eastfield, pitched my idea to colleges from Florida to Maine, gotten some financing from investors, and ruffled enough feathers in Eastfield to stuff mattresses for all the young artists and students I'd like to bring here. But I also have my own works to develop and market, assuming I can manage to stop breaking my wrist long enough to actually get anything done."

Arden turned into the curve of his shoulder and held his clean new cast in her embrace, like it was something dear to her. "Anne was very keen on my coming to Eastfield to hide out, and prevent you from taking over the cottage. She's going to think I failed in my mission."

"I'm not planning a hostile takeover of a place that's a quarter the size of my barn. It's all yours, as it always has been. You can live here if you choose. Or, if there's another place you'd like to live—I'm thinking of a farmhouse complete with a man and a dog and a cat—this can be your office. Or clothes closet, for that matter."

He turned them around to the large window, with its new green drapes framing the scene of fresh white snowdrifts. "But you really don't believe that Anne sent you here to save the cottage from me, do you? If so, you don't know your meddling sister half as well as I do."

He felt Arden stiffen. "I should have guessed. I would have guessed if I hadn't been so upset about everything at Bradford. This was a set up."

"Well, thanks for sounding so happy about it. But why not look at it from a practical point of view? We'll be the ones to finally resolve the oddity in the deed to both properties, and legally put the whole estate together again. It'll be like it was in the old days; the marriage of two great houses."

"You just said this cottage wasn't very great," Arden reminded him.

Alex hesitated, knowing he was going about this discussion in all the wrong ways. He wasn't much of a romantic, but an artist should be able to come up with something better than a business arrangement.

"I said it wasn't very large. But I would think that anywhere you are with the woman you love is, by definition, the greatest place on earth."

Judging by her response, in which she moved on from his cast to caress other things, he guessed he finally said the right thing. Miranda seemed to be satisfied as well.

After some time, during which he gave some passing thought to the possibility of someone watching them through the damned window, Arden tilted her face up to him. The sun glinted in her dark eyes and her smooth complexion was flushed.

"What do you think will happen to the two of them?" she asked.

"Miranda and Glinda? They'll live with us," Alex answered, incapable at the moment of any rational thought.

"I mean Hammond and Mike."

"Oh yes, the Riley boys. I hope you're not having any lingering regrets about the life you might have had with Hammond, living in the basement of Town Hall."

"That's not where he lives, is it?" Arden asked, horrified.

"I never really thought about it. But wherever he lives, it's got to be a lot nicer than prison. And I'm sure that's where he's going for a while. Maybe he'll get time off for good behavior, or have to do some hours of community service. We'll just wait and see, along with the rest of Eastfield."

"That's the saddest thing, of course," said Arden. "That two such men, the pillars of their society, should turn out to be common criminals."

"Heaven help us all if jolly old Eastfield had to rest on those two pillars. I'm sure it will be quite a blow to the community, and the talk of the town for years to come. But don't forget that you're a native daughter as well, and your claim to the town's traditions is just as strong as that of the Riley boys." He pressed his good hand to the cold surface of the window and braced himself. "Please tell me that you're going to marry me and stay here forever."

"Larry thinks I will be asked to come back to Bradford. There was so much protest from the museum benefactors that they're going to reopen, though on a smaller scale. And now that there's other incriminating evidence against Peter, he thinks the administration will beg me for forgiveness."

"Or beg you not to sue them," Alex said. "It may be somewhat awkward, since their students may come down here to intern in Eastfield with me. With us."

"I won't go back. As much as I love my apartment and living in Boston, I feel very settled here. Eastfield has given me friends, and a new purpose, a wonderful little painting, and a whole new landscape on my life."

"That's it?" Alex said.

"Or course not. It's also given me you." She tapped his cast gently. "And it's clear that you need a partner, not just in business, but in life. Honestly, I don't know how you managed before I got here."

"Eastfield looks after its own," he murmured

against her hair.

"So I've heard. Our news isn't going to surprise a single person is it?"

"Of course not. But I think we can be confident in knowing that you aren't the first resident of the cottage to provide gossip for the locals. It's a veritable tradition."

"So is the long line of spinsters who have lived here." Arden sighed.

"Will your worthy ancestors turn over in their graves if you break with that tradition?"

"I shall have to go back to the cemetery and ask for their forgiveness. After all, they were such fiercely independent women."

Alex decided it was time to pull the drapes closed. One never knew when the women of The Thrifty Means might come by to see if Arden needed an apple pie or a quart of milk.

"Remembering what I do of your dear Aunt Portia, I think you could also say that they were sad and lonely," Alex said.

Arden helped him with the drapes and the outside world was soon shut out.

"So they may have been," she said softly as she took his hand and started toward the bedroom. "But I prefer to believe that now they will finally be at peace. The story ends."

Alex fumbled with the lamp switch, until the glow of the light bulb bathed the room in warmth. The flowers on the wallpaper were in full bloom on this winter's night.

"Oh, no," he said. "It's just the beginning."

A word about the author...

A writer for most of her life, Sharon Sobel is the author of eight published novels, a novella, short stories, and many essays. She earned a PhD in English and American Literature from Brandeis University and is currently a professor of English at Norwalk Community College in Connecticut, where she actively tutors aspiring student writers and has chaired the annual Writers' Conference. She is a member of the Board of Directors of Romance Writers of America, a founding member of its Connecticut and Lower New York chapter, and is past president of The Beau Monde, the national chapter devoted to the interests of writers of the Regency period.

A native New Yorker, Sharon also lived in Boston and The Hague before moving to an eighteenth century farm in Connecticut with her husband and family.

A Cottage Affair follows *Thrifty Means* in a series of novels very loosely based on some of her experiences as a long-time volunteer and president of The Turnover Shop of Wilton, Connecticut. The Shop is not only the town's best-known resource for the exchange of excellent used merchandise, but is also a clearing house for local information and networking. If the events of *A Cottage Affair* had actually occurred, one would have heard about them first at The Turnover. In its sixty-five-year history, the wonderful women who volunteer there have contributed over a million dollars to local charities, and remain committed partners and good friends.

Thank you for purchasing
this Wild Rose Press publication.
For other wonderful stories of romance,
please visit our on-line bookstore at
www.thewildrosepress.com.

For questions or more information
contact us at
info@thewildrosepress.com.

The Wild Rose Press
www.TheWildRosePress.com

To visit with authors of The Wild Rose Press
join our yahoo loop at
http://groups.yahoo.com/group/thewildrosepress/